GNT
WIL

BIRTHRIGHT

VOLUME THREE
ALLIES AND ENEMIES

T 109913

SKYBOUND™
www.skybound.com

IMAGE COMICS, INC.
Robert Kirkman *Chief Operating Officer*
Erik Larsen *Chief Financial Officer*
Todd McFarlane *President*
Marc Silvestri *Chief Executive Officer*
Jim Valentino *Vice-President*

Eric Stephenson *Publisher*
Corey Murphy *Director of Sales*
Jeff Boison *Director of Publishing Planning & Book Trade Sales*
Jeremy Sullivan *Director of Digital Sales*
Kat Salazar *Director of PR & Marketing*
Emily Miller *Director of Operations*
Branwyn Bigglestone *Senior Accounts Manager*
Sarah Mello *Accounts Manager*

Drew Gill *Art Director*
Jonathan Chan *Production Manager*
Meredith Wallace *Print Manager*
Briah Skelly *Publicity Assistant*
Sasha Head *Sales & Marketing Production Designer*
Randy Okamura *Digital Production Designer*
David Brothers *Branding Manager*
Ally Power *Content Manager*
Addison Duke *Production Artist*
Vincent Kukua *Production Artist*
Tricia Ramos *Production Artist*
Jeff Stang *Direct Market Sales Representative*
Emilio Bautista *Digital Sales Associate*
Leanna Caunter *Accounting Assistant*
Chloe Ramos-Peterson *Administrative Assistant*

Robert Kirkman *CEO*
David Alpert *President*
Sean Mackiewicz *Editorial Director*
Shawn Kirkham *Director of Business Development*
Brian Huntington *Online Editorial Director*
June Alian *Publicity Director*
Jon Moisan *Editor*
Arielle Basich *Assistant Editor*
Andres Juarez *Graphic Designer*
Stephan Murillo *Business Development Assistant*
Johnny O'Dell *Online Editorial Assistant*
Emily Wald *Publicity Assistant*
Dan Petersen *Operations Manager*
Nick Palmer *Operations Coordinator*

International inquiries: foreign@skybound.com
Licensing inquiries: contact@skybound.com

www.imagecomics.com

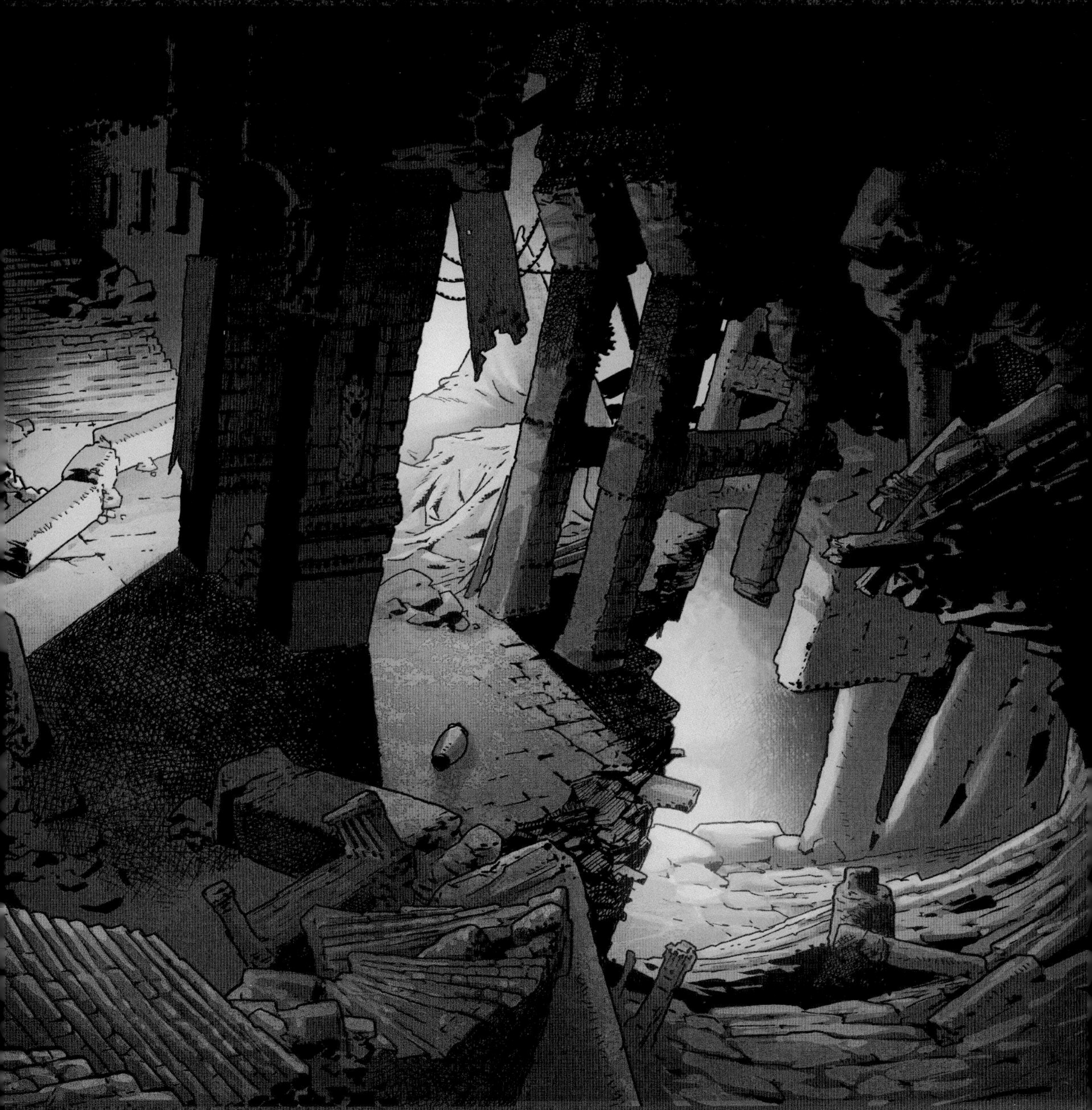

Joshua Williamson
creator, writer

Andrei Bressan
creator, artist

Adriano Lucas
colorist

Pat Brosseau
letterer

Arielle Basich
assistant editor

Sean Mackiewicz
editor

logo design by **Rian Hughes**

cover by **Andrei Bressan** *and* **Adriano Lucas**

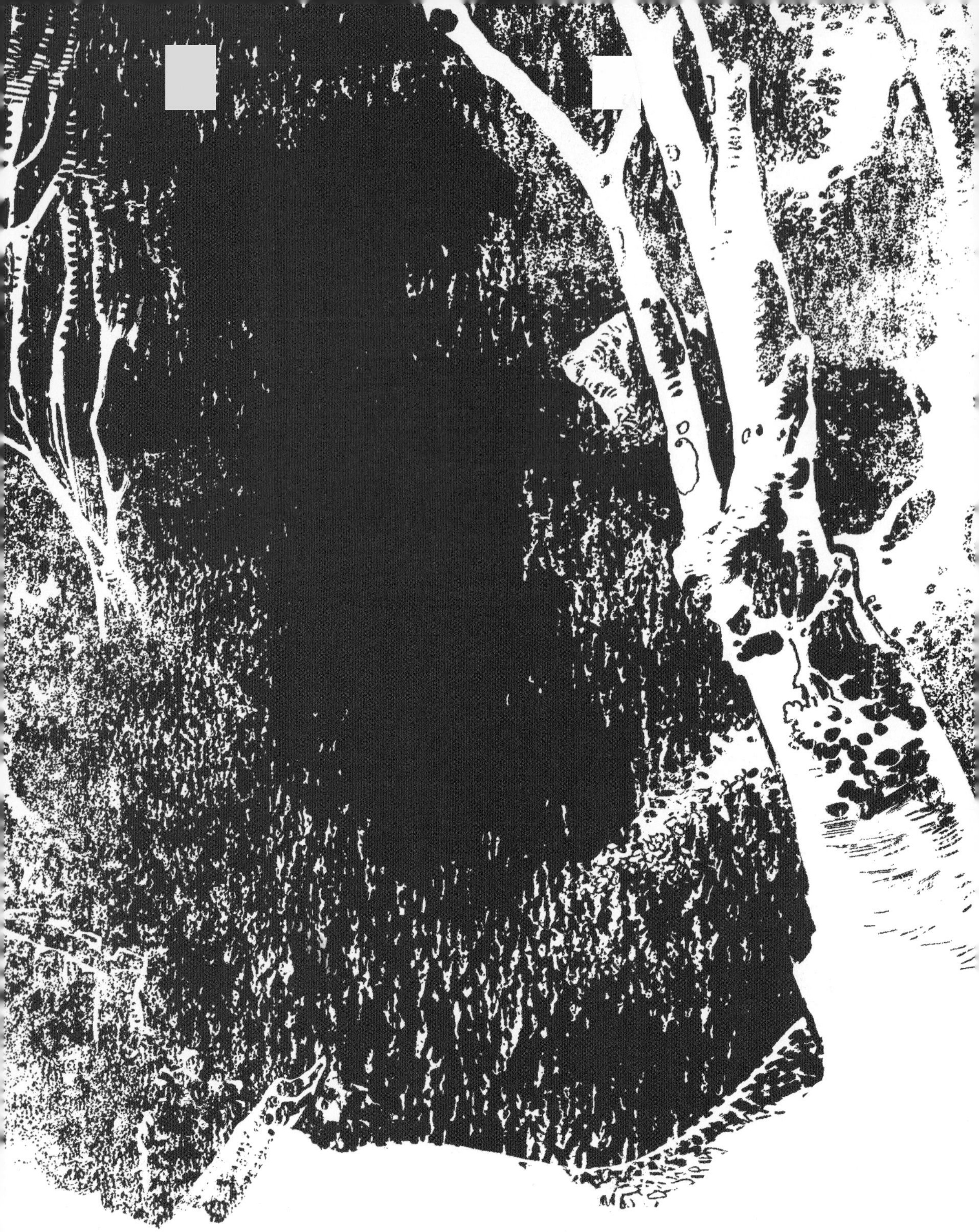

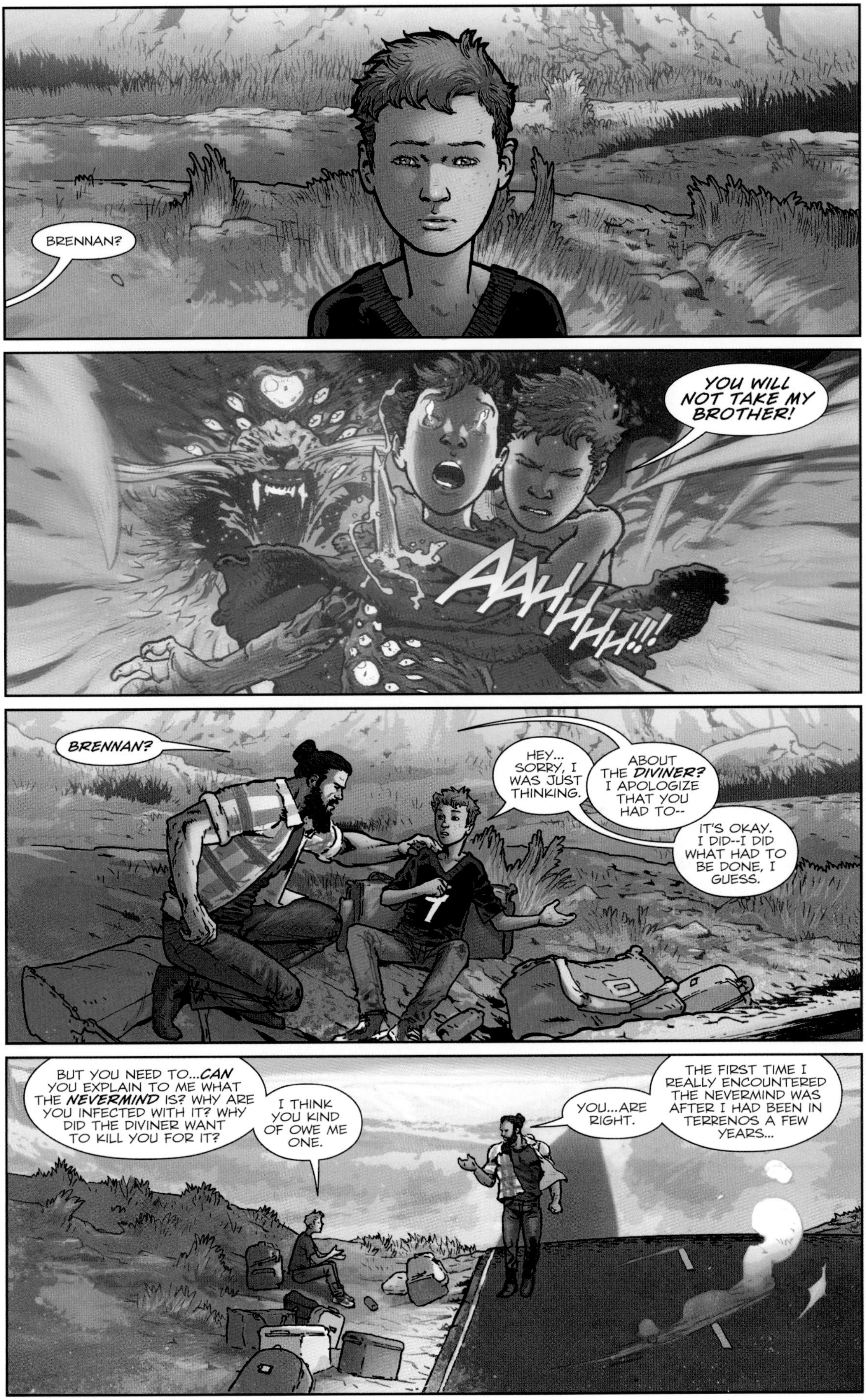
BRENNAN?
YOU WILL NOT TAKE MY BROTHER!
AAHHHH!!!
BRENNAN?
HEY... SORRY, I WAS JUST THINKING.
ABOUT THE DIVINER? I APOLOGIZE THAT YOU HAD TO--
IT'S OKAY. I DID--I DID WHAT HAD TO BE DONE, I GUESS.
BUT YOU NEED TO...CAN YOU EXPLAIN TO ME WHAT THE NEVERMIND IS? WHY ARE YOU INFECTED WITH IT? WHY DID THE DIVINER WANT TO KILL YOU FOR IT?
I THINK YOU KIND OF OWE ME ONE.
YOU...ARE RIGHT.
THE FIRST TIME I REALLY ENCOUNTERED THE NEVERMIND WAS AFTER I HAD BEEN IN TERRENOS A FEW YEARS...

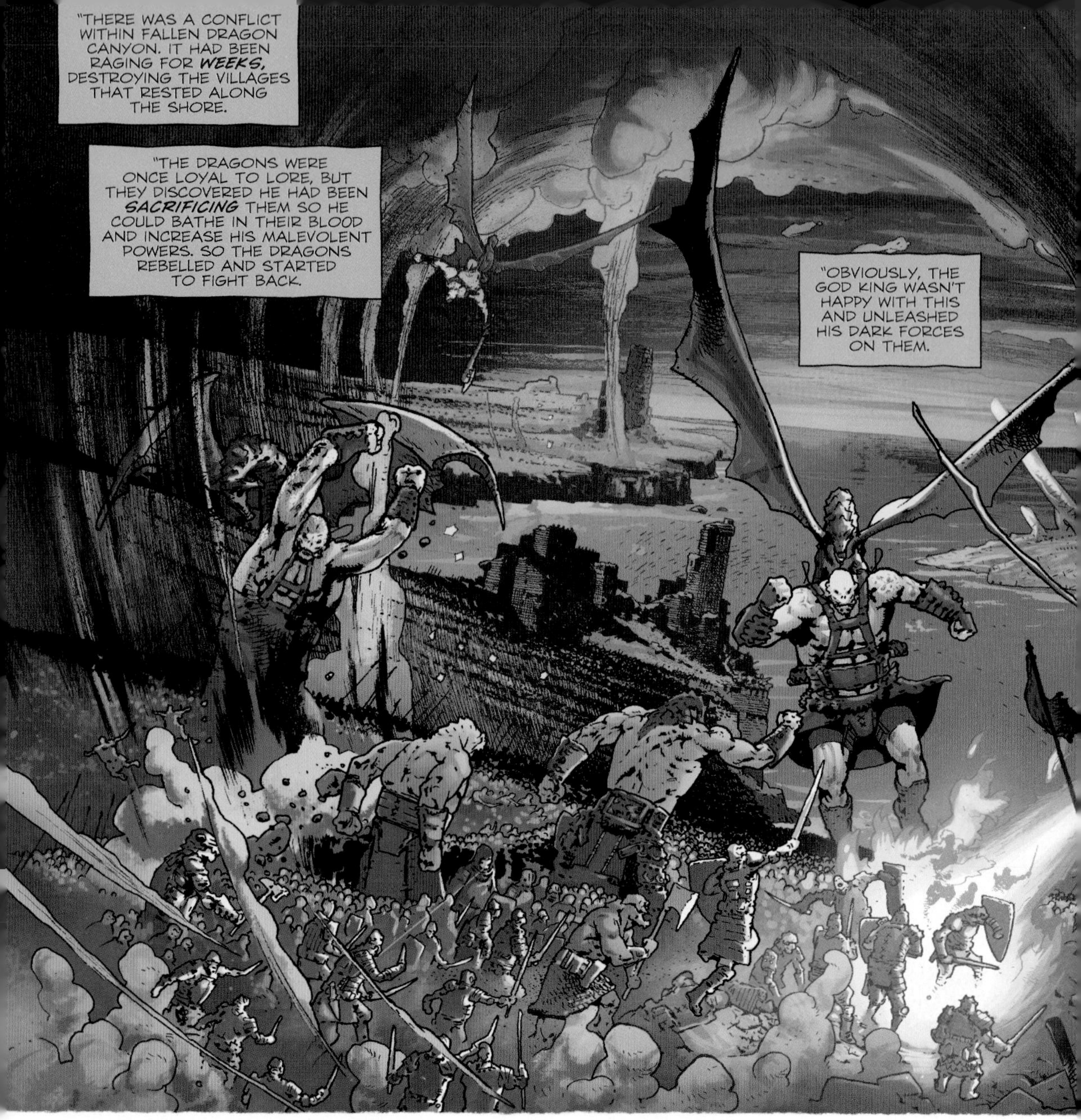
"THERE WAS A CONFLICT WITHIN FALLEN DRAGON CANYON. IT HAD BEEN RAGING FOR WEEKS, DESTROYING THE VILLAGES THAT RESTED ALONG THE SHORE.
"THE DRAGONS WERE ONCE LOYAL TO LORE, BUT THEY DISCOVERED HE HAD BEEN SACRIFICING THEM SO HE COULD BATHE IN THEIR BLOOD AND INCREASE HIS MALEVOLENT POWERS. SO THE DRAGONS REBELLED AND STARTED TO FIGHT BACK.
"OBVIOUSLY, THE GOD KING WASN'T HAPPY WITH THIS AND UNLEASHED HIS DARK FORCES ON THEM.

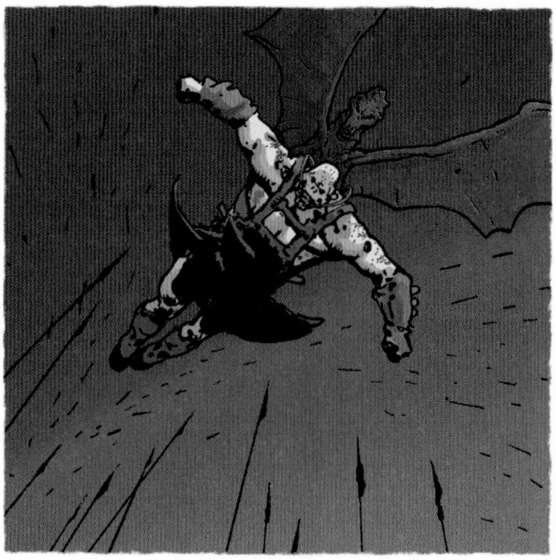

"AS A SIGN OF GOOD FAITH, WE WERE GOING THERE TO *HELP* THE DRAGONS. TO FORM A UNION.

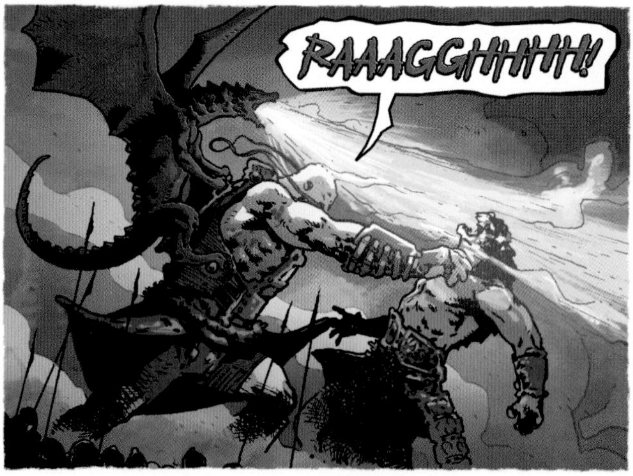
RAAAGGHHHHH!

"IN MY TIME IN TERRENOS, LORE HAD MADE MANY ATTEMPTS ON MY LIFE, BUT WITH EACH ONE I HAD SURVIVED AND MY LEGEND GREW.

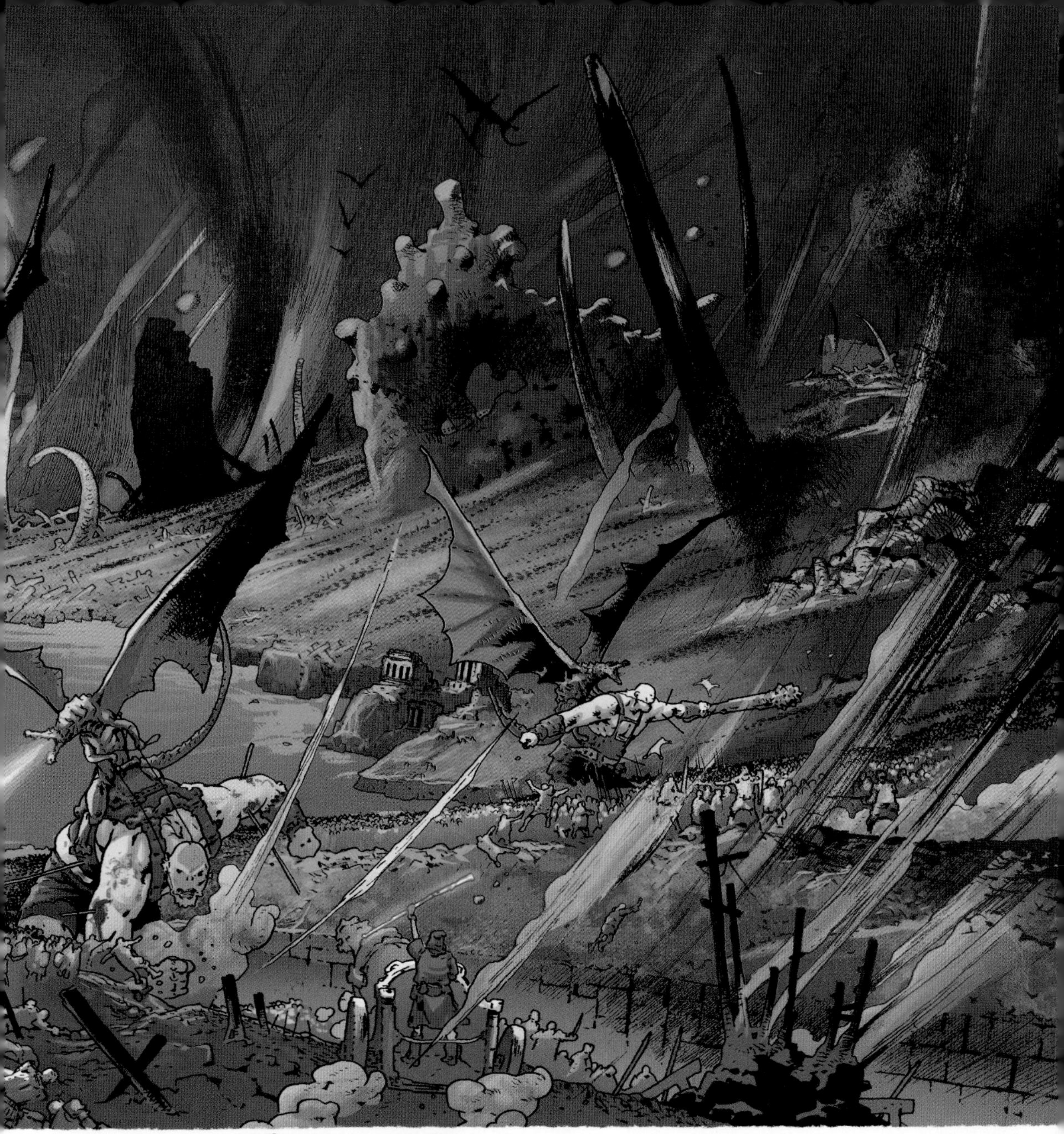

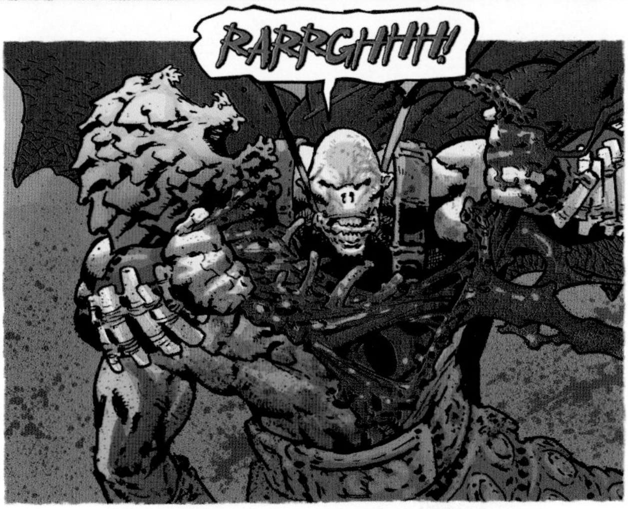
RARRGHHHH!

"ROOK WAS RIGHT...PEOPLE STARTED TO BELIEVE THAT I REALLY COULD BE THE ***CHOSEN ONE.*** THE DRAGONS WANTED TO SEE WITH THEIR OWN BLAZING EYES IF I WAS WORTH ALL THE TROUBLE.

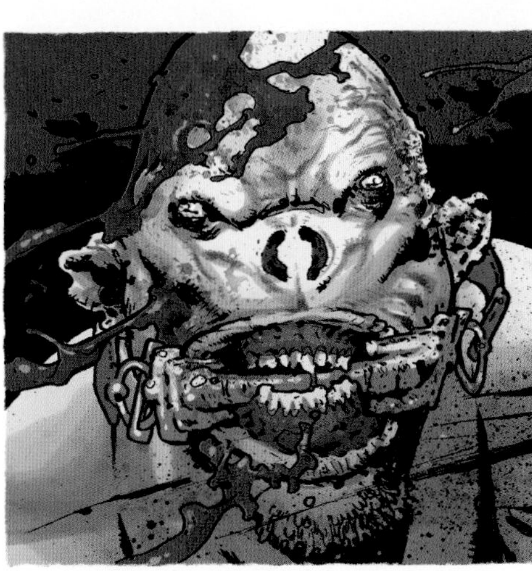

"AFTER MY TRAINING IN THE SWAMPS OF SERENITY AND THE FIELDS OF FOREVER, WE'D CROSSED THE OCEANS OF TERRENOS IN HOPES OF AIDING THE DRAGONS...

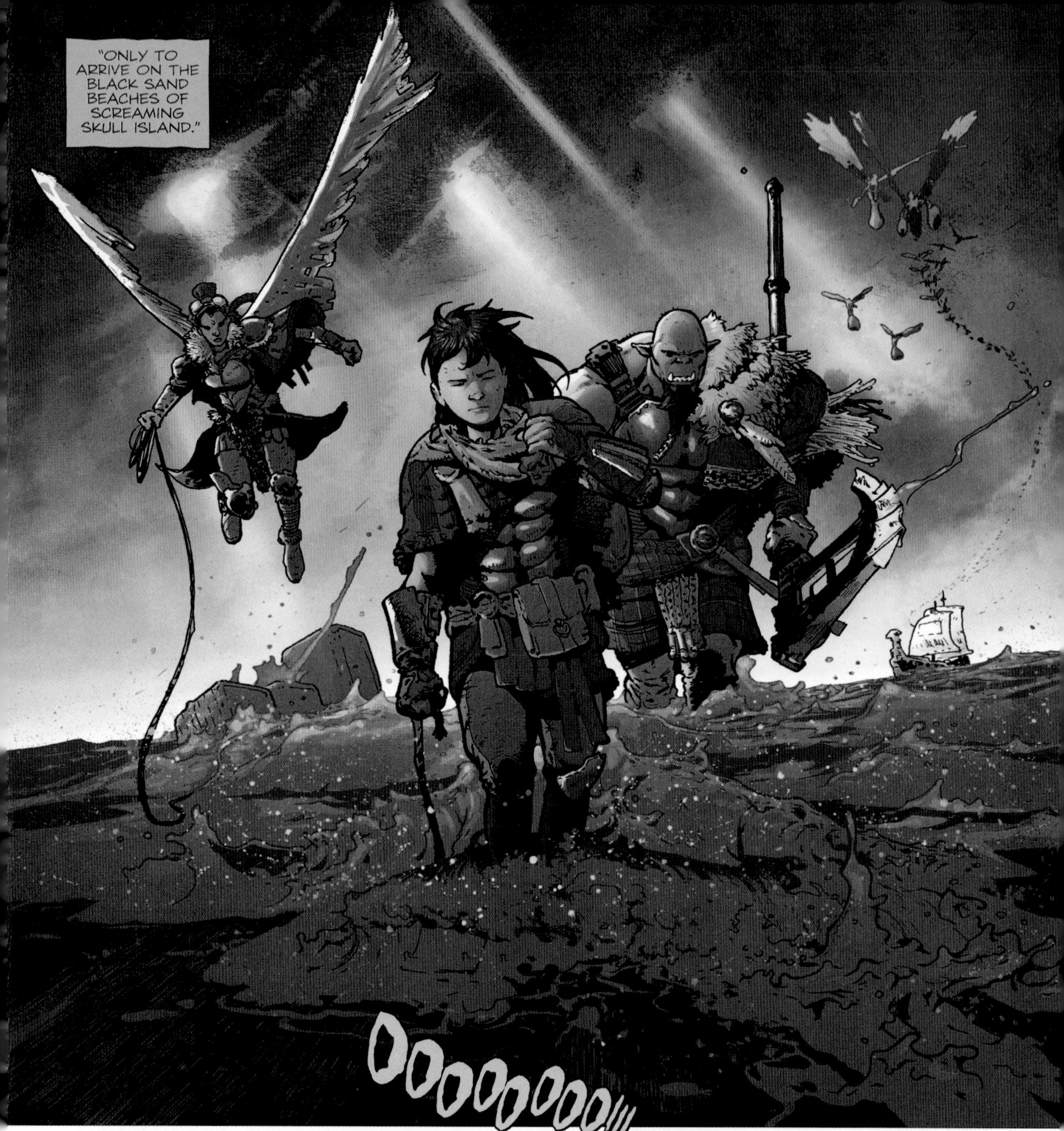
"ONLY TO ARRIVE ON THE BLACK SAND BEACHES OF SCREAMING SKULL ISLAND."
OOOOOOOOO!!!

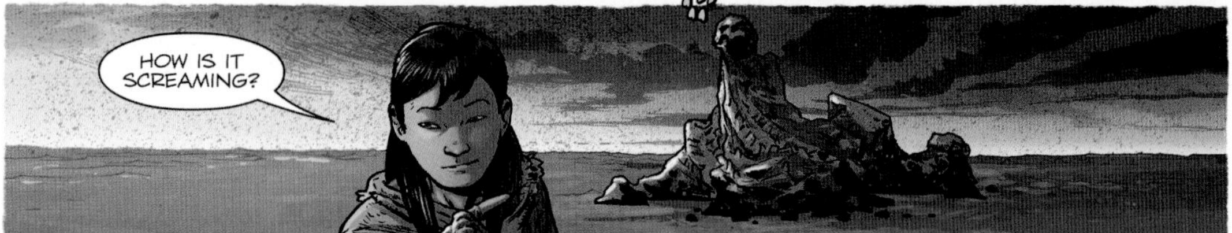
HOW IS IT SCREAMING?

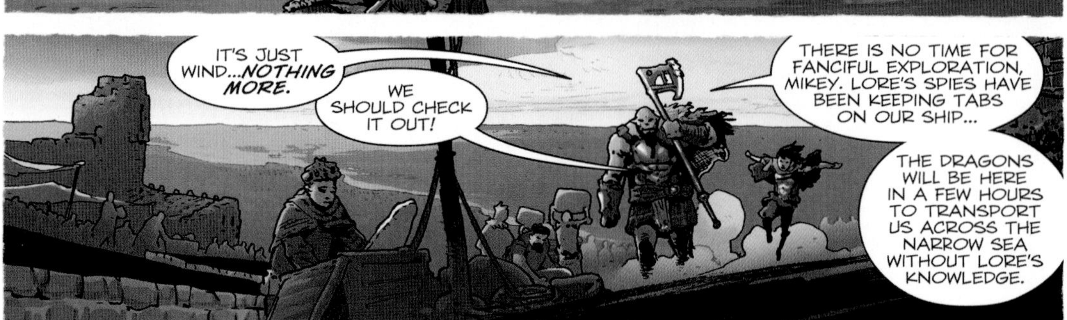
IT'S JUST WIND...NOTHING MORE.
WE SHOULD CHECK IT OUT!
THERE IS NO TIME FOR FANCIFUL EXPLORATION, MIKEY. LORE'S SPIES HAVE BEEN KEEPING TABS ON OUR SHIP...
THE DRAGONS WILL BE HERE IN A FEW HOURS TO TRANSPORT US ACROSS THE NARROW SEA WITHOUT LORE'S KNOWLEDGE.

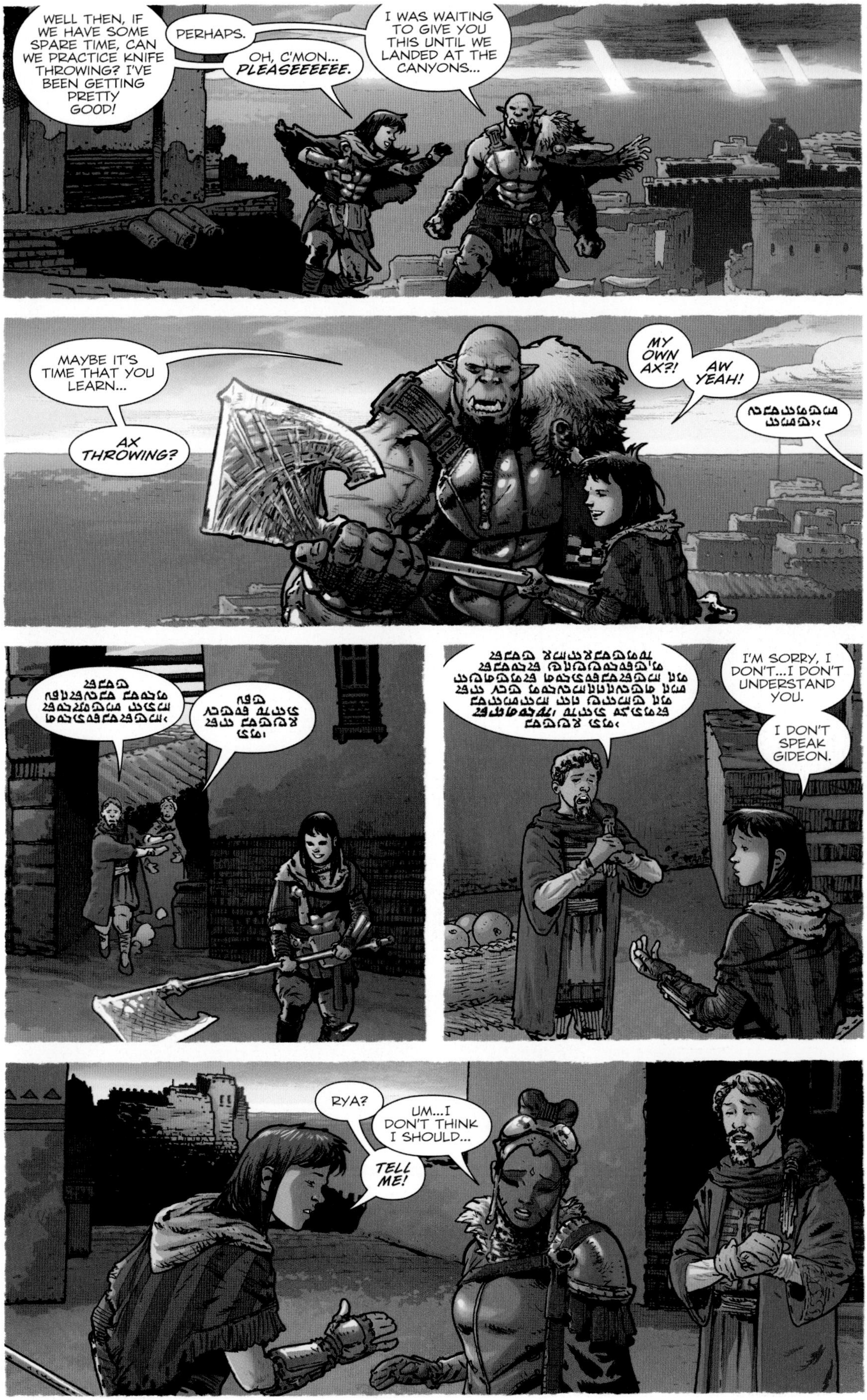
WELL THEN, IF WE HAVE SOME SPARE TIME, CAN WE PRACTICE KNIFE THROWING? I'VE BEEN GETTING PRETTY GOOD!
PERHAPS.
OH, C'MON... ***PLEASEEEEEEE.***
I WAS WAITING TO GIVE YOU THIS UNTIL WE LANDED AT THE CANYONS...
MAYBE IT'S TIME THAT YOU LEARN...
AX THROWING?
MY OWN AX?!
AW YEAH!
I'M SORRY, I DON'T...I DON'T UNDERSTAND YOU.
I DON'T SPEAK GIDEON.
RYA?
UM...I DON'T THINK I SHOULD...
TELL ME!

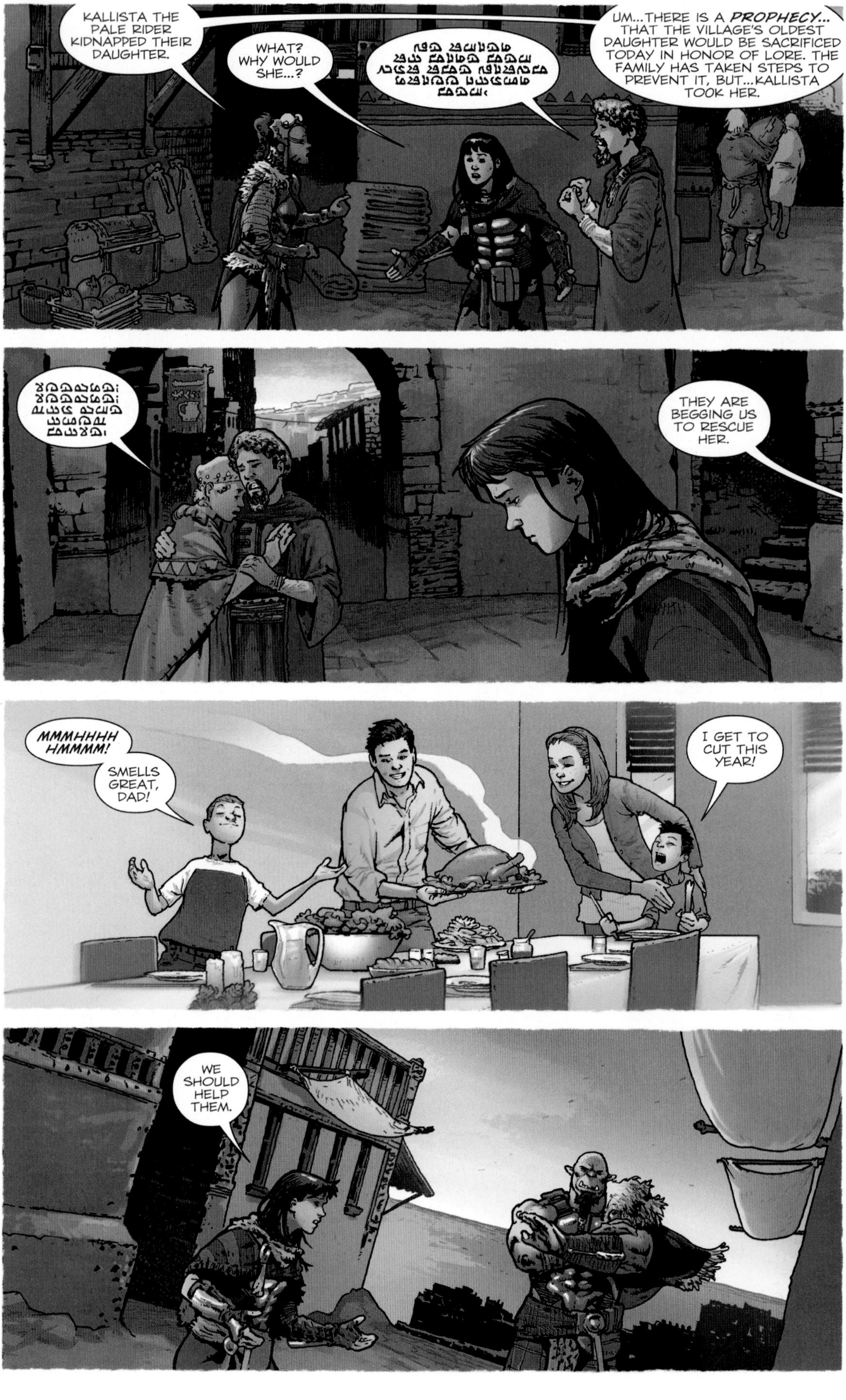
KALLISTA THE PALE RIDER KIDNAPPED THEIR DAUGHTER.
WHAT? WHY WOULD SHE...?
UM...THERE IS A ***PROPHECY...*** THAT THE VILLAGE'S OLDEST DAUGHTER WOULD BE SACRIFICED TODAY IN HONOR OF LORE. THE FAMILY HAS TAKEN STEPS TO PREVENT IT, BUT...KALLISTA TOOK HER.
THEY ARE BEGGING US TO RESCUE HER.
MMMHHHH HMMMM!
SMELLS GREAT, DAD!
I GET TO CUT THIS YEAR!
WE SHOULD HELP THEM.

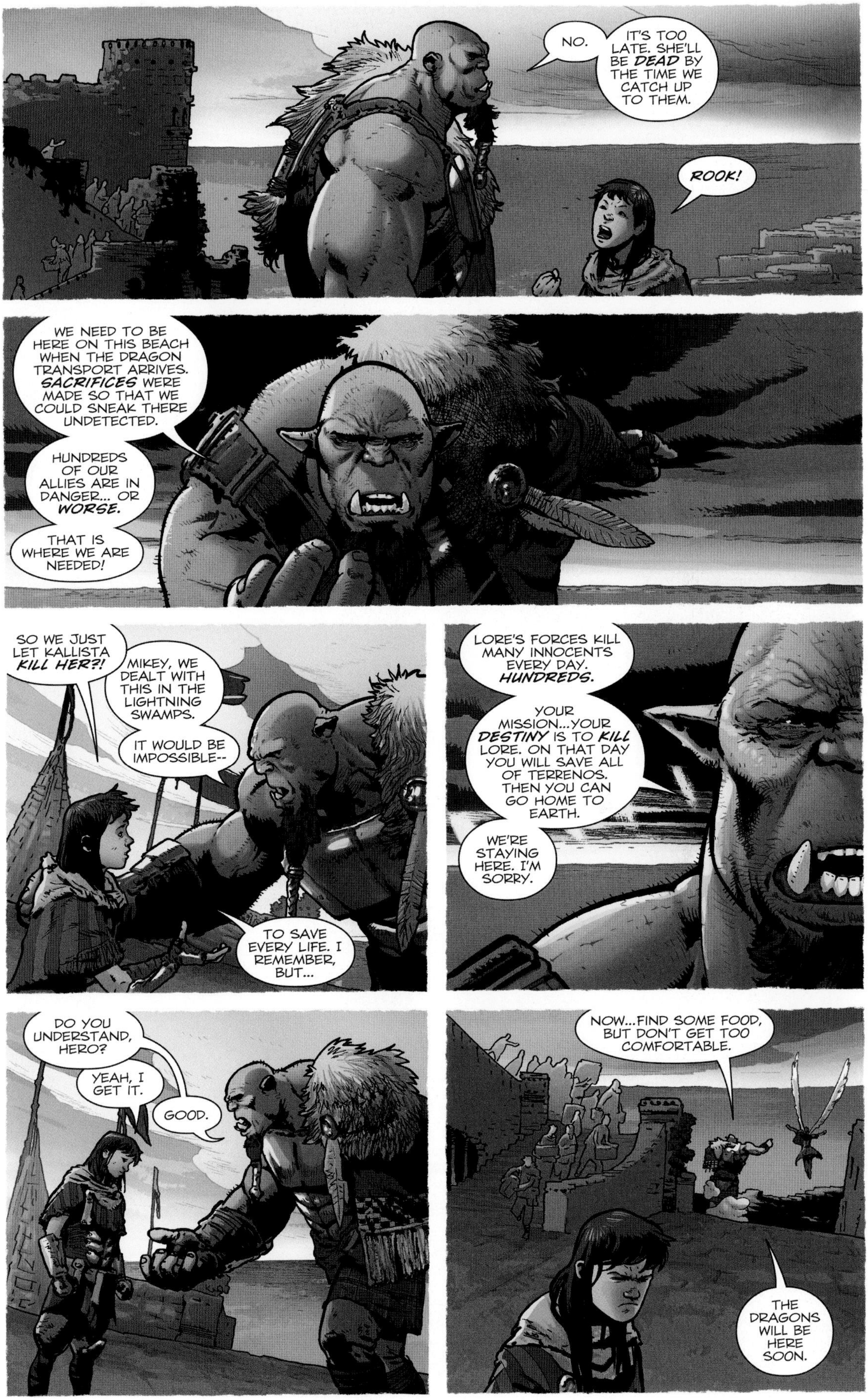
NO.
IT'S TOO LATE. SHE'LL BE DEAD BY THE TIME WE CATCH UP TO THEM.
ROOK!
WE NEED TO BE HERE ON THIS BEACH WHEN THE DRAGON TRANSPORT ARRIVES. SACRIFICES WERE MADE SO THAT WE COULD SNEAK THERE UNDETECTED.
HUNDREDS OF OUR ALLIES ARE IN DANGER... OR WORSE.
THAT IS WHERE WE ARE NEEDED!
SO WE JUST LET KALLISTA KILL HER?!
MIKEY, WE DEALT WITH THIS IN THE LIGHTNING SWAMPS.
IT WOULD BE IMPOSSIBLE--
TO SAVE EVERY LIFE. I REMEMBER, BUT...
LORE'S FORCES KILL MANY INNOCENTS EVERY DAY. HUNDREDS.
YOUR MISSION...YOUR DESTINY IS TO KILL LORE. ON THAT DAY YOU WILL SAVE ALL OF TERRENOS. THEN YOU CAN GO HOME TO EARTH.
WE'RE STAYING HERE. I'M SORRY.
DO YOU UNDERSTAND, HERO?
YEAH, I GET IT.
GOOD.
NOW...FIND SOME FOOD, BUT DON'T GET TOO COMFORTABLE.
THE DRAGONS WILL BE HERE SOON.

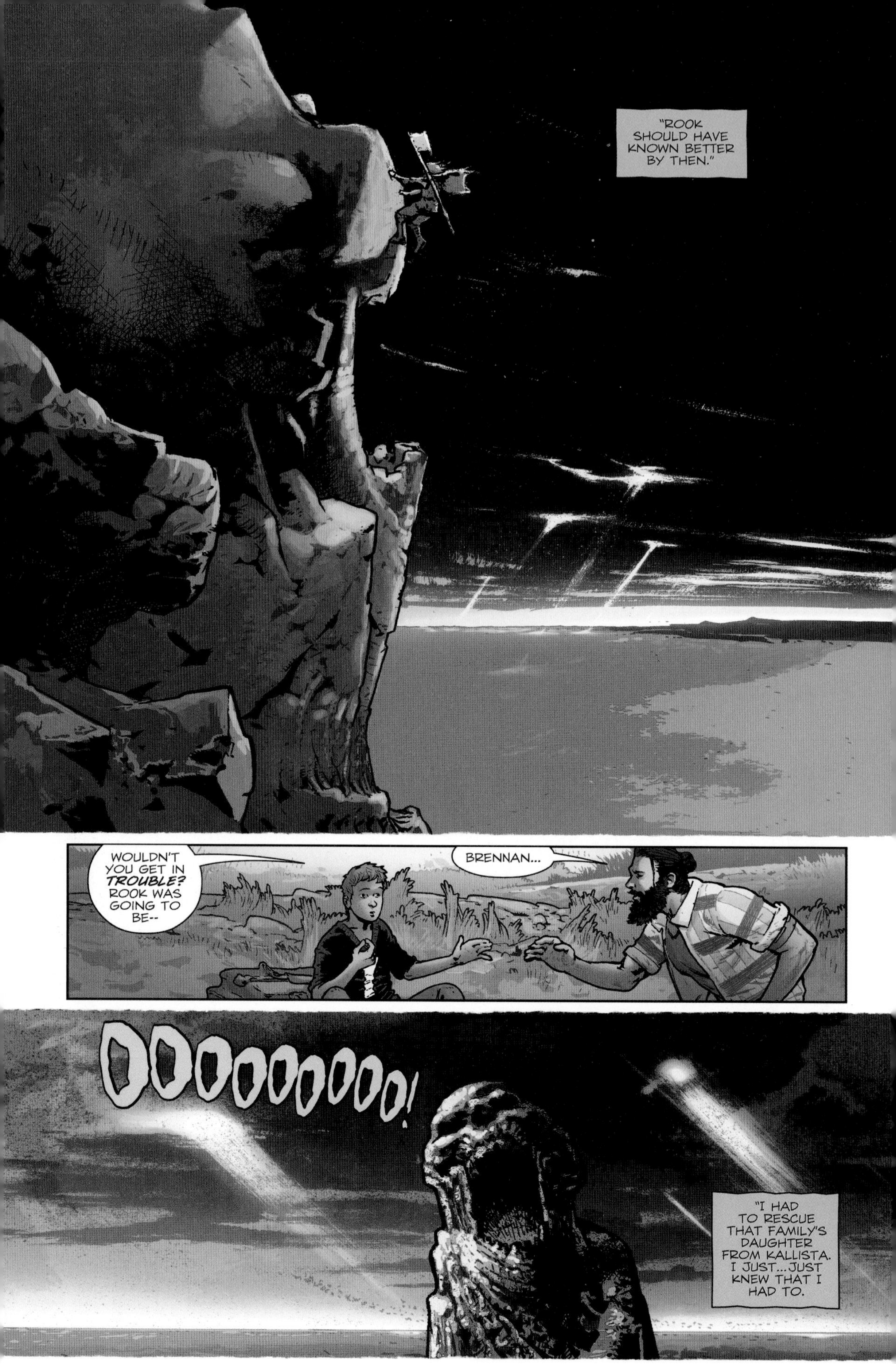
"ROOK SHOULD HAVE KNOWN BETTER BY THEN."
WOULDN'T YOU GET IN *TROUBLE?* ROOK WAS GOING TO BE--
BRENNAN...
OOOOOOOOO!
"I HAD TO RESCUE THAT FAMILY'S DAUGHTER FROM KALLISTA. I JUST...JUST KNEW THAT I HAD TO.

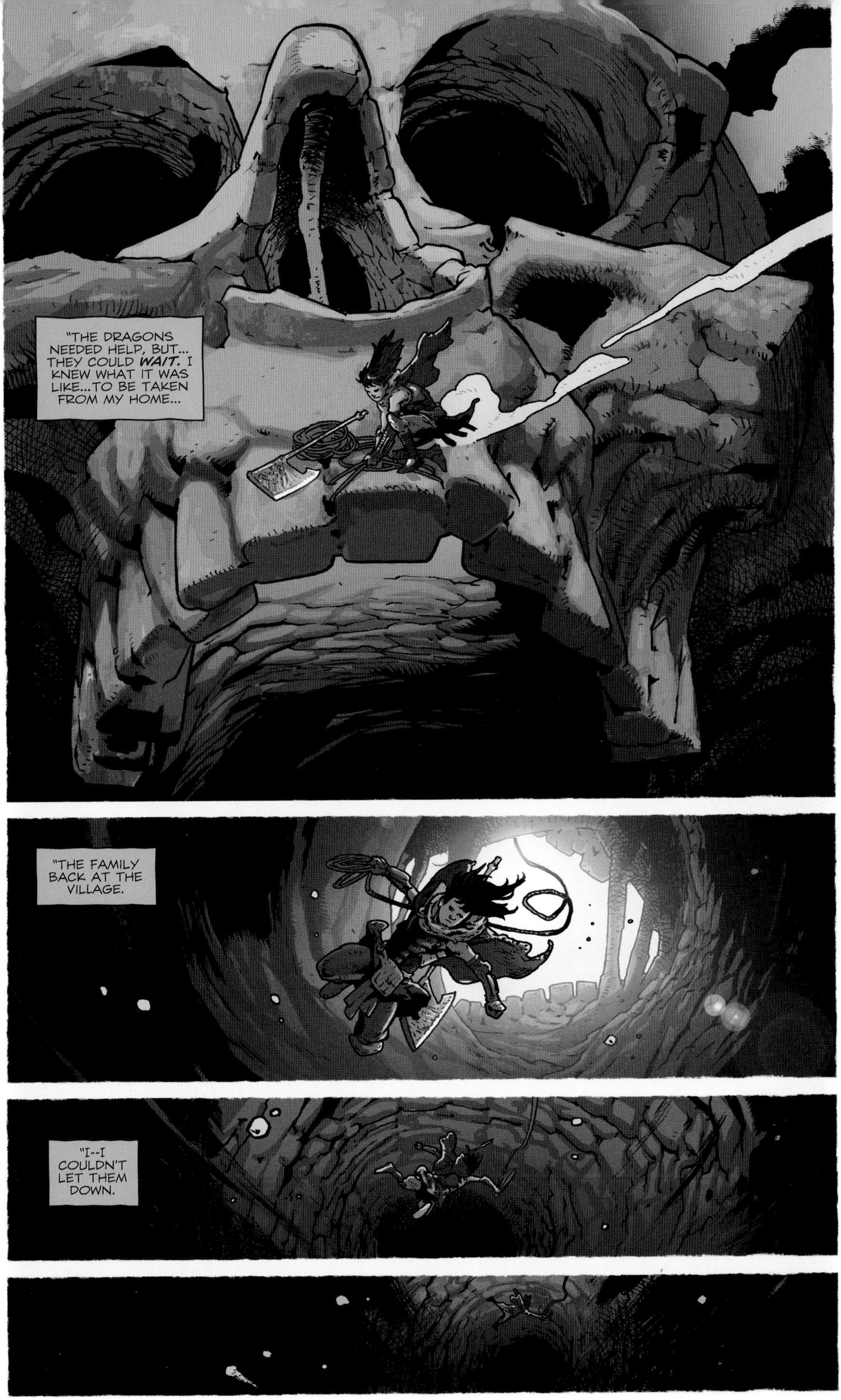
"THE DRAGONS NEEDED HELP, BUT... THEY COULD *WAIT.* I KNEW WHAT IT WAS LIKE...TO BE TAKEN FROM MY HOME...
"THE FAMILY BACK AT THE VILLAGE.
"I--I COULDN'T LET THEM DOWN.

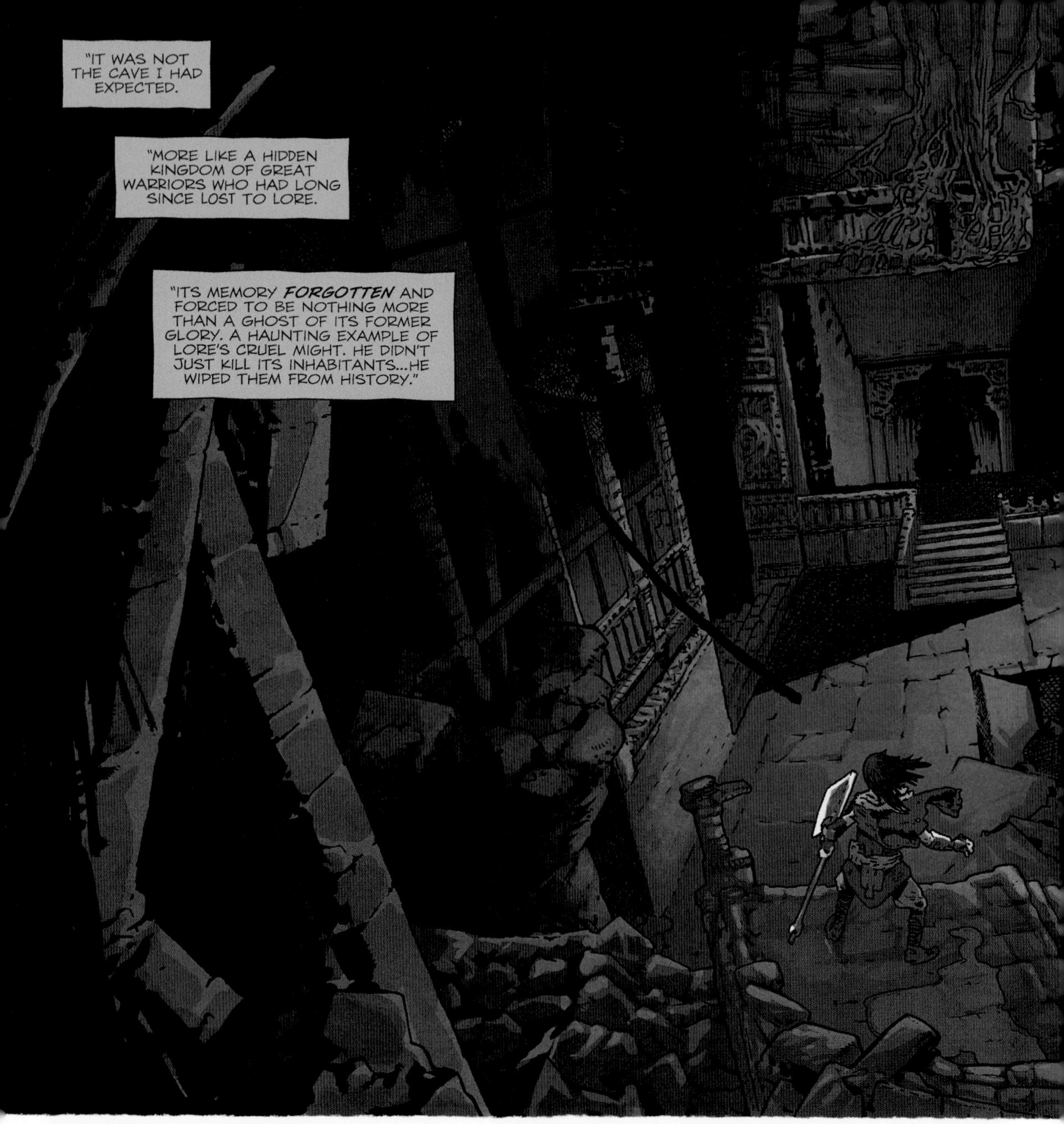
"IT WAS NOT THE CAVE I HAD EXPECTED.
"MORE LIKE A HIDDEN KINGDOM OF GREAT WARRIORS WHO HAD LONG SINCE LOST TO LORE.
"ITS MEMORY FORGOTTEN AND FORCED TO BE NOTHING MORE THAN A GHOST OF ITS FORMER GLORY. A HAUNTING EXAMPLE OF LORE'S CRUEL MIGHT. HE DIDN'T JUST KILL ITS INHABITANTS...HE WIPED THEM FROM HISTORY."
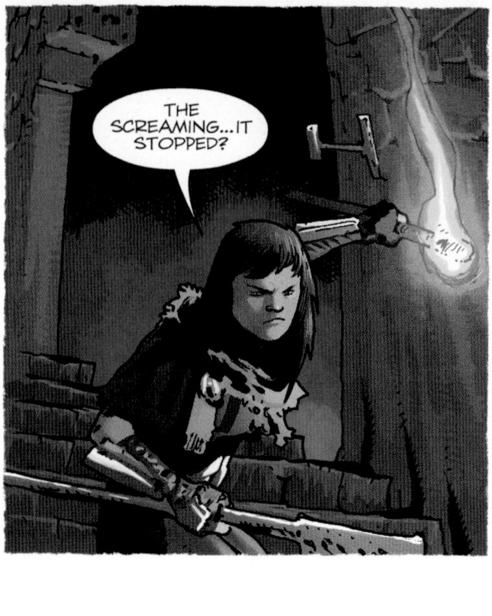
THE SCREAMING...IT STOPPED?
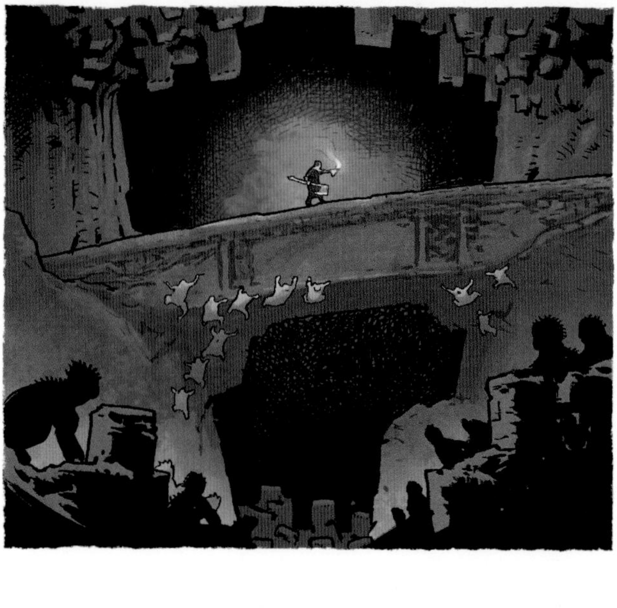

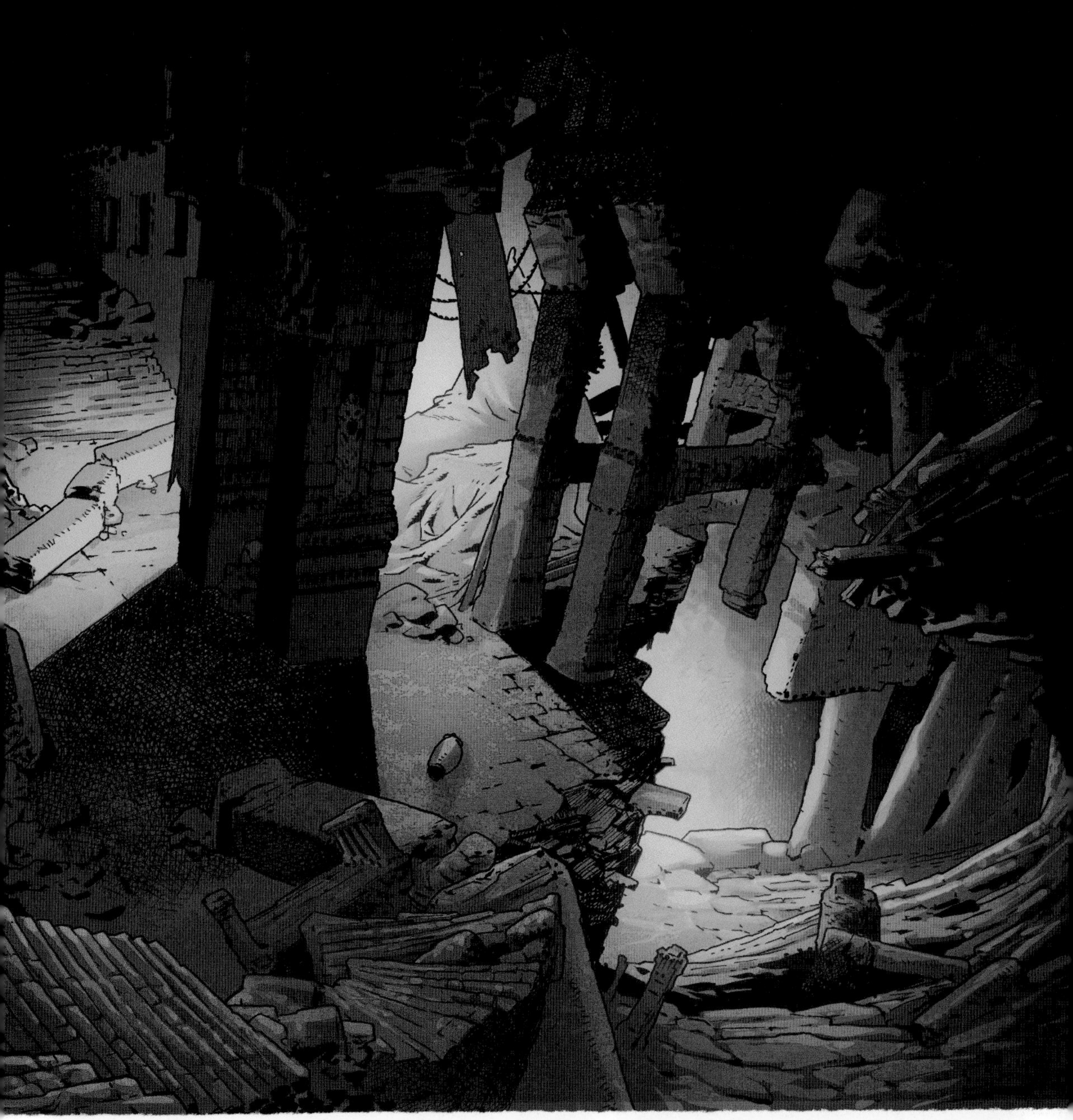

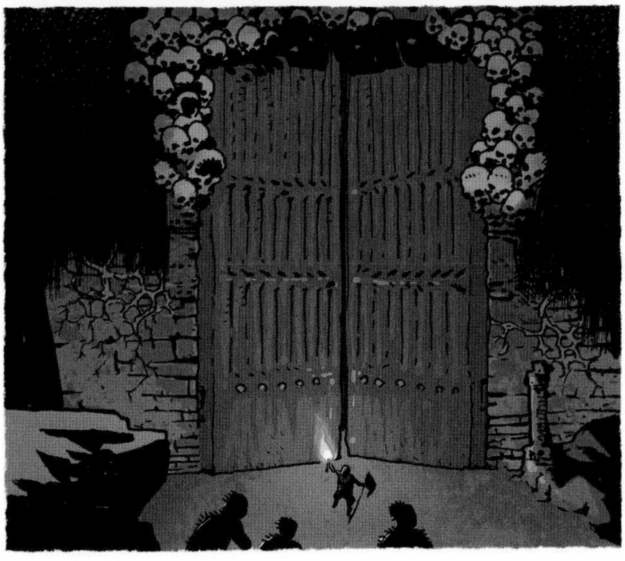

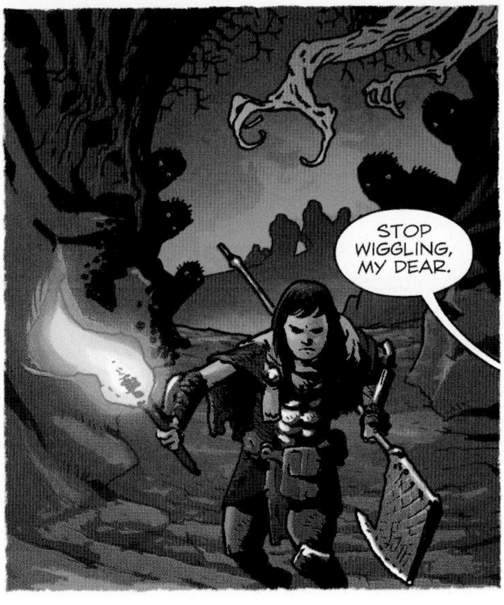
STOP WIGGLING, MY DEAR.

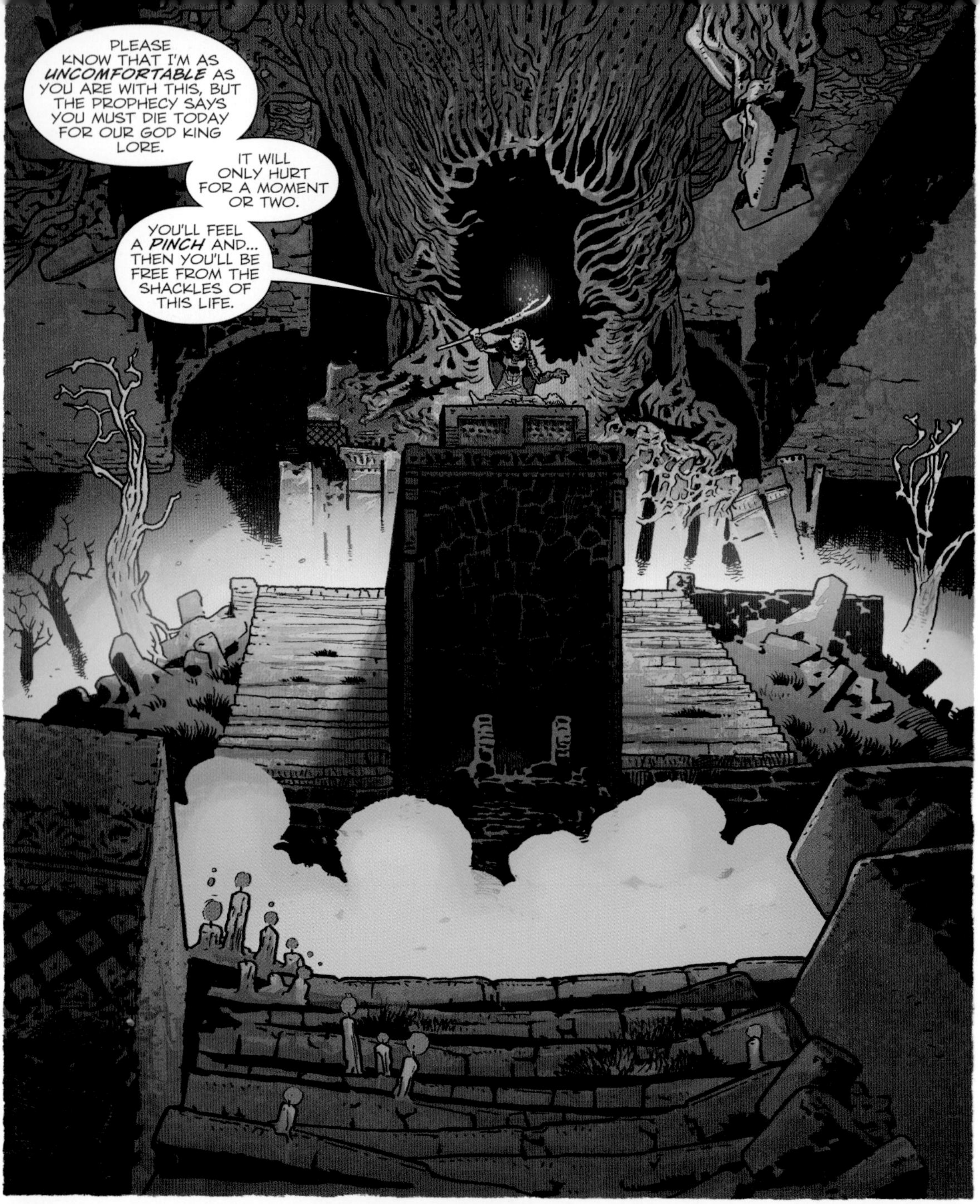
PLEASE KNOW THAT I'M AS *UNCOMFORTABLE* AS YOU ARE WITH THIS, BUT THE PROPHECY SAYS YOU MUST DIE TODAY FOR OUR GOD KING LORE.
IT WILL ONLY HURT FOR A MOMENT OR TWO.
YOU'LL FEEL A *PINCH* AND... THEN YOU'LL BE FREE FROM THE SHACKLES OF THIS LIFE.
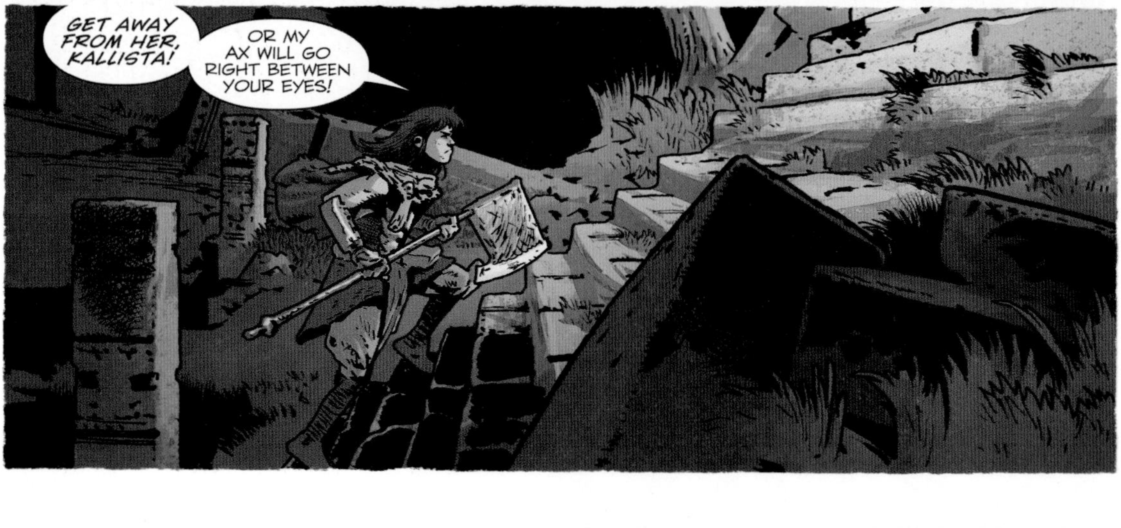
GET AWAY FROM HER, KALLISTA!
OR MY AX WILL GO RIGHT BETWEEN YOUR EYES!

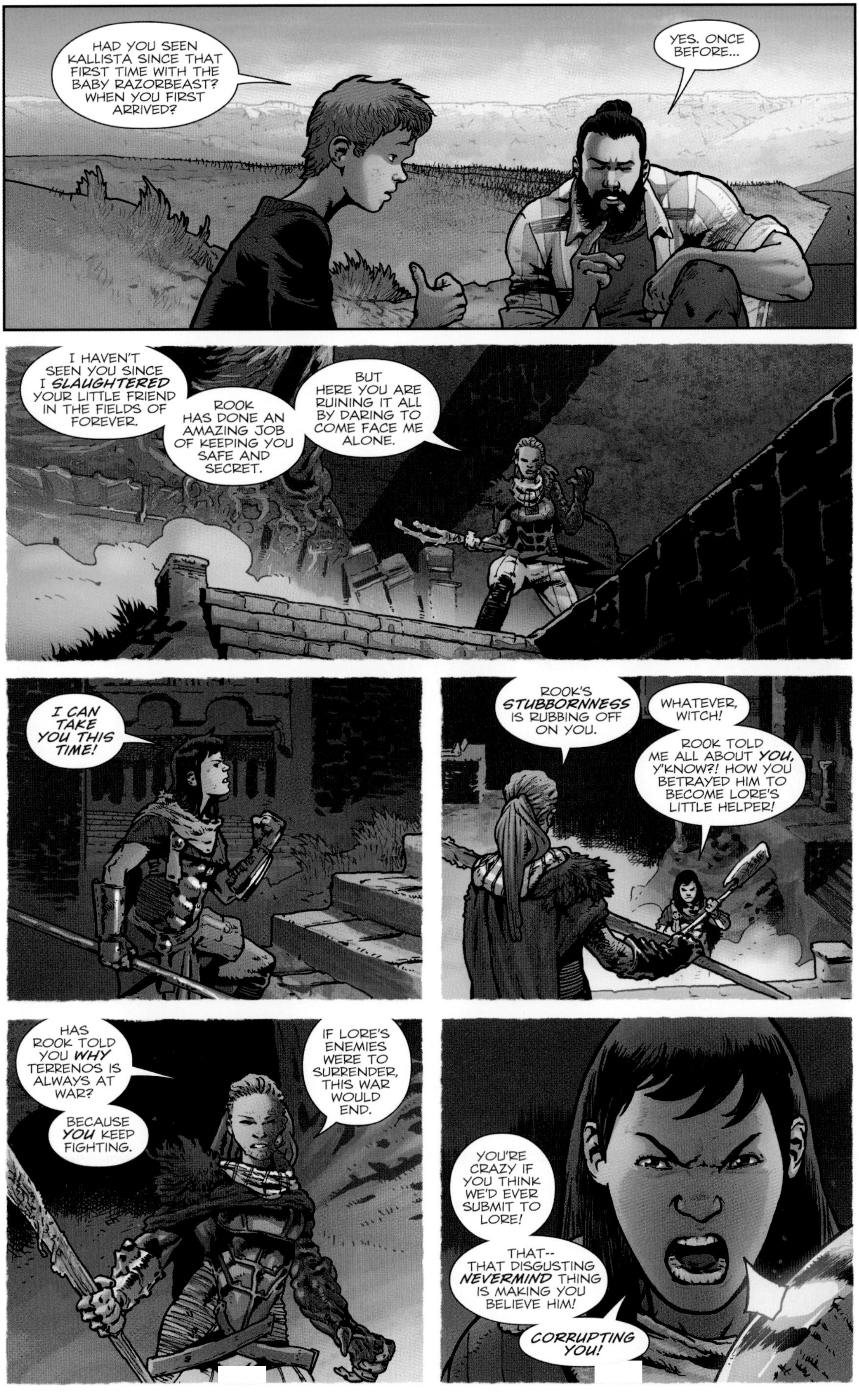
HAD YOU SEEN KALLISTA SINCE THAT FIRST TIME WITH THE BABY RAZORBEAST? WHEN YOU FIRST ARRIVED?
YES. ONCE BEFORE...
I HAVEN'T SEEN YOU SINCE I SLAUGHTERED YOUR LITTLE FRIEND IN THE FIELDS OF FOREVER.
ROOK HAS DONE AN AMAZING JOB OF KEEPING YOU SAFE AND SECRET.
BUT HERE YOU ARE RUINING IT ALL BY DARING TO COME FACE ME ALONE.
I CAN TAKE YOU THIS TIME!
ROOK'S STUBBORNNESS IS RUBBING OFF ON YOU.
WHATEVER, WITCH!
ROOK TOLD ME ALL ABOUT YOU, Y'KNOW?! HOW YOU BETRAYED HIM TO BECOME LORE'S LITTLE HELPER!
HAS ROOK TOLD YOU WHY TERRENOS IS ALWAYS AT WAR?
BECAUSE YOU KEEP FIGHTING.
IF LORE'S ENEMIES WERE TO SURRENDER, THIS WAR WOULD END.
YOU'RE CRAZY IF YOU THINK WE'D EVER SUBMIT TO LORE!
THAT-- THAT DISGUSTING NEVERMIND THING IS MAKING YOU BELIEVE HIM!
CORRUPTING YOU!

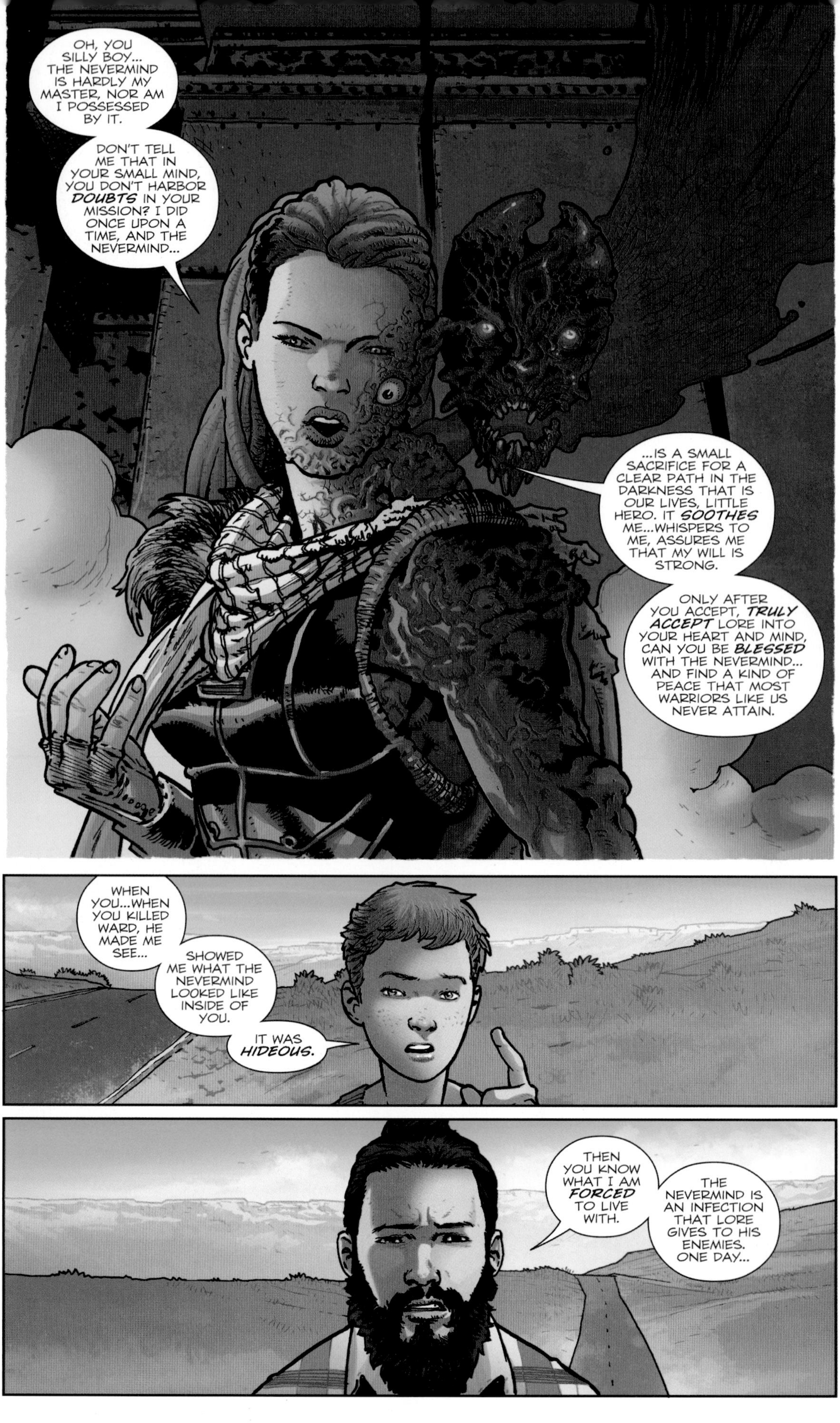
OH, YOU SILLY BOY... THE NEVERMIND IS HARDLY MY MASTER, NOR AM I POSSESSED BY IT.
DON'T TELL ME THAT IN YOUR SMALL MIND, YOU DON'T HARBOR DOUBTS IN YOUR MISSION? I DID ONCE UPON A TIME, AND THE NEVERMIND...
...IS A SMALL SACRIFICE FOR A CLEAR PATH IN THE DARKNESS THAT IS OUR LIVES, LITTLE HERO. IT SOOTHES ME...WHISPERS TO ME, ASSURES ME THAT MY WILL IS STRONG.
ONLY AFTER YOU ACCEPT, TRULY ACCEPT LORE INTO YOUR HEART AND MIND, CAN YOU BE BLESSED WITH THE NEVERMIND... AND FIND A KIND OF PEACE THAT MOST WARRIORS LIKE US NEVER ATTAIN.
WHEN YOU...WHEN YOU KILLED WARD, HE MADE ME SEE...
SHOWED ME WHAT THE NEVERMIND LOOKED LIKE INSIDE OF YOU.
IT WAS HIDEOUS.
THEN YOU KNOW WHAT I AM FORCED TO LIVE WITH.
THE NEVERMIND IS AN INFECTION THAT LORE GIVES TO HIS ENEMIES. ONE DAY...

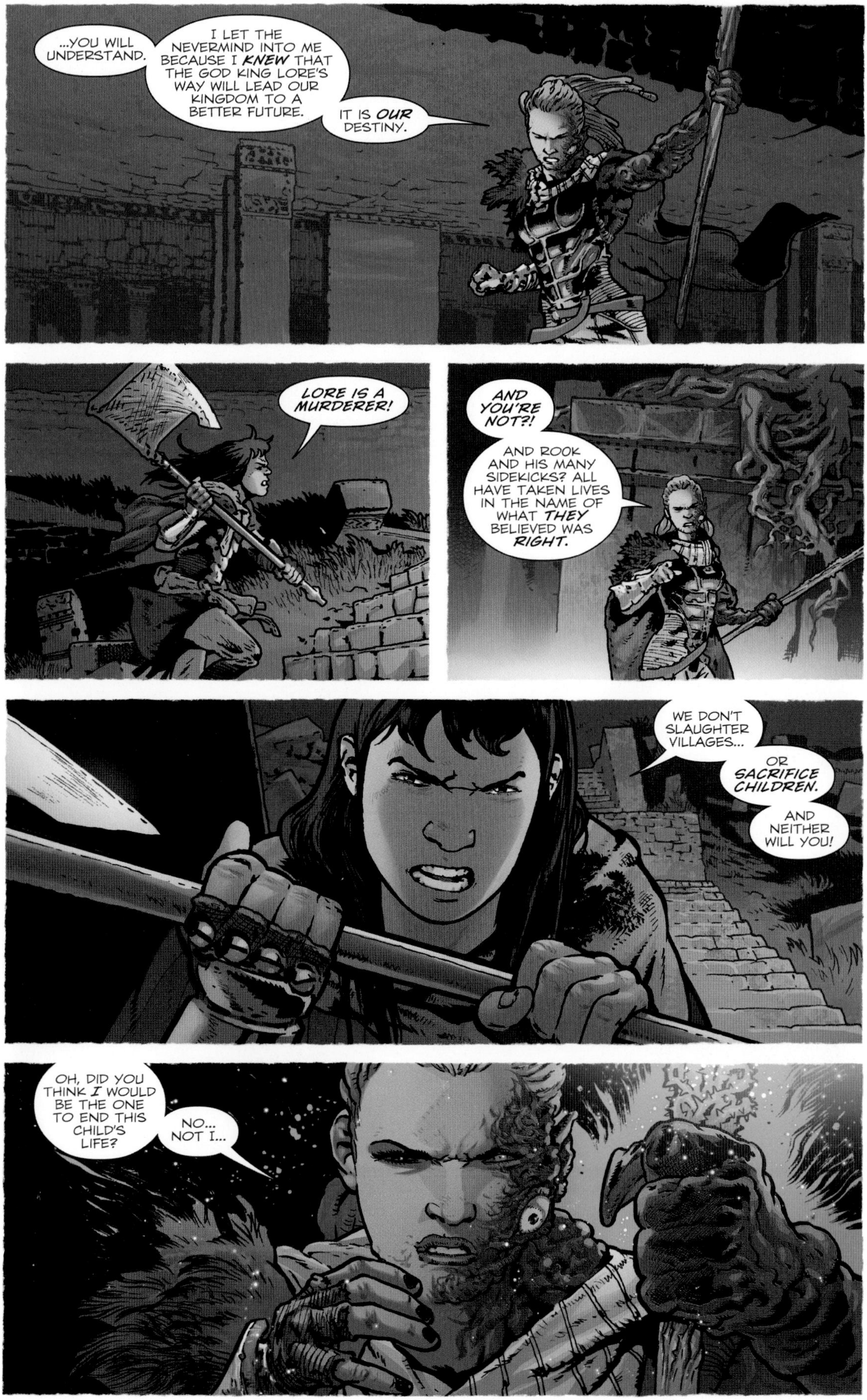
...YOU WILL UNDERSTAND.
I LET THE NEVERMIND INTO ME BECAUSE I KNEW THAT THE GOD KING LORE'S WAY WILL LEAD OUR KINGDOM TO A BETTER FUTURE.
IT IS OUR DESTINY.
LORE IS A MURDERER!
AND YOU'RE NOT?!
AND ROOK AND HIS MANY SIDEKICKS? ALL HAVE TAKEN LIVES IN THE NAME OF WHAT THEY BELIEVED WAS RIGHT.
WE DON'T SLAUGHTER VILLAGES...
OR SACRIFICE CHILDREN.
AND NEITHER WILL YOU!
OH, DID YOU THINK I WOULD BE THE ONE TO END THIS CHILD'S LIFE?
NO... NOT I...

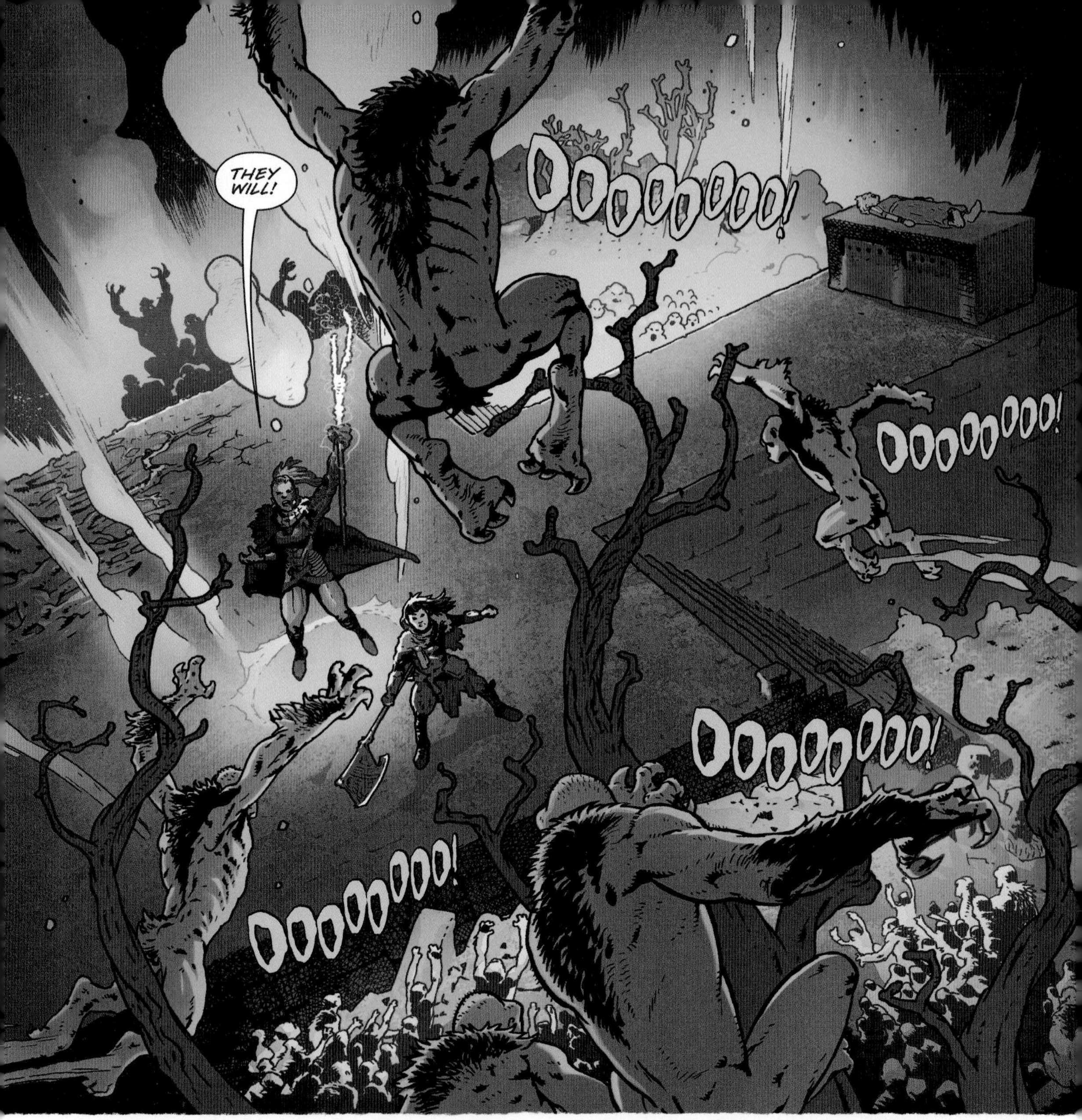
THEY WILL!
OOOOOOOOO!
OOOOOOOOO!
OOOOOOOOOO!
OOOOOOOOOO!

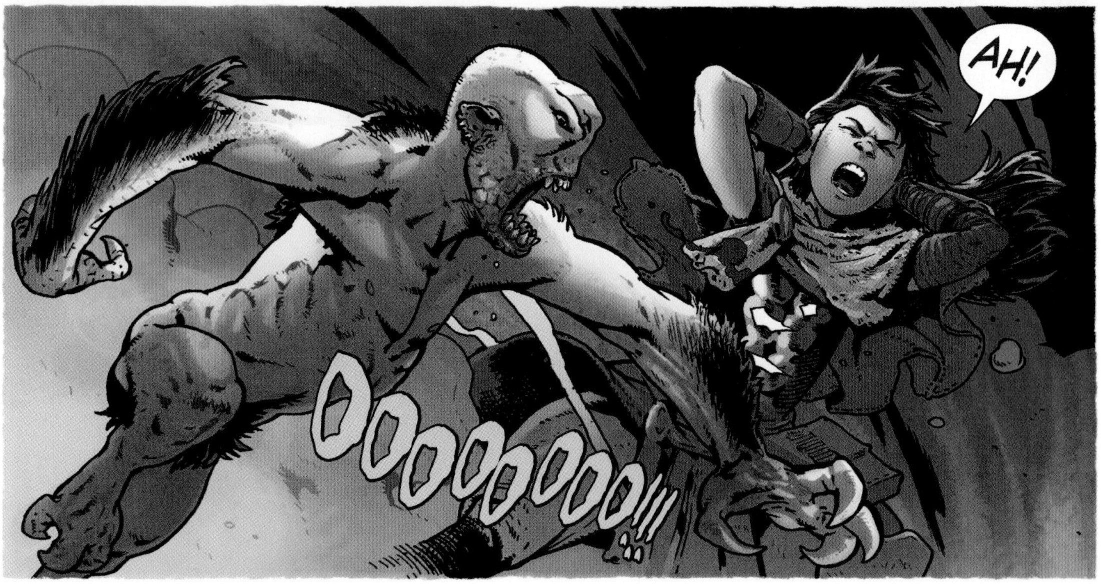
AH!
OOOOOOOOOO!!!

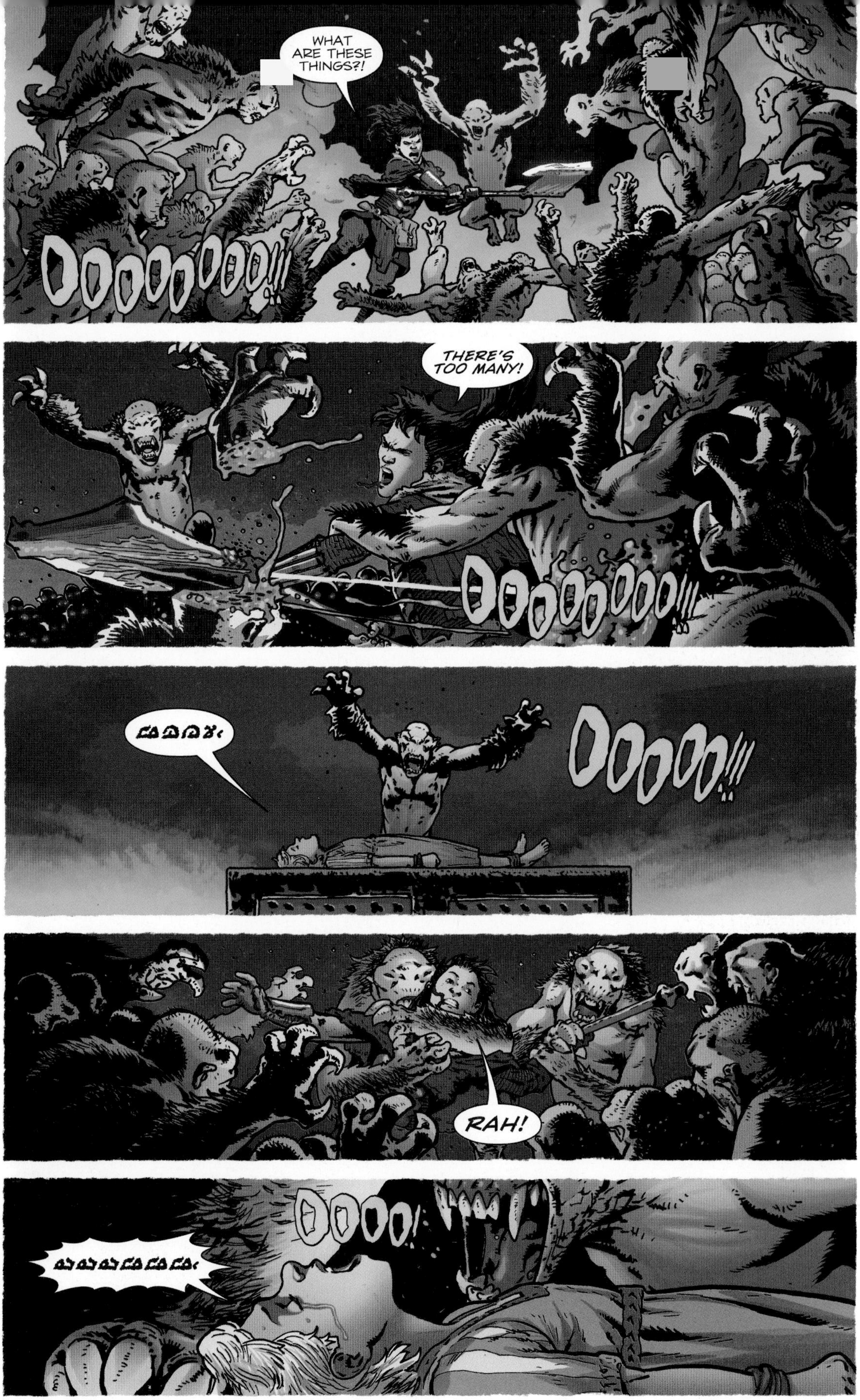
WHAT ARE THESE THINGS?!
OOOOOOOOO!!!
THERE'S TOO MANY!
OOOOOOOOO!!!
OOOOO!!!
RAH!
OOOO!

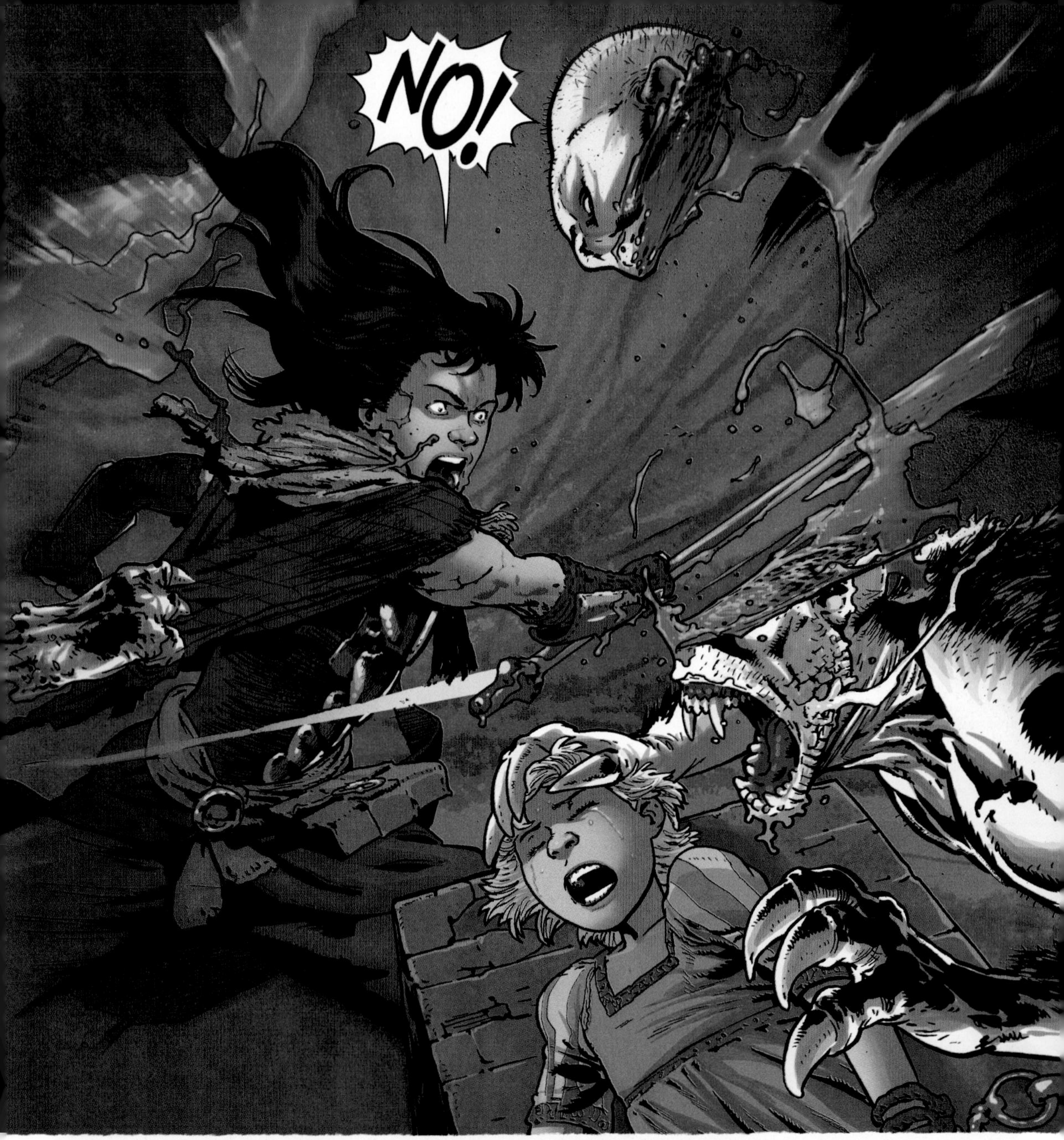
NO!

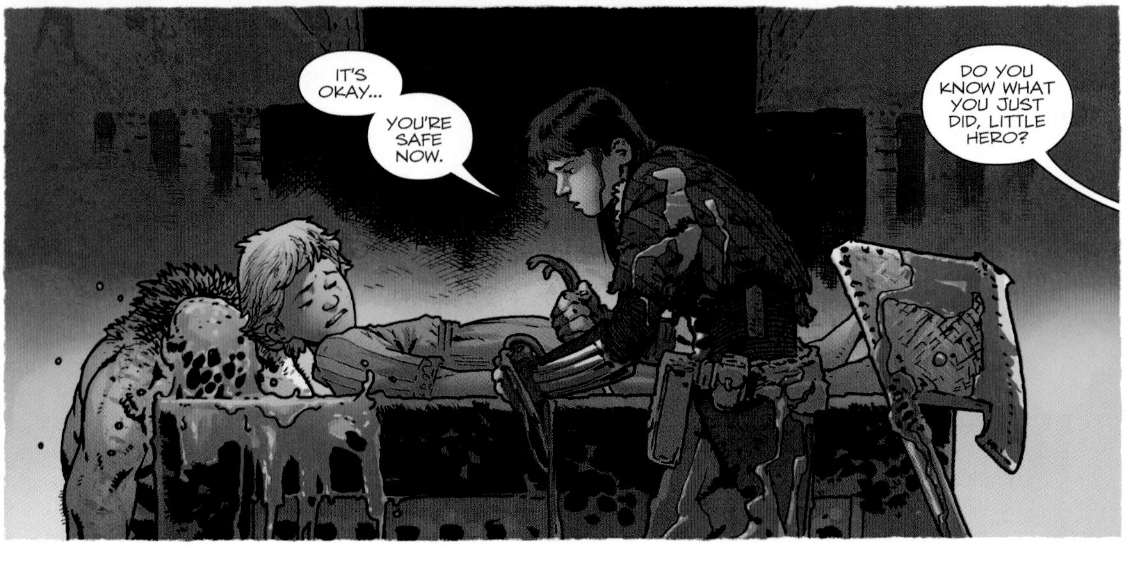
IT'S OKAY...
YOU'RE SAFE NOW.
DO YOU KNOW WHAT YOU JUST DID, LITTLE HERO?

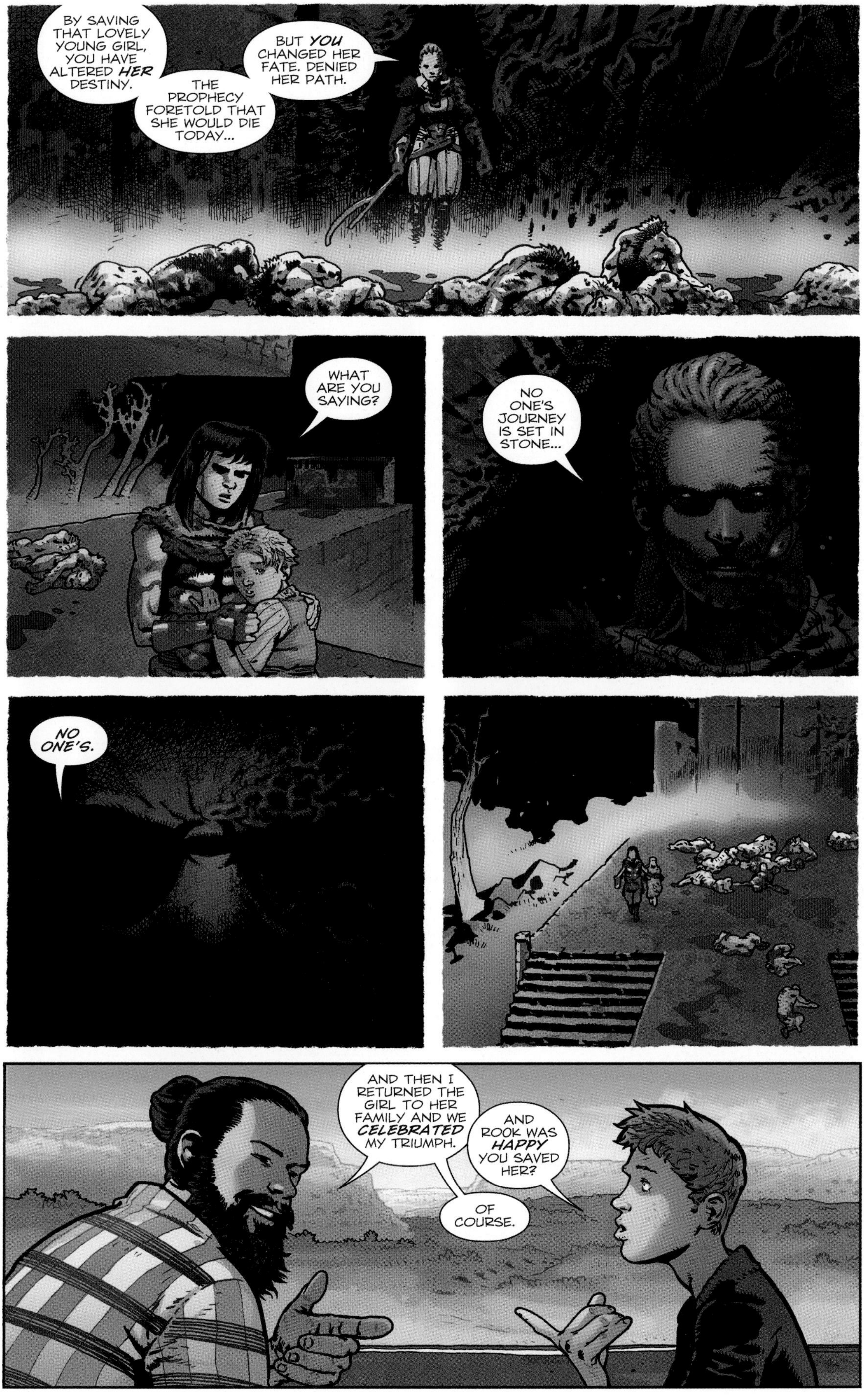
BY SAVING THAT LOVELY YOUNG GIRL, YOU HAVE ALTERED HER DESTINY.
THE PROPHECY FORETOLD THAT SHE WOULD DIE TODAY...
BUT YOU CHANGED HER FATE. DENIED HER PATH.
WHAT ARE YOU SAYING?
NO ONE'S JOURNEY IS SET IN STONE...
NO ONE'S.
AND THEN I RETURNED THE GIRL TO HER FAMILY AND WE CELEBRATED MY TRIUMPH.
AND ROOK WAS HAPPY YOU SAVED HER?
OF COURSE.

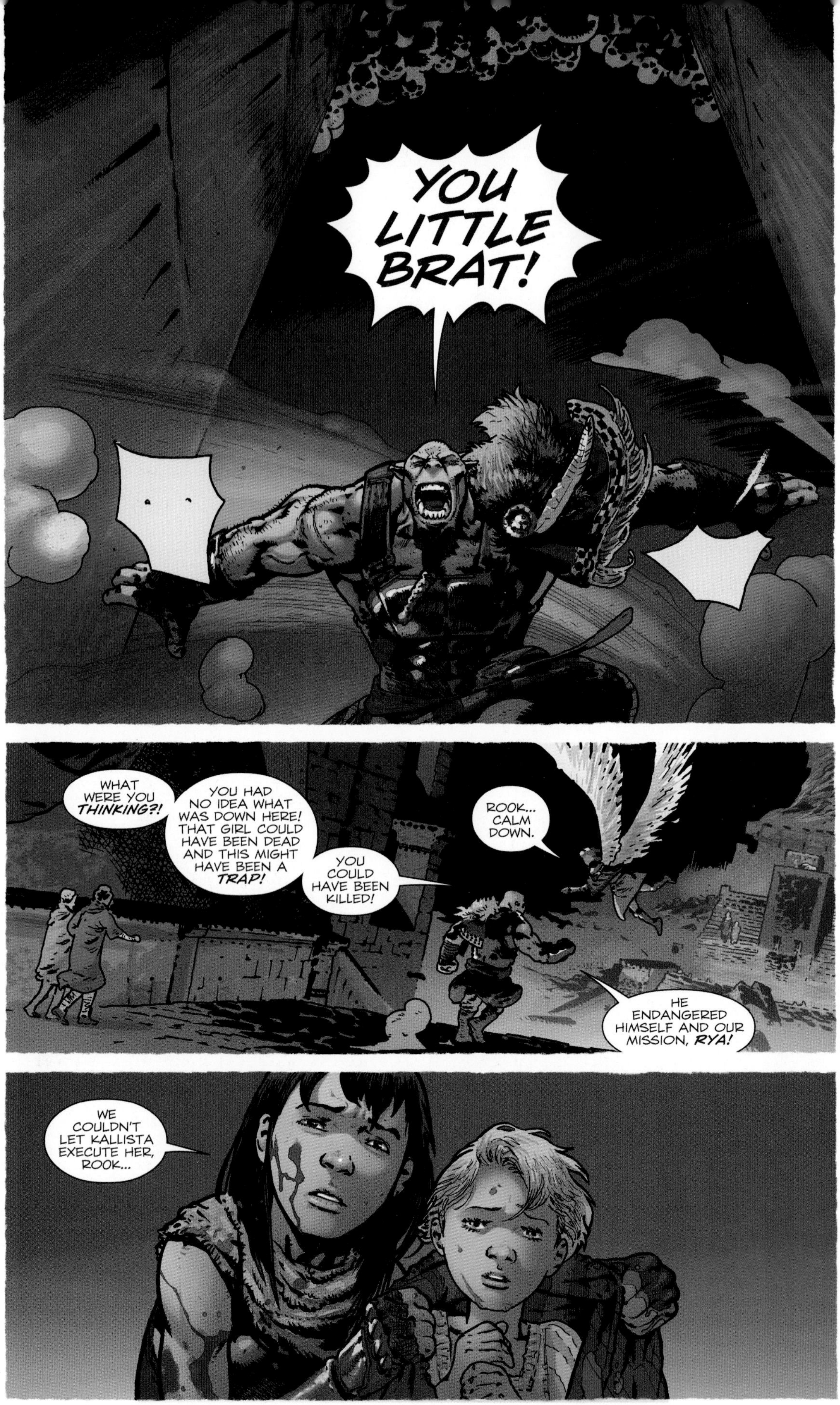
YOU LITTLE BRAT!
WHAT WERE YOU THINKING?!
YOU HAD NO IDEA WHAT WAS DOWN HERE! THAT GIRL COULD HAVE BEEN DEAD AND THIS MIGHT HAVE BEEN A TRAP!
YOU COULD HAVE BEEN KILLED!
ROOK... CALM DOWN.
HE ENDANGERED HIMSELF AND OUR MISSION, RYA!
WE COULDN'T LET KALLISTA EXECUTE HER, ROOK...

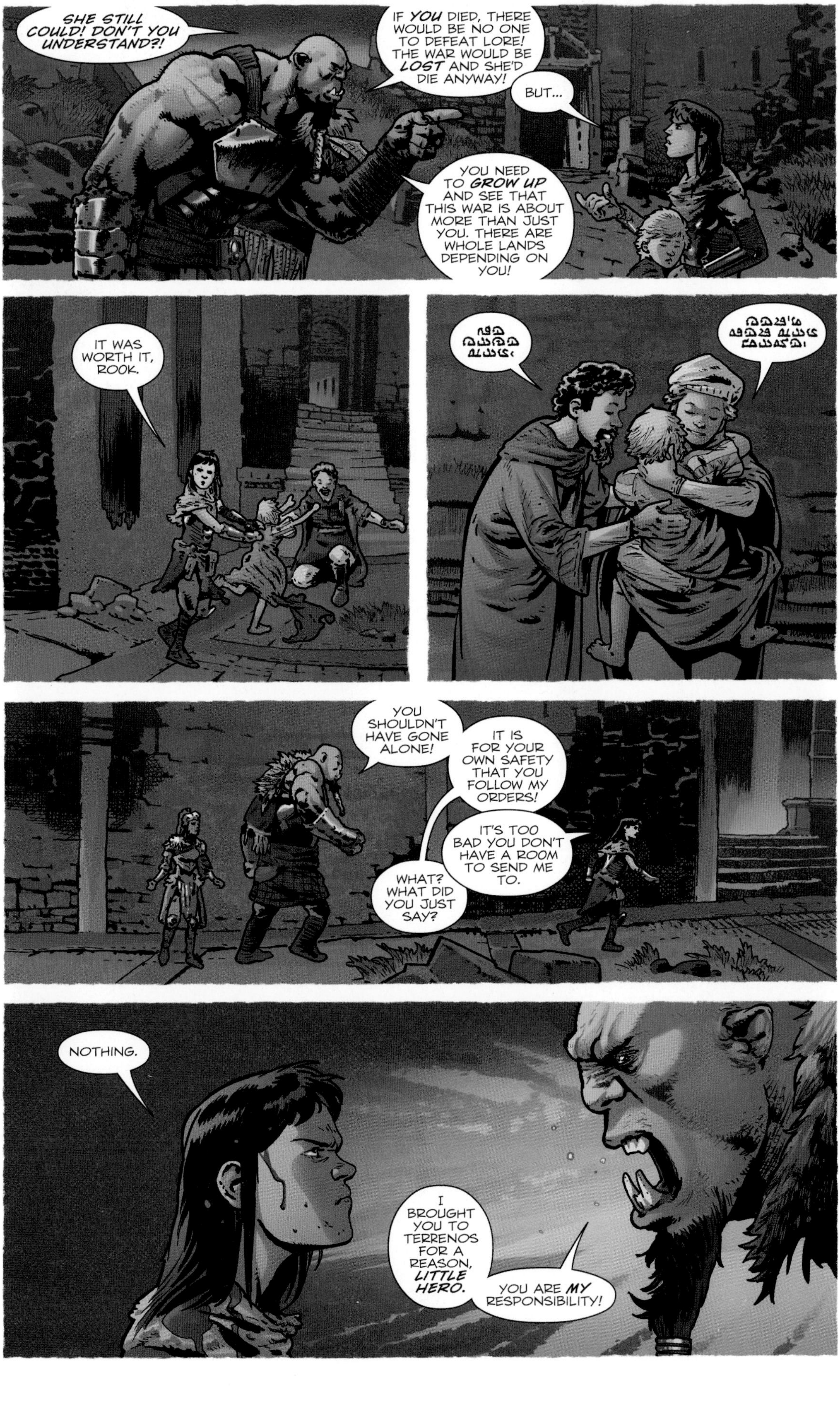
SHE STILL COULD! DON'T YOU UNDERSTAND?!
IF YOU DIED, THERE WOULD BE NO ONE TO DEFEAT LORE! THE WAR WOULD BE LOST AND SHE'D DIE ANYWAY!
BUT...
YOU NEED TO GROW UP AND SEE THAT THIS WAR IS ABOUT MORE THAN JUST YOU. THERE ARE WHOLE LANDS DEPENDING ON YOU!
IT WAS WORTH IT, ROOK.
YOU SHOULDN'T HAVE GONE ALONE!
IT IS FOR YOUR OWN SAFETY THAT YOU FOLLOW MY ORDERS!
IT'S TOO BAD YOU DON'T HAVE A ROOM TO SEND ME TO.
WHAT? WHAT DID YOU JUST SAY?
NOTHING.
I BROUGHT YOU TO TERRENOS FOR A REASON, LITTLE HERO.
YOU ARE MY RESPONSIBILITY!

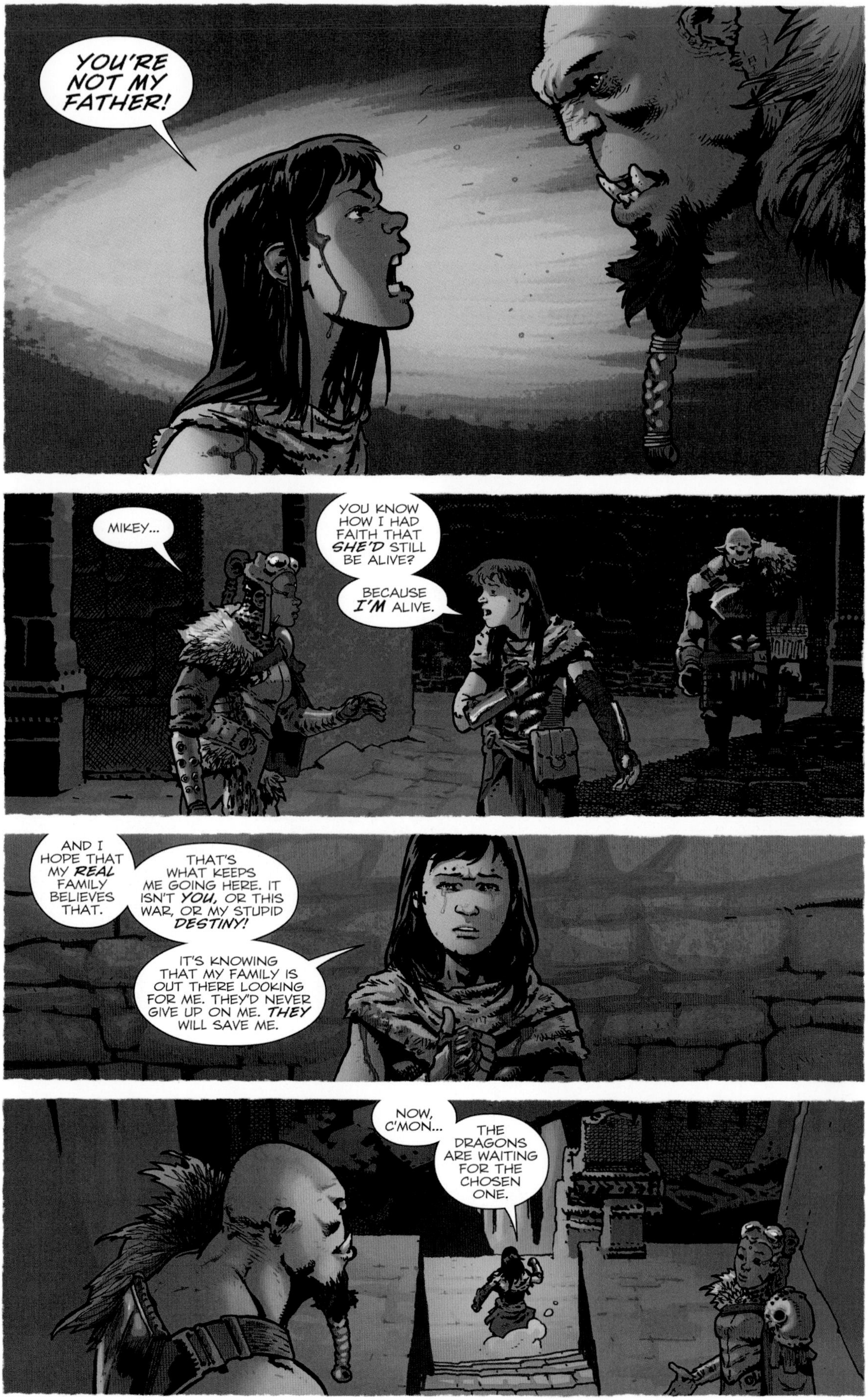
YOU'RE NOT MY FATHER!
MIKEY...
YOU KNOW HOW I HAD FAITH THAT SHE'D STILL BE ALIVE?
BECAUSE I'M ALIVE.
AND I HOPE THAT MY REAL FAMILY BELIEVES THAT.
THAT'S WHAT KEEPS ME GOING HERE. IT ISN'T YOU, OR THIS WAR, OR MY STUPID DESTINY!
IT'S KNOWING THAT MY FAMILY IS OUT THERE LOOKING FOR ME. THEY'D NEVER GIVE UP ON ME. THEY WILL SAVE ME.
NOW, C'MON...
THE DRAGONS ARE WAITING FOR THE CHOSEN ONE.

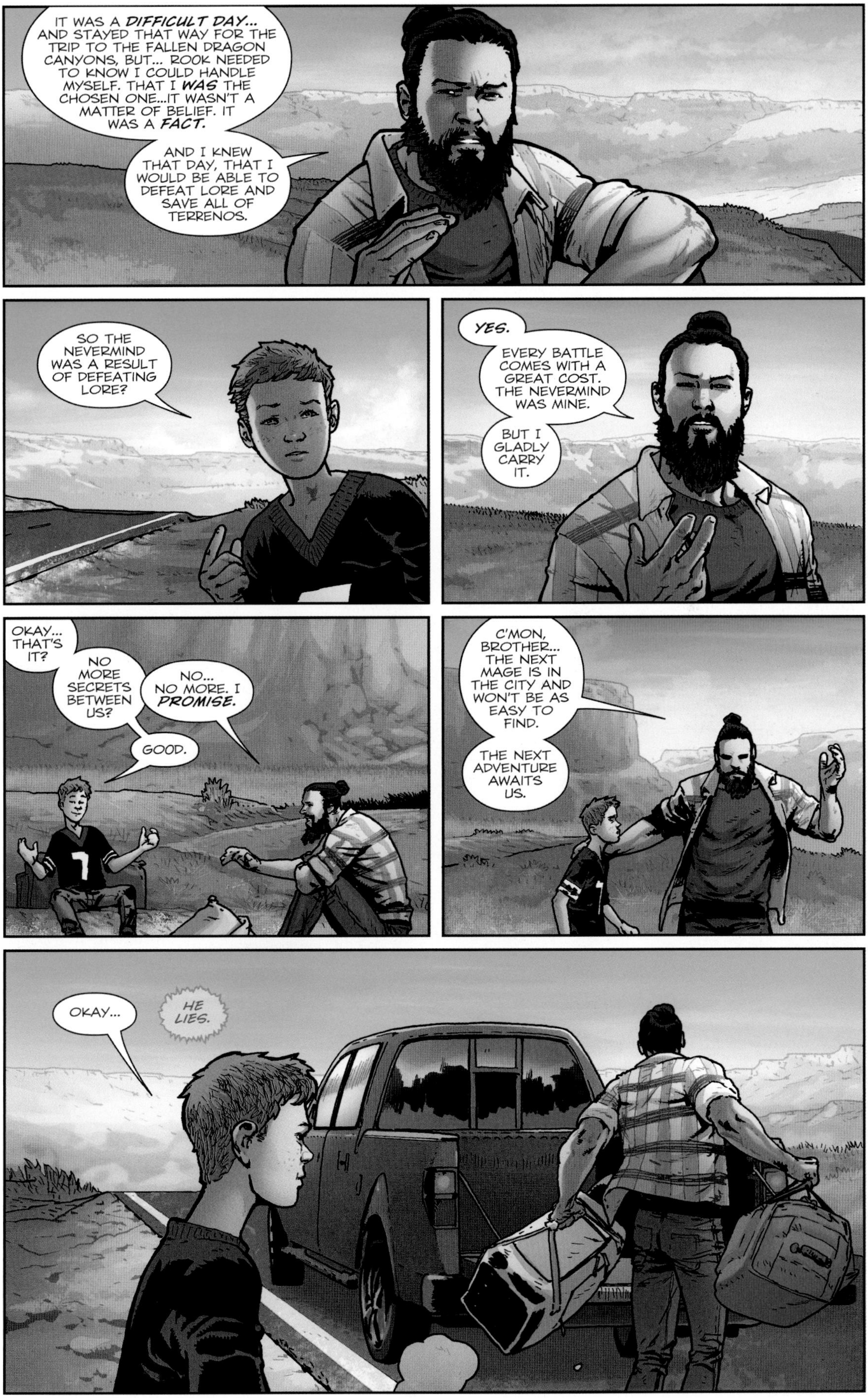
IT WAS A DIFFICULT DAY... AND STAYED THAT WAY FOR THE TRIP TO THE FALLEN DRAGON CANYONS, BUT... ROOK NEEDED TO KNOW I COULD HANDLE MYSELF. THAT I WAS THE CHOSEN ONE...IT WASN'T A MATTER OF BELIEF. IT WAS A FACT.
AND I KNEW THAT DAY, THAT I WOULD BE ABLE TO DEFEAT LORE AND SAVE ALL OF TERRENOS.
SO THE NEVERMIND WAS A RESULT OF DEFEATING LORE?
YES.
EVERY BATTLE COMES WITH A GREAT COST. THE NEVERMIND WAS MINE.
BUT I GLADLY CARRY IT.
OKAY... THAT'S IT?
NO MORE SECRETS BETWEEN US?
NO... NO MORE. I PROMISE.
GOOD.
C'MON, BROTHER... THE NEXT MAGE IS IN THE CITY AND WON'T BE AS EASY TO FIND.
THE NEXT ADVENTURE AWAITS US.
OKAY...
HE LIES.

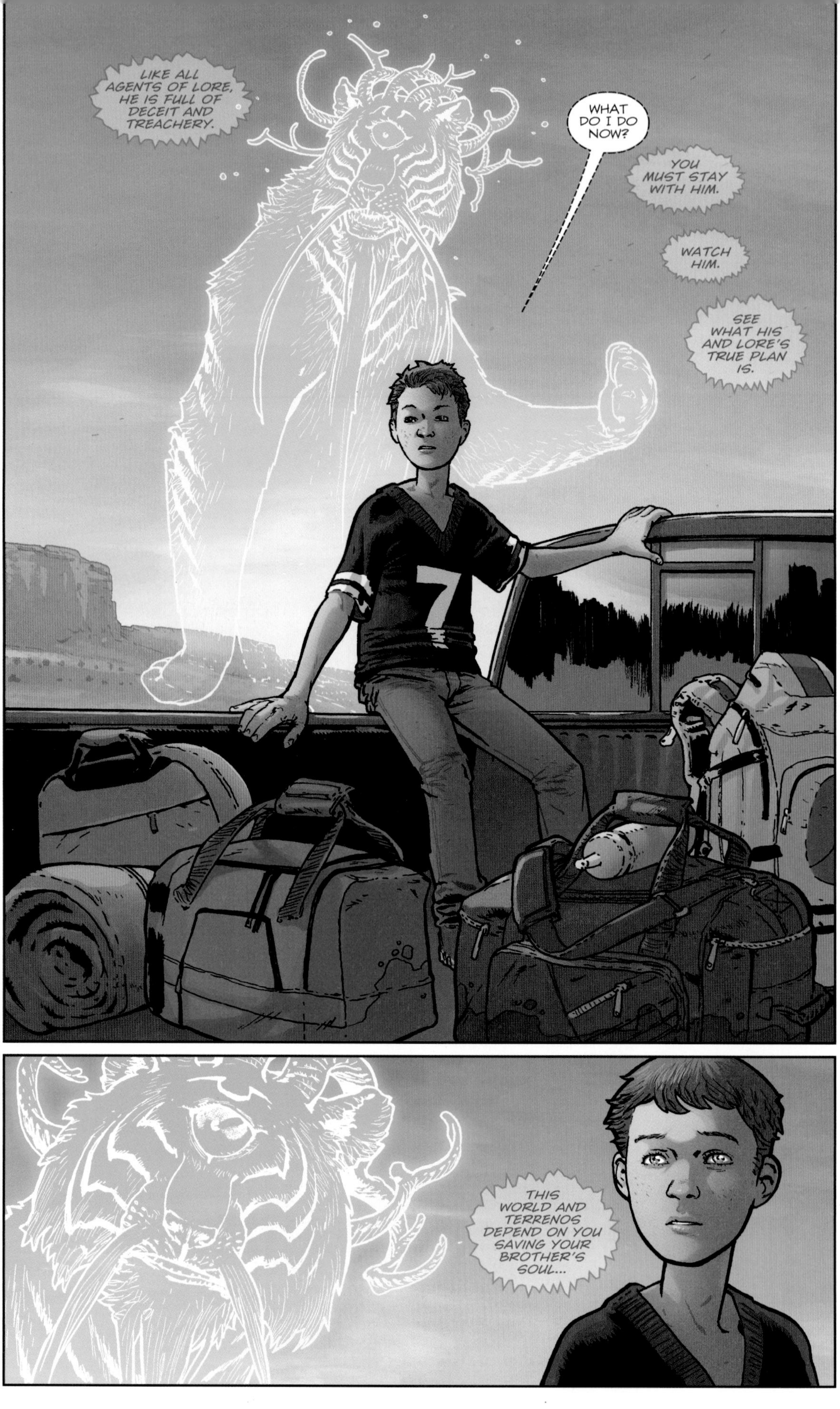
LIKE ALL AGENTS OF LORE, HE IS FULL OF DECEIT AND TREACHERY.
WHAT DO I DO NOW?
YOU MUST STAY WITH HIM.
WATCH HIM.
SEE WHAT HIS AND LORE'S TRUE PLAN IS.
THIS WORLD AND TERRENOS DEPEND ON YOU SAVING YOUR BROTHER'S SOUL...

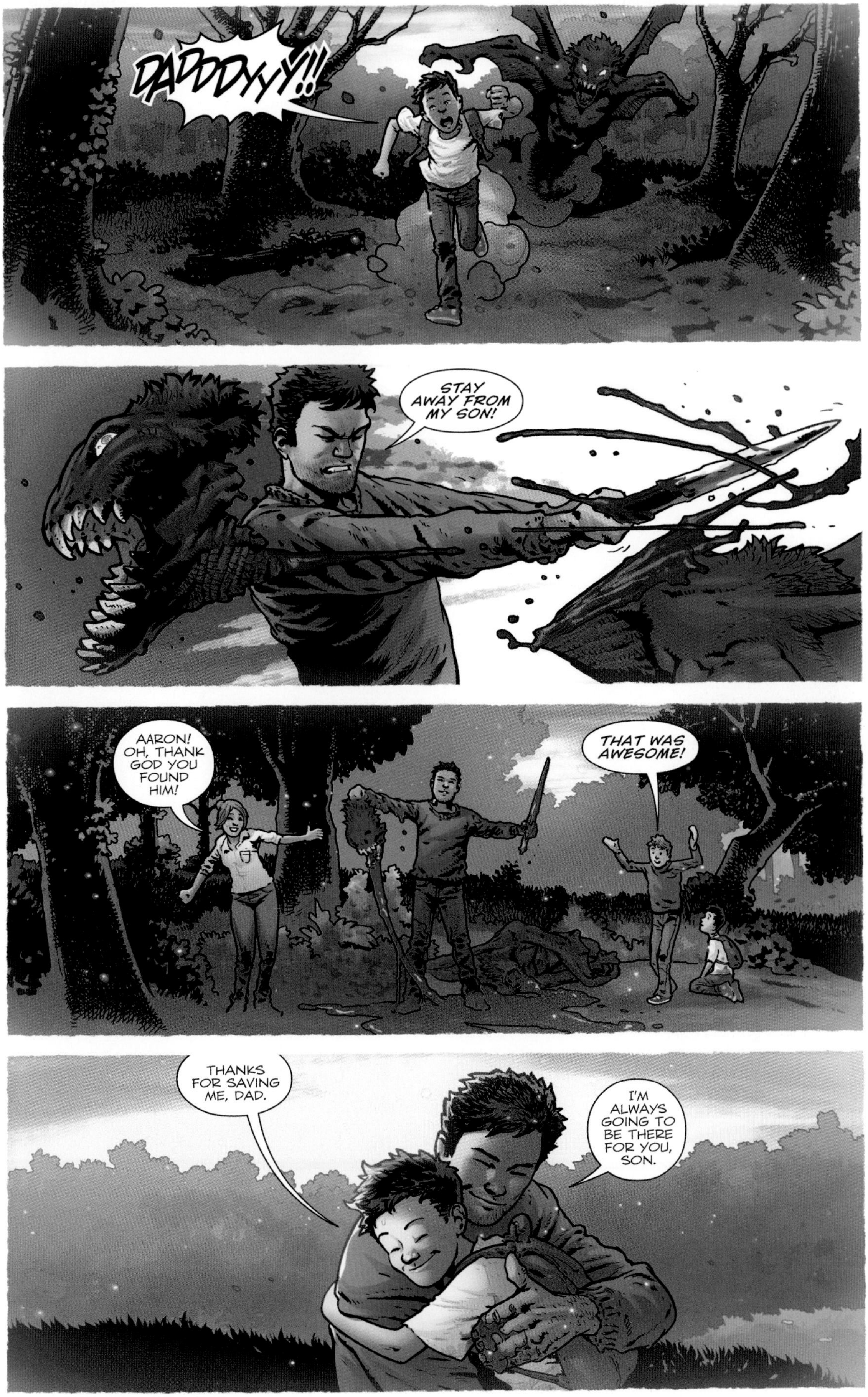
DADDDYYY!!
STAY AWAY FROM MY SON!
AARON! OH, THANK GOD YOU FOUND HIM!
THAT WAS AWESOME!
THANKS FOR SAVING ME, DAD.
I'M ALWAYS GOING TO BE THERE FOR YOU, SON.

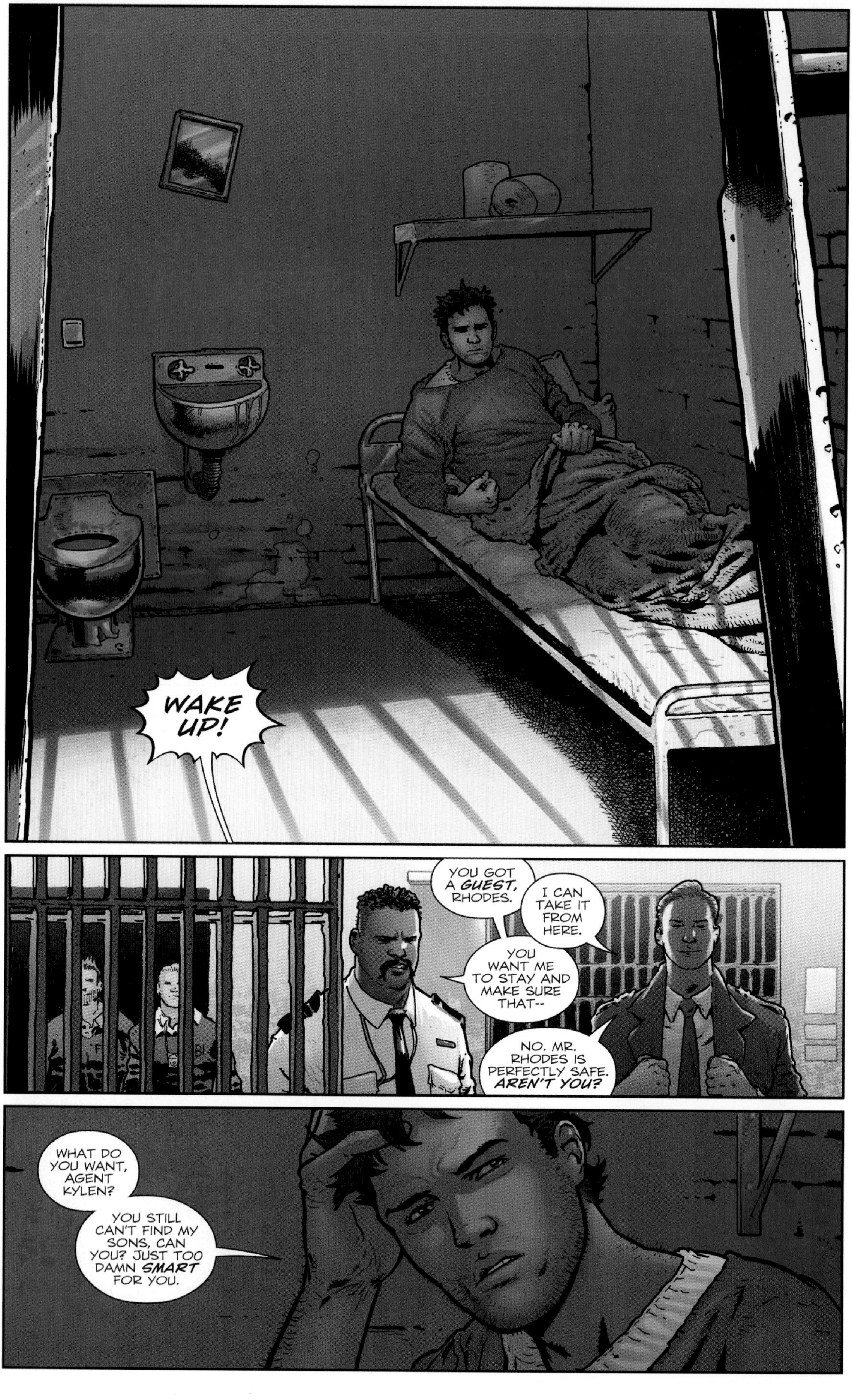
WAKE UP!
YOU GOT A GUEST, RHODES.
I CAN TAKE IT FROM HERE.
YOU WANT ME TO STAY AND MAKE SURE THAT--
NO. MR. RHODES IS PERFECTLY SAFE. AREN'T YOU?
FBI
WHAT DO YOU WANT, AGENT KYLEN?
YOU STILL CAN'T FIND MY SONS, CAN YOU? JUST TOO DAMN SMART FOR YOU.

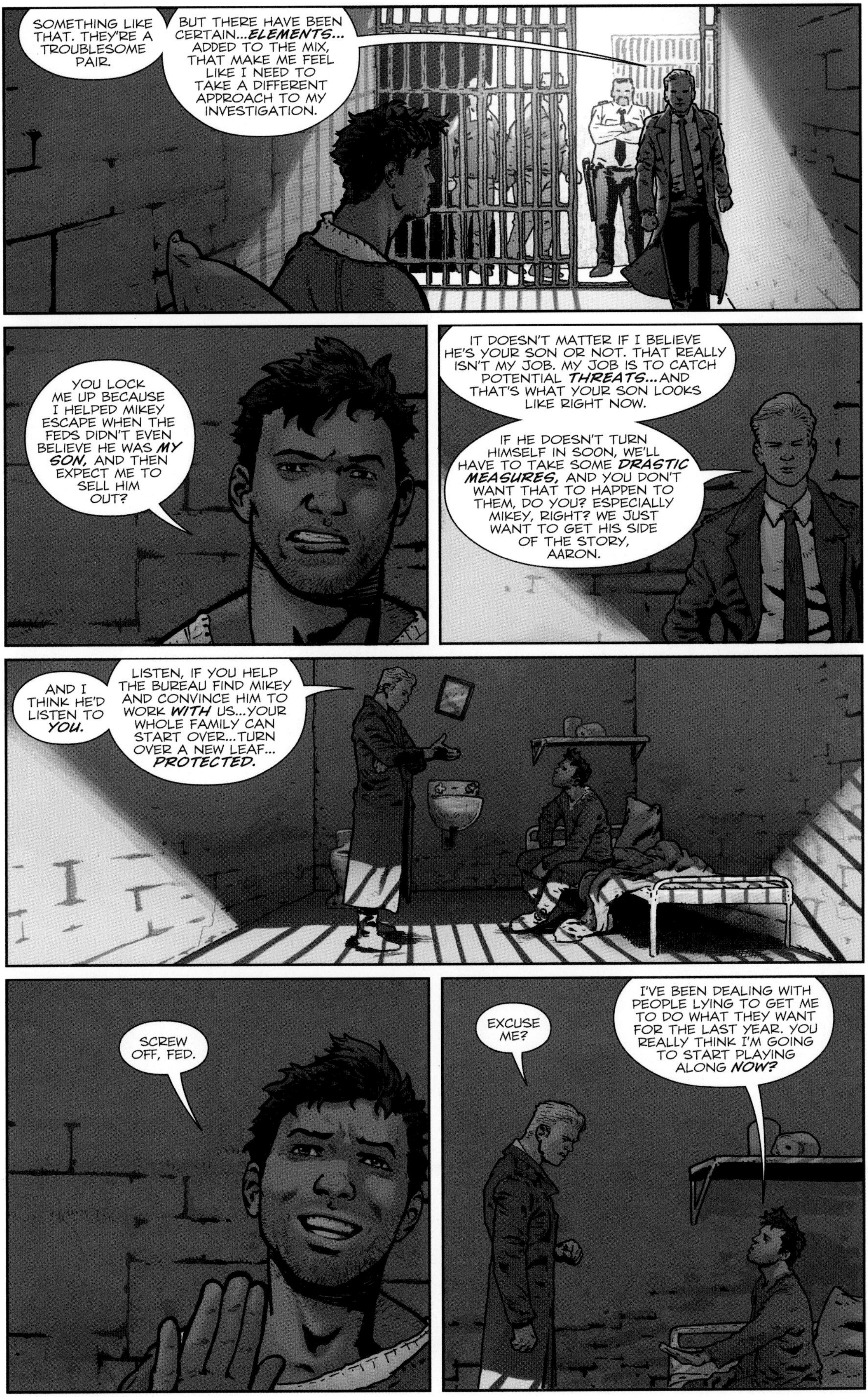
SOMETHING LIKE THAT. THEY'RE A TROUBLESOME PAIR.
BUT THERE HAVE BEEN CERTAIN...ELEMENTS... ADDED TO THE MIX, THAT MAKE ME FEEL LIKE I NEED TO TAKE A DIFFERENT APPROACH TO MY INVESTIGATION.
YOU LOCK ME UP BECAUSE I HELPED MIKEY ESCAPE WHEN THE FEDS DIDN'T EVEN BELIEVE HE WAS MY SON, AND THEN EXPECT ME TO SELL HIM OUT?
IT DOESN'T MATTER IF I BELIEVE HE'S YOUR SON OR NOT. THAT REALLY ISN'T MY JOB. MY JOB IS TO CATCH POTENTIAL THREATS...AND THAT'S WHAT YOUR SON LOOKS LIKE RIGHT NOW.
IF HE DOESN'T TURN HIMSELF IN SOON, WE'LL HAVE TO TAKE SOME DRASTIC MEASURES, AND YOU DON'T WANT THAT TO HAPPEN TO THEM, DO YOU? ESPECIALLY MIKEY, RIGHT? WE JUST WANT TO GET HIS SIDE OF THE STORY, AARON.
AND I THINK HE'D LISTEN TO YOU.
LISTEN, IF YOU HELP THE BUREAU FIND MIKEY AND CONVINCE HIM TO WORK WITH US...YOUR WHOLE FAMILY CAN START OVER...TURN OVER A NEW LEAF... PROTECTED.
SCREW OFF, FED.
EXCUSE ME?
I'VE BEEN DEALING WITH PEOPLE LYING TO GET ME TO DO WHAT THEY WANT FOR THE LAST YEAR. YOU REALLY THINK I'M GOING TO START PLAYING ALONG NOW?

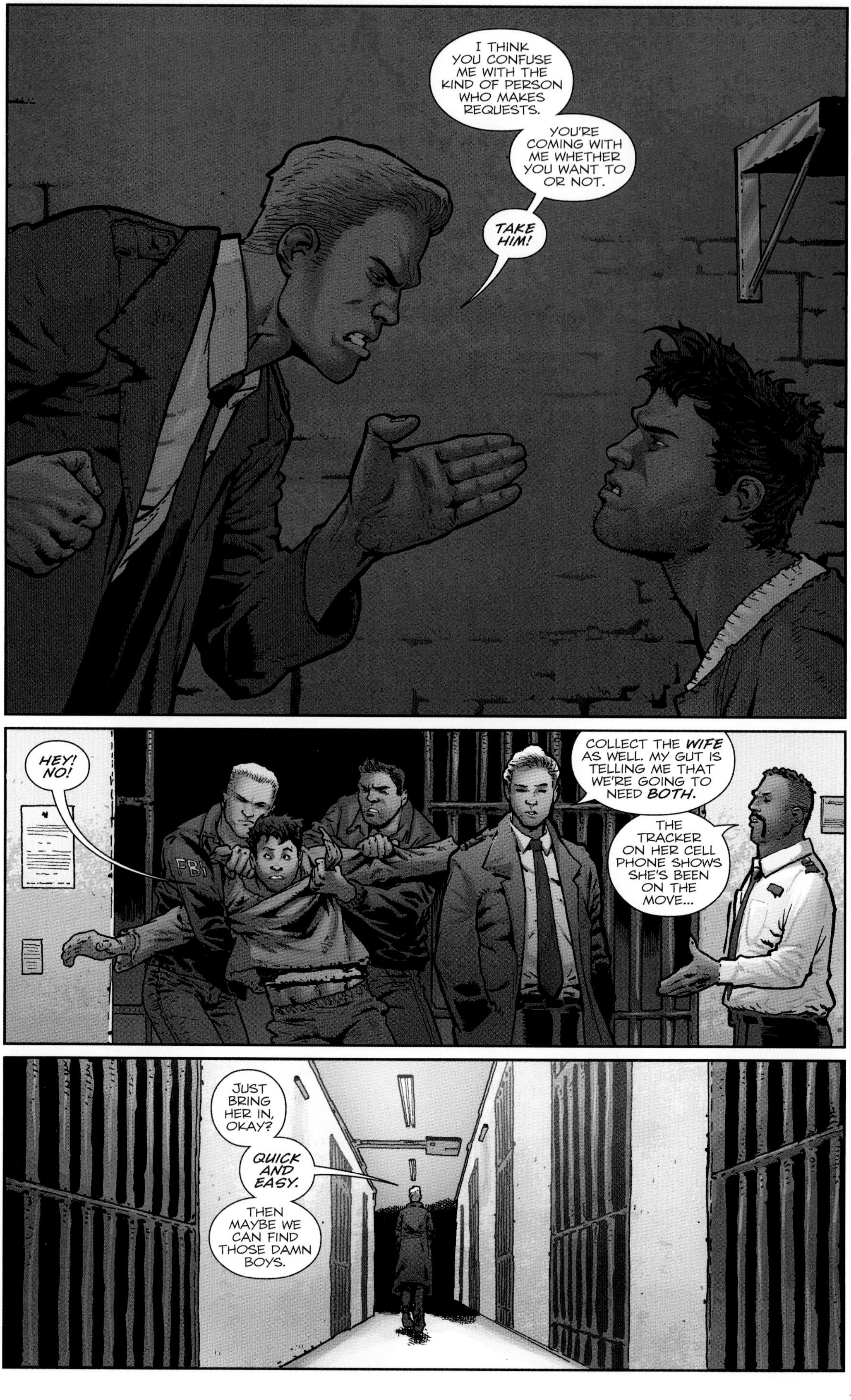
I THINK YOU CONFUSE ME WITH THE KIND OF PERSON WHO MAKES REQUESTS.
YOU'RE COMING WITH ME WHETHER YOU WANT TO OR NOT.
TAKE HIM!
HEY! NO!
FBI
COLLECT THE WIFE AS WELL. MY GUT IS TELLING ME THAT WE'RE GOING TO NEED BOTH.
THE TRACKER ON HER CELL PHONE SHOWS SHE'S BEEN ON THE MOVE...
JUST BRING HER IN, OKAY?
QUICK AND EASY.
THEN MAYBE WE CAN FIND THOSE DAMN BOYS.

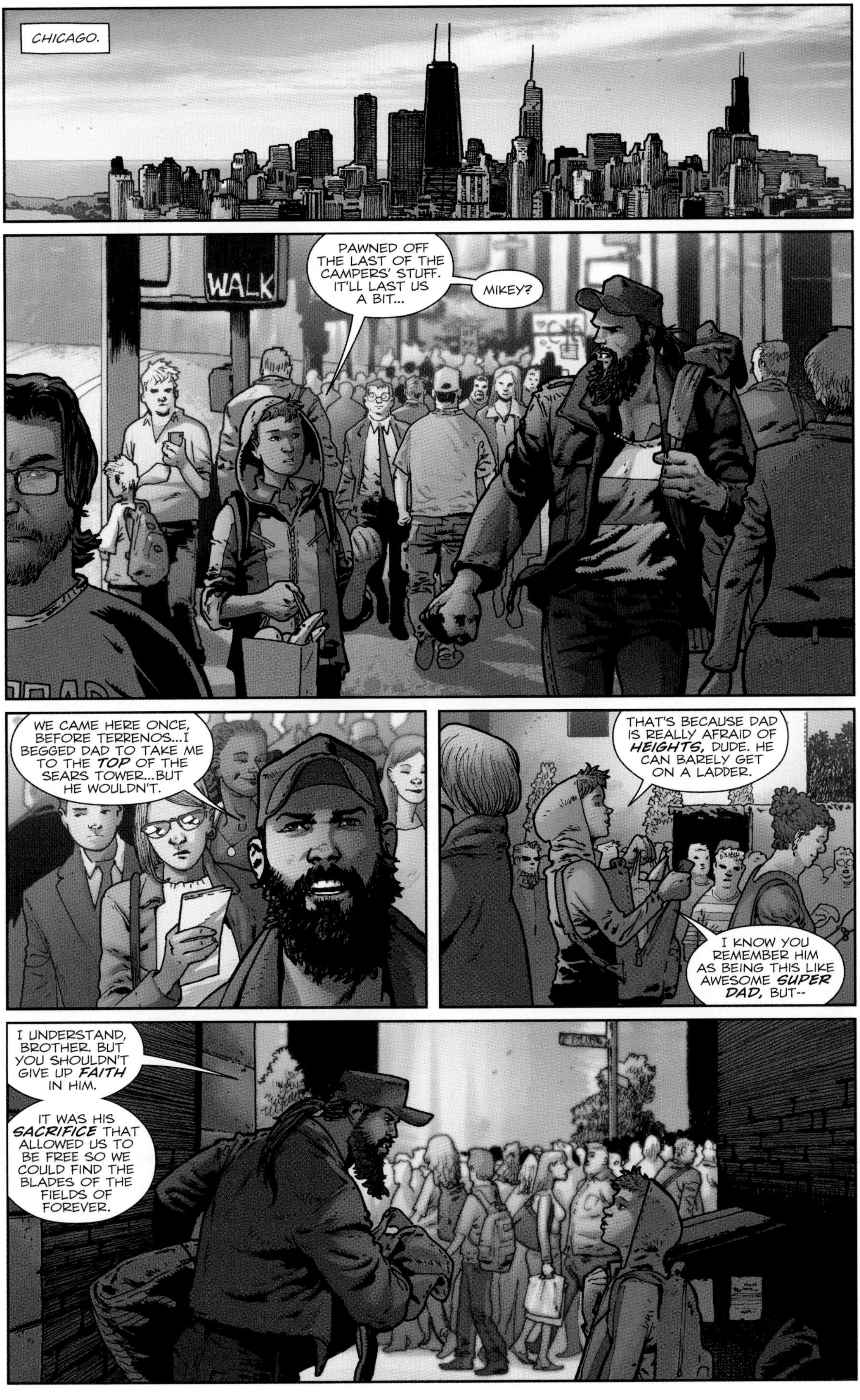
CHICAGO.
WALK
PAWNED OFF THE LAST OF THE CAMPERS' STUFF. IT'LL LAST US A BIT...
MIKEY?
WE CAME HERE ONCE, BEFORE TERRENOS...I BEGGED DAD TO TAKE ME TO THE TOP OF THE SEARS TOWER...BUT HE WOULDN'T.
THAT'S BECAUSE DAD IS REALLY AFRAID OF HEIGHTS, DUDE. HE CAN BARELY GET ON A LADDER.
I KNOW YOU REMEMBER HIM AS BEING THIS LIKE AWESOME SUPER DAD, BUT--
I UNDERSTAND, BROTHER. BUT YOU SHOULDN'T GIVE UP FAITH IN HIM.
IT WAS HIS SACRIFICE THAT ALLOWED US TO BE FREE SO WE COULD FIND THE BLADES OF THE FIELDS OF FOREVER.

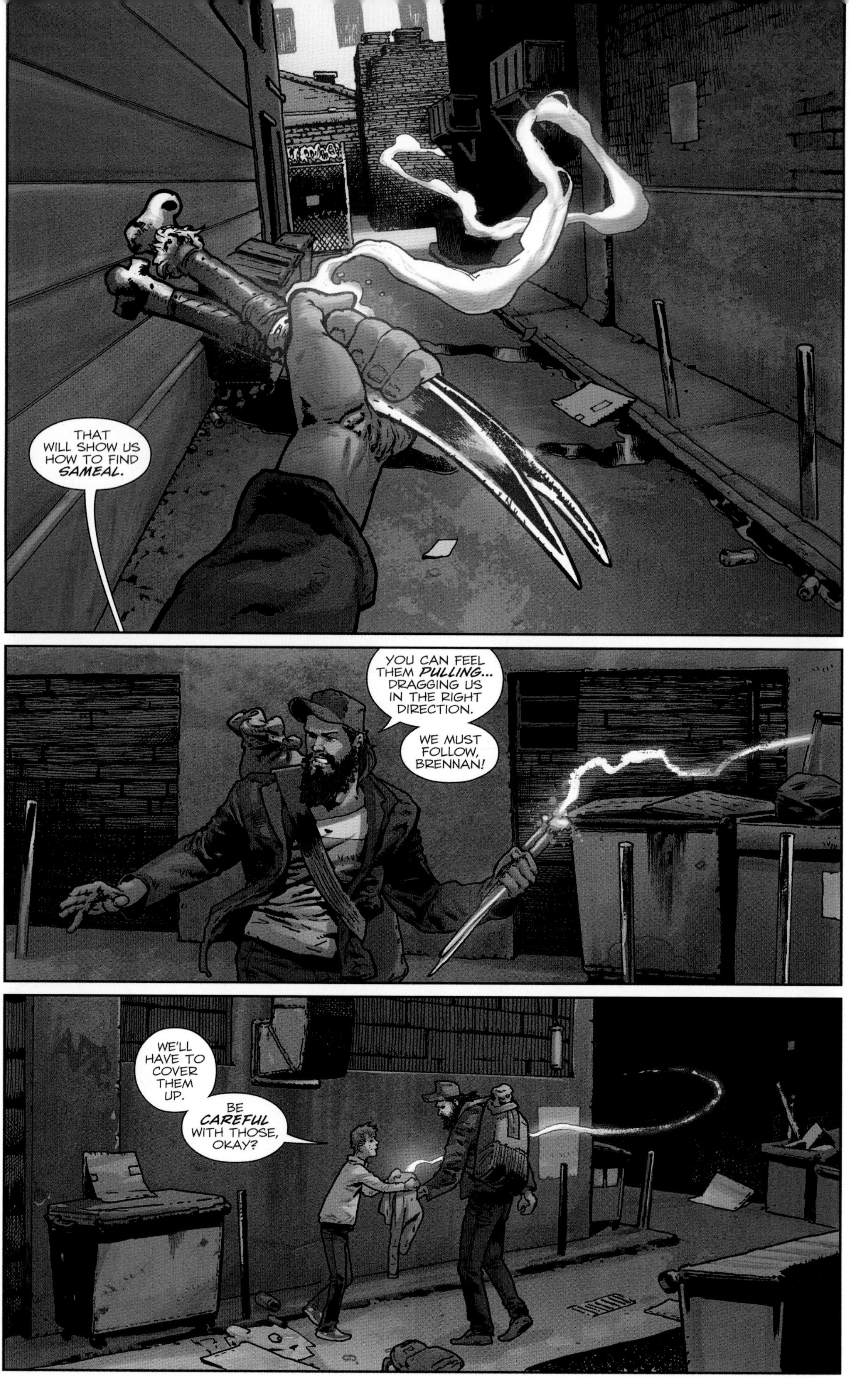
THAT WILL SHOW US HOW TO FIND *SAMEAL.*
YOU CAN FEEL THEM *PULLING...* DRAGGING US IN THE RIGHT DIRECTION.
WE MUST FOLLOW, BRENNAN!
WE'LL HAVE TO COVER THEM UP.
BE *CAREFUL* WITH THOSE, OKAY?

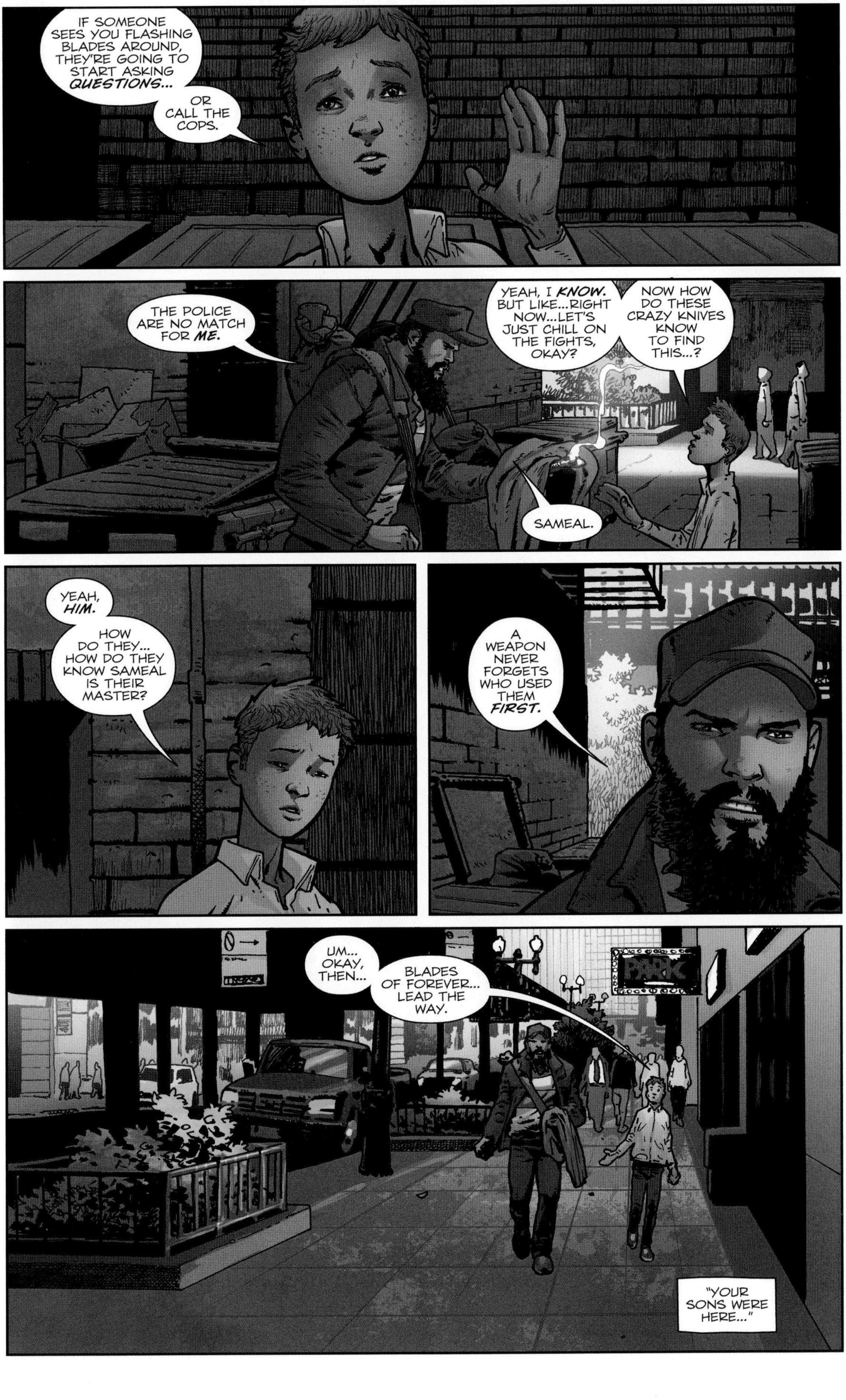
IF SOMEONE SEES YOU FLASHING BLADES AROUND, THEY'RE GOING TO START ASKING *QUESTIONS*...
OR CALL THE COPS.
THE POLICE ARE NO MATCH FOR *ME*.
YEAH, I *KNOW*. BUT LIKE...RIGHT NOW...LET'S JUST CHILL ON THE FIGHTS, OKAY?
NOW HOW DO THESE CRAZY KNIVES KNOW TO FIND THIS...?
SAMEAL.
YEAH, *HIM*.
HOW DO THEY... HOW DO THEY KNOW SAMEAL IS THEIR MASTER?
A WEAPON NEVER FORGETS WHO USED THEM *FIRST*.
UM... OKAY, THEN...
BLADES OF FOREVER... LEAD THE WAY.
PARK
"YOUR SONS WERE HERE..."

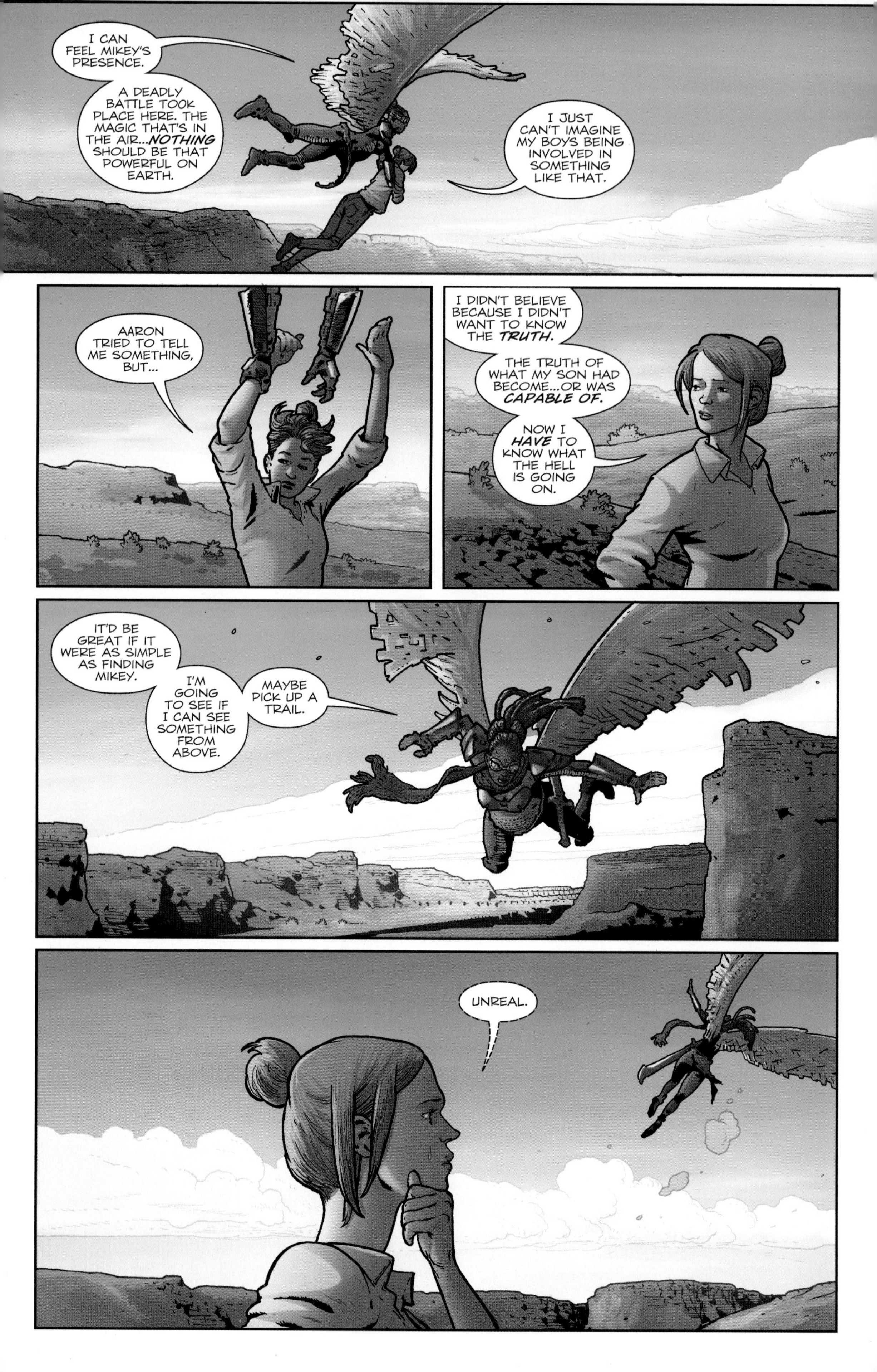
I CAN FEEL MIKEY'S PRESENCE.
A DEADLY BATTLE TOOK PLACE HERE. THE MAGIC THAT'S IN THE AIR...NOTHING SHOULD BE THAT POWERFUL ON EARTH.
I JUST CAN'T IMAGINE MY BOYS BEING INVOLVED IN SOMETHING LIKE THAT.
AARON TRIED TO TELL ME SOMETHING, BUT...
I DIDN'T BELIEVE BECAUSE I DIDN'T WANT TO KNOW THE TRUTH.
THE TRUTH OF WHAT MY SON HAD BECOME...OR WAS CAPABLE OF.
NOW I HAVE TO KNOW WHAT THE HELL IS GOING ON.
IT'D BE GREAT IF IT WERE AS SIMPLE AS FINDING MIKEY.
I'M GOING TO SEE IF I CAN SEE SOMETHING FROM ABOVE.
MAYBE PICK UP A TRAIL.
UNREAL.

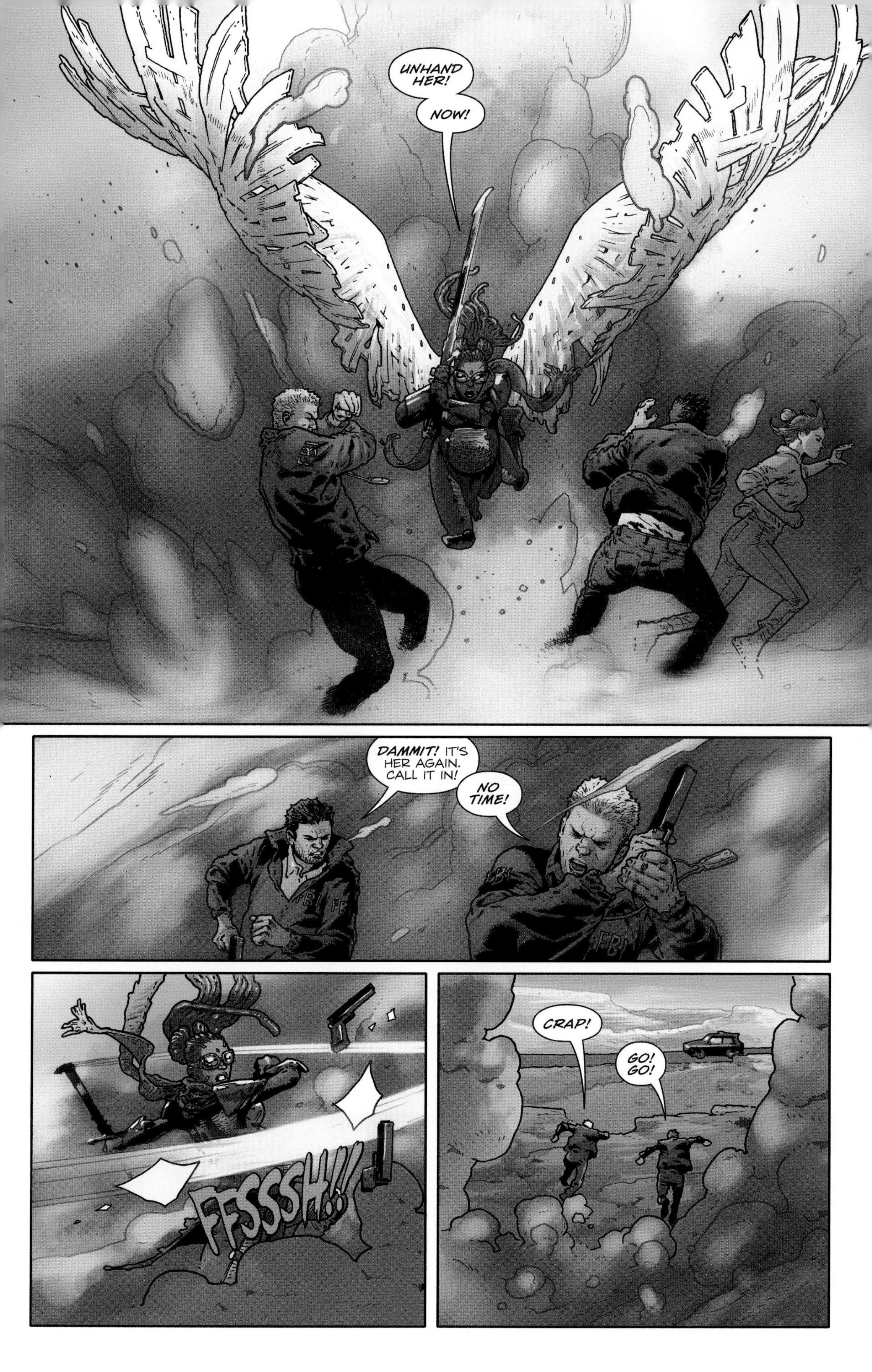
UNHAND HER!
NOW!
DAMMIT! IT'S HER AGAIN. CALL IT IN!
NO TIME!
FFSSSH!!!
CRAP!
GO! GO!

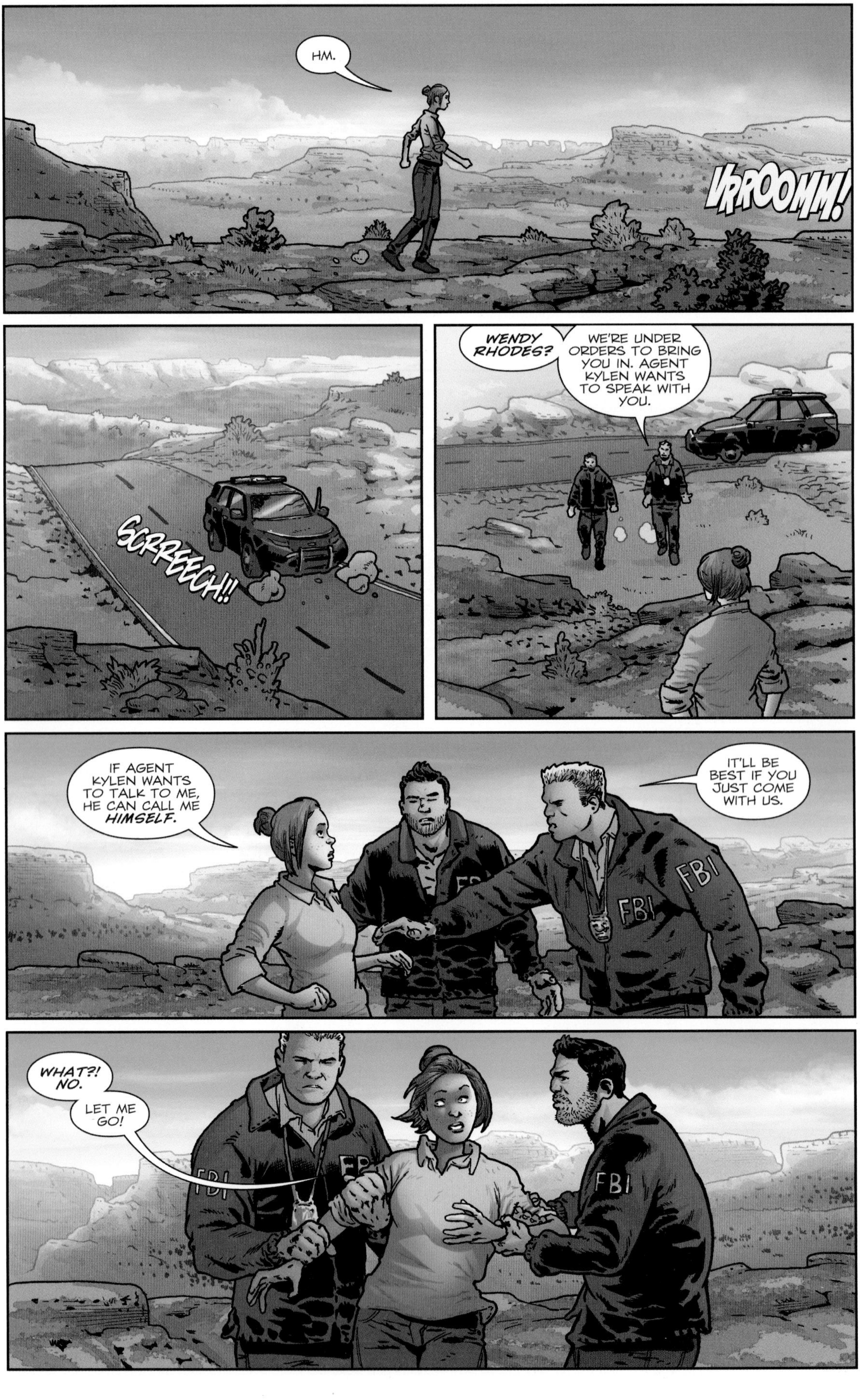

HM.
VRROOMM!
SCRREEECH!!
WENDY RHODES?
WE'RE UNDER ORDERS TO BRING YOU IN. AGENT KYLEN WANTS TO SPEAK WITH YOU.
IF AGENT KYLEN WANTS TO TALK TO ME, HE CAN CALL ME HIMSELF.
IT'LL BE BEST IF YOU JUST COME WITH US.
FBI
WHAT?! NO.
LET ME GO!

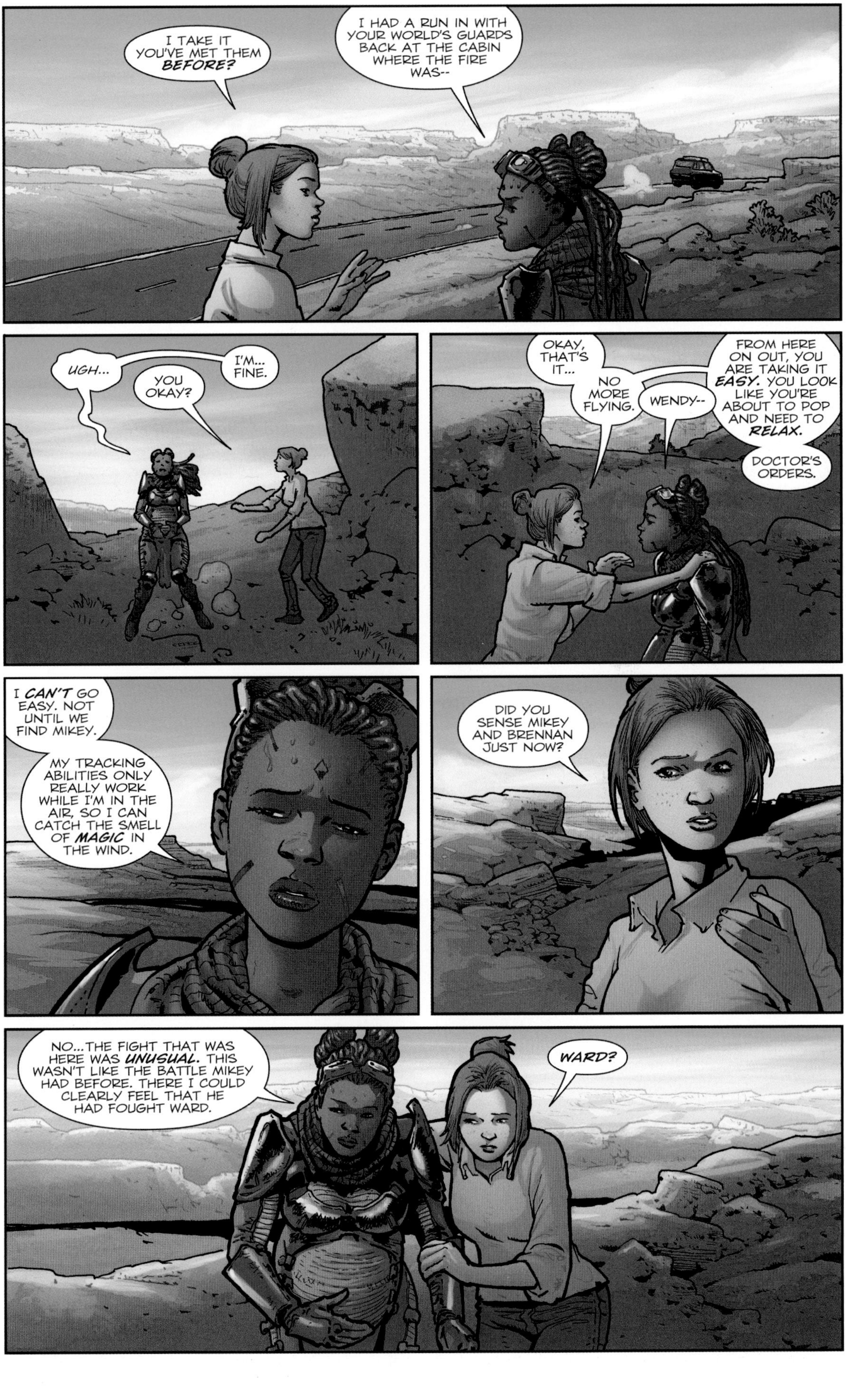
I TAKE IT YOU'VE MET THEM ***BEFORE?***
I HAD A RUN IN WITH YOUR WORLD'S GUARDS BACK AT THE CABIN WHERE THE FIRE WAS--
UGH...
I'M... FINE.
YOU OKAY?
OKAY, THAT'S IT...
NO MORE FLYING.
WENDY--
FROM HERE ON OUT, YOU ARE TAKING IT ***EASY.*** YOU LOOK LIKE YOU'RE ABOUT TO POP AND NEED TO ***RELAX.***
DOCTOR'S ORDERS.
I ***CAN'T*** GO EASY. NOT UNTIL WE FIND MIKEY.
MY TRACKING ABILITIES ONLY REALLY WORK WHILE I'M IN THE AIR, SO I CAN CATCH THE SMELL OF ***MAGIC*** IN THE WIND.
DID YOU SENSE MIKEY AND BRENNAN JUST NOW?
NO... THE FIGHT THAT WAS HERE WAS ***UNUSUAL.*** THIS WASN'T LIKE THE BATTLE MIKEY HAD BEFORE. THERE I COULD CLEARLY FEEL THAT HE HAD FOUGHT WARD.
WARD?

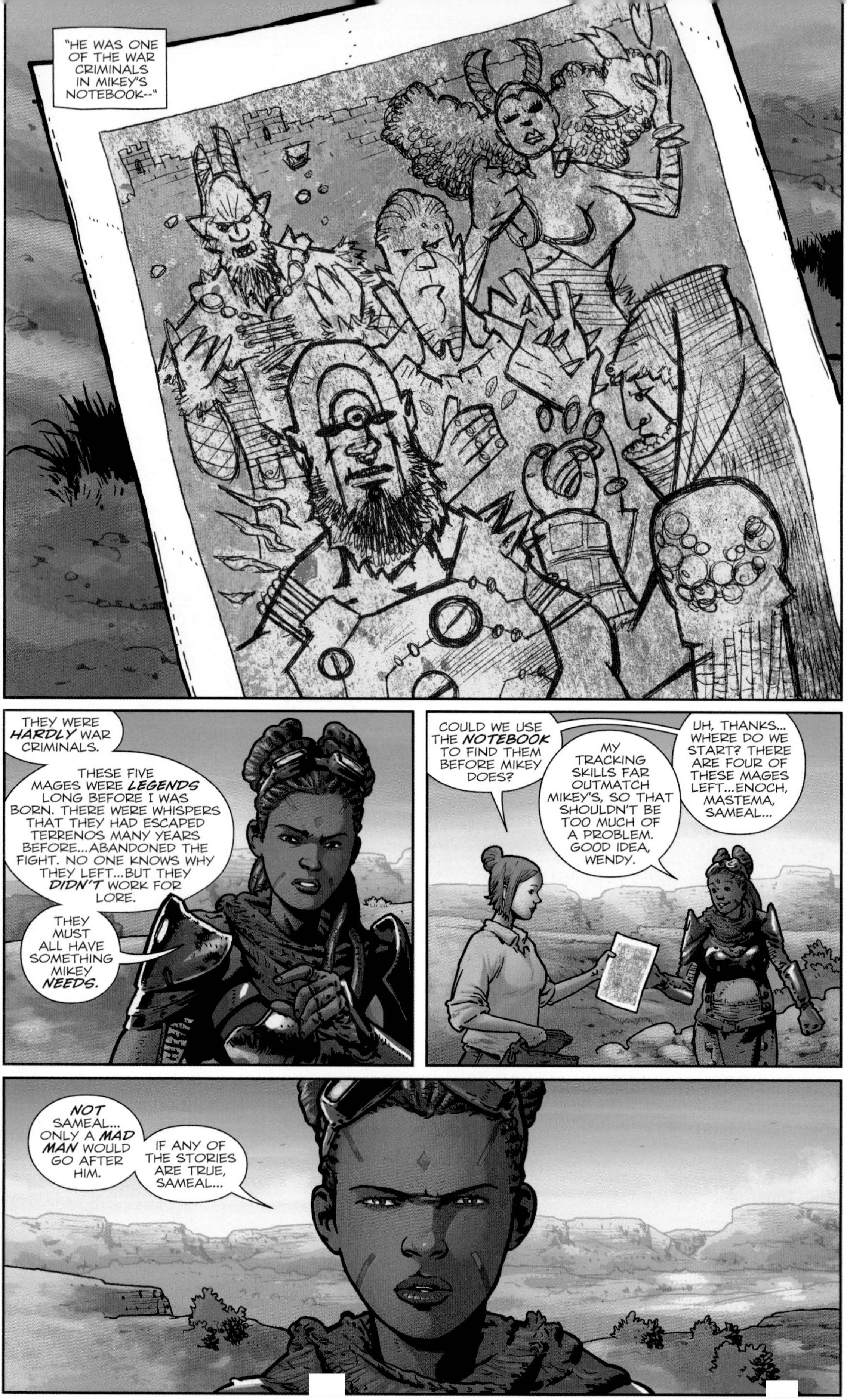
"HE WAS ONE OF THE WAR CRIMINALS IN MIKEY'S NOTEBOOK--"
THEY WERE HARDLY WAR CRIMINALS.
THESE FIVE MAGES WERE LEGENDS LONG BEFORE I WAS BORN. THERE WERE WHISPERS THAT THEY HAD ESCAPED TERRENOS MANY YEARS BEFORE...ABANDONED THE FIGHT. NO ONE KNOWS WHY THEY LEFT...BUT THEY DIDN'T WORK FOR LORE.
THEY MUST ALL HAVE SOMETHING MIKEY NEEDS.
COULD WE USE THE NOTEBOOK TO FIND THEM BEFORE MIKEY DOES?
MY TRACKING SKILLS FAR OUTMATCH MIKEY'S, SO THAT SHOULDN'T BE TOO MUCH OF A PROBLEM. GOOD IDEA, WENDY.
UH, THANKS... WHERE DO WE START? THERE ARE FOUR OF THESE MAGES LEFT...ENOCH, MASTEMA, SAMEAL...
NOT SAMEAL... ONLY A MAD MAN WOULD GO AFTER HIM.
IF ANY OF THE STORIES ARE TRUE, SAMEAL...

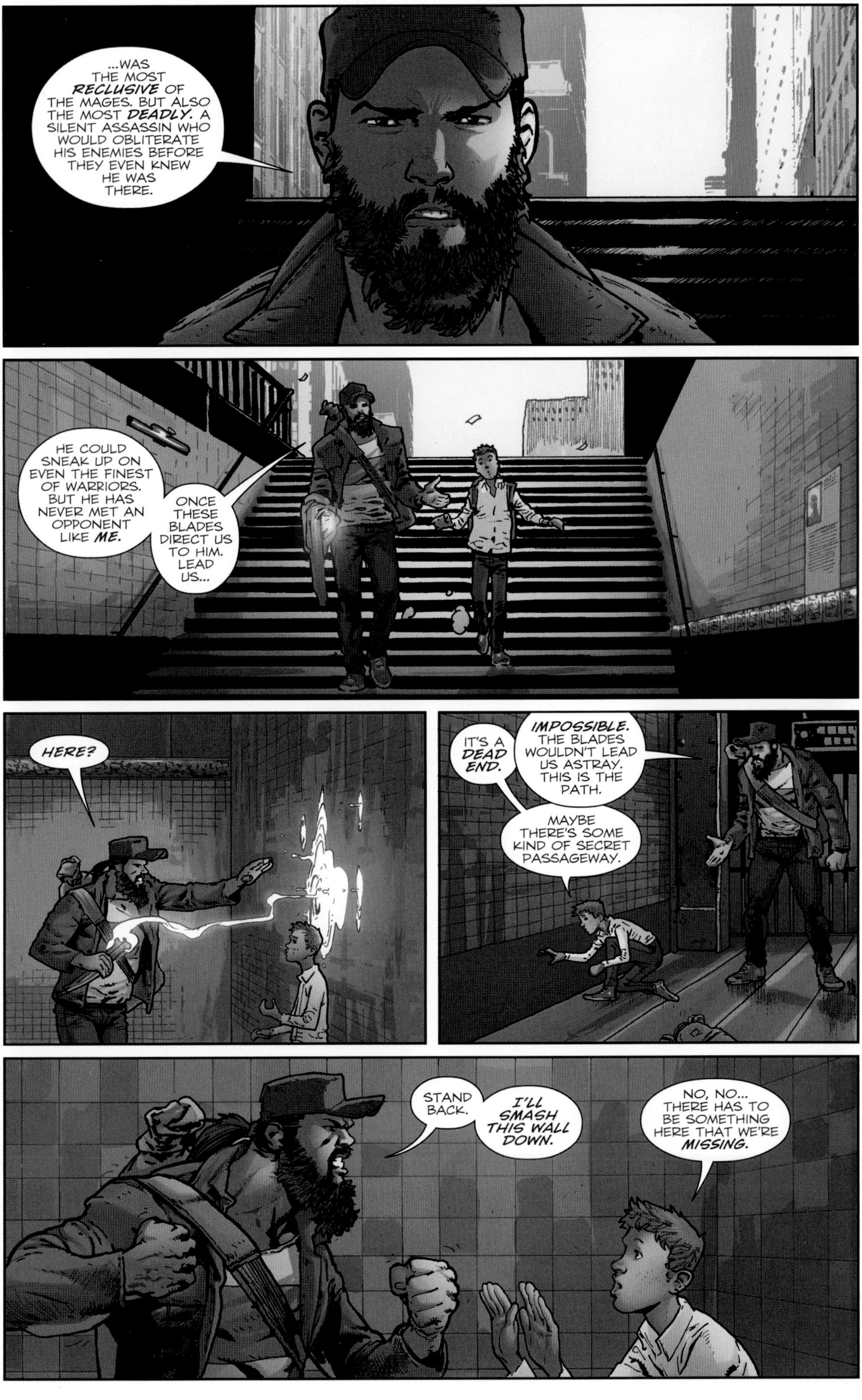

...WAS THE MOST *RECLUSIVE* OF THE MAGES. BUT ALSO THE MOST *DEADLY.* A SILENT ASSASSIN WHO WOULD OBLITERATE HIS ENEMIES BEFORE THEY EVEN KNEW HE WAS THERE.
HE COULD SNEAK UP ON EVEN THE FINEST OF WARRIORS. BUT HE HAS NEVER MET AN OPPONENT LIKE *ME.*
ONCE THESE BLADES DIRECT US TO HIM. LEAD US...
HERE?
IT'S A *DEAD END.*
IMPOSSIBLE. THE BLADES WOULDN'T LEAD US ASTRAY. THIS IS THE PATH.
MAYBE THERE'S SOME KIND OF SECRET PASSAGEWAY.
STAND BACK.
I'LL SMASH THIS WALL DOWN.
NO, NO... THERE HAS TO BE SOMETHING HERE THAT WE'RE *MISSING.*

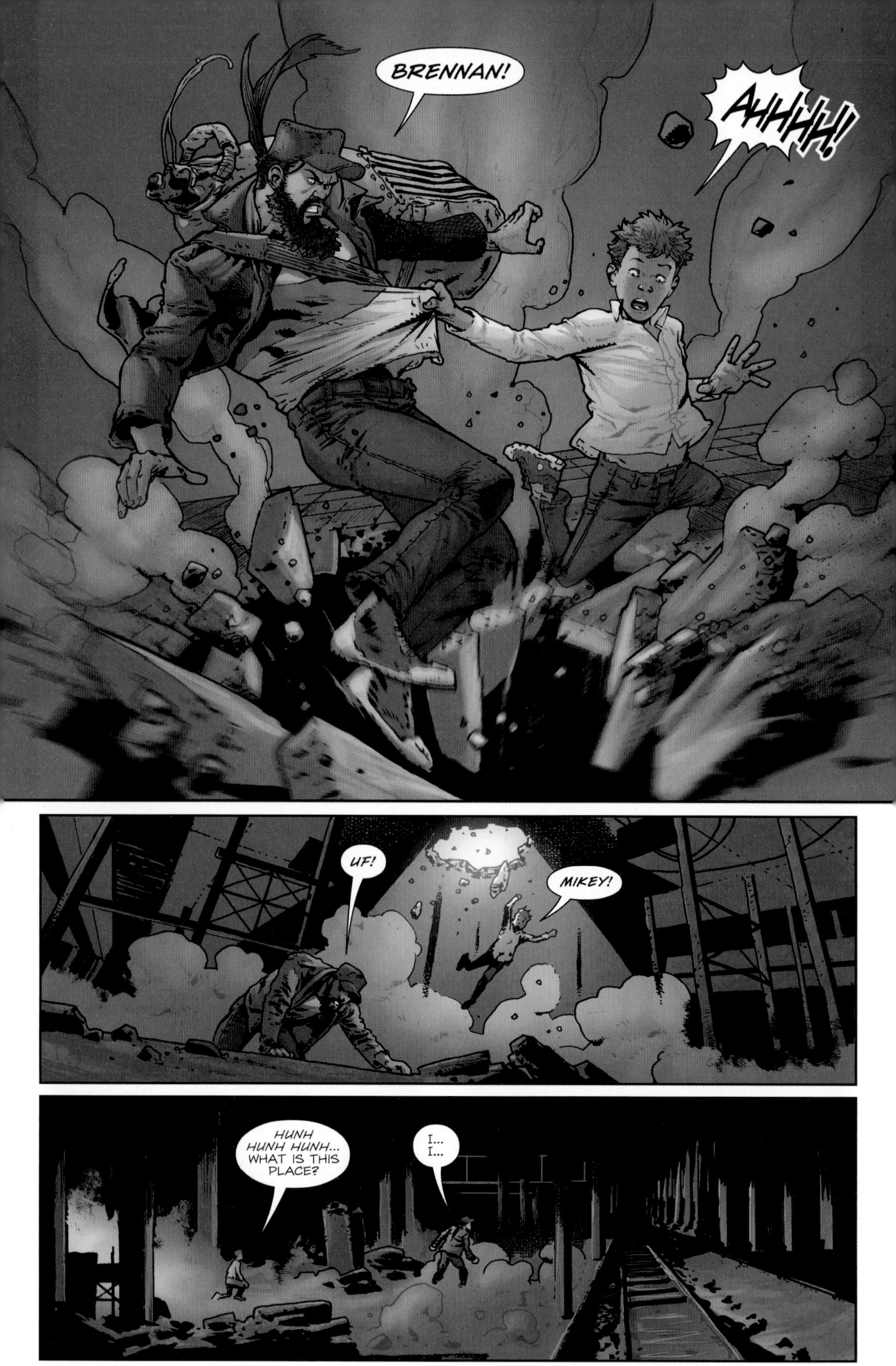
BRENNAN!
AHHHH!
UF!
MIKEY!
HUNH HUNH HUNH... WHAT IS THIS PLACE?
I... I...

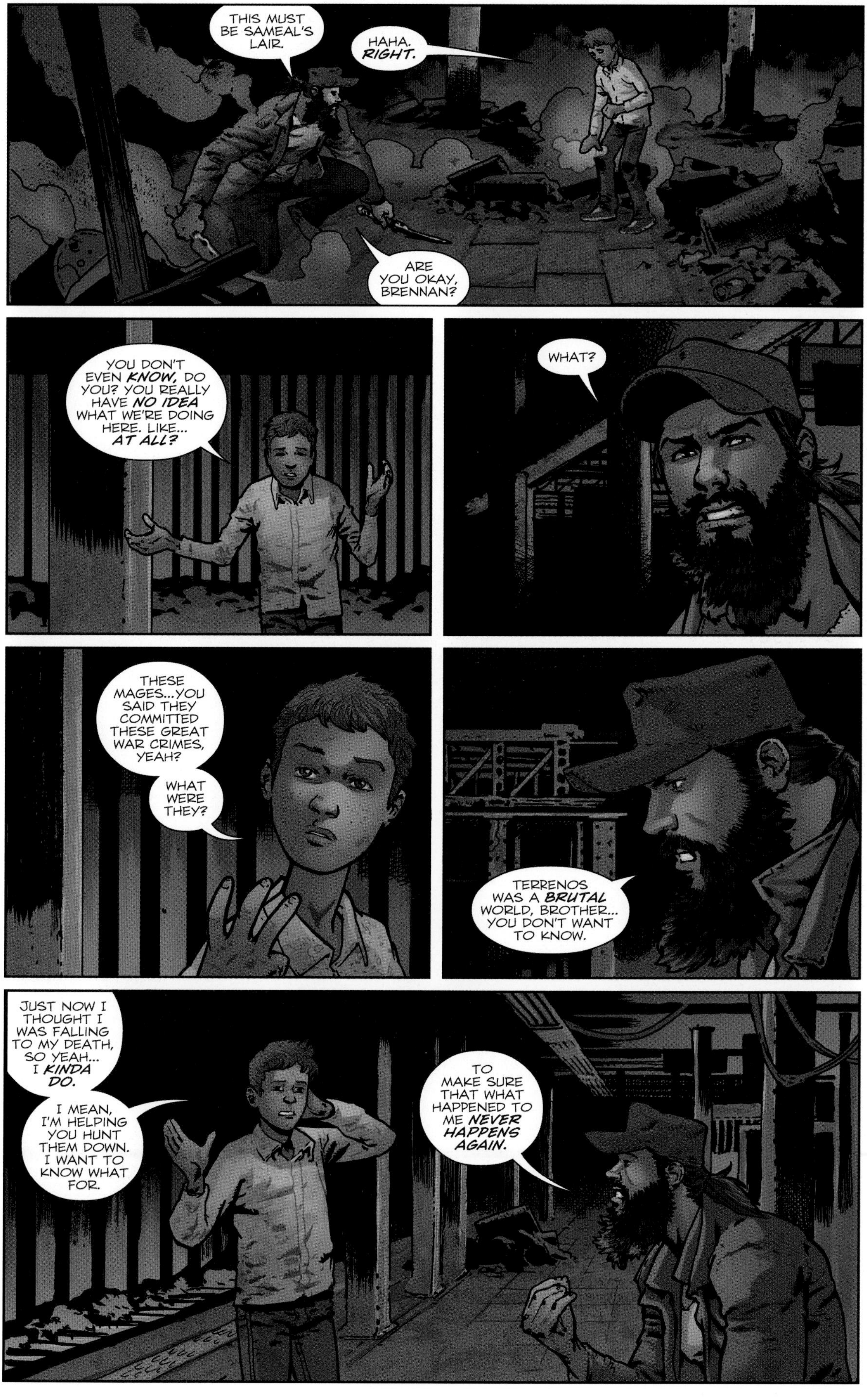
THIS MUST BE SAMEAL'S LAIR.
HAHA. *RIGHT.*
ARE YOU OKAY, BRENNAN?
YOU DON'T EVEN *KNOW,* DO YOU? YOU REALLY HAVE *NO IDEA* WHAT WE'RE DOING HERE. LIKE... *AT ALL?*
WHAT?
THESE MAGES...YOU SAID THEY COMMITTED THESE GREAT WAR CRIMES, YEAH?
WHAT WERE THEY?
TERRENOS WAS A *BRUTAL* WORLD, BROTHER... YOU DON'T WANT TO KNOW.
JUST NOW I THOUGHT I WAS FALLING TO MY DEATH, SO YEAH... I *KINDA DO.*
I MEAN, I'M HELPING YOU HUNT THEM DOWN. I WANT TO KNOW WHAT FOR.
TO MAKE SURE THAT WHAT HAPPENED TO ME *NEVER HAPPENS AGAIN.*

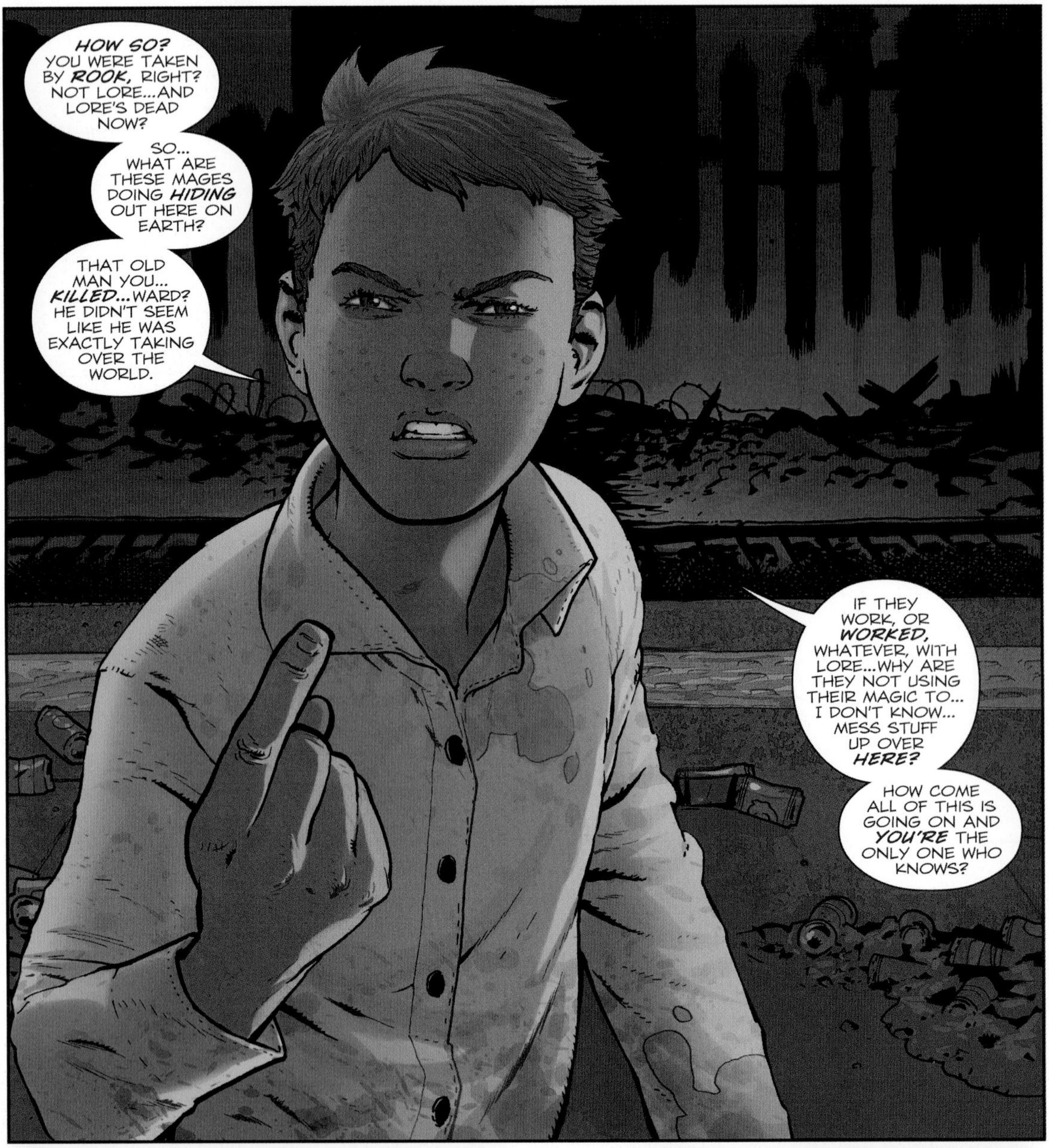
HOW SO? YOU WERE TAKEN BY ROOK, RIGHT? NOT LORE...AND LORE'S DEAD NOW?
SO... WHAT ARE THESE MAGES DOING HIDING OUT HERE ON EARTH?
THAT OLD MAN YOU... KILLED...WARD? HE DIDN'T SEEM LIKE HE WAS EXACTLY TAKING OVER THE WORLD.
IF THEY WORK, OR WORKED, WHATEVER, WITH LORE...WHY ARE THEY NOT USING THEIR MAGIC TO... I DON'T KNOW... MESS STUFF UP OVER HERE?
HOW COME ALL OF THIS IS GOING ON AND YOU'RE THE ONLY ONE WHO KNOWS?

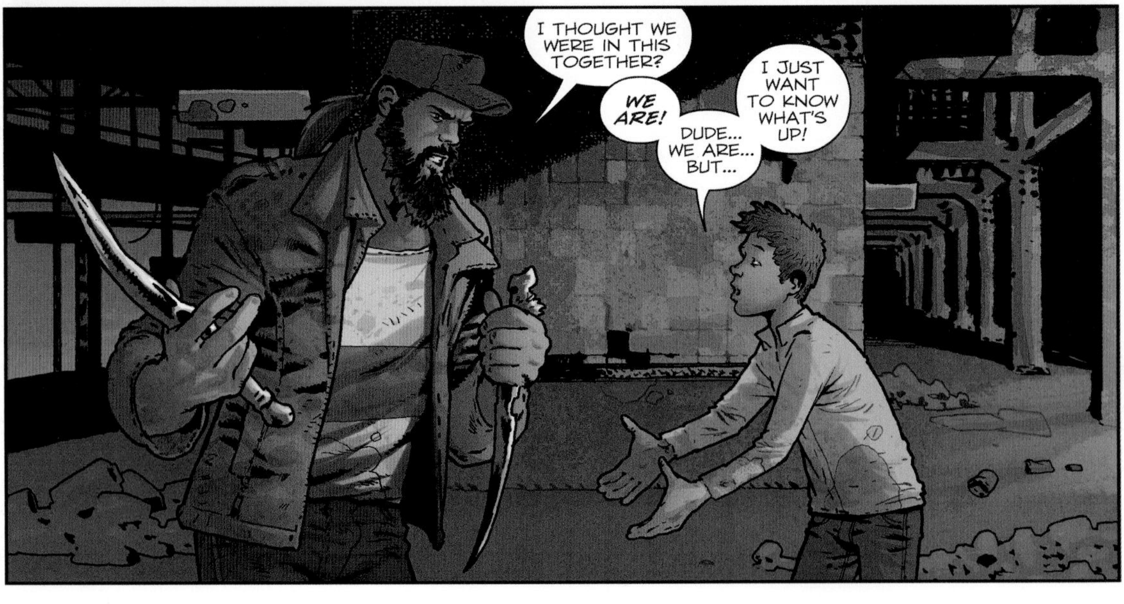
I THOUGHT WE WERE IN THIS TOGETHER?
WE ARE!
DUDE... WE ARE... BUT...
I JUST WANT TO KNOW WHAT'S UP!

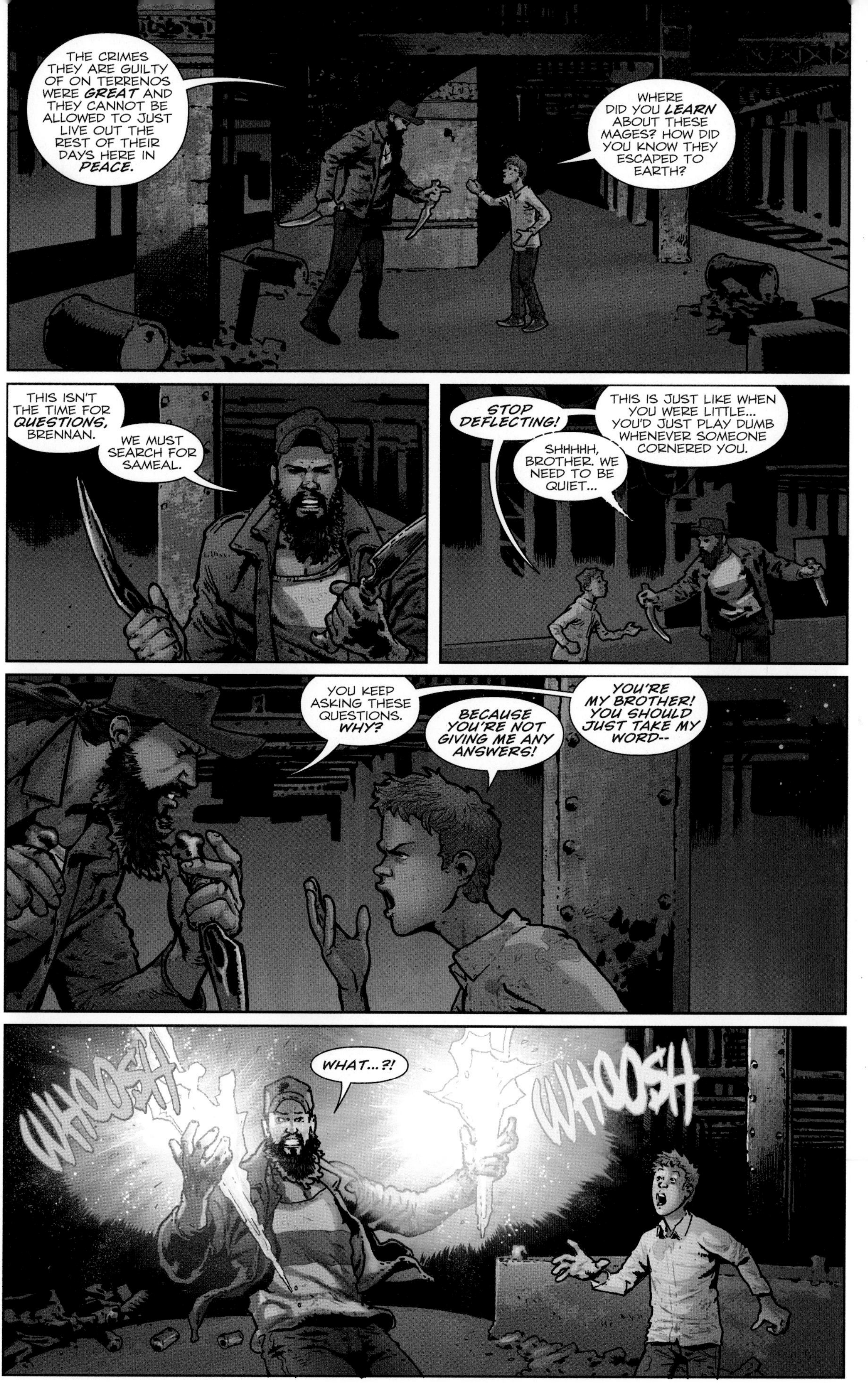
THE CRIMES THEY ARE GUILTY OF ON TERRENOS WERE GREAT AND THEY CANNOT BE ALLOWED TO JUST LIVE OUT THE REST OF THEIR DAYS HERE IN PEACE.
WHERE DID YOU LEARN ABOUT THESE MAGES? HOW DID YOU KNOW THEY ESCAPED TO EARTH?
THIS ISN'T THE TIME FOR QUESTIONS, BRENNAN.
WE MUST SEARCH FOR SAMEAL.
STOP DEFLECTING!
THIS IS JUST LIKE WHEN YOU WERE LITTLE... YOU'D JUST PLAY DUMB WHENEVER SOMEONE CORNERED YOU.
SHHHHH, BROTHER. WE NEED TO BE QUIET...
YOU KEEP ASKING THESE QUESTIONS. WHY?
BECAUSE YOU'RE NOT GIVING ME ANY ANSWERS!
YOU'RE MY BROTHER! YOU SHOULD JUST TAKE MY WORD--
WHOOSH
WHAT...?!
WHOOSH

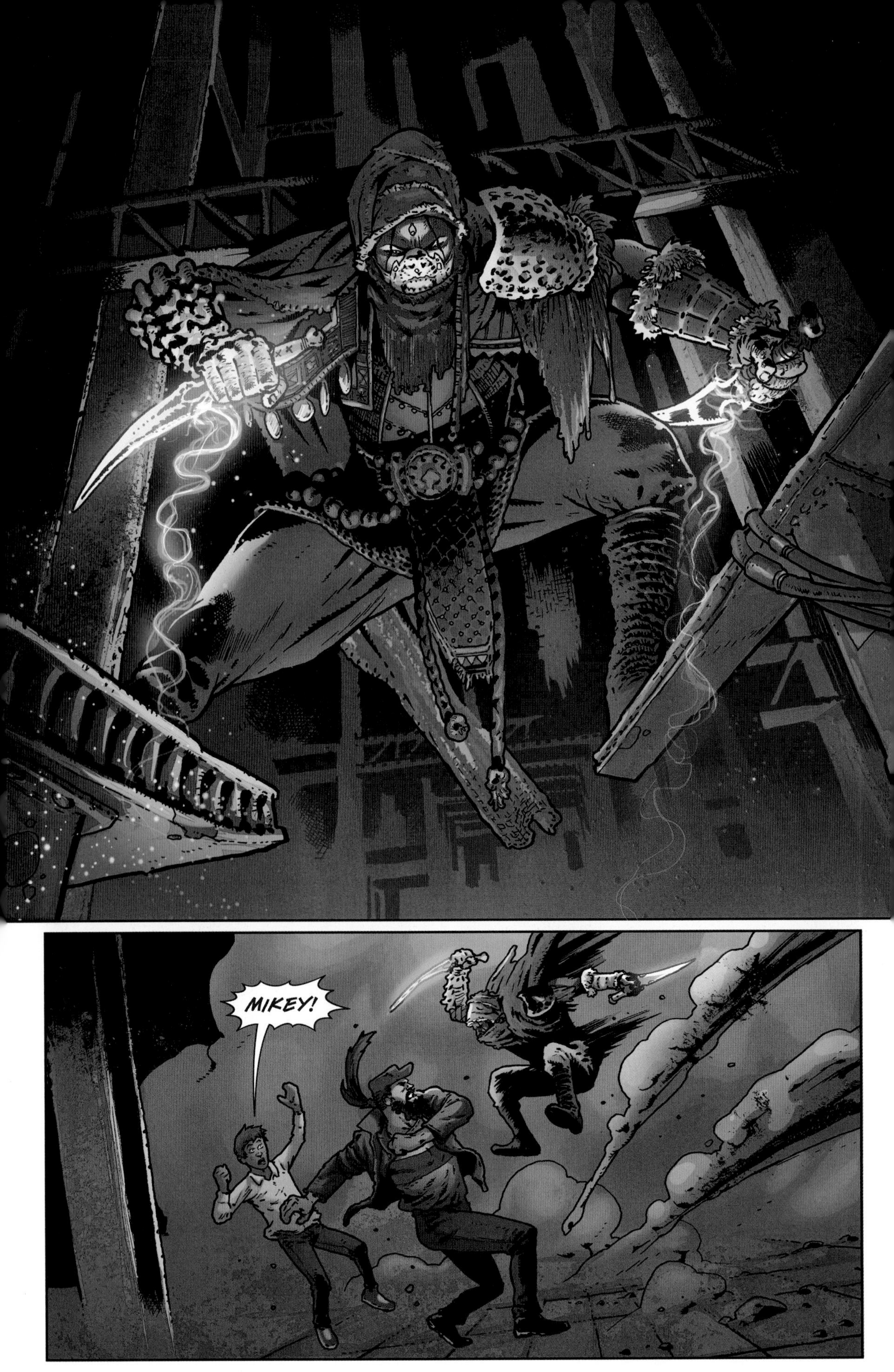
MIKEY!

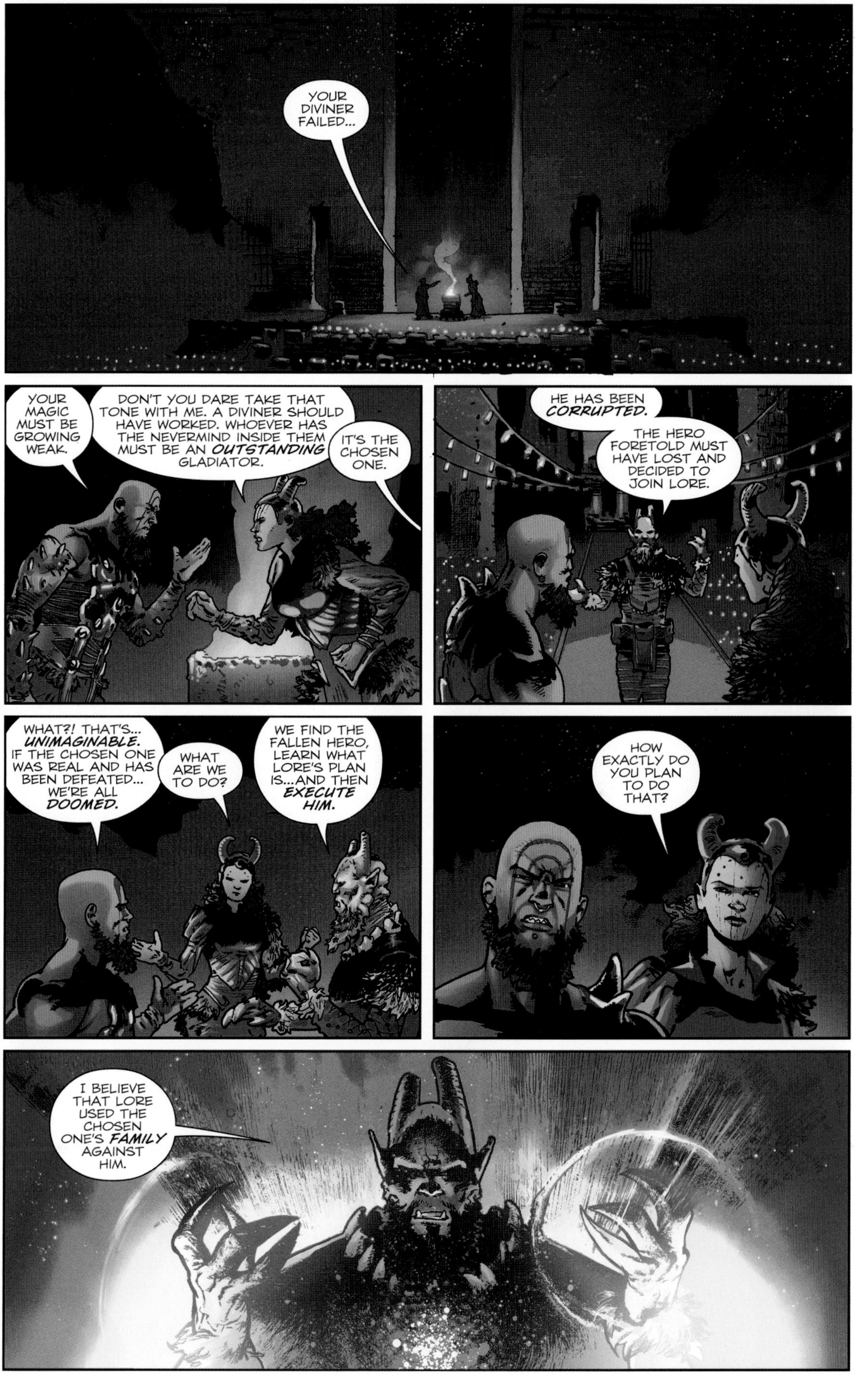
YOUR DIVINER FAILED...
YOUR MAGIC MUST BE GROWING WEAK.
DON'T YOU DARE TAKE THAT TONE WITH ME. A DIVINER SHOULD HAVE WORKED. WHOEVER HAS THE NEVERMIND INSIDE THEM MUST BE AN *OUTSTANDING* GLADIATOR.
IT'S THE CHOSEN ONE.
HE HAS BEEN *CORRUPTED.*
THE HERO FORETOLD MUST HAVE LOST AND DECIDED TO JOIN LORE.
WHAT?! THAT'S... *UNIMAGINABLE.* IF THE CHOSEN ONE WAS REAL AND HAS BEEN DEFEATED... WE'RE ALL *DOOMED.*
WHAT ARE WE TO DO?
WE FIND THE FALLEN HERO, LEARN WHAT LORE'S PLAN IS...AND THEN *EXECUTE HIM.*
HOW EXACTLY DO YOU PLAN TO DO THAT?
I BELIEVE THAT LORE USED THE CHOSEN ONE'S *FAMILY* AGAINST HIM.

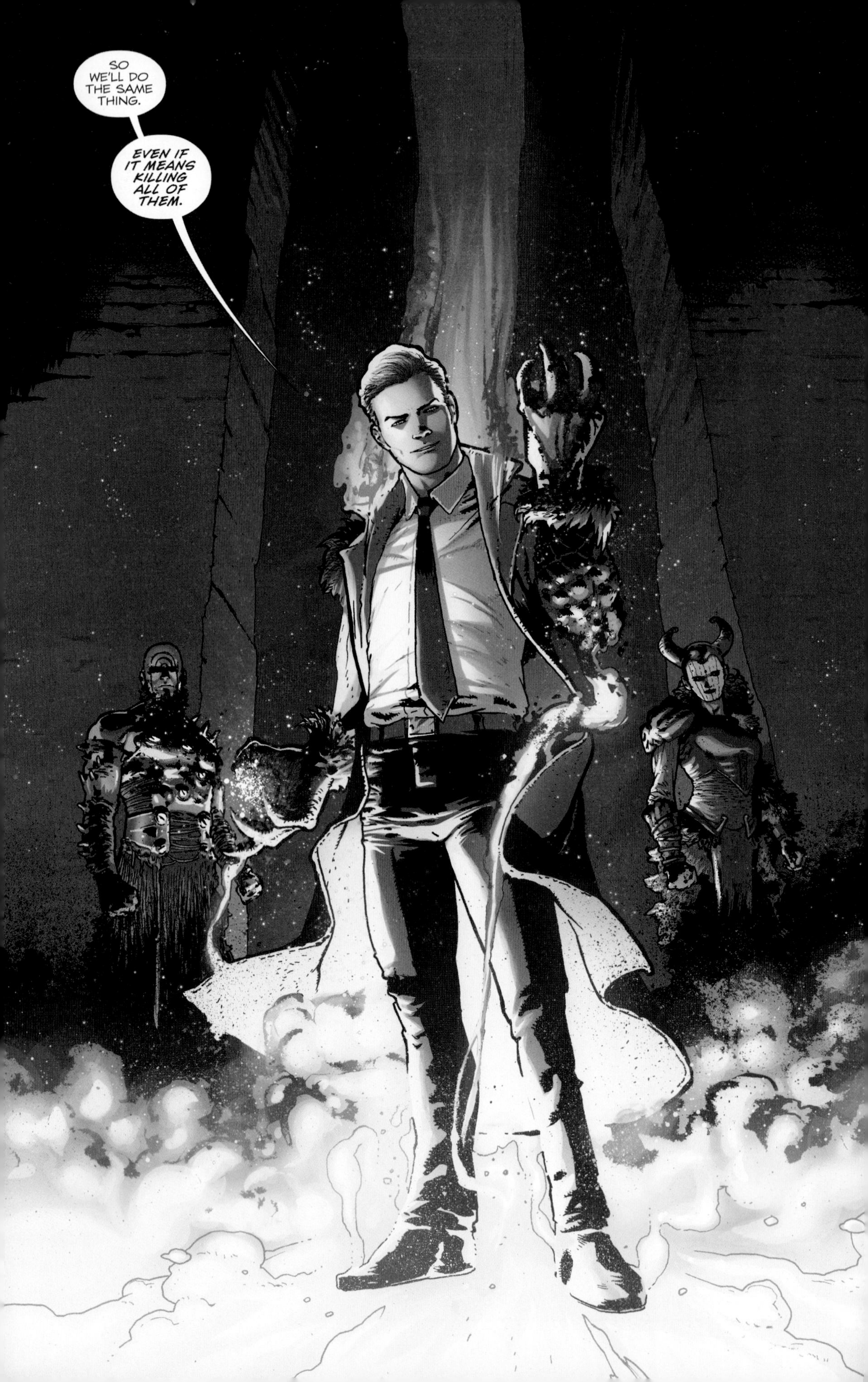
SO WE'LL DO THE SAME THING.
EVEN IF IT MEANS KILLING ALL OF THEM.

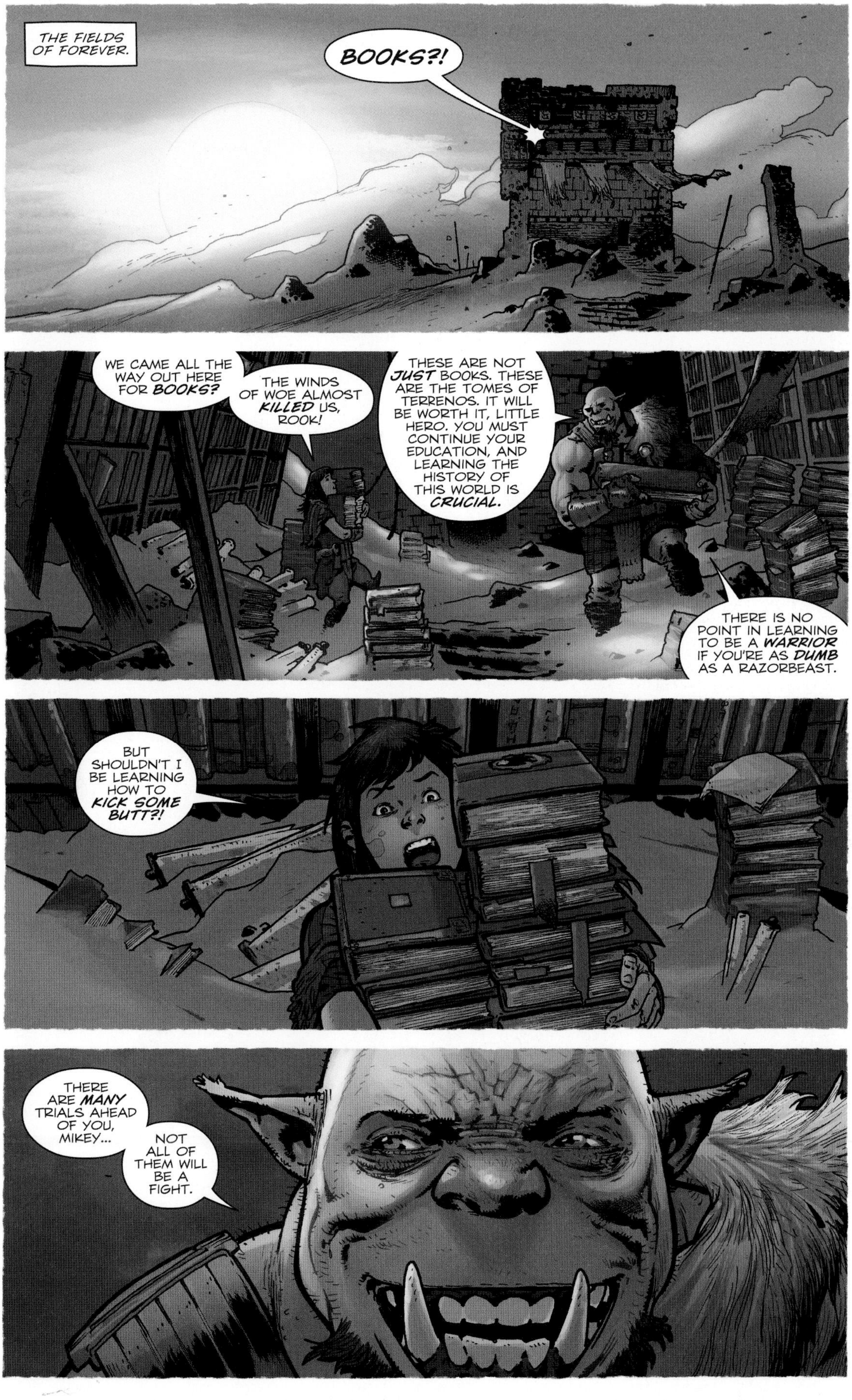
THE FIELDS OF FOREVER.
BOOKS?!
WE CAME ALL THE WAY OUT HERE FOR BOOKS?
THE WINDS OF WOE ALMOST KILLED US, ROOK!
THESE ARE NOT JUST BOOKS. THESE ARE THE TOMES OF TERRENOS. IT WILL BE WORTH IT, LITTLE HERO. YOU MUST CONTINUE YOUR EDUCATION, AND LEARNING THE HISTORY OF THIS WORLD IS CRUCIAL.
THERE IS NO POINT IN LEARNING TO BE A WARRIOR IF YOU'RE AS DUMB AS A RAZORBEAST.
BUT SHOULDN'T I BE LEARNING HOW TO KICK SOME BUTT?!
THERE ARE MANY TRIALS AHEAD OF YOU, MIKEY...
NOT ALL OF THEM WILL BE A FIGHT.

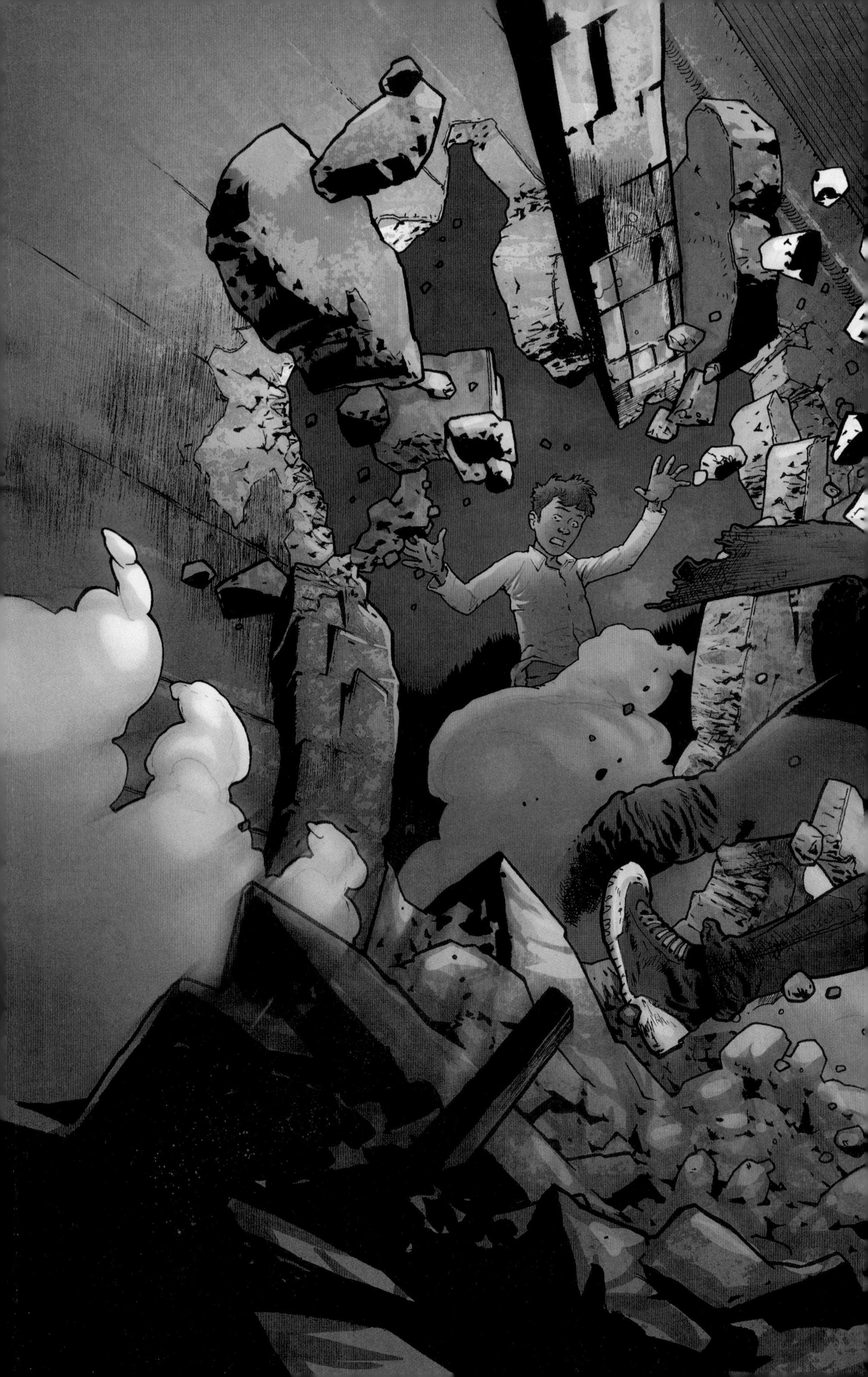

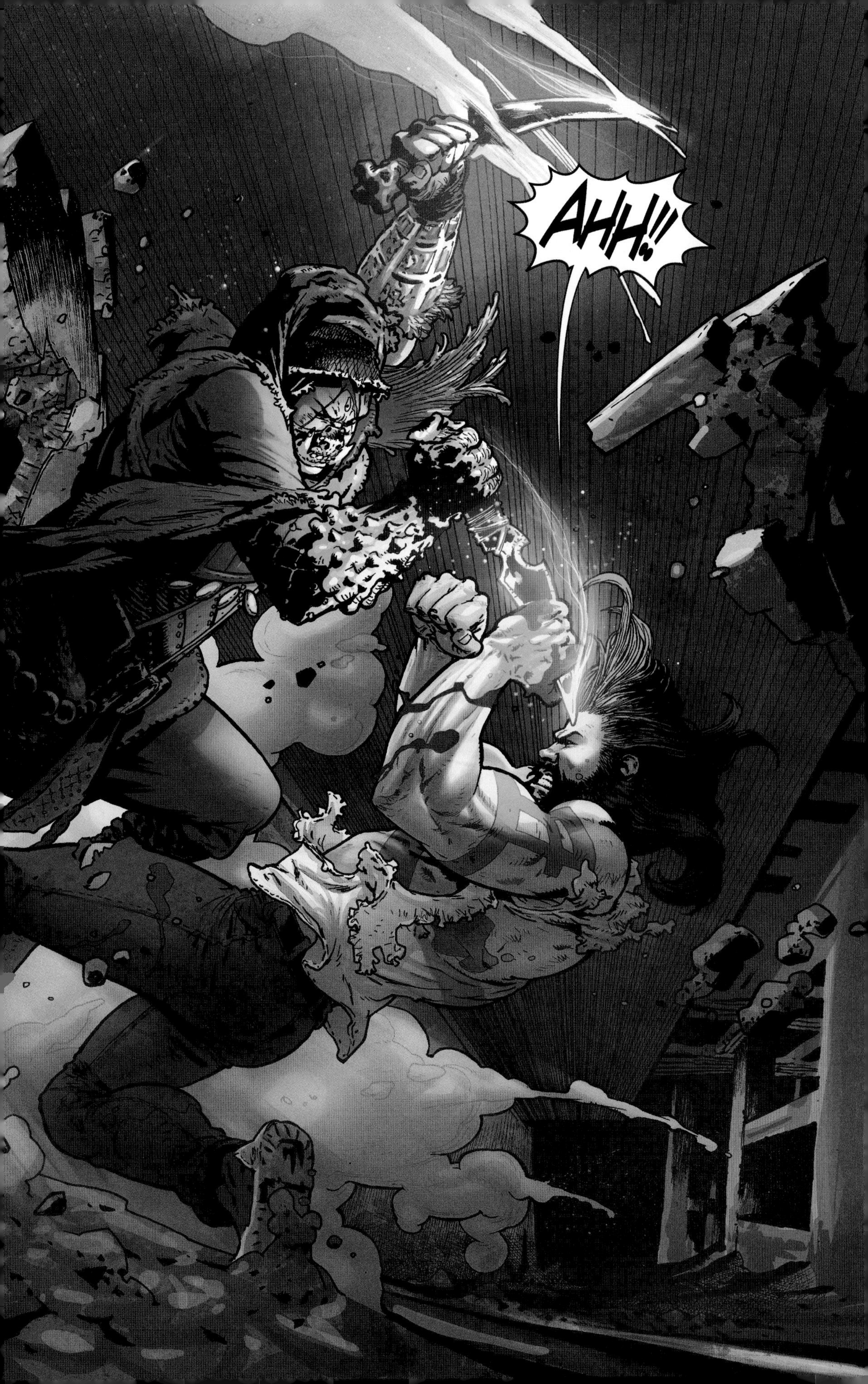
AHH!!

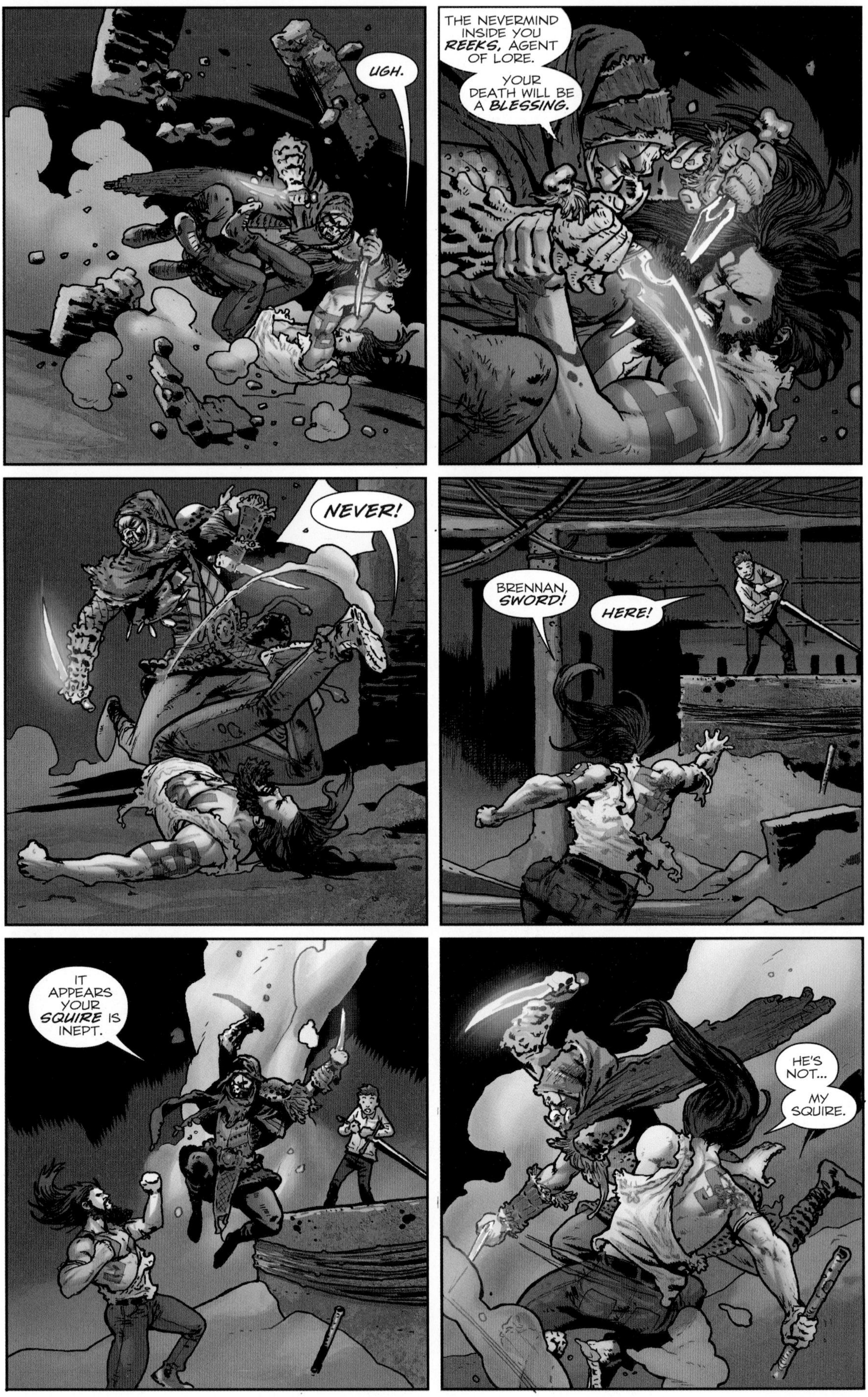
UGH.
THE NEVERMIND INSIDE YOU REEKS, AGENT OF LORE.
YOUR DEATH WILL BE A BLESSING.
NEVER!
BRENNAN, SWORD!
HERE!
IT APPEARS YOUR SQUIRE IS INEPT.
HE'S NOT...
MY SQUIRE.

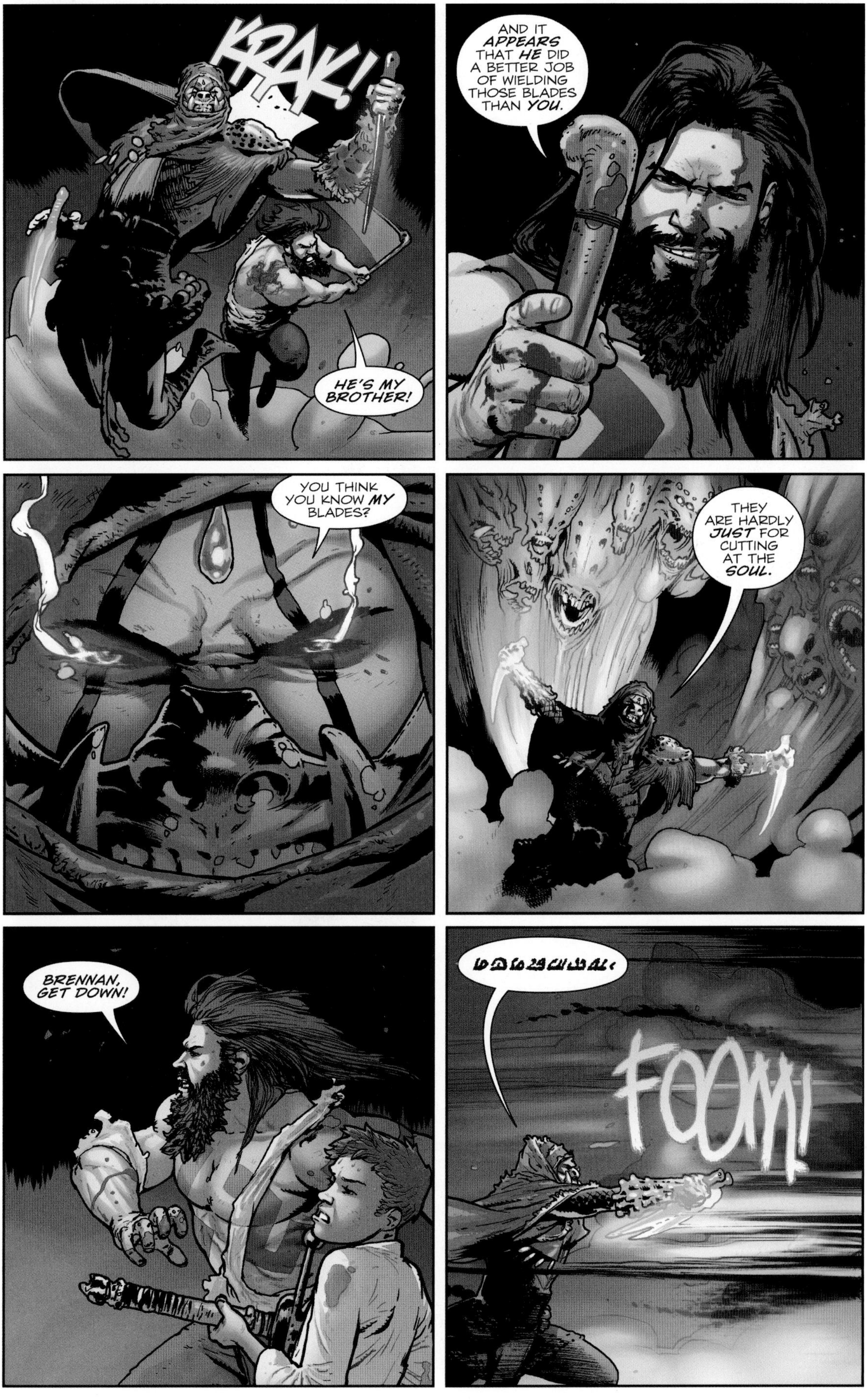
KRAK!
HE'S MY BROTHER!
AND IT APPEARS THAT HE DID A BETTER JOB OF WIELDING THOSE BLADES THAN YOU.
YOU THINK YOU KNOW MY BLADES?
THEY ARE HARDLY JUST FOR CUTTING AT THE SOUL.
BRENNAN, GET DOWN!
FOOM!

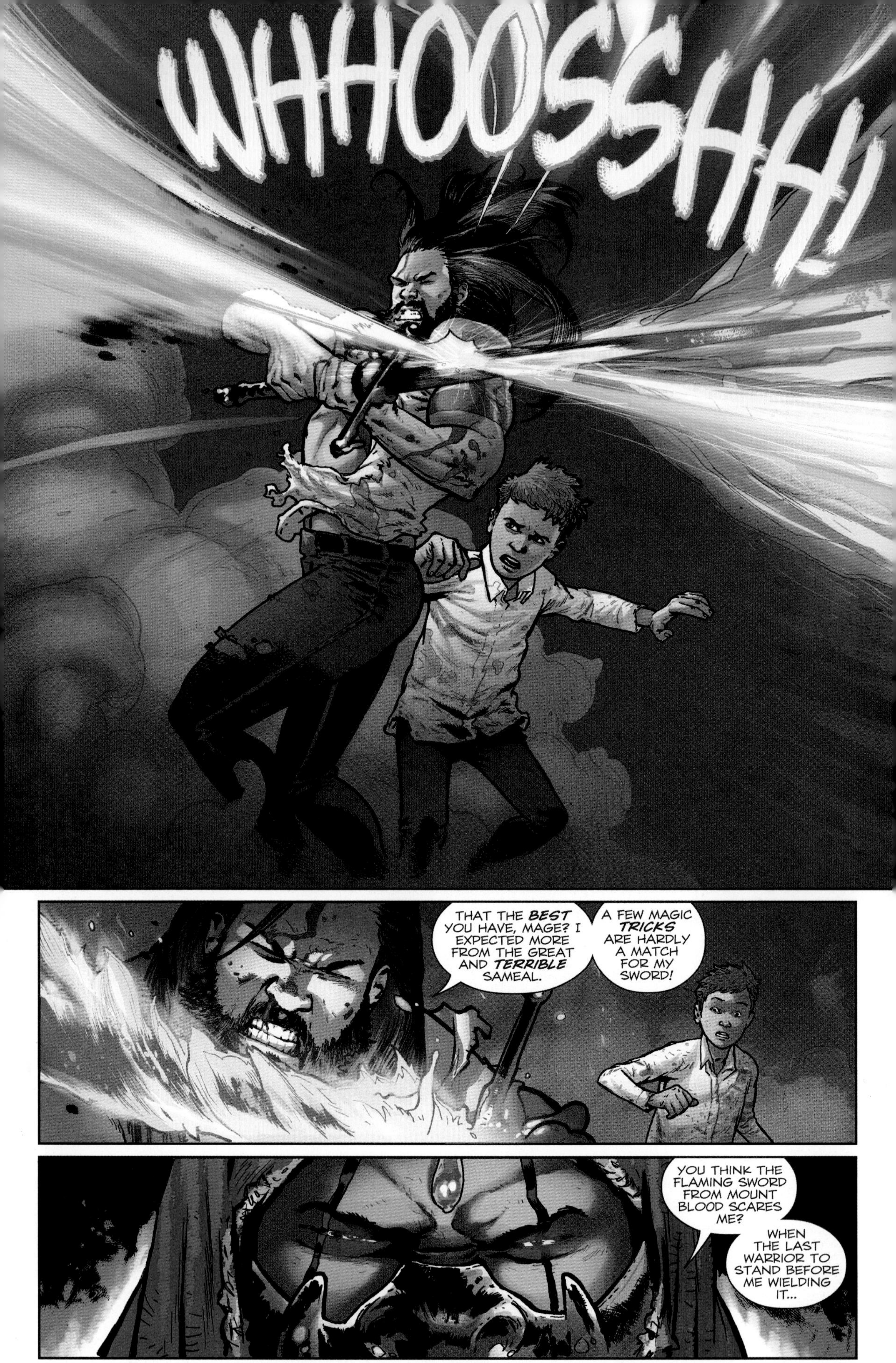
WHHOOSSHH!
THAT THE BEST YOU HAVE, MAGE? I EXPECTED MORE FROM THE GREAT AND TERRIBLE SAMEAL.
A FEW MAGIC TRICKS ARE HARDLY A MATCH FOR MY SWORD!
YOU THINK THE FLAMING SWORD FROM MOUNT BLOOD SCARES ME?
WHEN THE LAST WARRIOR TO STAND BEFORE ME WIELDING IT...

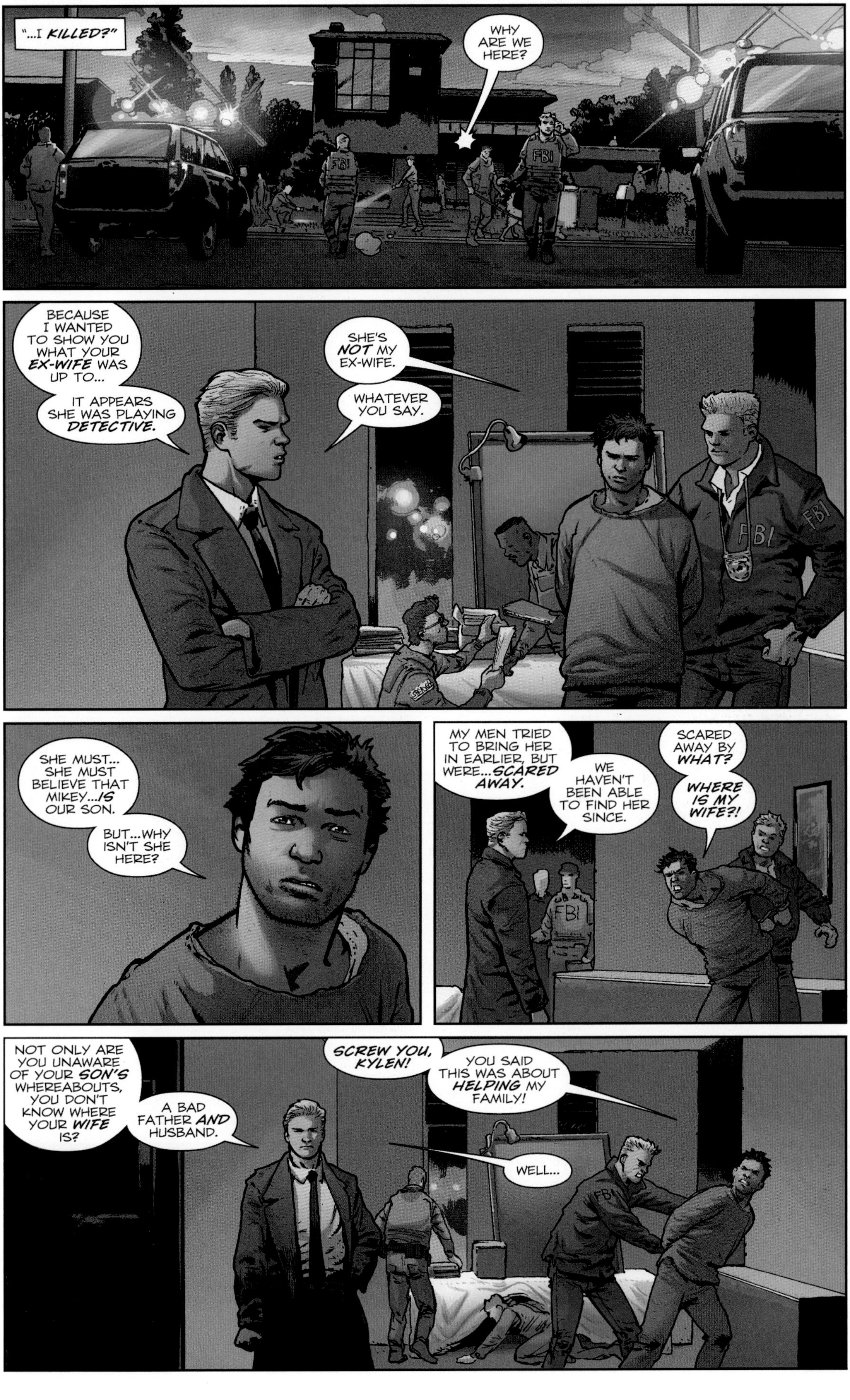
"...I KILLED?"
WHY ARE WE HERE?
BECAUSE I WANTED TO SHOW YOU WHAT YOUR EX-WIFE WAS UP TO...
IT APPEARS SHE WAS PLAYING DETECTIVE.
SHE'S NOT MY EX-WIFE.
WHATEVER YOU SAY.
FBI
SHE MUST... SHE MUST BELIEVE THAT MIKEY...IS OUR SON.
BUT...WHY ISN'T SHE HERE?
MY MEN TRIED TO BRING HER IN EARLIER, BUT WERE...SCARED AWAY.
WE HAVEN'T BEEN ABLE TO FIND HER SINCE.
SCARED AWAY BY WHAT?
WHERE IS MY WIFE?!
NOT ONLY ARE YOU UNAWARE OF YOUR SON'S WHEREABOUTS, YOU DON'T KNOW WHERE YOUR WIFE IS?
A BAD FATHER AND HUSBAND.
SCREW YOU, KYLEN!
YOU SAID THIS WAS ABOUT HELPING MY FAMILY!
WELL...

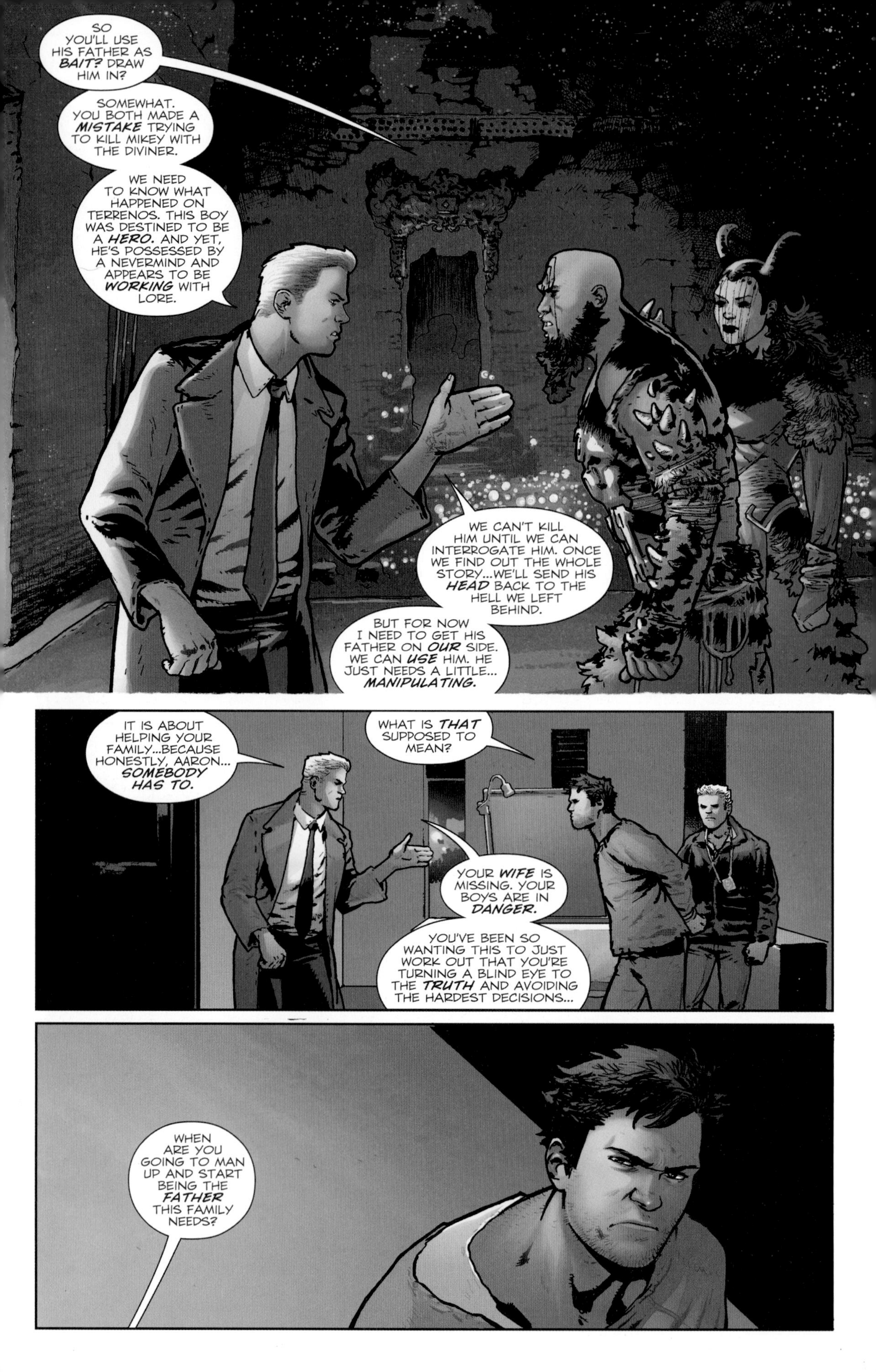
SO YOU'LL USE HIS FATHER AS BAIT? DRAW HIM IN?
SOMEWHAT. YOU BOTH MADE A MISTAKE TRYING TO KILL MIKEY WITH THE DIVINER.
WE NEED TO KNOW WHAT HAPPENED ON TERRENOS. THIS BOY WAS DESTINED TO BE A HERO. AND YET, HE'S POSSESSED BY A NEVERMIND AND APPEARS TO BE WORKING WITH LORE.
WE CAN'T KILL HIM UNTIL WE CAN INTERROGATE HIM. ONCE WE FIND OUT THE WHOLE STORY...WE'LL SEND HIS HEAD BACK TO THE HELL WE LEFT BEHIND.
BUT FOR NOW I NEED TO GET HIS FATHER ON OUR SIDE. WE CAN USE HIM. HE JUST NEEDS A LITTLE... MANIPULATING.
IT IS ABOUT HELPING YOUR FAMILY...BECAUSE HONESTLY, AARON... SOMEBODY HAS TO.
WHAT IS THAT SUPPOSED TO MEAN?
YOUR WIFE IS MISSING. YOUR BOYS ARE IN DANGER.
YOU'VE BEEN SO WANTING THIS TO JUST WORK OUT THAT YOU'RE TURNING A BLIND EYE TO THE TRUTH AND AVOIDING THE HARDEST DECISIONS...
WHEN ARE YOU GOING TO MAN UP AND START BEING THE FATHER THIS FAMILY NEEDS?

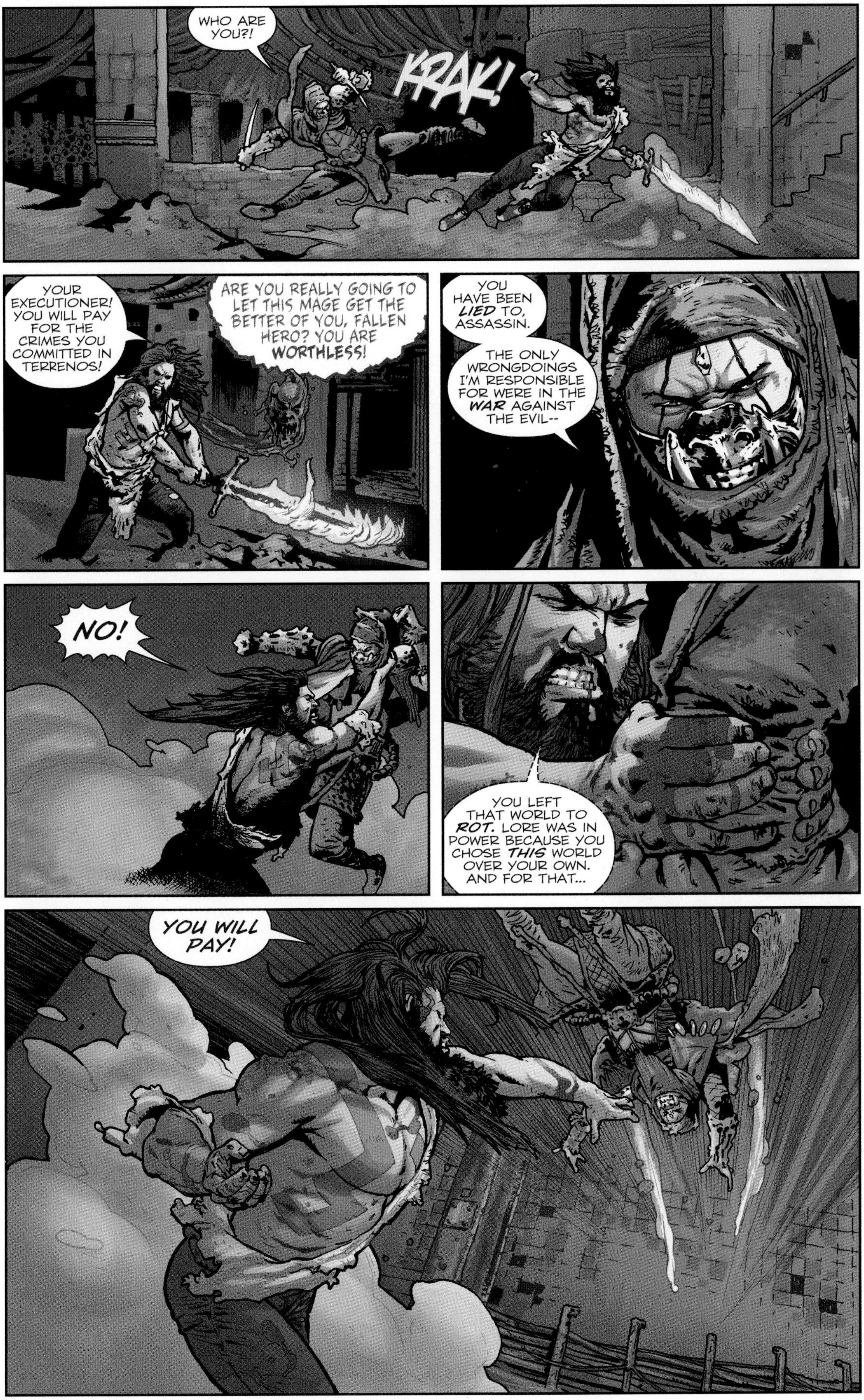
WHO ARE YOU?!
KRAK!
YOUR EXECUTIONER! YOU WILL PAY FOR THE CRIMES YOU COMMITTED IN TERRENOS!
ARE YOU REALLY GOING TO LET THIS MAGE GET THE BETTER OF YOU, FALLEN HERO? YOU ARE WORTHLESS!
YOU HAVE BEEN LIED TO, ASSASSIN.
THE ONLY WRONGDOINGS I'M RESPONSIBLE FOR WERE IN THE WAR AGAINST THE EVIL--
NO!
YOU LEFT THAT WORLD TO ROT. LORE WAS IN POWER BECAUSE YOU CHOSE THIS WORLD OVER YOUR OWN. AND FOR THAT...
YOU WILL PAY!

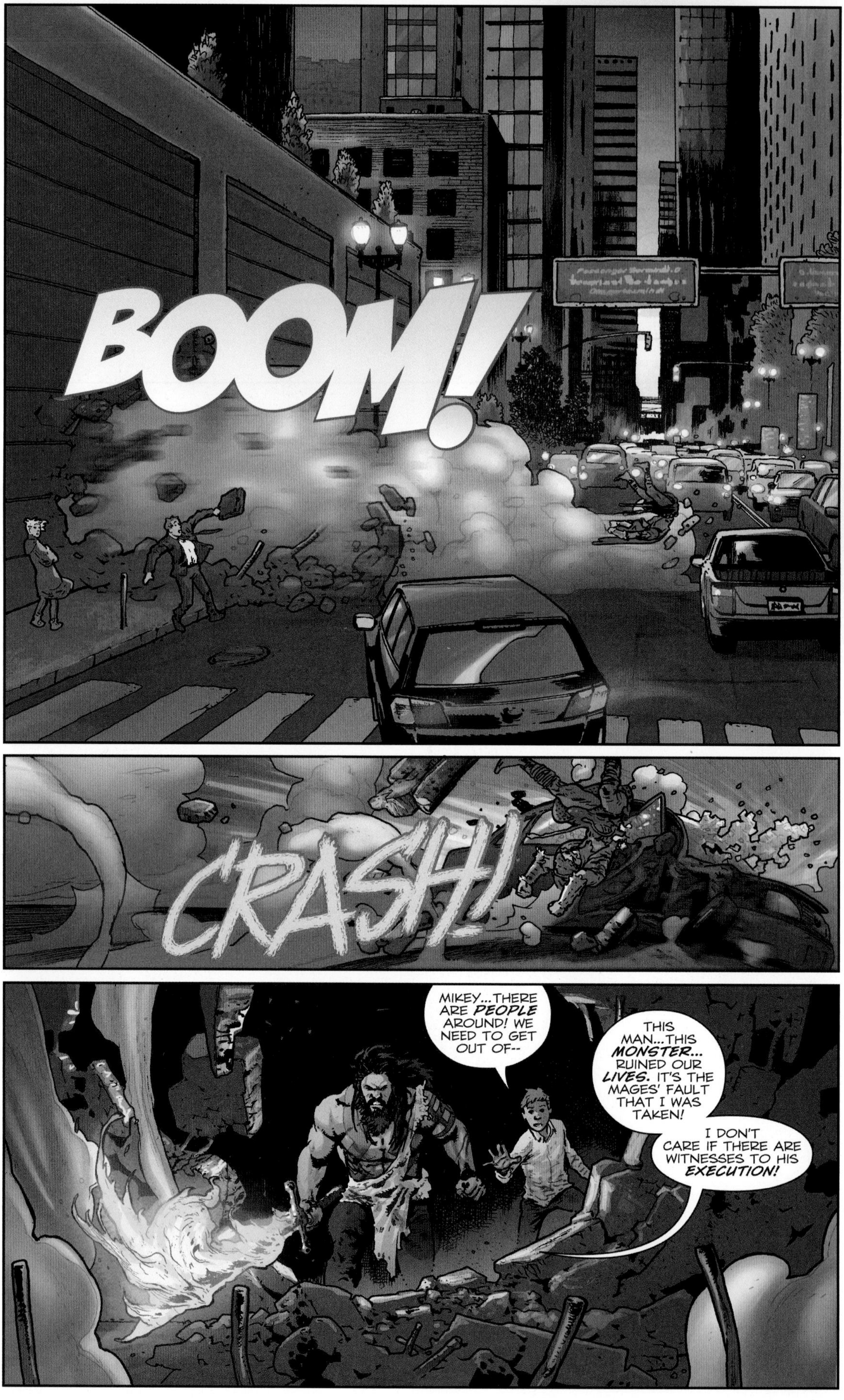
BOOM!
CRASH!
MIKEY...THERE ARE PEOPLE AROUND! WE NEED TO GET OUT OF--
THIS MAN...THIS MONSTER... RUINED OUR LIVES. IT'S THE MAGES' FAULT THAT I WAS TAKEN!
I DON'T CARE IF THERE ARE WITNESSES TO HIS EXECUTION!

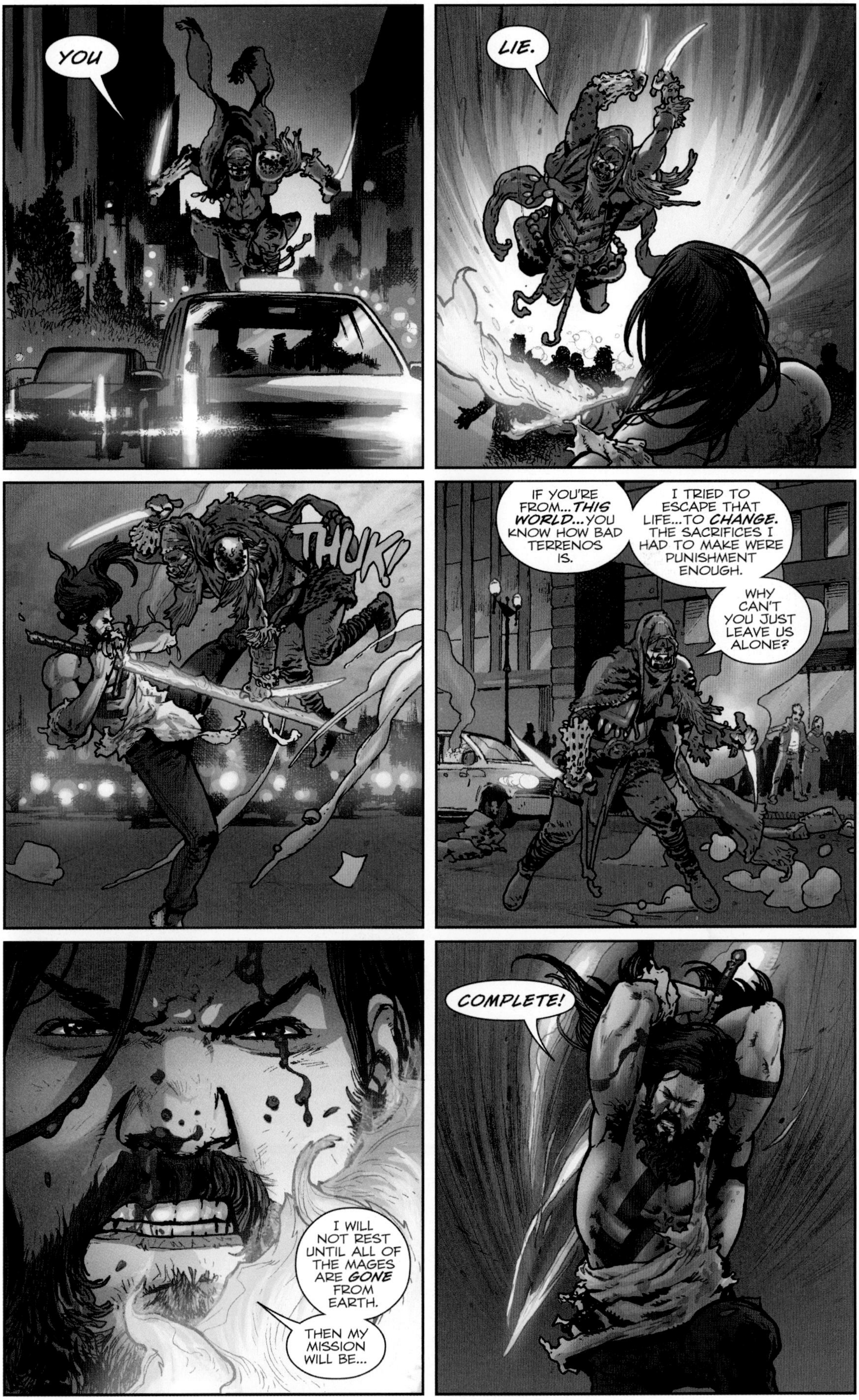
YOU
LIE.
THUK!
IF YOU'RE FROM...THIS WORLD...YOU KNOW HOW BAD TERRENOS IS.
I TRIED TO ESCAPE THAT LIFE...TO CHANGE. THE SACRIFICES I HAD TO MAKE WERE PUNISHMENT ENOUGH.
WHY CAN'T YOU JUST LEAVE US ALONE?
I WILL NOT REST UNTIL ALL OF THE MAGES ARE GONE FROM EARTH.
THEN MY MISSION WILL BE...
COMPLETE!

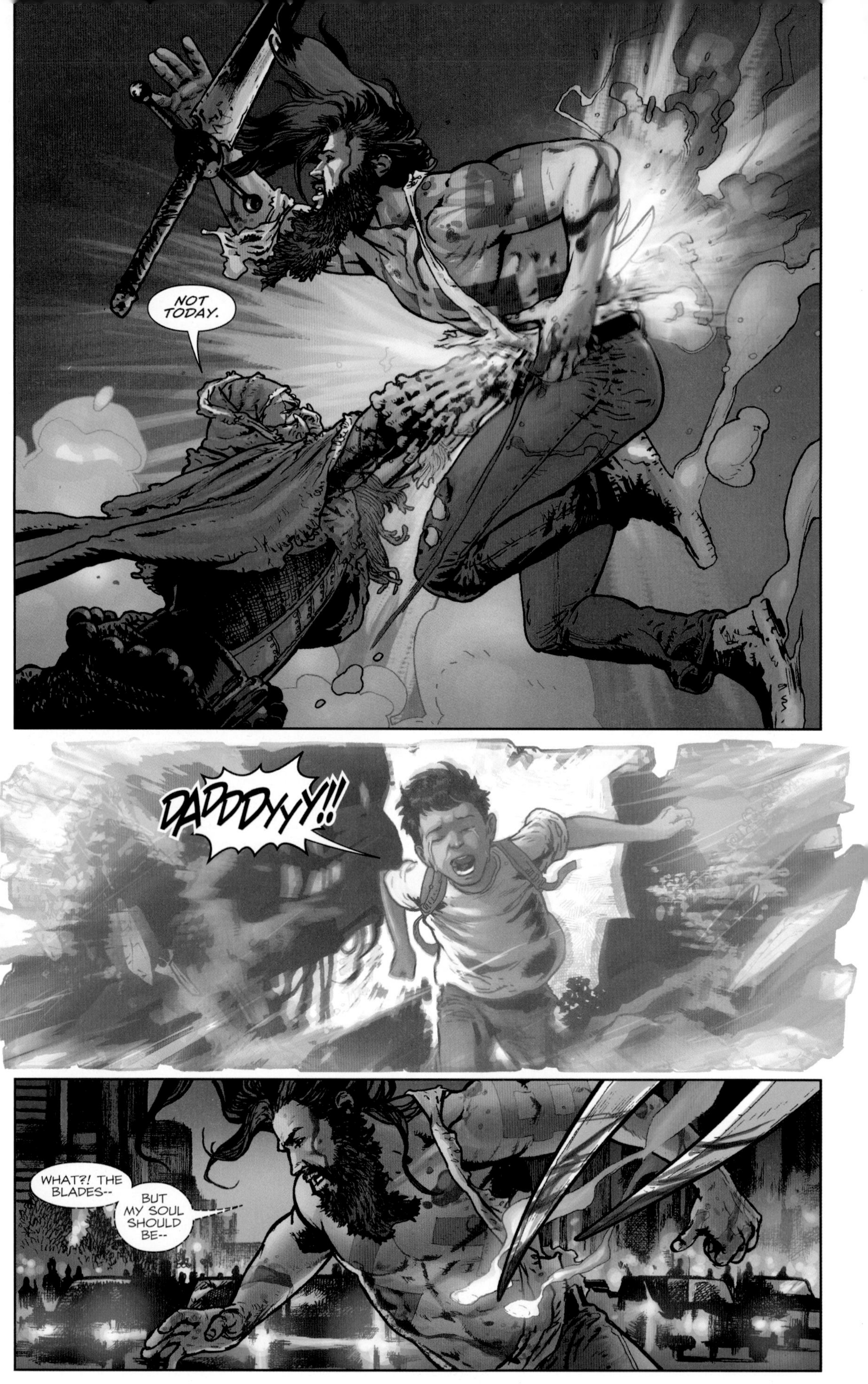
NOT TODAY.
DADDDYYY!!
WHAT?! THE BLADES--
BUT MY SOUL SHOULD BE--

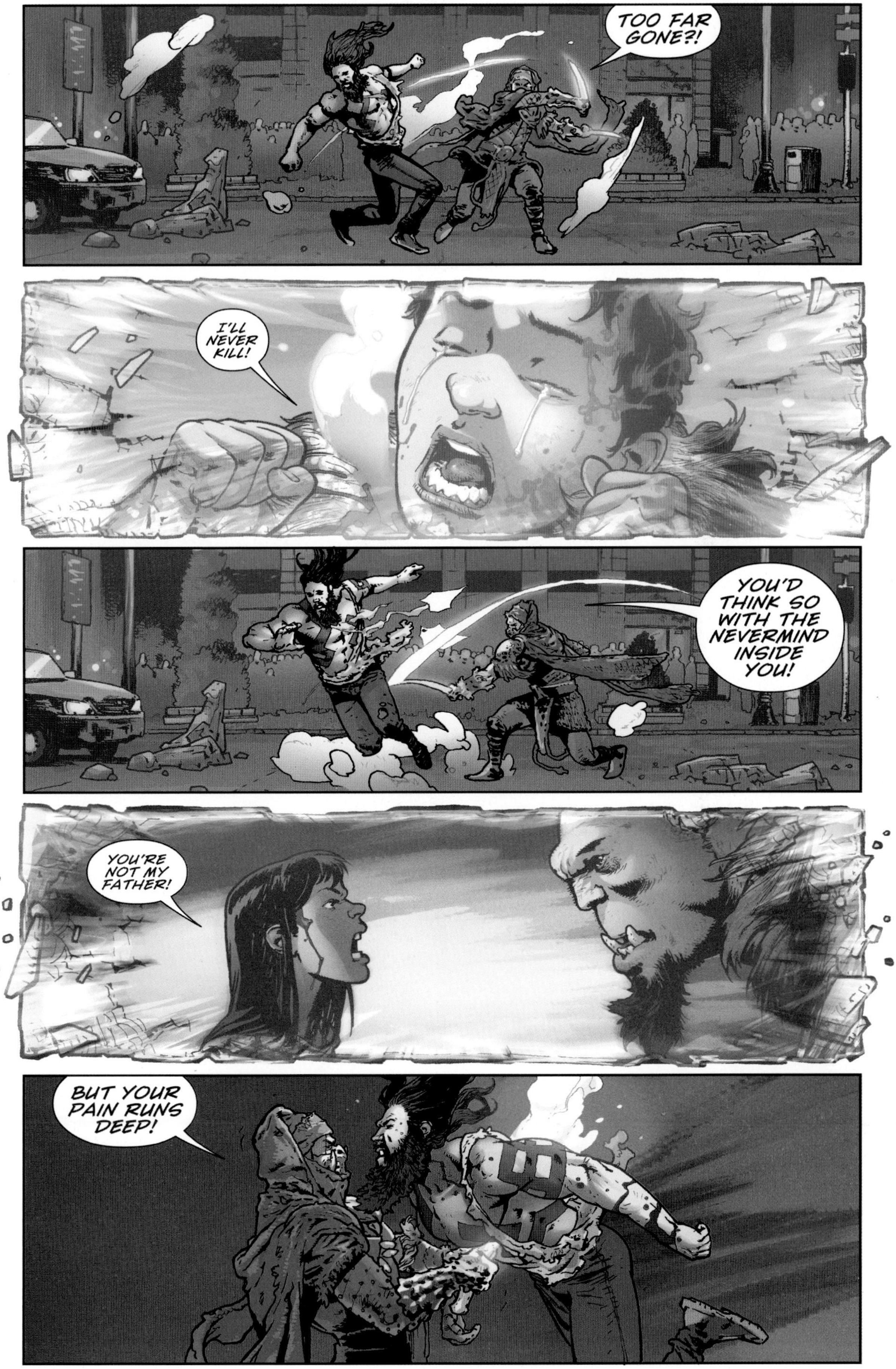
TOO FAR GONE?!
I'LL NEVER KILL!
YOU'D THINK SO WITH THE NEVERMIND INSIDE YOU!
YOU'RE NOT MY FATHER!
BUT YOUR PAIN RUNS DEEP!

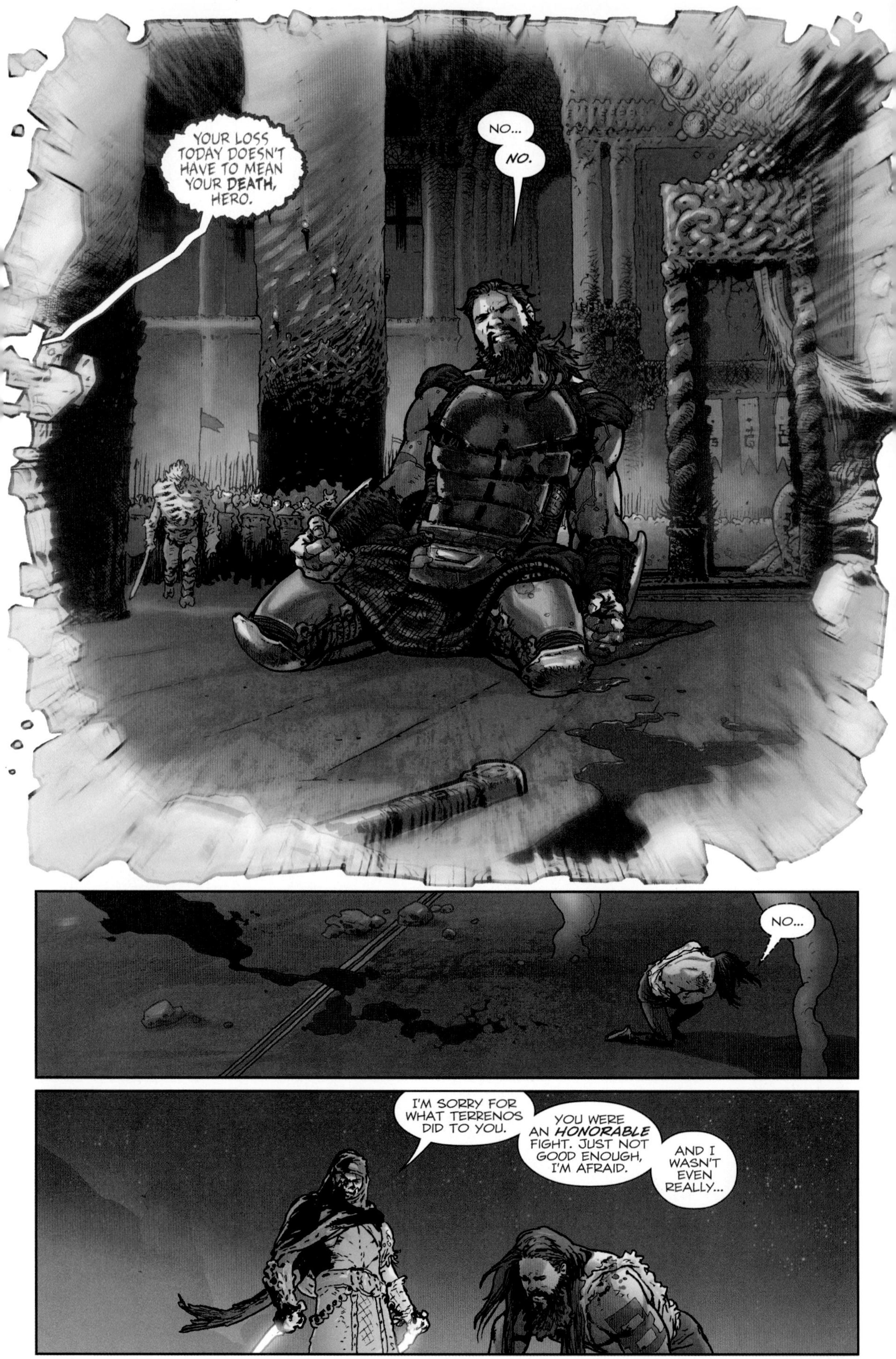
YOUR LOSS TODAY DOESN'T HAVE TO MEAN YOUR DEATH, HERO.
NO... NO.
NO...
I'M SORRY FOR WHAT TERRENOS DID TO YOU.
YOU WERE AN HONORABLE FIGHT. JUST NOT GOOD ENOUGH, I'M AFRAID.
AND I WASN'T EVEN REALLY...

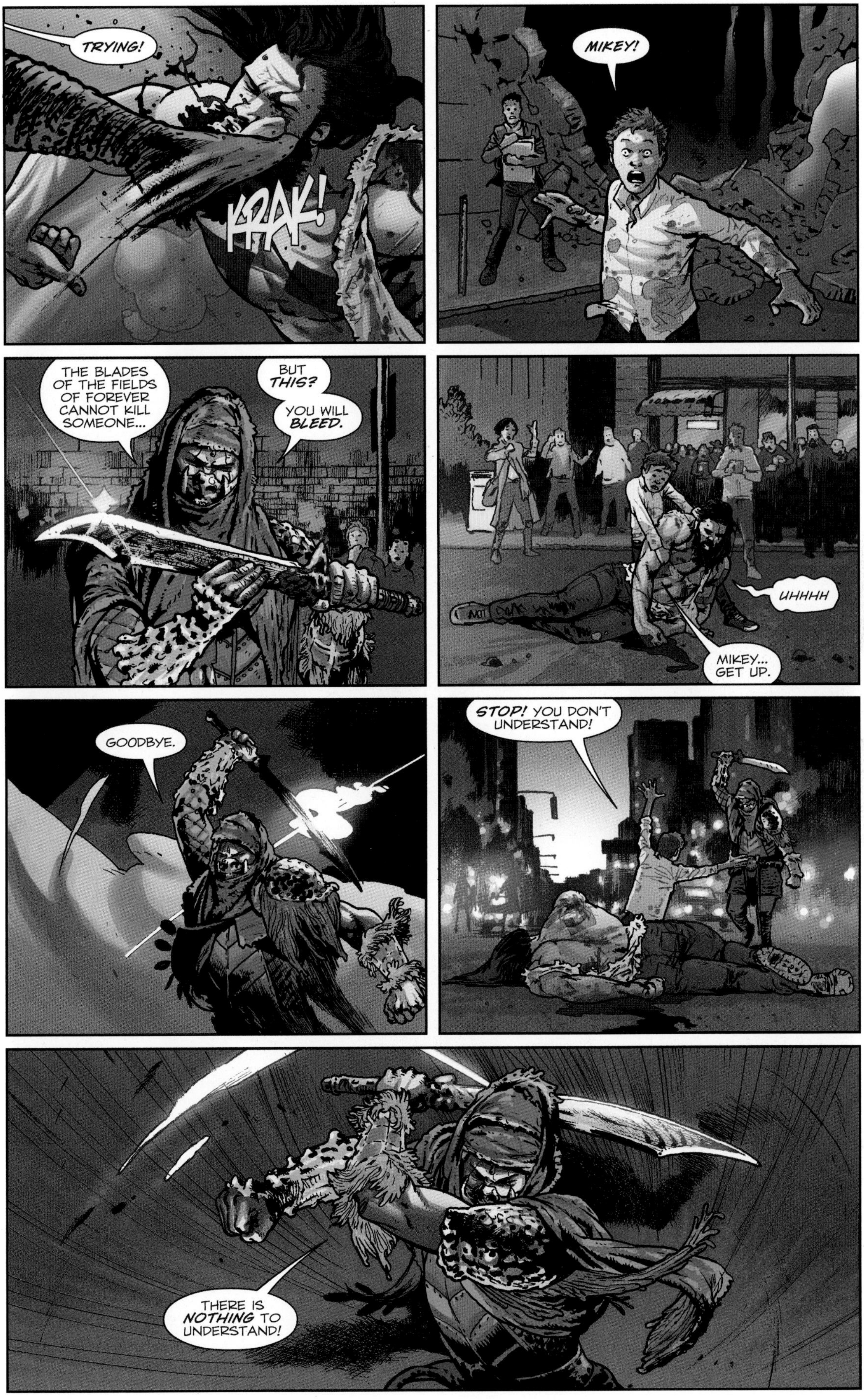
TRYING!
KRAK!
MIKEY!
THE BLADES OF THE FIELDS OF FOREVER CANNOT KILL SOMEONE...
BUT THIS?
YOU WILL BLEED.
UHHHH
MIKEY... GET UP.
GOODBYE.
STOP! YOU DON'T UNDERSTAND!
THERE IS NOTHING TO UNDERSTAND!

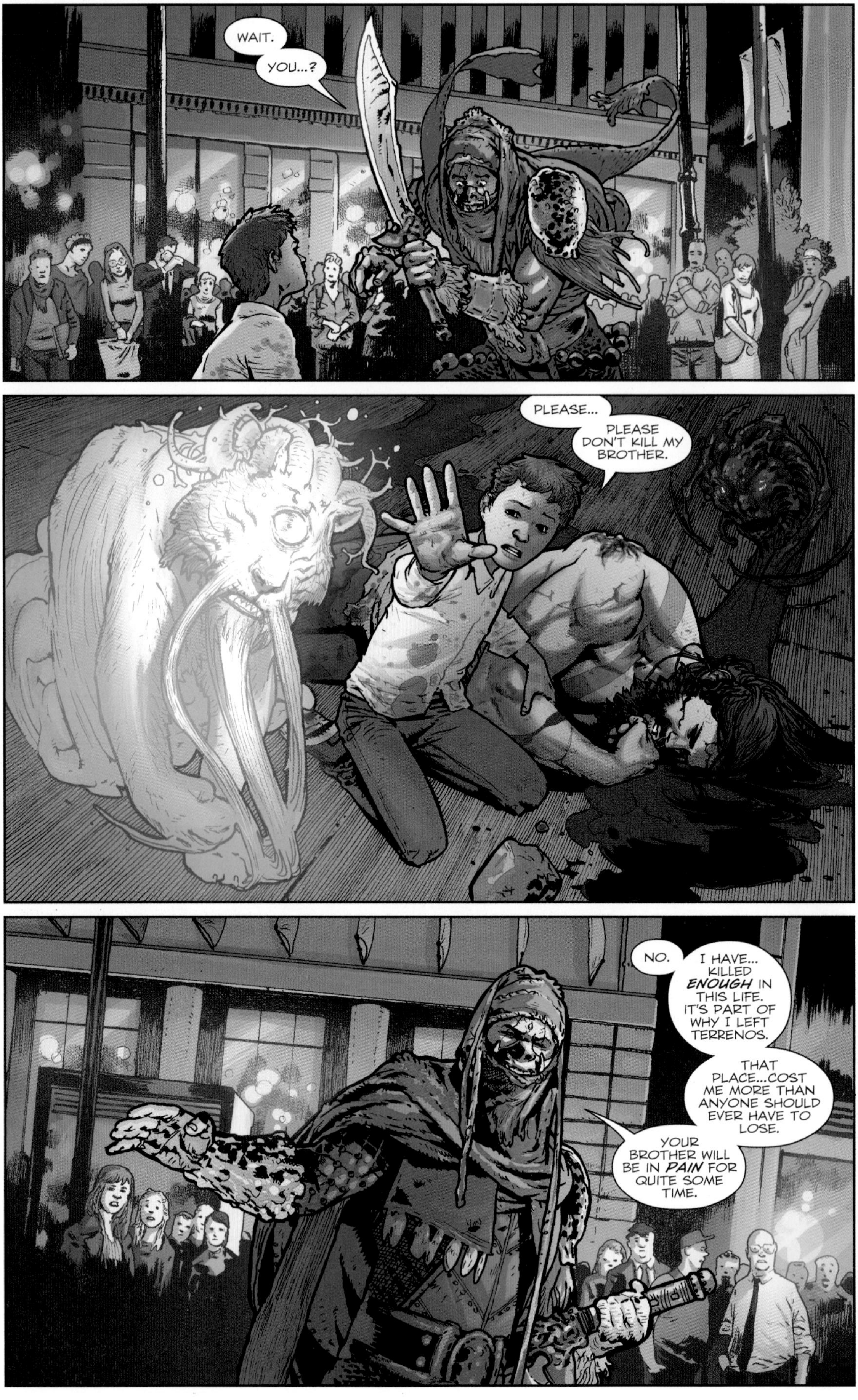
WAIT.
YOU...?
PLEASE...
PLEASE DON'T KILL MY BROTHER.
NO.
I HAVE... KILLED ENOUGH IN THIS LIFE. IT'S PART OF WHY I LEFT TERRENOS.
THAT PLACE...COST ME MORE THAN ANYONE SHOULD EVER HAVE TO LOSE.
YOUR BROTHER WILL BE IN PAIN FOR QUITE SOME TIME.

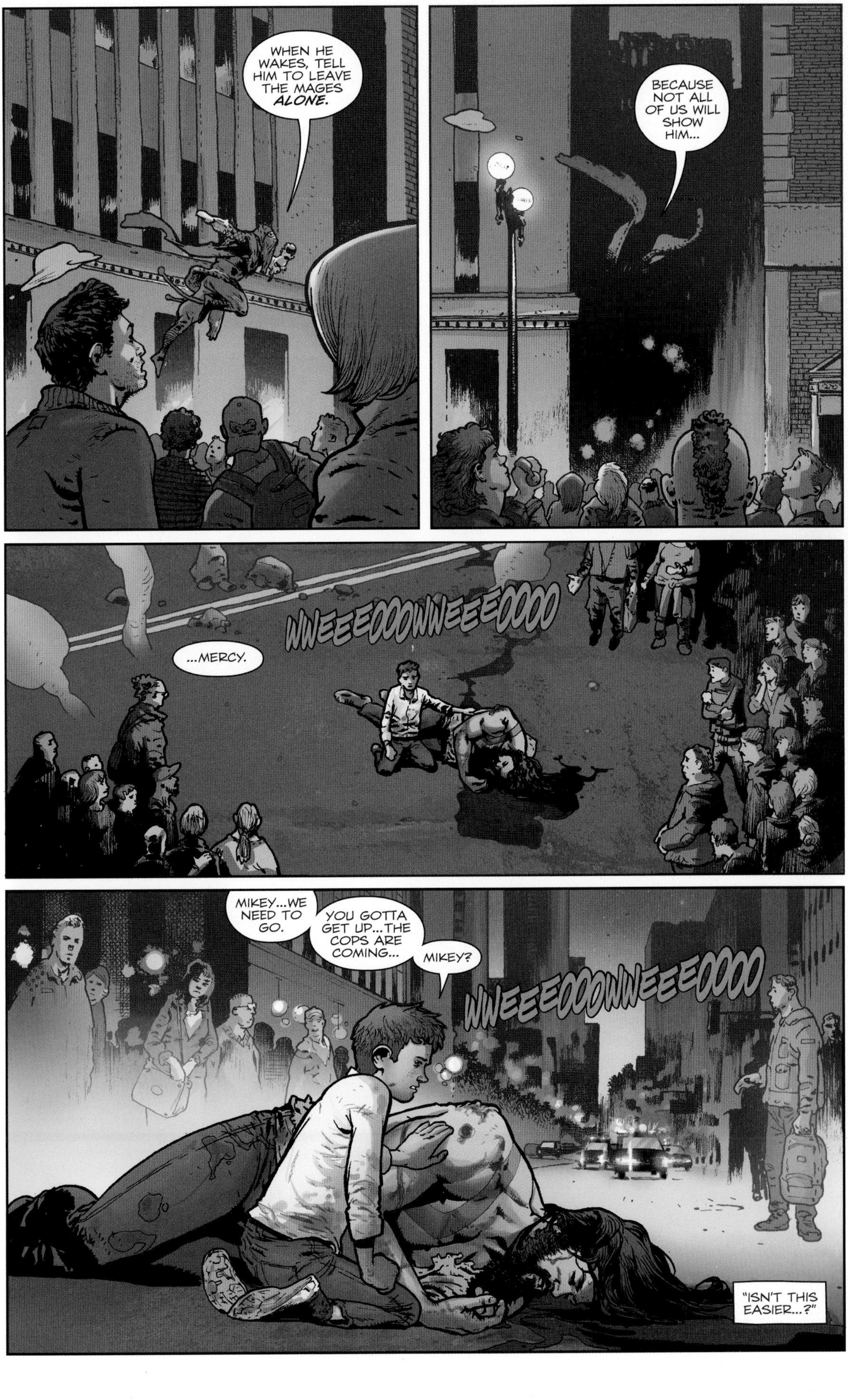
WHEN HE WAKES, TELL HIM TO LEAVE THE MAGES *ALONE*.
BECAUSE NOT ALL OF US WILL SHOW HIM...
WWEEEOOOWWEEEOOOO
...MERCY.
MIKEY...WE NEED TO GO.
YOU GOTTA GET UP...THE COPS ARE COMING...
MIKEY?
WWEEEOOOWWEEEOOOO
"ISN'T THIS EASIER...?"

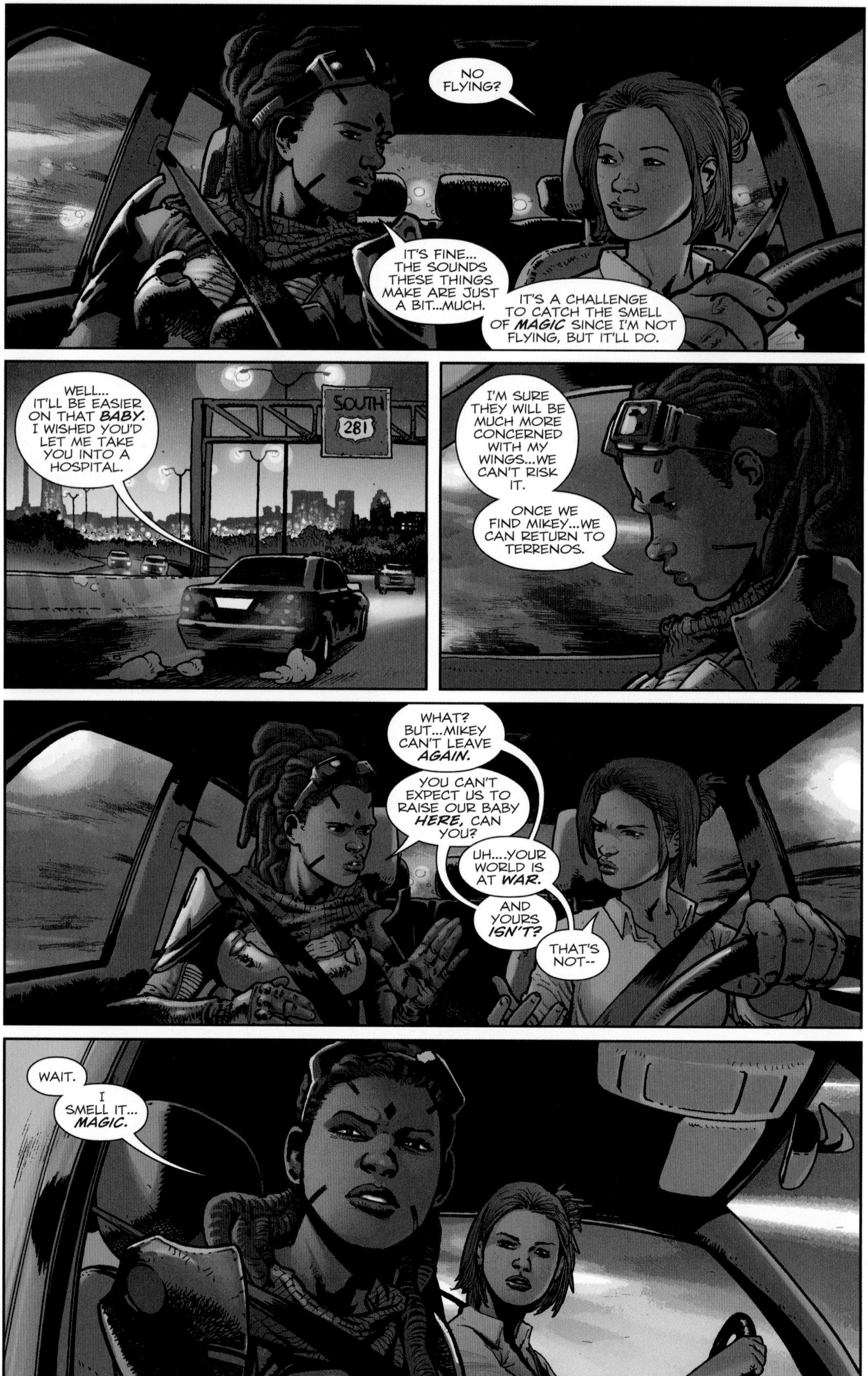
NO FLYING?
IT'S FINE... THE SOUNDS THESE THINGS MAKE ARE JUST A BIT...MUCH.
IT'S A CHALLENGE TO CATCH THE SMELL OF MAGIC SINCE I'M NOT FLYING, BUT IT'LL DO.
WELL... IT'LL BE EASIER ON THAT BABY. I WISHED YOU'D LET ME TAKE YOU INTO A HOSPITAL.
SOUTH
281
I'M SURE THEY WILL BE MUCH MORE CONCERNED WITH MY WINGS...WE CAN'T RISK IT.
ONCE WE FIND MIKEY...WE CAN RETURN TO TERRENOS.
WHAT? BUT...MIKEY CAN'T LEAVE AGAIN.
YOU CAN'T EXPECT US TO RAISE OUR BABY HERE, CAN YOU?
UH....YOUR WORLD IS AT WAR.
AND YOURS ISN'T?
THAT'S NOT--
WAIT.
I SMELL IT... MAGIC.

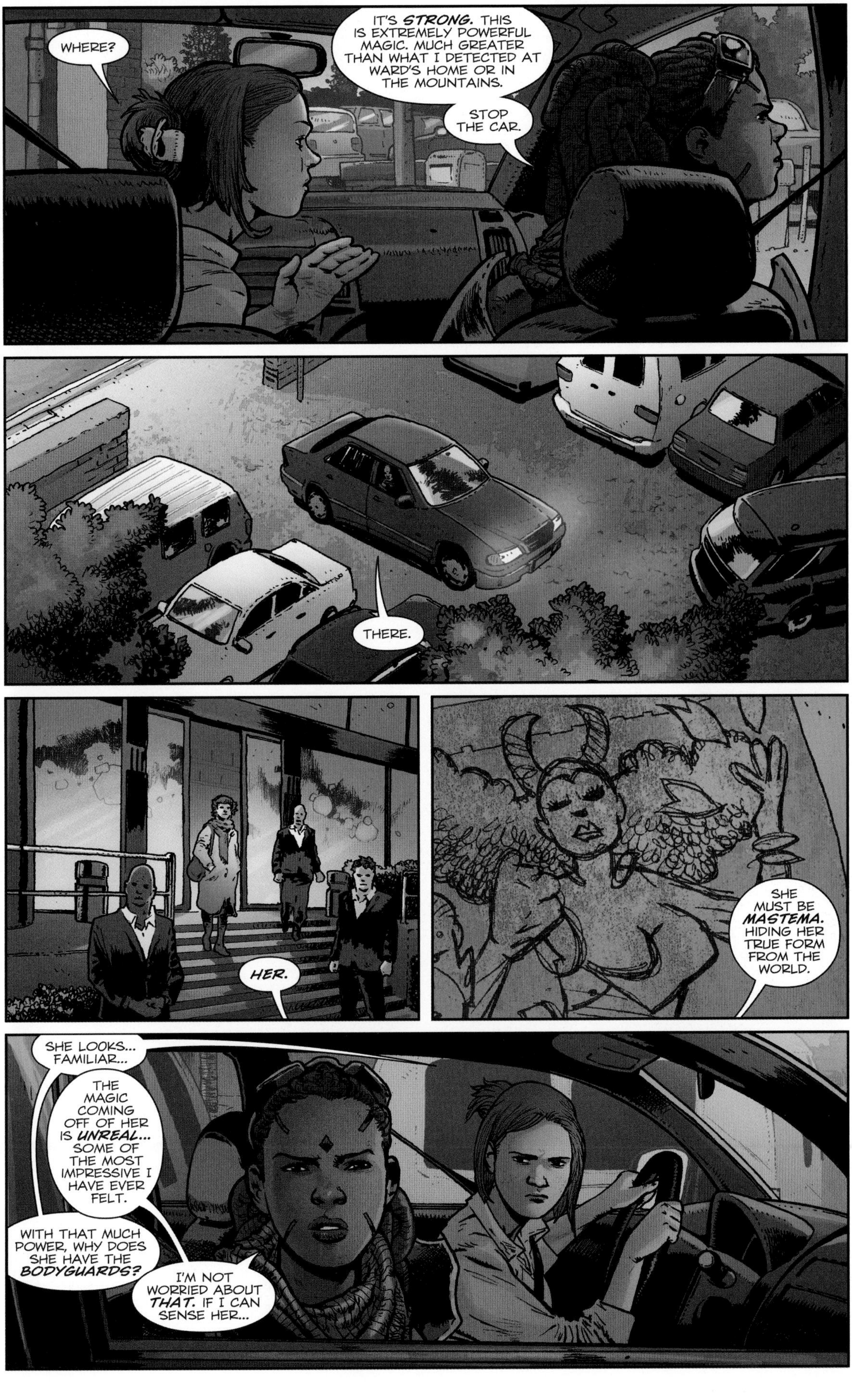
WHERE?
IT'S STRONG. THIS IS EXTREMELY POWERFUL MAGIC. MUCH GREATER THAN WHAT I DETECTED AT WARD'S HOME OR IN THE MOUNTAINS.
STOP THE CAR.
THERE.
HER.
SHE MUST BE MASTEMA. HIDING HER TRUE FORM FROM THE WORLD.
SHE LOOKS... FAMILIAR...
THE MAGIC COMING OFF OF HER IS UNREAL... SOME OF THE MOST IMPRESSIVE I HAVE EVER FELT.
WITH THAT MUCH POWER, WHY DOES SHE HAVE THE BODYGUARDS?
I'M NOT WORRIED ABOUT THAT. IF I CAN SENSE HER...

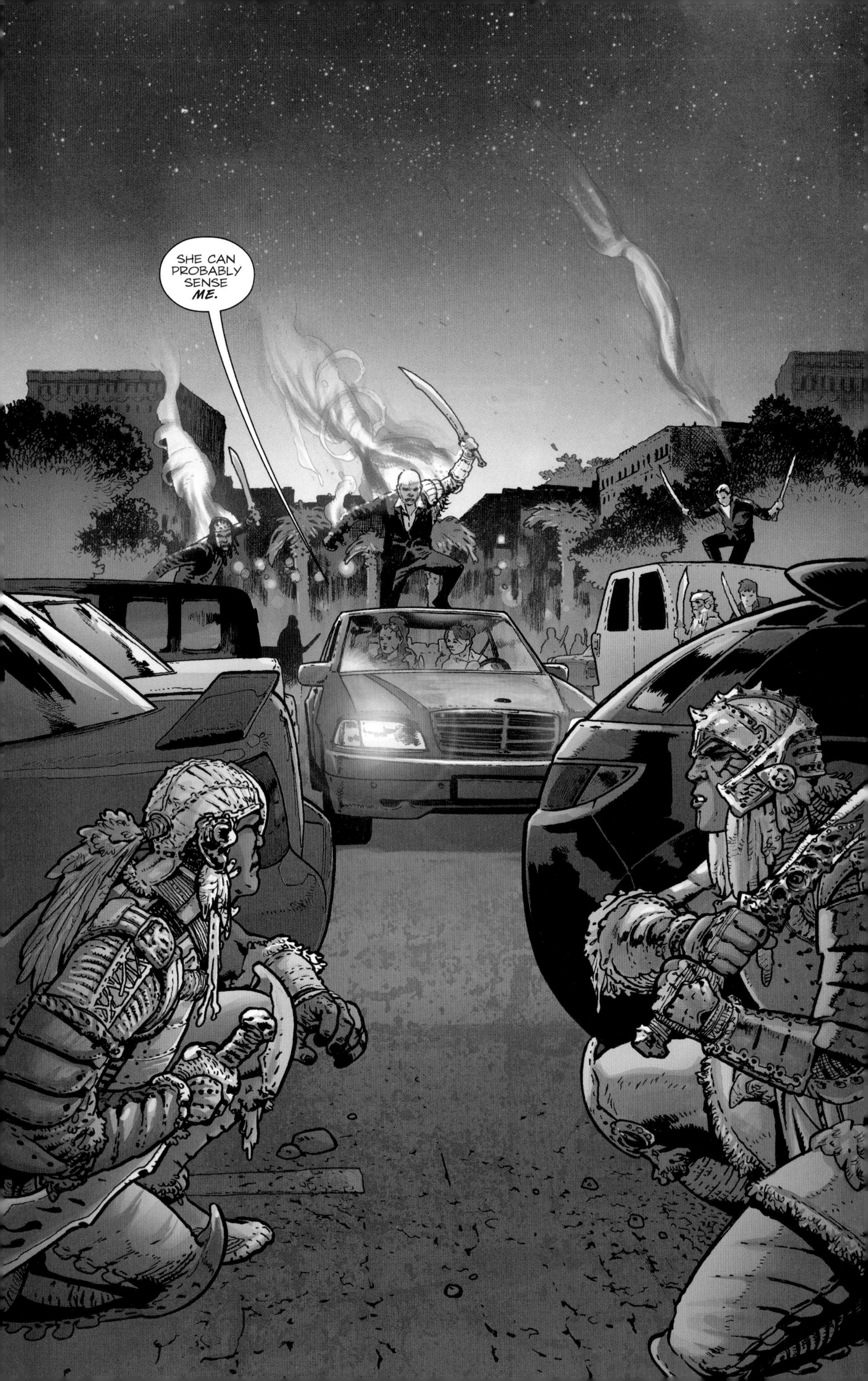
SHE CAN PROBABLY SENSE ***ME.***

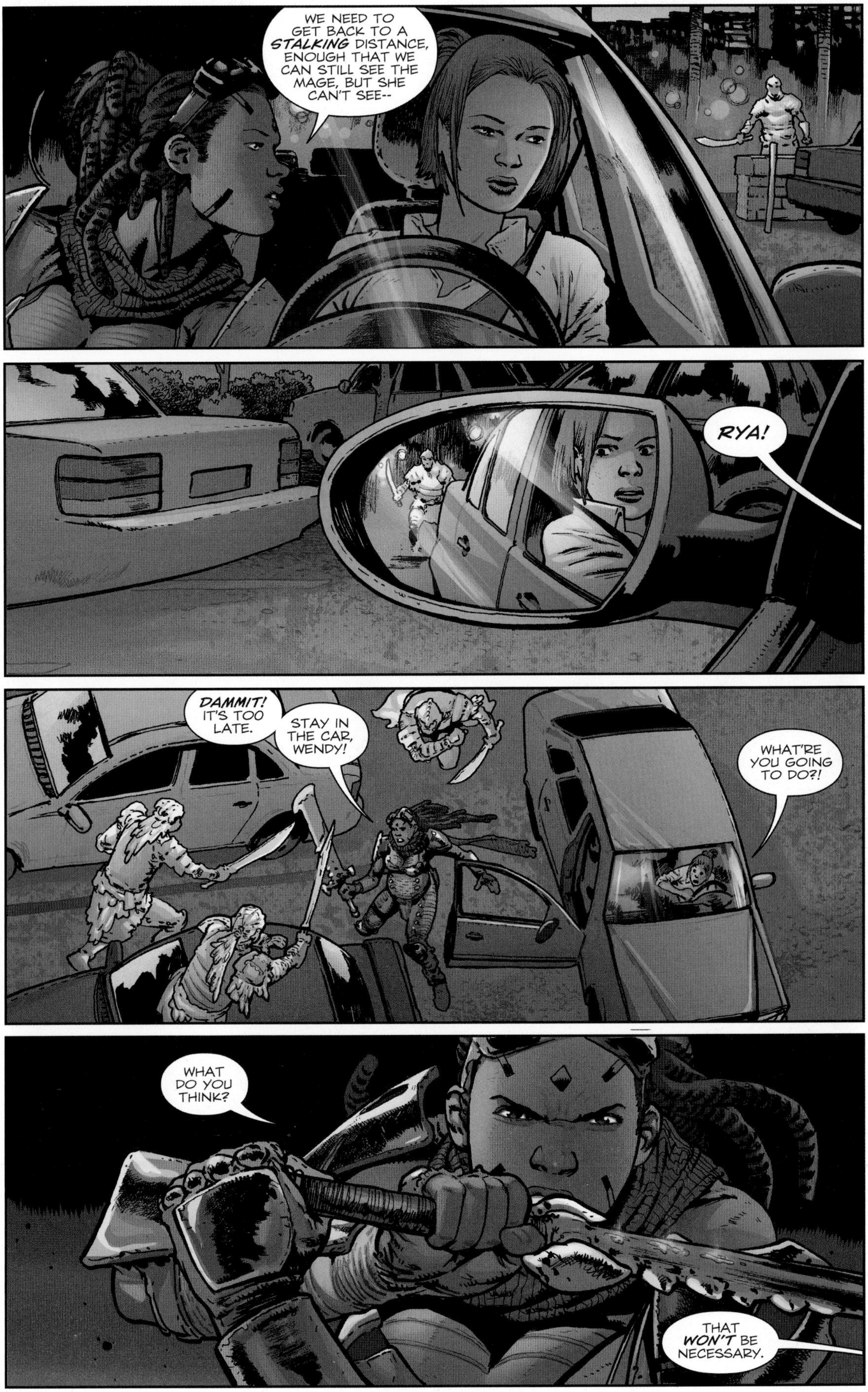
WE NEED TO GET BACK TO A STALKING DISTANCE, ENOUGH THAT WE CAN STILL SEE THE MAGE, BUT SHE CAN'T SEE--
RYA!
DAMMIT! IT'S TOO LATE.
STAY IN THE CAR, WENDY!
WHAT'RE YOU GOING TO DO?!
WHAT DO YOU THINK?
THAT WON'T BE NECESSARY.

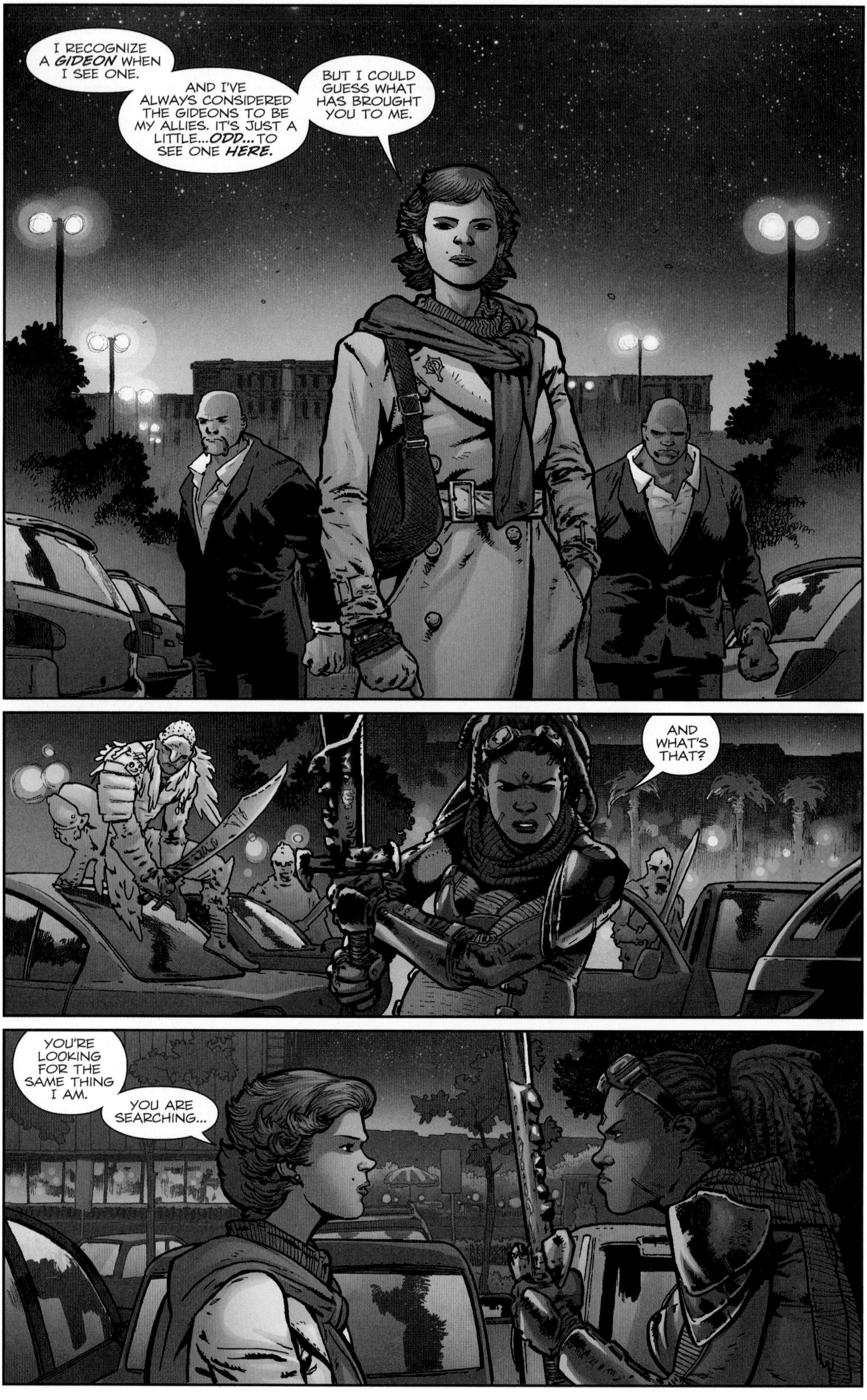
I RECOGNIZE A GIDEON WHEN I SEE ONE.
AND I'VE ALWAYS CONSIDERED THE GIDEONS TO BE MY ALLIES. IT'S JUST A LITTLE...ODD...TO SEE ONE HERE.
BUT I COULD GUESS WHAT HAS BROUGHT YOU TO ME.
AND WHAT'S THAT?
YOU'RE LOOKING FOR THE SAME THING I AM.
YOU ARE SEARCHING...

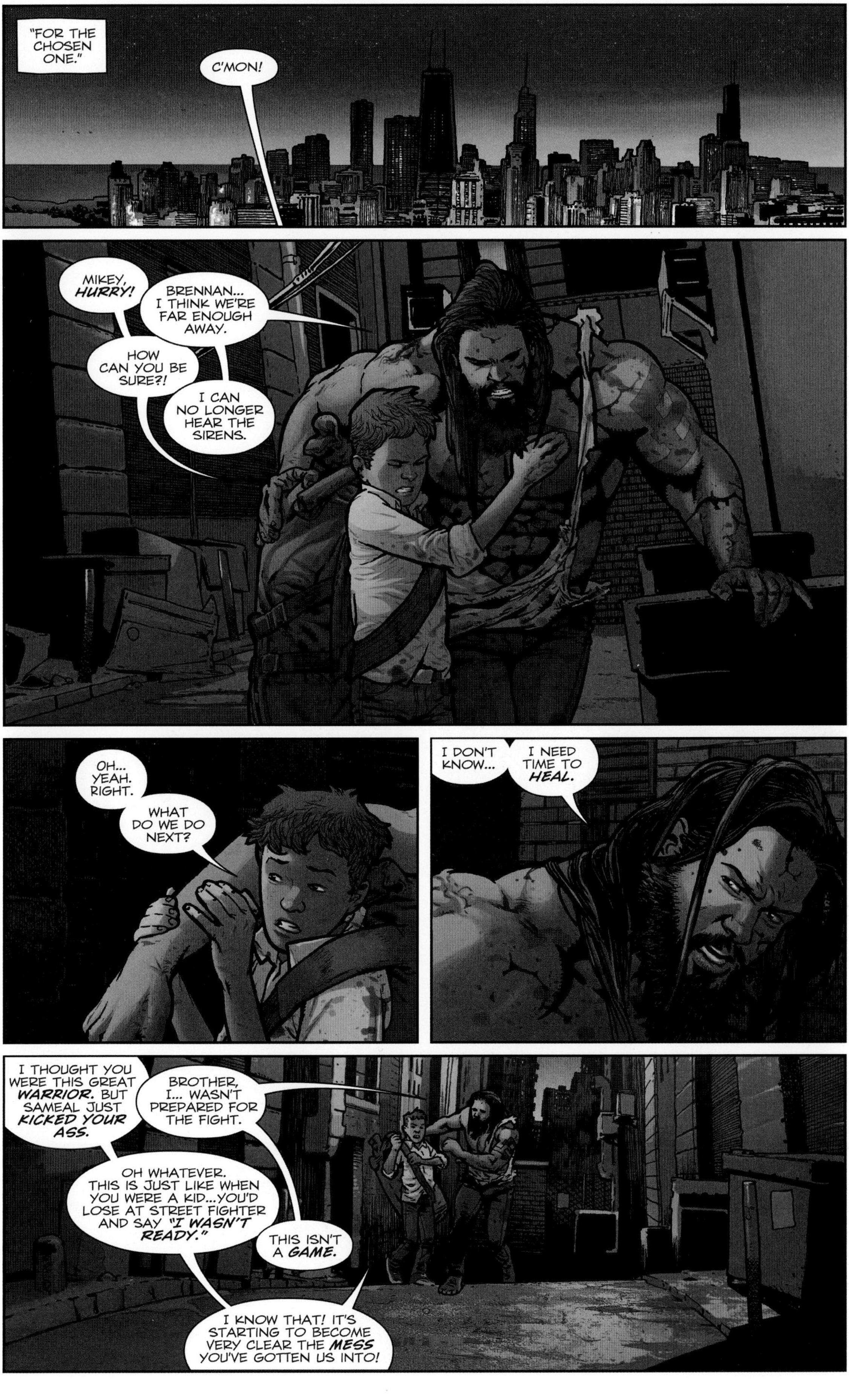
"FOR THE CHOSEN ONE."
C'MON!
MIKEY, **HURRY!**
BRENNAN... I THINK WE'RE FAR ENOUGH AWAY.
HOW CAN YOU BE SURE?!
I CAN NO LONGER HEAR THE SIRENS.
OH... YEAH. RIGHT.
WHAT DO WE DO NEXT?
I DON'T KNOW...
I NEED TIME TO **HEAL.**
I THOUGHT YOU WERE THIS GREAT **WARRIOR.** BUT SAMEAL JUST **KICKED YOUR ASS.**
BROTHER, I... WASN'T PREPARED FOR THE FIGHT.
OH WHATEVER. THIS IS JUST LIKE WHEN YOU WERE A KID...YOU'D LOSE AT STREET FIGHTER AND SAY ***"I WASN'T READY."***
THIS ISN'T A **GAME.**
I KNOW THAT! IT'S STARTING TO BECOME VERY CLEAR THE **MESS** YOU'VE GOTTEN US INTO!

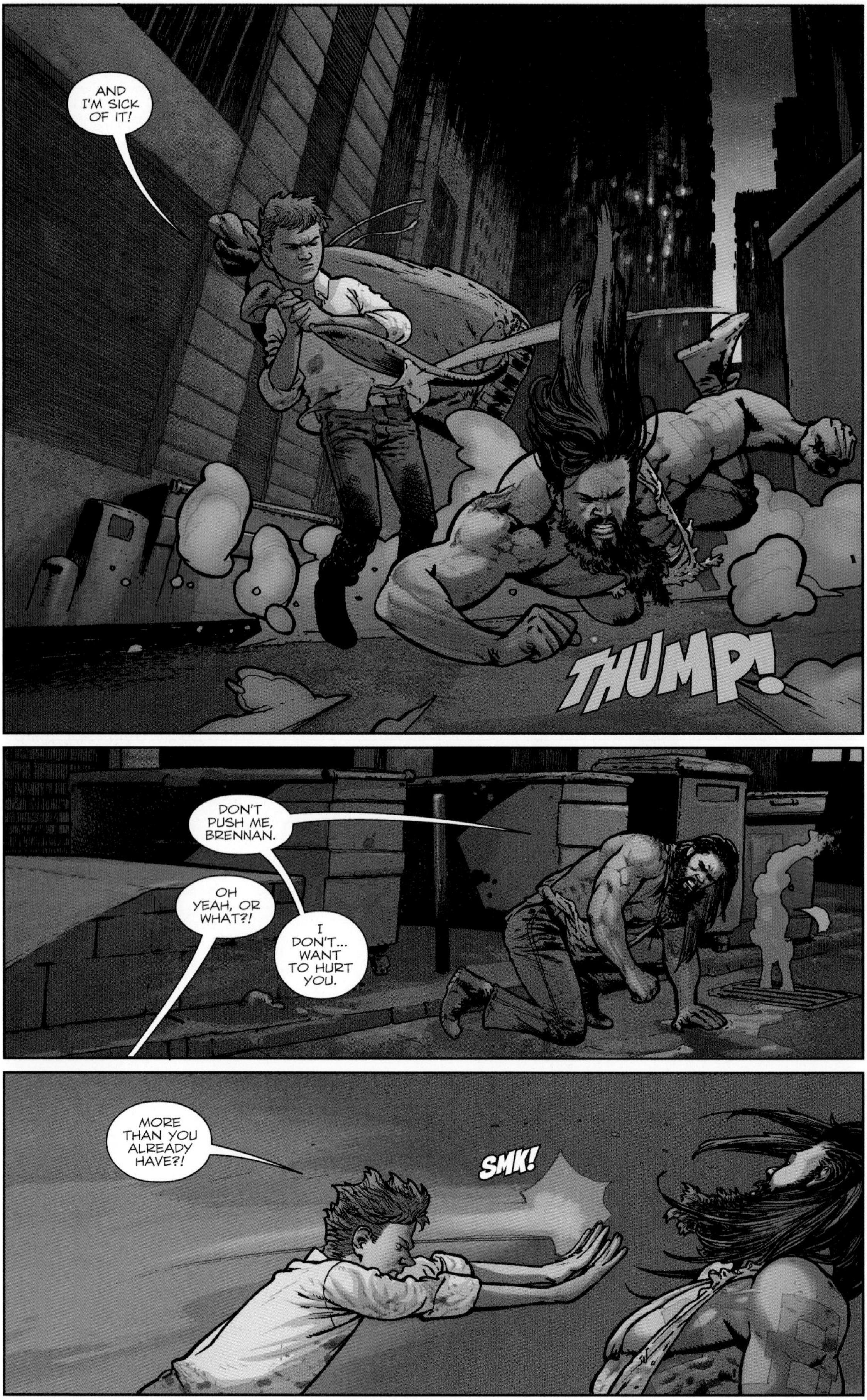
AND I'M SICK OF IT!
THUMP!
DON'T PUSH ME, BRENNAN.
OH YEAH, OR WHAT?!
I DON'T... WANT TO HURT YOU.
MORE THAN YOU ALREADY HAVE?!
SMK!

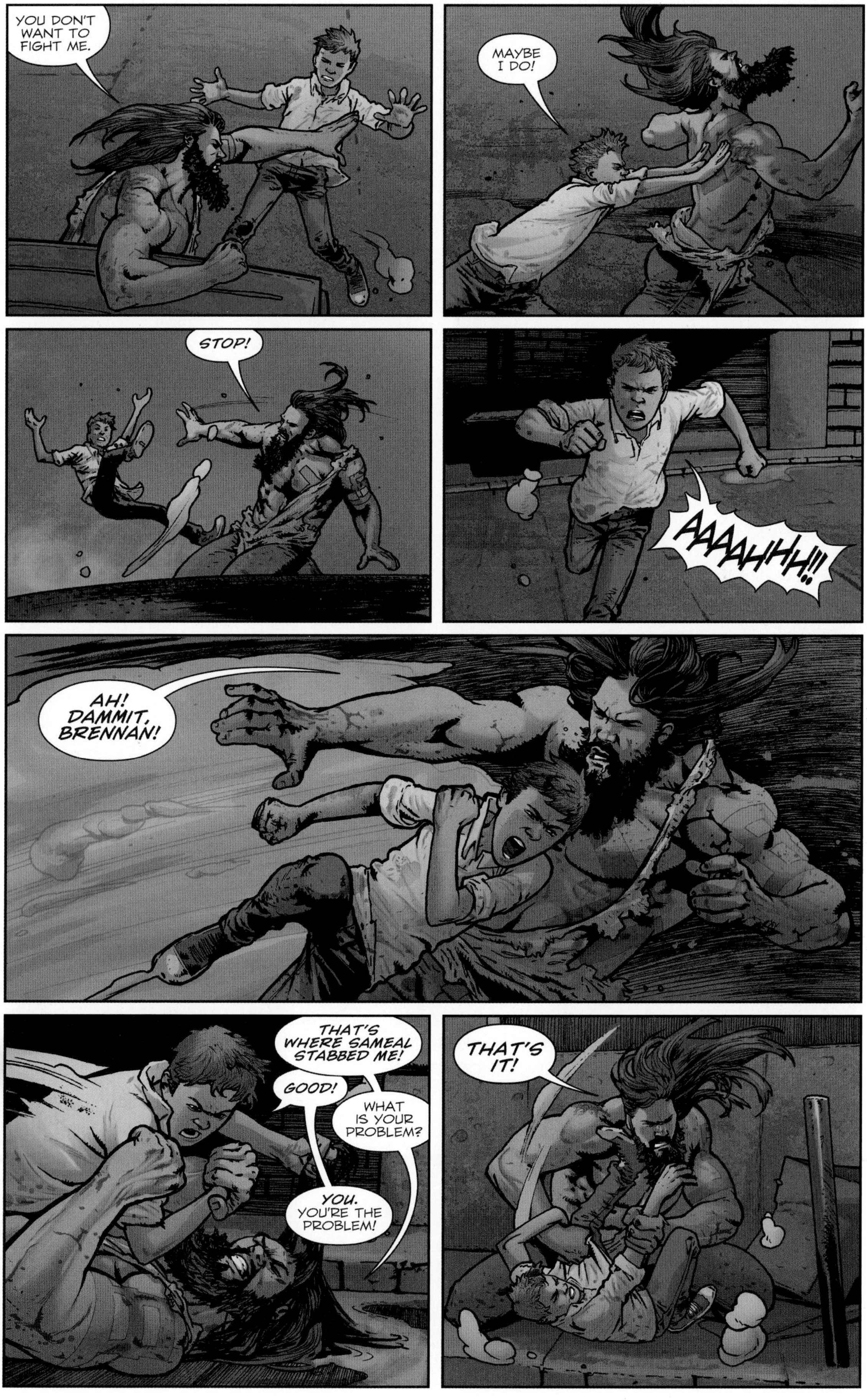
YOU DON'T WANT TO FIGHT ME.
MAYBE I DO!
STOP!
AAAAHHH!!
AH! DAMMIT, BRENNAN!
THAT'S WHERE SAMEAL STABBED ME!
GOOD!
WHAT IS YOUR PROBLEM?
YOU. YOU'RE THE PROBLEM!
THAT'S IT!

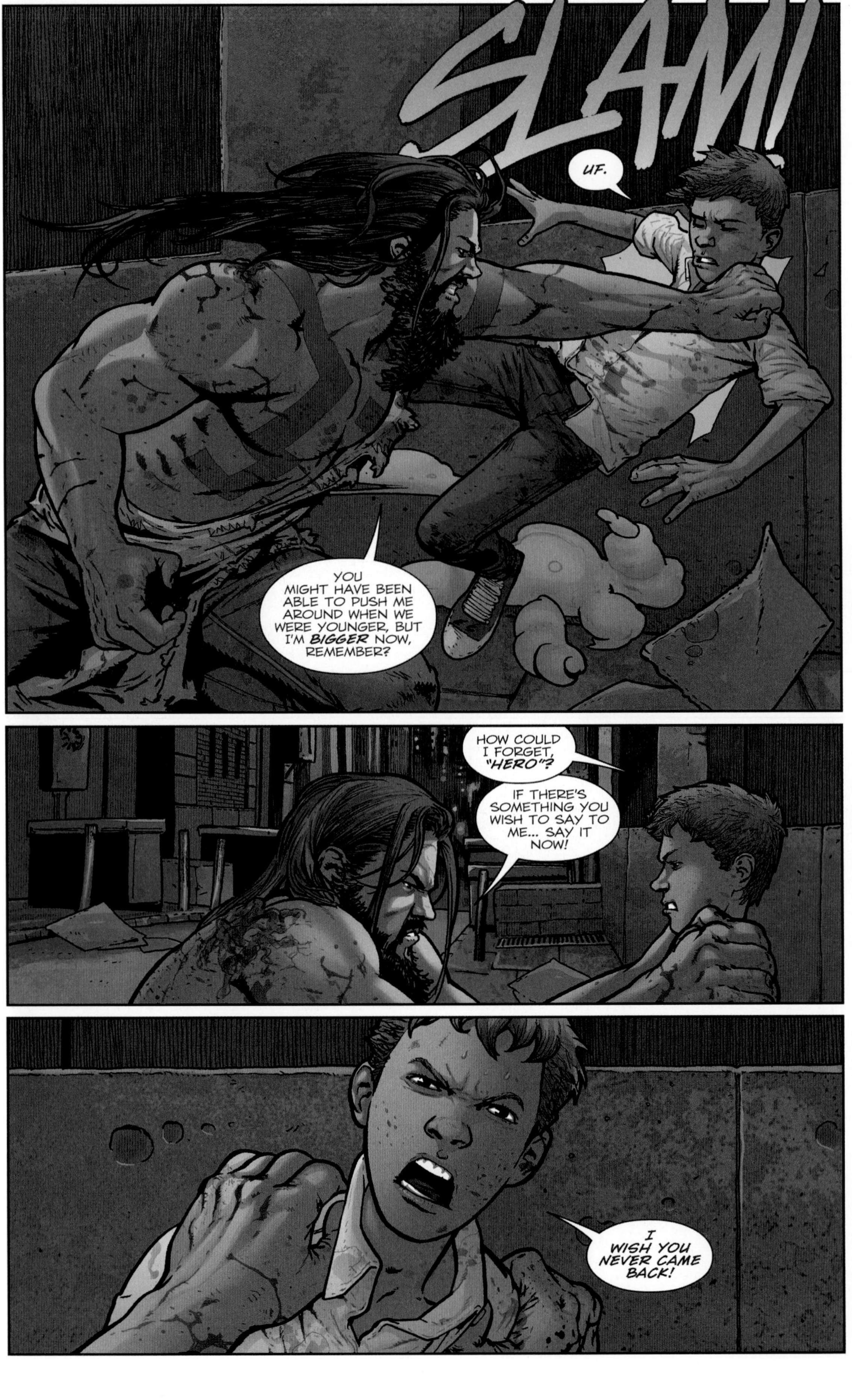
SLAM!
UF.
YOU MIGHT HAVE BEEN ABLE TO PUSH ME AROUND WHEN WE WERE YOUNGER, BUT I'M **BIGGER** NOW, REMEMBER?
HOW COULD I FORGET, ***"HERO"***?
IF THERE'S SOMETHING YOU WISH TO SAY TO ME... SAY IT NOW!
I WISH YOU NEVER CAME BACK!

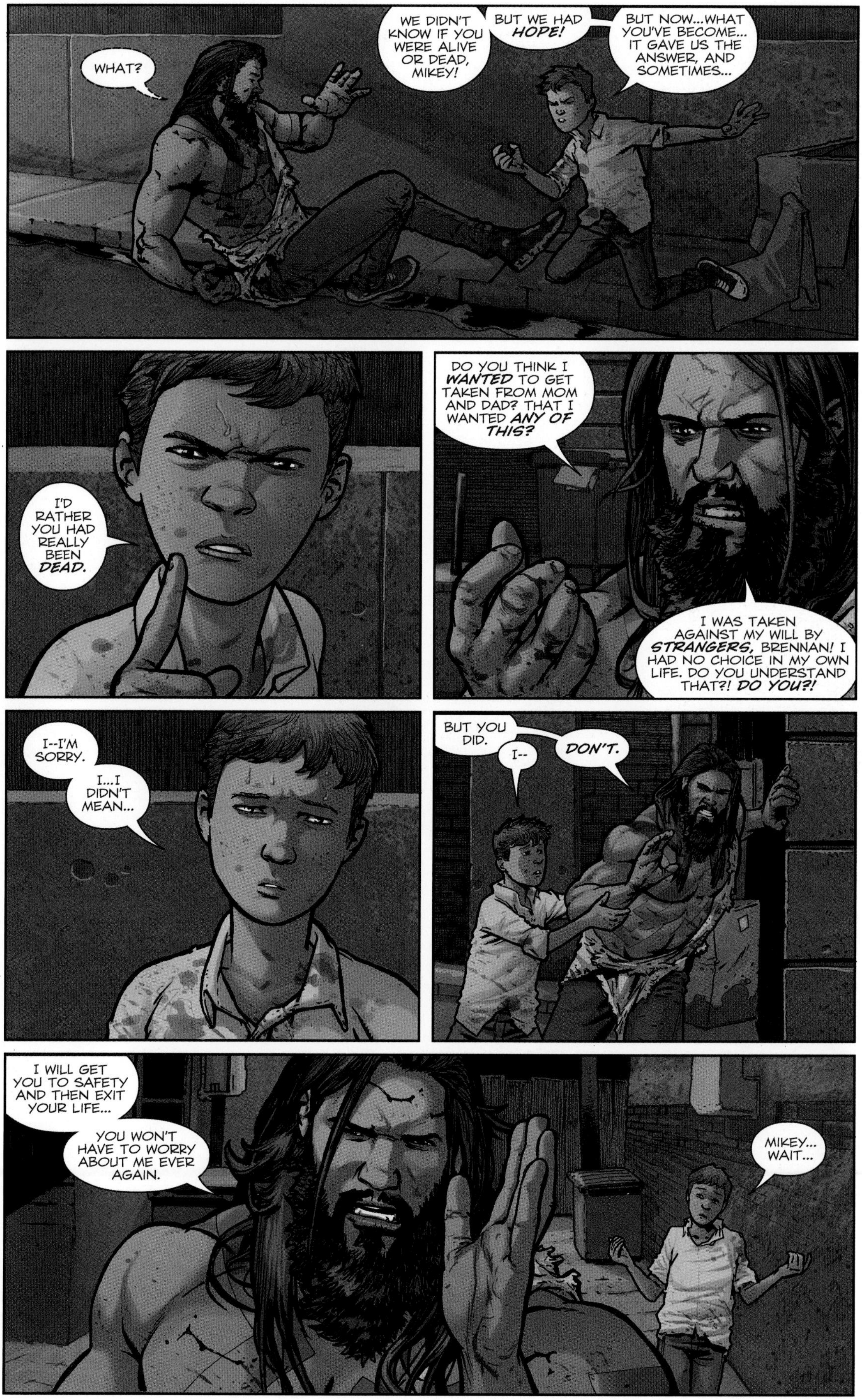
WHAT?
WE DIDN'T KNOW IF YOU WERE ALIVE OR DEAD, MIKEY!
BUT WE HAD HOPE!
BUT NOW...WHAT YOU'VE BECOME... IT GAVE US THE ANSWER, AND SOMETIMES...
I'D RATHER YOU HAD REALLY BEEN DEAD.
DO YOU THINK I WANTED TO GET TAKEN FROM MOM AND DAD? THAT I WANTED ANY OF THIS?
I WAS TAKEN AGAINST MY WILL BY STRANGERS, BRENNAN! I HAD NO CHOICE IN MY OWN LIFE. DO YOU UNDERSTAND THAT?! DO YOU?!
I--I'M SORRY.
I...I DIDN'T MEAN...
BUT YOU DID.
I--
DON'T.
I WILL GET YOU TO SAFETY AND THEN EXIT YOUR LIFE...
YOU WON'T HAVE TO WORRY ABOUT ME EVER AGAIN.
MIKEY... WAIT...

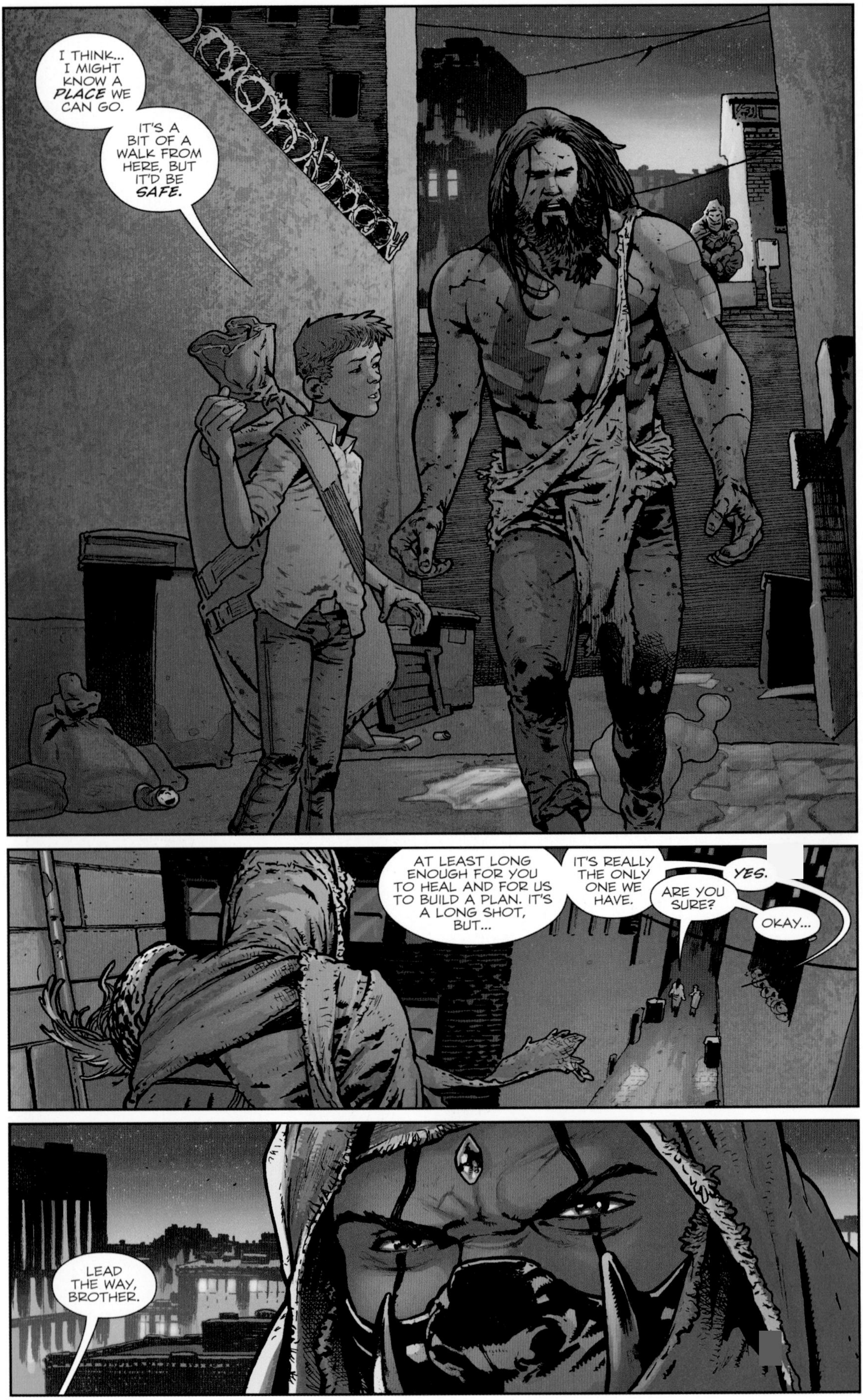

I THINK... I MIGHT KNOW A PLACE WE CAN GO.
IT'S A BIT OF A WALK FROM HERE, BUT IT'D BE SAFE.
AT LEAST LONG ENOUGH FOR YOU TO HEAL AND FOR US TO BUILD A PLAN. IT'S A LONG SHOT, BUT...
IT'S REALLY THE ONLY ONE WE HAVE.
ARE YOU SURE?
YES.
OKAY...
LEAD THE WAY, BROTHER.

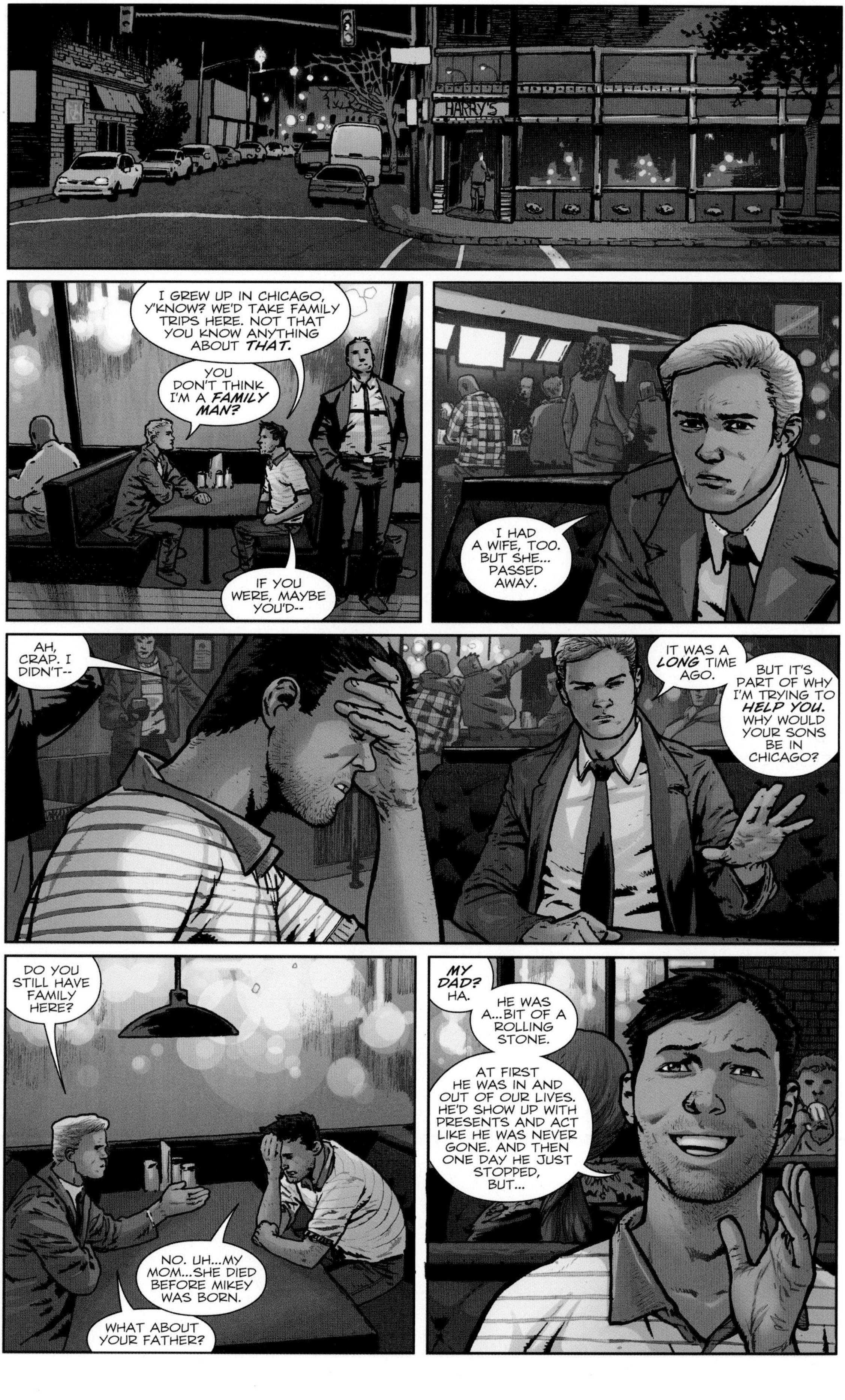
HARRY'S
I GREW UP IN CHICAGO, Y'KNOW? WE'D TAKE FAMILY TRIPS HERE. NOT THAT YOU KNOW ANYTHING ABOUT THAT.
YOU DON'T THINK I'M A FAMILY MAN?
IF YOU WERE, MAYBE YOU'D--
I HAD A WIFE, TOO. BUT SHE... PASSED AWAY.
AH, CRAP. I DIDN'T--
IT WAS A LONG TIME AGO.
BUT IT'S PART OF WHY I'M TRYING TO HELP YOU. WHY WOULD YOUR SONS BE IN CHICAGO?
DO YOU STILL HAVE FAMILY HERE?
NO. UH...MY MOM...SHE DIED BEFORE MIKEY WAS BORN.
WHAT ABOUT YOUR FATHER?
MY DAD? HA.
HE WAS A...BIT OF A ROLLING STONE.
AT FIRST HE WAS IN AND OUT OF OUR LIVES. HE'D SHOW UP WITH PRESENTS AND ACT LIKE HE WAS NEVER GONE. AND THEN ONE DAY HE JUST STOPPED, BUT...

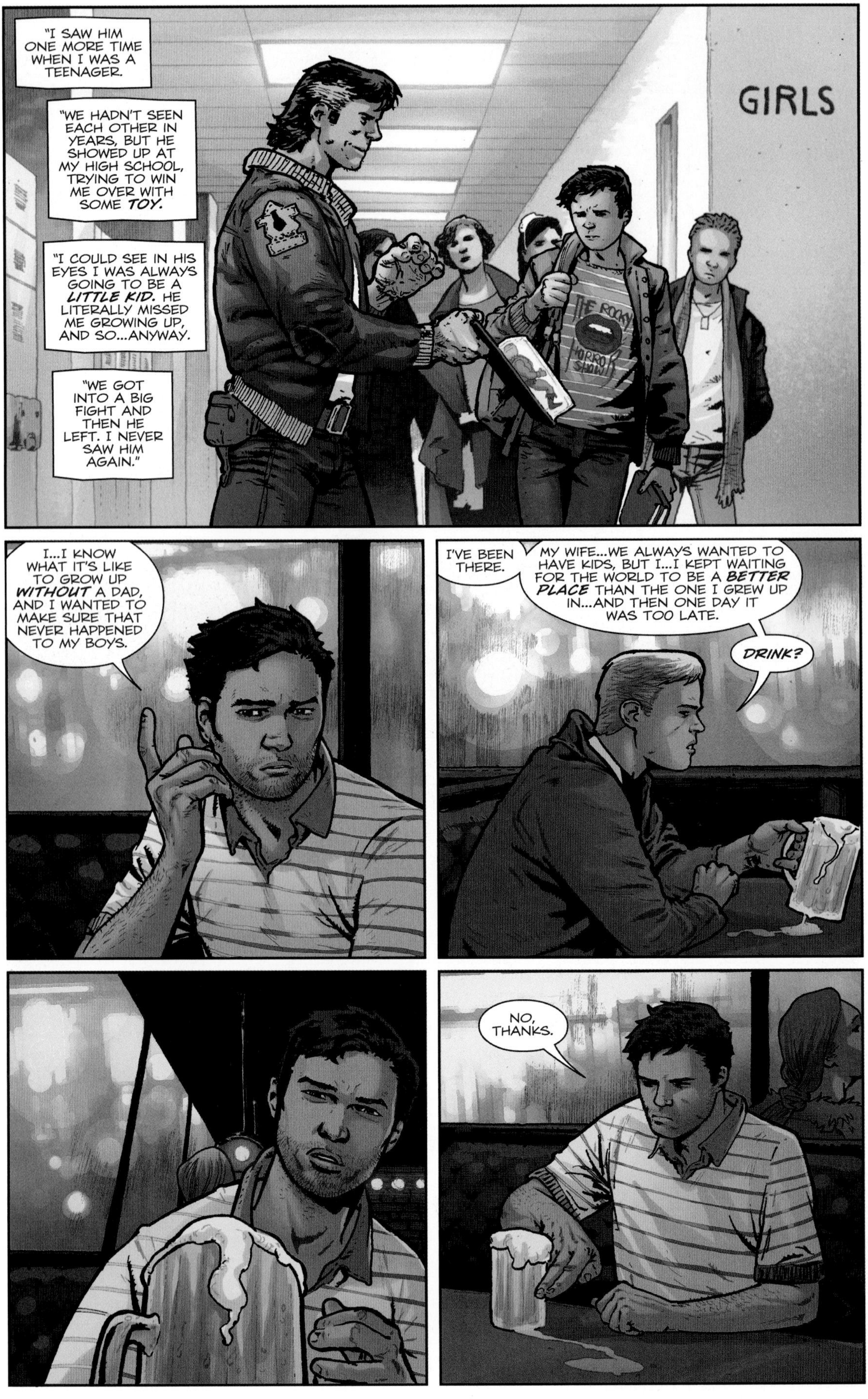
"I SAW HIM ONE MORE TIME WHEN I WAS A TEENAGER.
"WE HADN'T SEEN EACH OTHER IN YEARS, BUT HE SHOWED UP AT MY HIGH SCHOOL, TRYING TO WIN ME OVER WITH SOME TOY.
"I COULD SEE IN HIS EYES I WAS ALWAYS GOING TO BE A LITTLE KID. HE LITERALLY MISSED ME GROWING UP, AND SO...ANYWAY.
"WE GOT INTO A BIG FIGHT AND THEN HE LEFT. I NEVER SAW HIM AGAIN."
GIRLS
THE ROCKY HORROR SHOW
I...I KNOW WHAT IT'S LIKE TO GROW UP WITHOUT A DAD, AND I WANTED TO MAKE SURE THAT NEVER HAPPENED TO MY BOYS.
I'VE BEEN THERE.
MY WIFE...WE ALWAYS WANTED TO HAVE KIDS, BUT I...I KEPT WAITING FOR THE WORLD TO BE A BETTER PLACE THAN THE ONE I GREW UP IN...AND THEN ONE DAY IT WAS TOO LATE.
DRINK?
NO, THANKS.

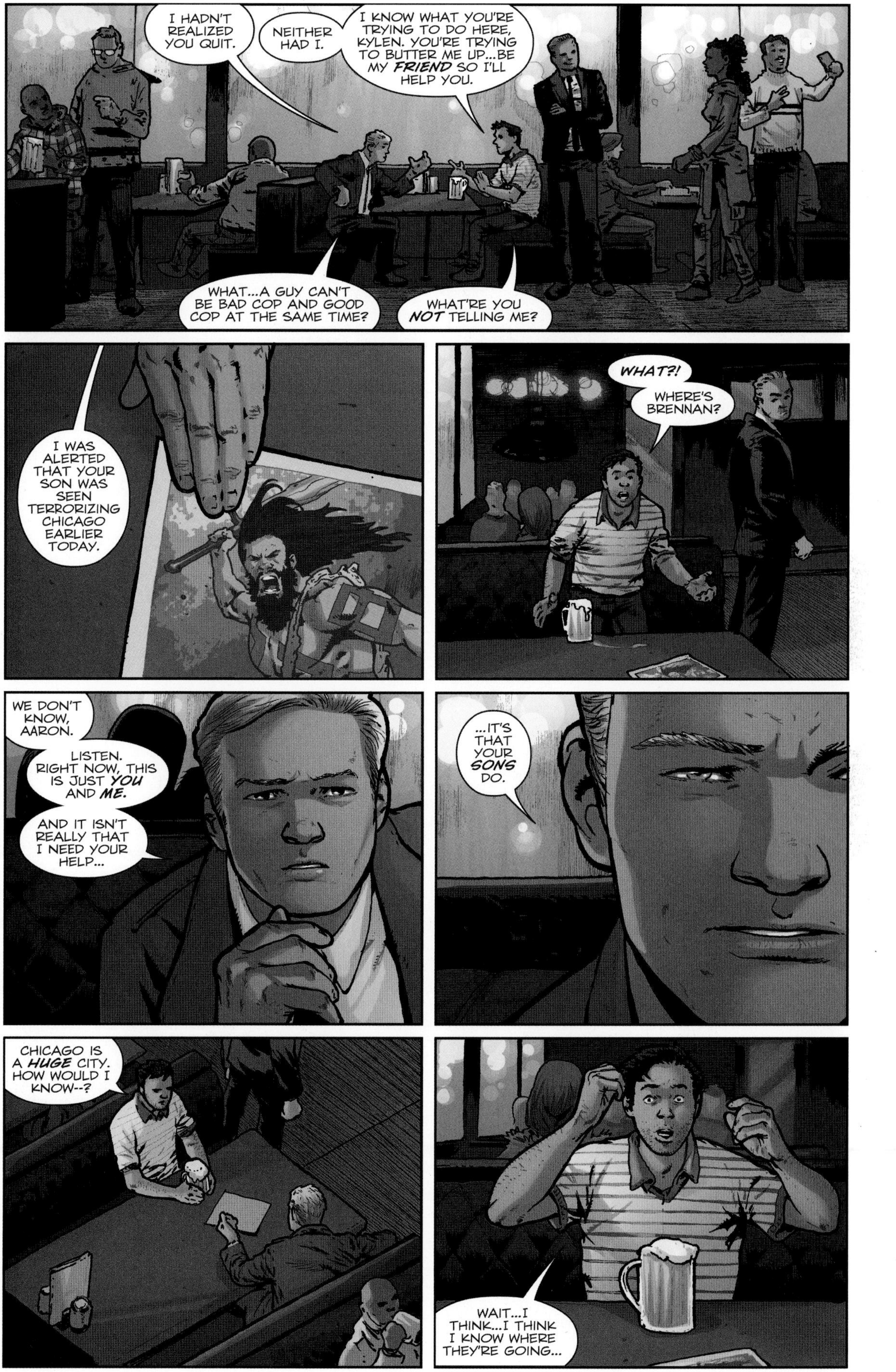
I HADN'T REALIZED YOU QUIT.
NEITHER HAD I.
I KNOW WHAT YOU'RE TRYING TO DO HERE, KYLEN. YOU'RE TRYING TO BUTTER ME UP...BE MY FRIEND SO I'LL HELP YOU.
WHAT...A GUY CAN'T BE BAD COP AND GOOD COP AT THE SAME TIME?
WHAT'RE YOU NOT TELLING ME?
I WAS ALERTED THAT YOUR SON WAS SEEN TERRORIZING CHICAGO EARLIER TODAY.
WHAT?!
WHERE'S BRENNAN?
WE DON'T KNOW, AARON.
LISTEN. RIGHT NOW, THIS IS JUST YOU AND ME.
AND IT ISN'T REALLY THAT I NEED YOUR HELP...
...IT'S THAT YOUR SONS DO.
CHICAGO IS A HUGE CITY. HOW WOULD I KNOW--?
WAIT...I THINK...I THINK I KNOW WHERE THEY'RE GOING...

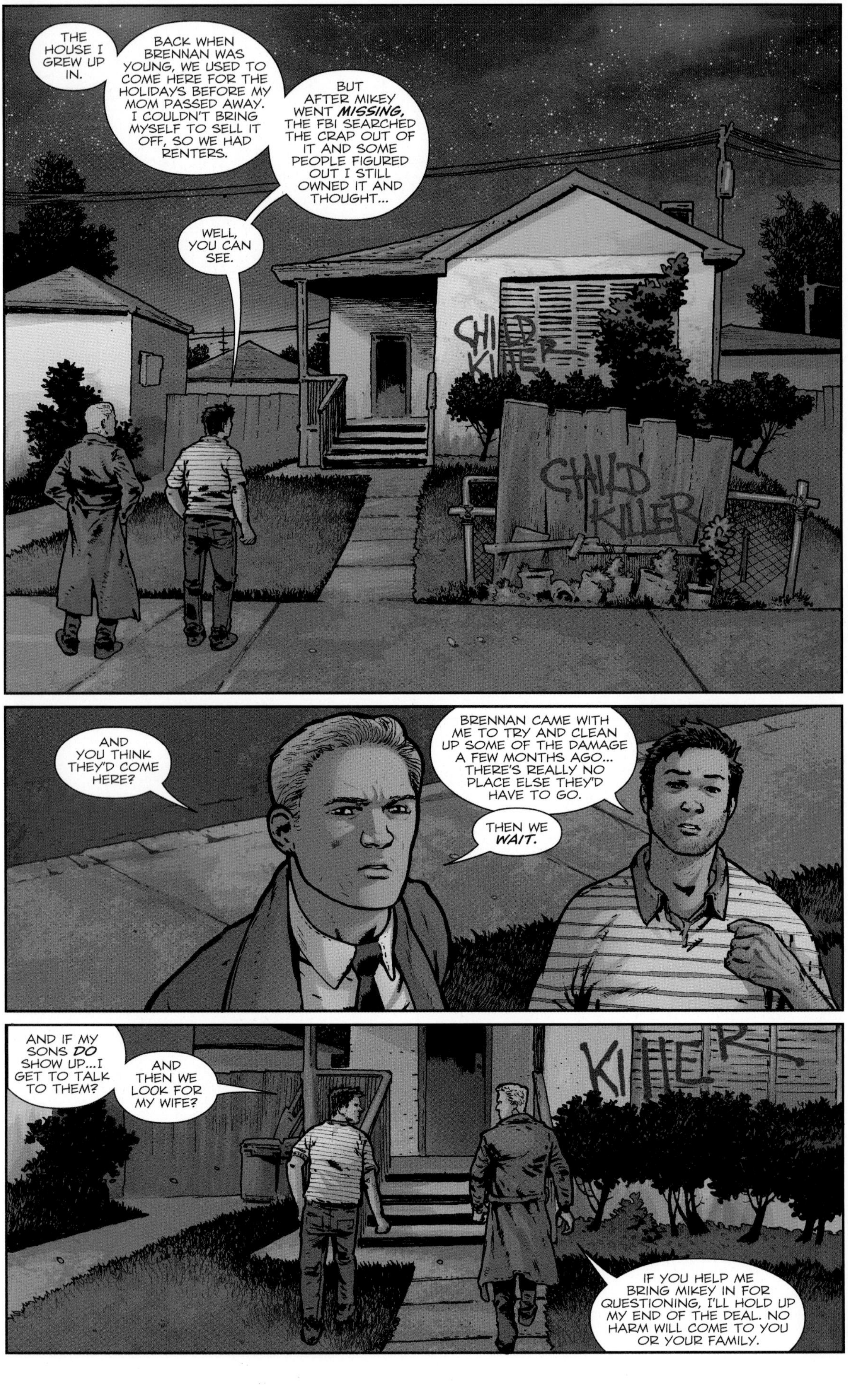
THE HOUSE I GREW UP IN.
BACK WHEN BRENNAN WAS YOUNG, WE USED TO COME HERE FOR THE HOLIDAYS BEFORE MY MOM PASSED AWAY. I COULDN'T BRING MYSELF TO SELL IT OFF, SO WE HAD RENTERS.
BUT AFTER MIKEY WENT MISSING, THE FBI SEARCHED THE CRAP OUT OF IT AND SOME PEOPLE FIGURED OUT I STILL OWNED IT AND THOUGHT...
WELL, YOU CAN SEE.
CHILD KILLER
CHILD KILLER
AND YOU THINK THEY'D COME HERE?
BRENNAN CAME WITH ME TO TRY AND CLEAN UP SOME OF THE DAMAGE A FEW MONTHS AGO... THERE'S REALLY NO PLACE ELSE THEY'D HAVE TO GO.
THEN WE WAIT.
AND IF MY SONS DO SHOW UP...I GET TO TALK TO THEM?
AND THEN WE LOOK FOR MY WIFE?
KILLER
IF YOU HELP ME BRING MIKEY IN FOR QUESTIONING, I'LL HOLD UP MY END OF THE DEAL. NO HARM WILL COME TO YOU OR YOUR FAMILY.

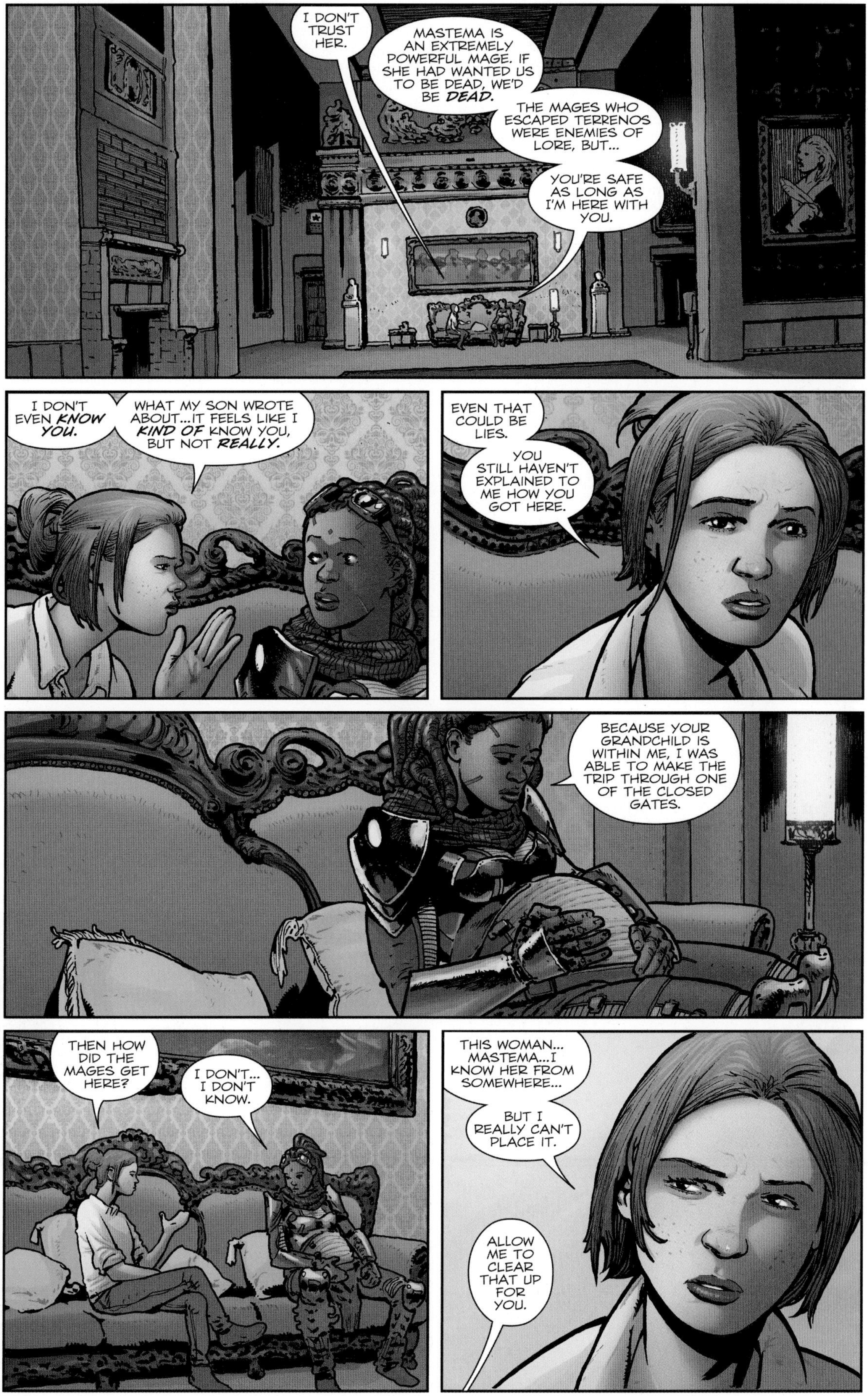
I DON'T TRUST HER.
MASTEMA IS AN EXTREMELY POWERFUL MAGE. IF SHE HAD WANTED US TO BE DEAD, WE'D BE *DEAD*.
THE MAGES WHO ESCAPED TERRENOS WERE ENEMIES OF LORE, BUT...
YOU'RE SAFE AS LONG AS I'M HERE WITH YOU.
I DON'T EVEN *KNOW YOU*.
WHAT MY SON WROTE ABOUT...IT FEELS LIKE I *KIND OF* KNOW YOU, BUT NOT *REALLY*.
EVEN THAT COULD BE LIES.
YOU STILL HAVEN'T EXPLAINED TO ME HOW YOU GOT HERE.
BECAUSE YOUR GRANDCHILD IS WITHIN ME, I WAS ABLE TO MAKE THE TRIP THROUGH ONE OF THE CLOSED GATES.
THEN HOW DID THE MAGES GET HERE?
I DON'T... I DON'T KNOW.
THIS WOMAN... MASTEMA...I KNOW HER FROM SOMEWHERE...
BUT I REALLY CAN'T PLACE IT.
ALLOW ME TO CLEAR THAT UP FOR YOU.

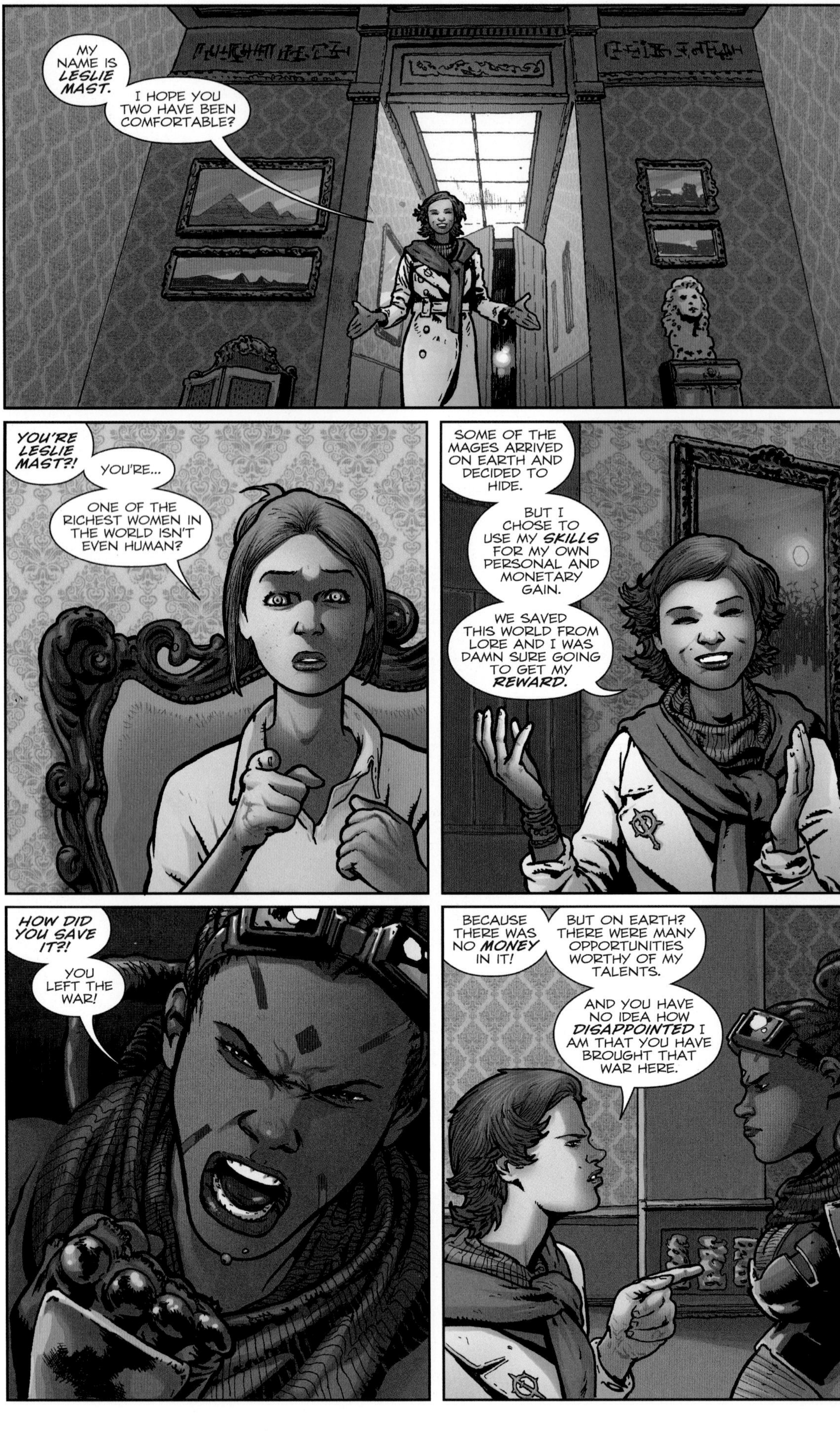

MY NAME IS *LESLIE MAST.*
I HOPE YOU TWO HAVE BEEN COMFORTABLE?
YOU'RE LESLIE MAST?!
YOU'RE...
ONE OF THE RICHEST WOMEN IN THE WORLD ISN'T EVEN HUMAN?
SOME OF THE MAGES ARRIVED ON EARTH AND DECIDED TO HIDE.
BUT I CHOSE TO USE MY *SKILLS* FOR MY OWN PERSONAL AND MONETARY GAIN.
WE SAVED THIS WORLD FROM LORE AND I WAS DAMN SURE GOING TO GET MY *REWARD.*
HOW DID YOU SAVE IT?!
YOU LEFT THE WAR!
BECAUSE THERE WAS NO *MONEY* IN IT!
BUT ON EARTH? THERE WERE MANY OPPORTUNITIES WORTHY OF MY TALENTS.
AND YOU HAVE NO IDEA HOW *DISAPPOINTED* I AM THAT YOU HAVE BROUGHT THAT WAR HERE.

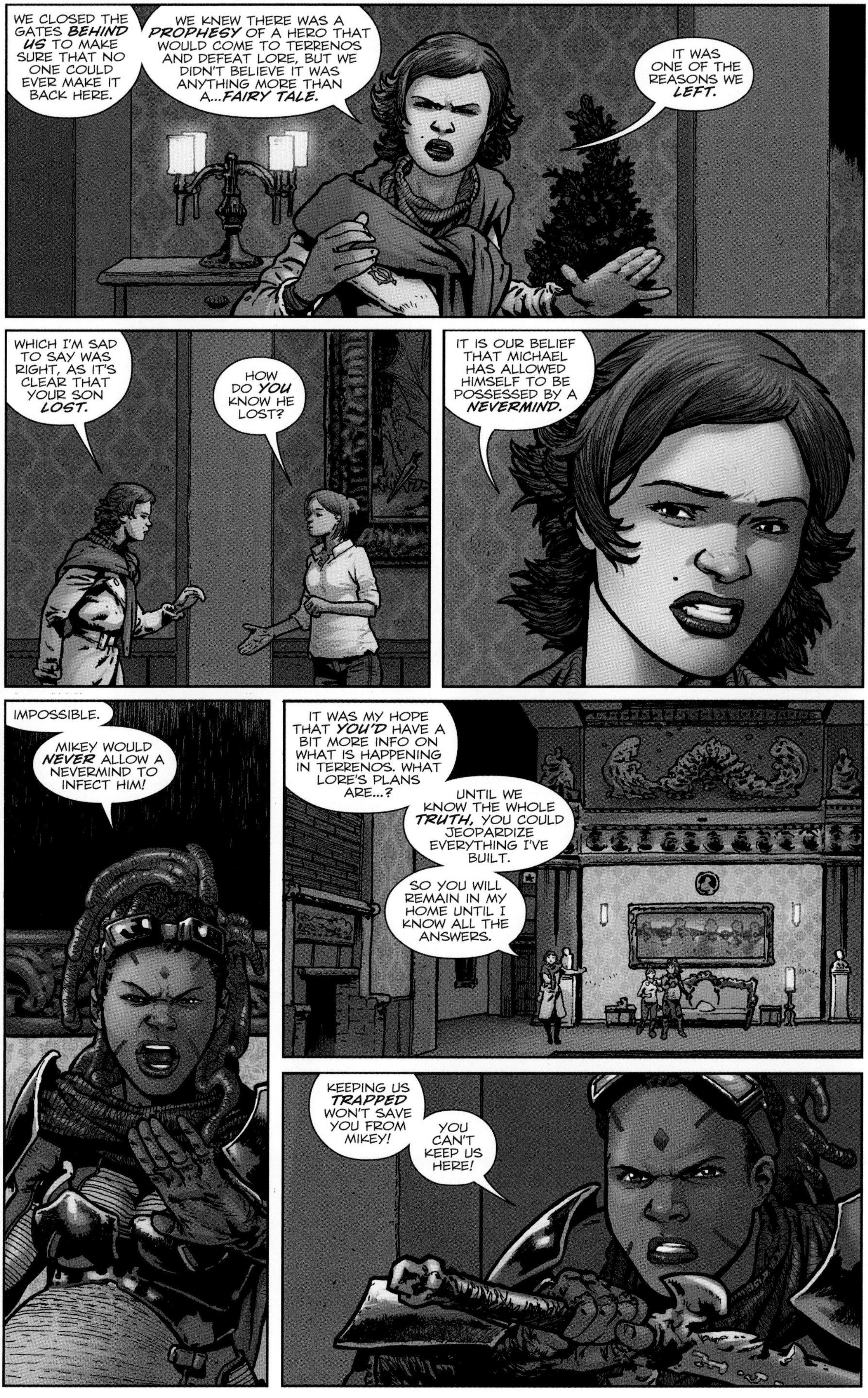
WE CLOSED THE GATES BEHIND US TO MAKE SURE THAT NO ONE COULD EVER MAKE IT BACK HERE.
WE KNEW THERE WAS A PROPHESY OF A HERO THAT WOULD COME TO TERRENOS AND DEFEAT LORE, BUT WE DIDN'T BELIEVE IT WAS ANYTHING MORE THAN A...FAIRY TALE.
IT WAS ONE OF THE REASONS WE LEFT.
WHICH I'M SAD TO SAY WAS RIGHT, AS IT'S CLEAR THAT YOUR SON LOST.
HOW DO YOU KNOW HE LOST?
IT IS OUR BELIEF THAT MICHAEL HAS ALLOWED HIMSELF TO BE POSSESSED BY A NEVERMIND.
IMPOSSIBLE.
MIKEY WOULD NEVER ALLOW A NEVERMIND TO INFECT HIM!
IT WAS MY HOPE THAT YOU'D HAVE A BIT MORE INFO ON WHAT IS HAPPENING IN TERRENOS. WHAT LORE'S PLANS ARE...?
UNTIL WE KNOW THE WHOLE TRUTH, YOU COULD JEOPARDIZE EVERYTHING I'VE BUILT.
SO YOU WILL REMAIN IN MY HOME UNTIL I KNOW ALL THE ANSWERS.
KEEPING US TRAPPED WON'T SAVE YOU FROM MIKEY!
YOU CAN'T KEEP US HERE!

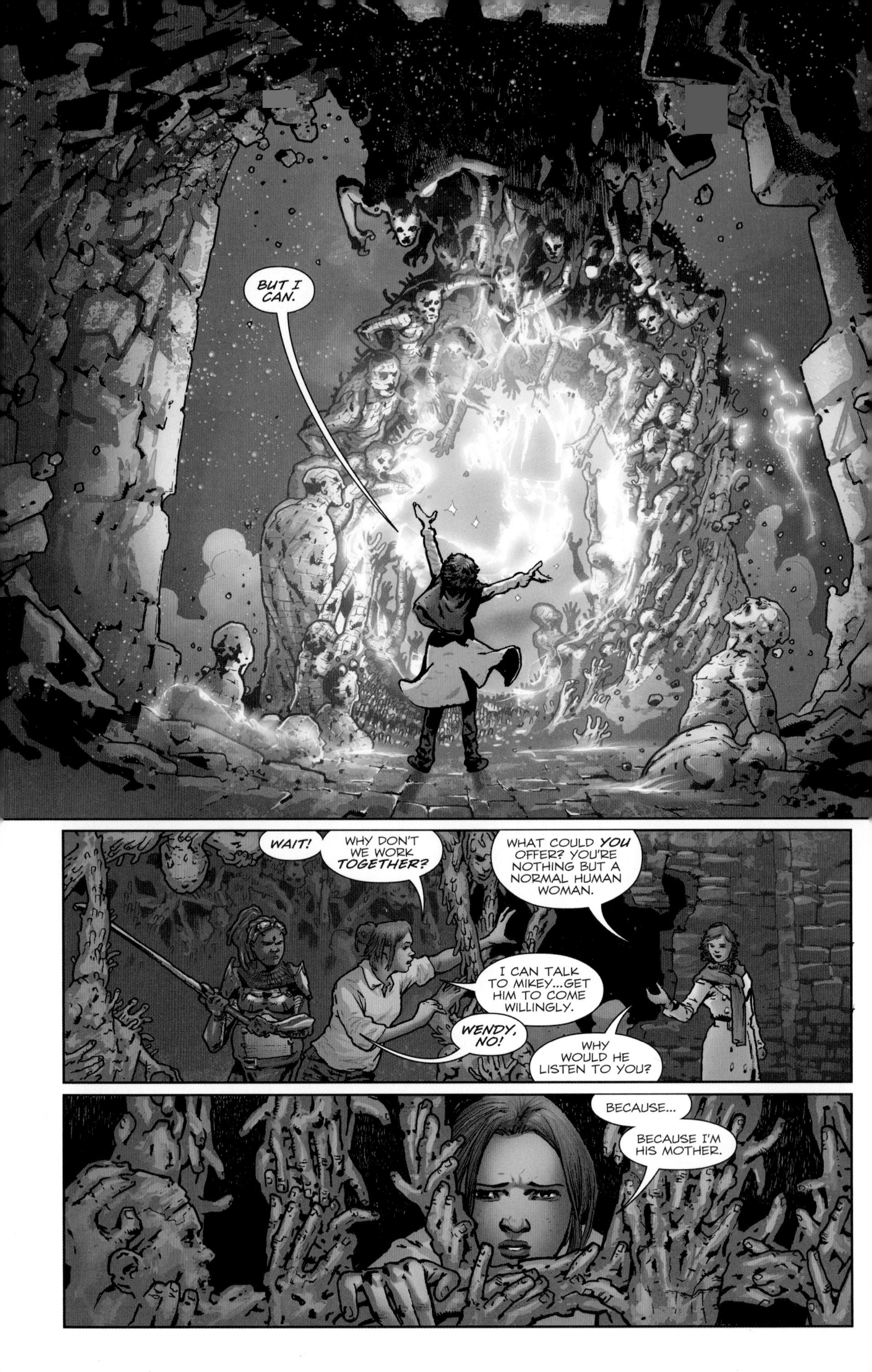
BUT I CAN.
WAIT!
WHY DON'T WE WORK TOGETHER?
WHAT COULD YOU OFFER? YOU'RE NOTHING BUT A NORMAL HUMAN WOMAN.
I CAN TALK TO MIKEY...GET HIM TO COME WILLINGLY.
WENDY, NO!
WHY WOULD HE LISTEN TO YOU?
BECAUSE...
BECAUSE I'M HIS MOTHER.

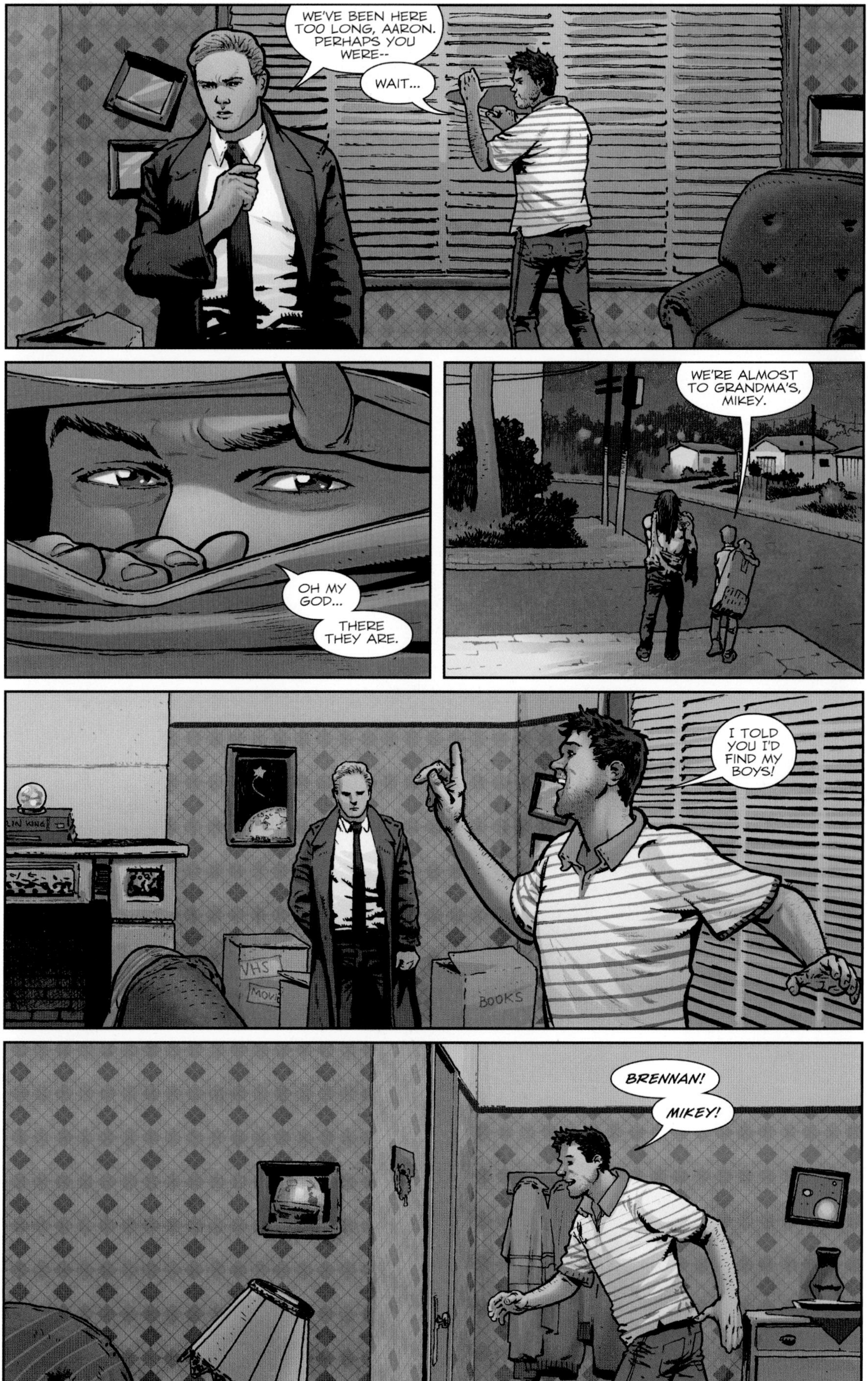
WE'VE BEEN HERE TOO LONG, AARON. PERHAPS YOU WERE--
WAIT...
OH MY GOD...
THERE THEY ARE.
WE'RE ALMOST TO GRANDMA'S, MIKEY.
I TOLD YOU I'D FIND MY BOYS!
BRENNAN!
MIKEY!
VHS
MOVIE
BOOKS

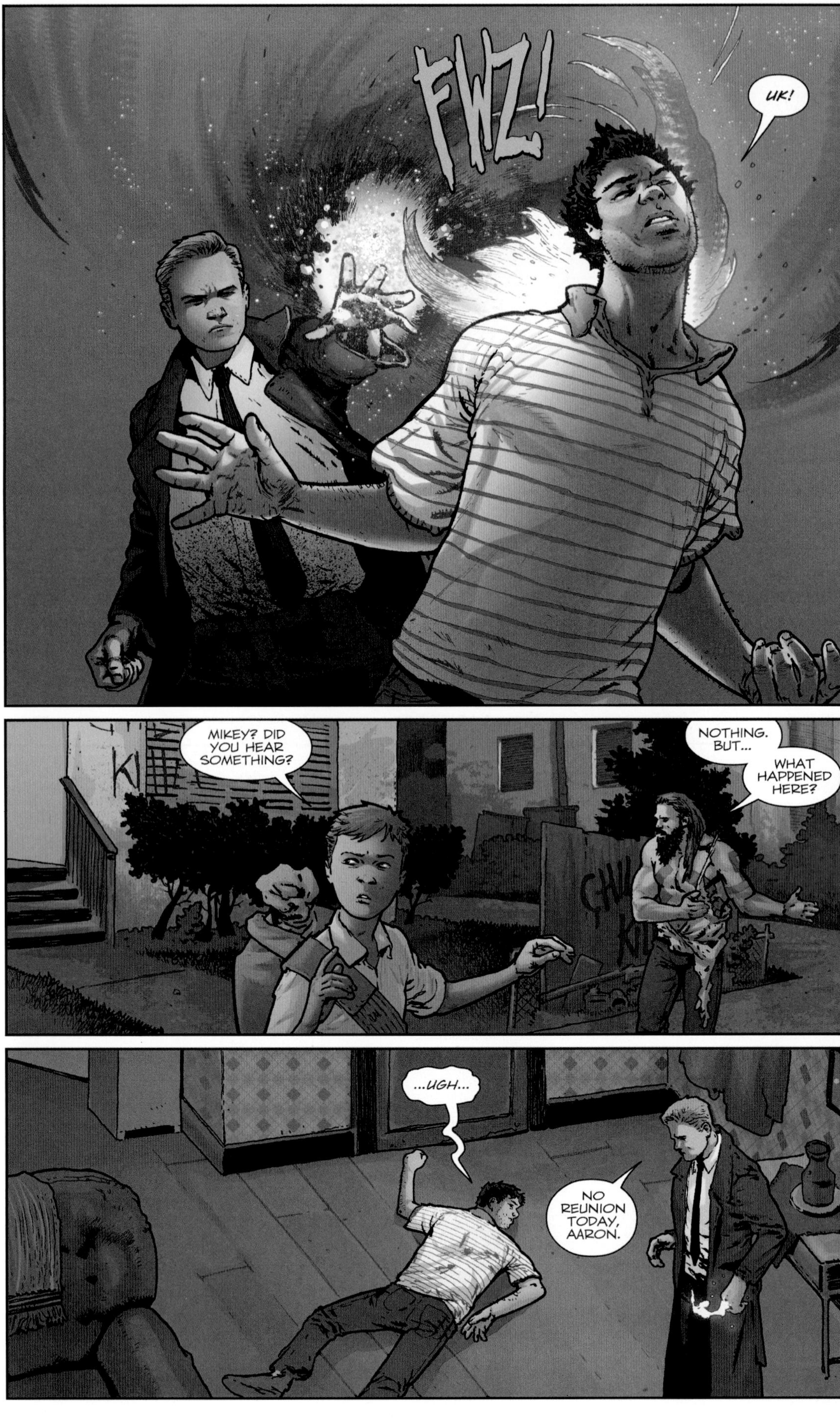
FWZ!
UK!
MIKEY? DID YOU HEAR SOMETHING?
NOTHING. BUT...
WHAT HAPPENED HERE?
...UGH...
NO REUNION TODAY, AARON.

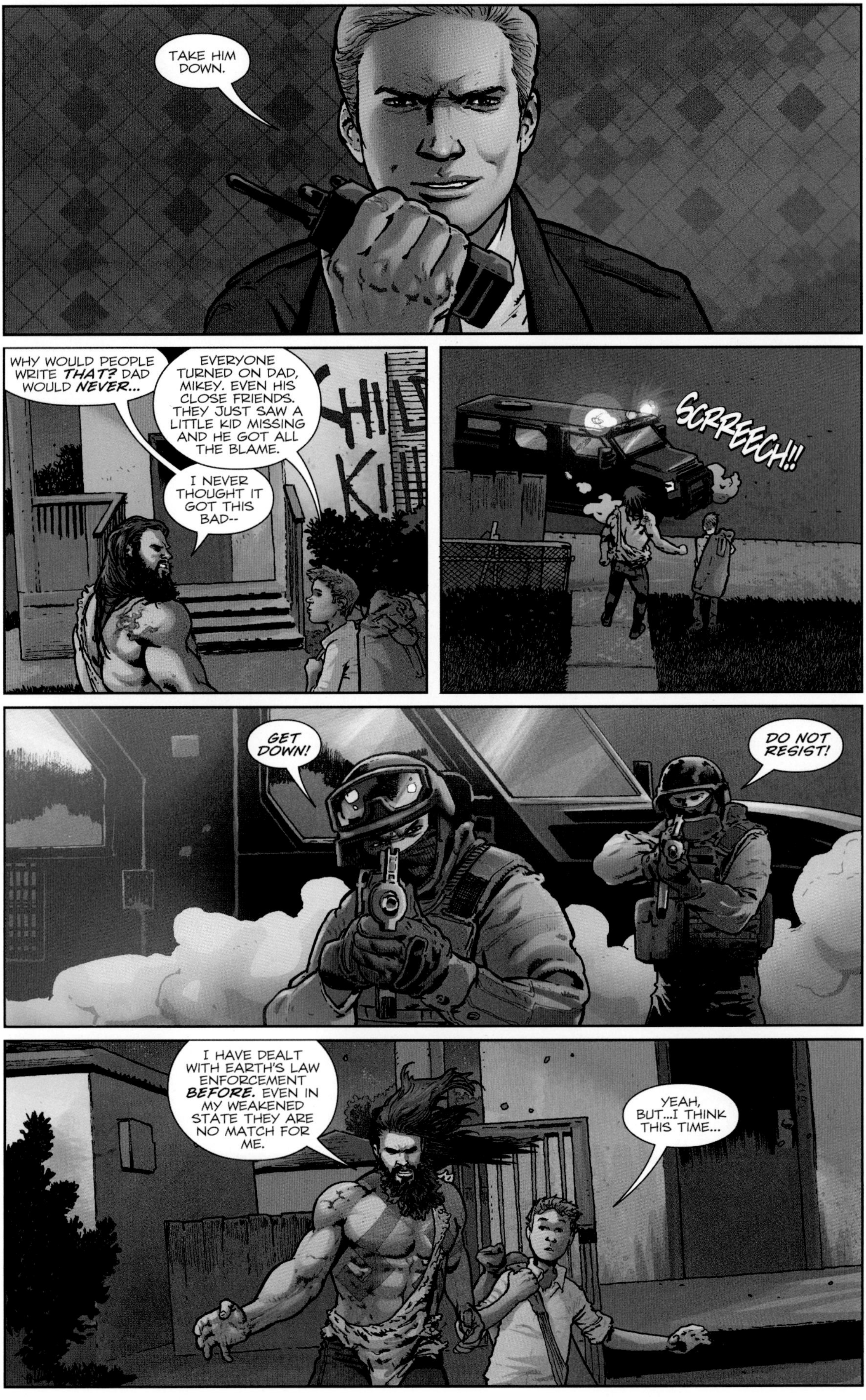
TAKE HIM DOWN.
WHY WOULD PEOPLE WRITE THAT? DAD WOULD NEVER...
EVERYONE TURNED ON DAD, MIKEY. EVEN HIS CLOSE FRIENDS. THEY JUST SAW A LITTLE KID MISSING AND HE GOT ALL THE BLAME.
I NEVER THOUGHT IT GOT THIS BAD--
SCRREECH!!
GET DOWN!
DO NOT RESIST!
I HAVE DEALT WITH EARTH'S LAW ENFORCEMENT BEFORE. EVEN IN MY WEAKENED STATE THEY ARE NO MATCH FOR ME.
YEAH, BUT...I THINK THIS TIME...

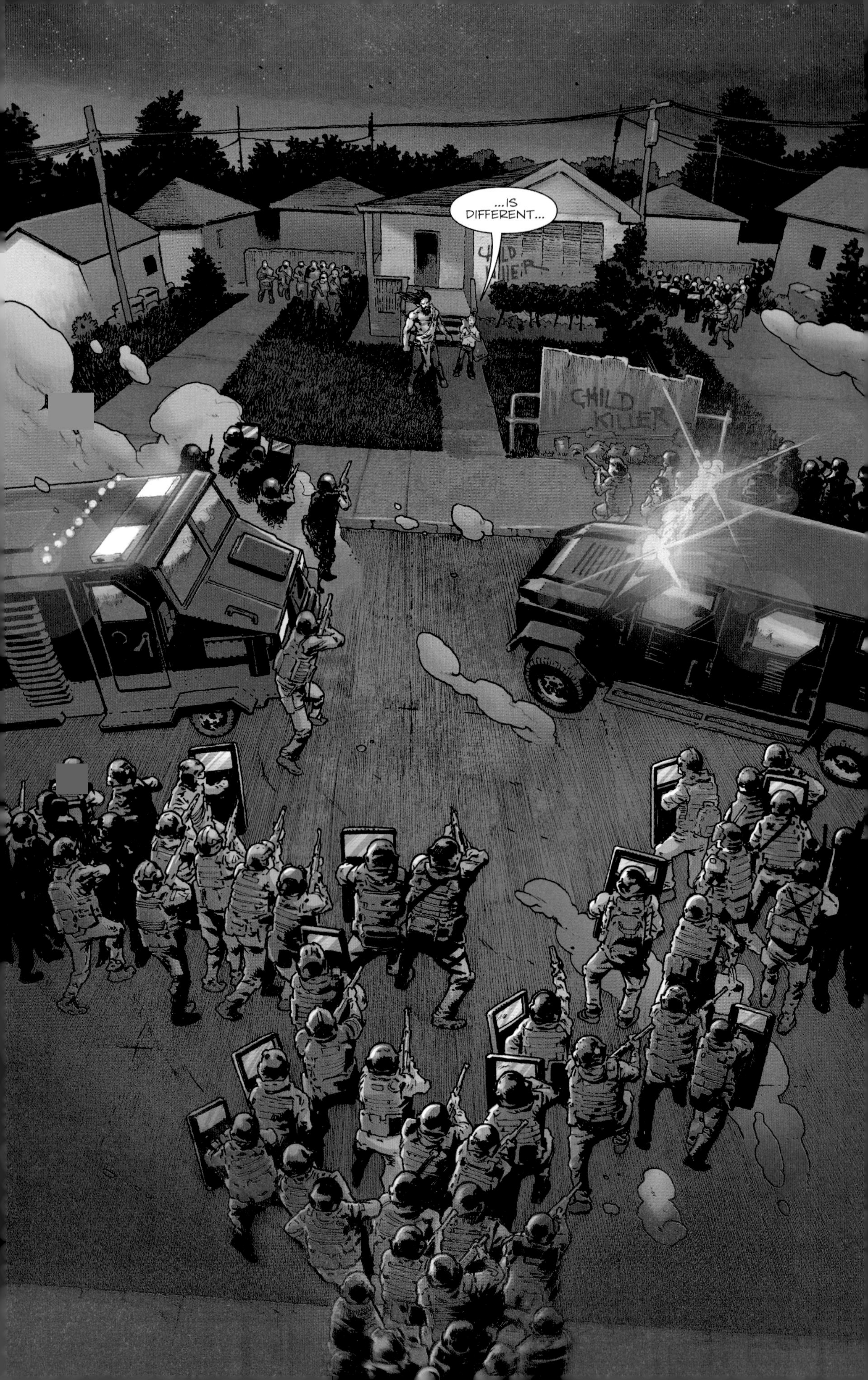
...IS DIFFERENT...
CHILD KILLER

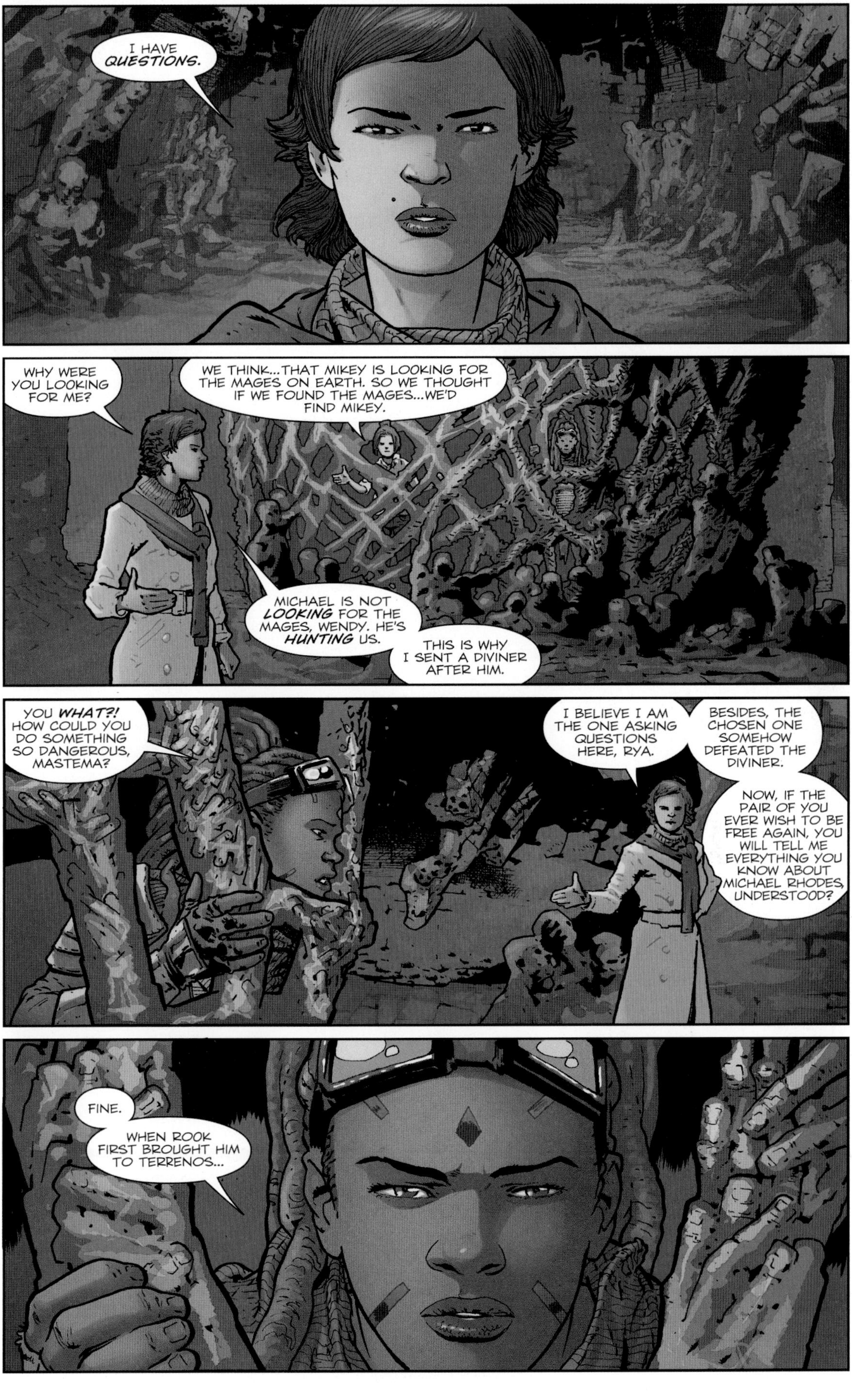
I HAVE QUESTIONS.
WHY WERE YOU LOOKING FOR ME?
WE THINK...THAT MIKEY IS LOOKING FOR THE MAGES ON EARTH. SO WE THOUGHT IF WE FOUND THE MAGES...WE'D FIND MIKEY.
MICHAEL IS NOT LOOKING FOR THE MAGES, WENDY. HE'S HUNTING US.
THIS IS WHY I SENT A DIVINER AFTER HIM.
YOU WHAT?! HOW COULD YOU DO SOMETHING SO DANGEROUS, MASTEMA?
I BELIEVE I AM THE ONE ASKING QUESTIONS HERE, RYA.
BESIDES, THE CHOSEN ONE SOMEHOW DEFEATED THE DIVINER.
NOW, IF THE PAIR OF YOU EVER WISH TO BE FREE AGAIN, YOU WILL TELL ME EVERYTHING YOU KNOW ABOUT MICHAEL RHODES, UNDERSTOOD?
FINE.
WHEN ROOK FIRST BROUGHT HIM TO TERRENOS...

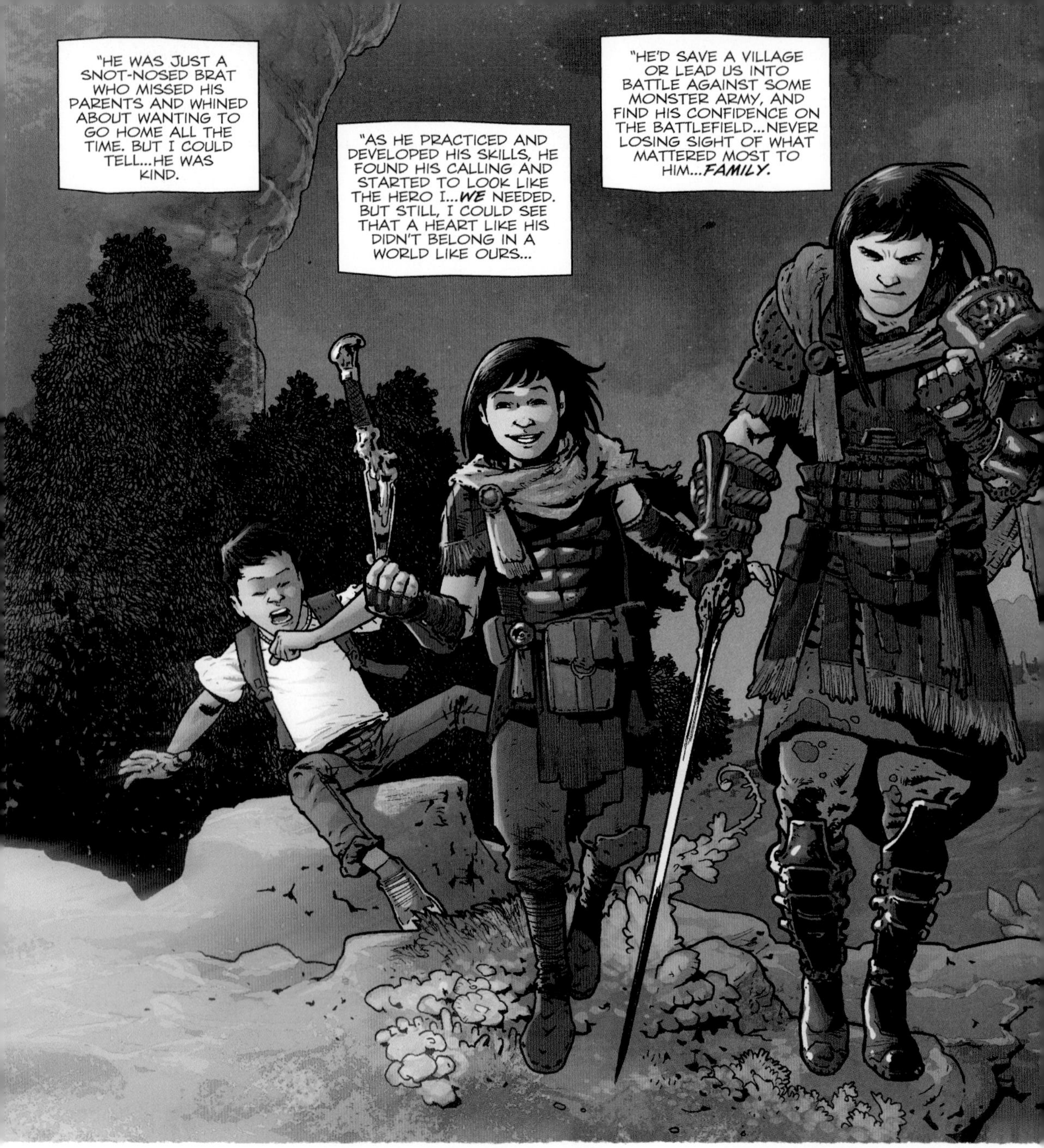
"HE WAS JUST A SNOT-NOSED BRAT WHO MISSED HIS PARENTS AND WHINED ABOUT WANTING TO GO HOME ALL THE TIME. BUT I COULD TELL...HE WAS KIND.
"AS HE PRACTICED AND DEVELOPED HIS SKILLS, HE FOUND HIS CALLING AND STARTED TO LOOK LIKE THE HERO I...*WE* NEEDED. BUT STILL, I COULD SEE THAT A HEART LIKE HIS DIDN'T BELONG IN A WORLD LIKE OURS...
"HE'D SAVE A VILLAGE OR LEAD US INTO BATTLE AGAINST SOME MONSTER ARMY, AND FIND HIS CONFIDENCE ON THE BATTLEFIELD...NEVER LOSING SIGHT OF WHAT MATTERED MOST TO HIM...*FAMILY.*
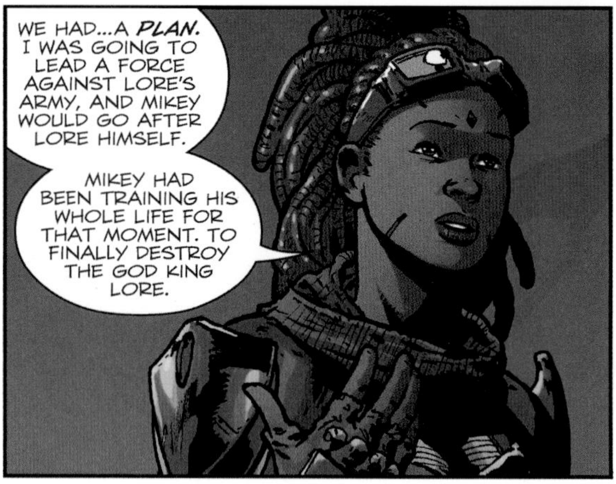
WE HAD...A *PLAN.* I WAS GOING TO LEAD A FORCE AGAINST LORE'S ARMY, AND MIKEY WOULD GO AFTER LORE HIMSELF.
MIKEY HAD BEEN TRAINING HIS WHOLE LIFE FOR THAT MOMENT. TO FINALLY DESTROY THE GOD KING LORE.
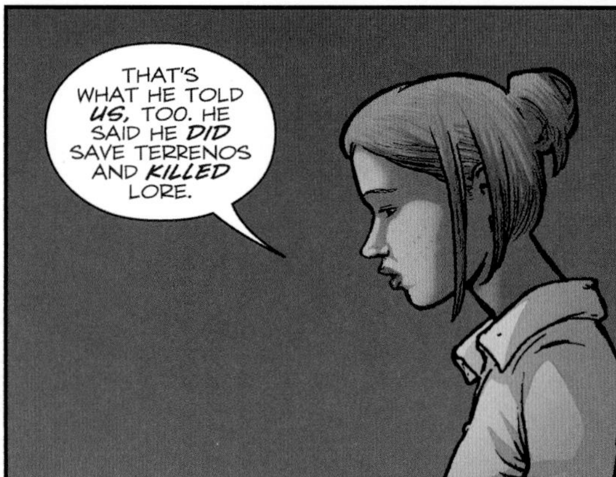
THAT'S WHAT HE TOLD *US,* TOO. HE SAID HE *DID* SAVE TERRENOS AND *KILLED* LORE.

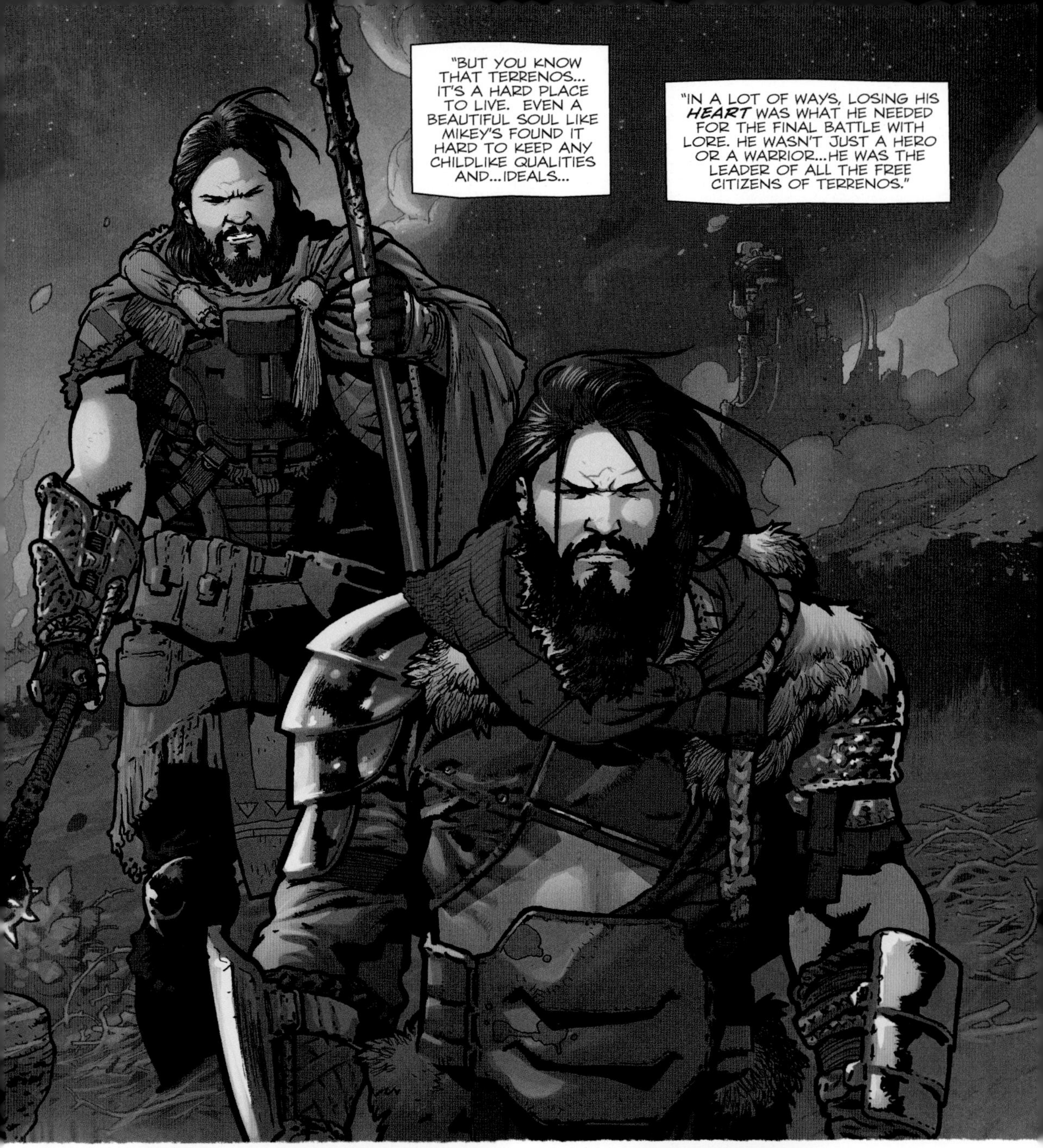
"BUT YOU KNOW THAT TERRENOS... IT'S A HARD PLACE TO LIVE. EVEN A BEAUTIFUL SOUL LIKE MIKEY'S FOUND IT HARD TO KEEP ANY CHILDLIKE QUALITIES AND...IDEALS...
"IN A LOT OF WAYS, LOSING HIS *HEART* WAS WHAT HE NEEDED FOR THE FINAL BATTLE WITH LORE. HE WASN'T JUST A HERO OR A WARRIOR...HE WAS THE LEADER OF ALL THE FREE CITIZENS OF TERRENOS."

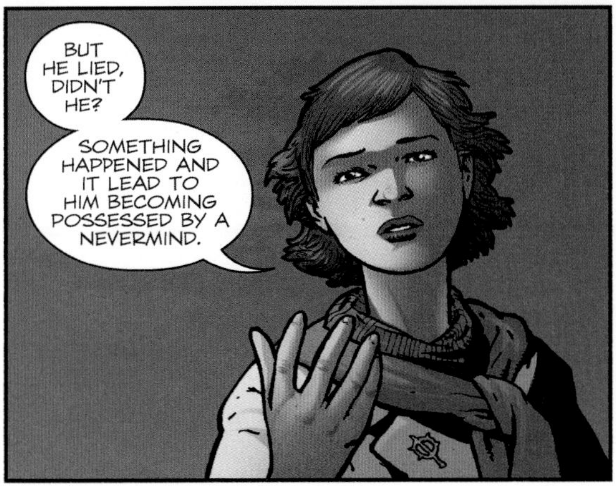
BUT HE LIED, DIDN'T HE?
SOMETHING HAPPENED AND IT LEAD TO HIM BECOMING POSSESSED BY A NEVERMIND.

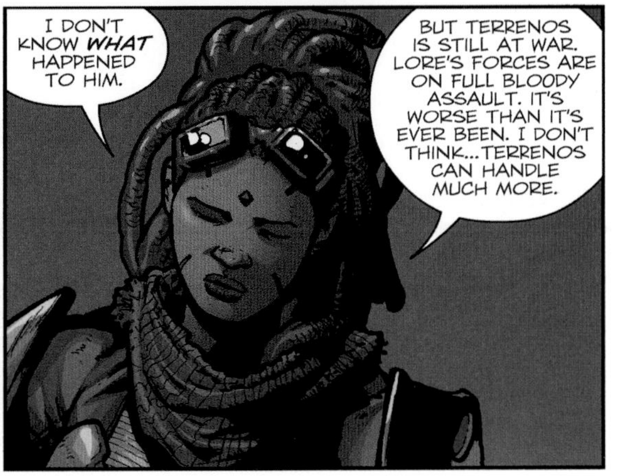
I DON'T KNOW *WHAT* HAPPENED TO HIM.
BUT TERRENOS IS STILL AT WAR. LORE'S FORCES ARE ON FULL BLOODY ASSAULT. IT'S WORSE THAN IT'S EVER BEEN. I DON'T THINK...TERRENOS CAN HANDLE MUCH MORE.

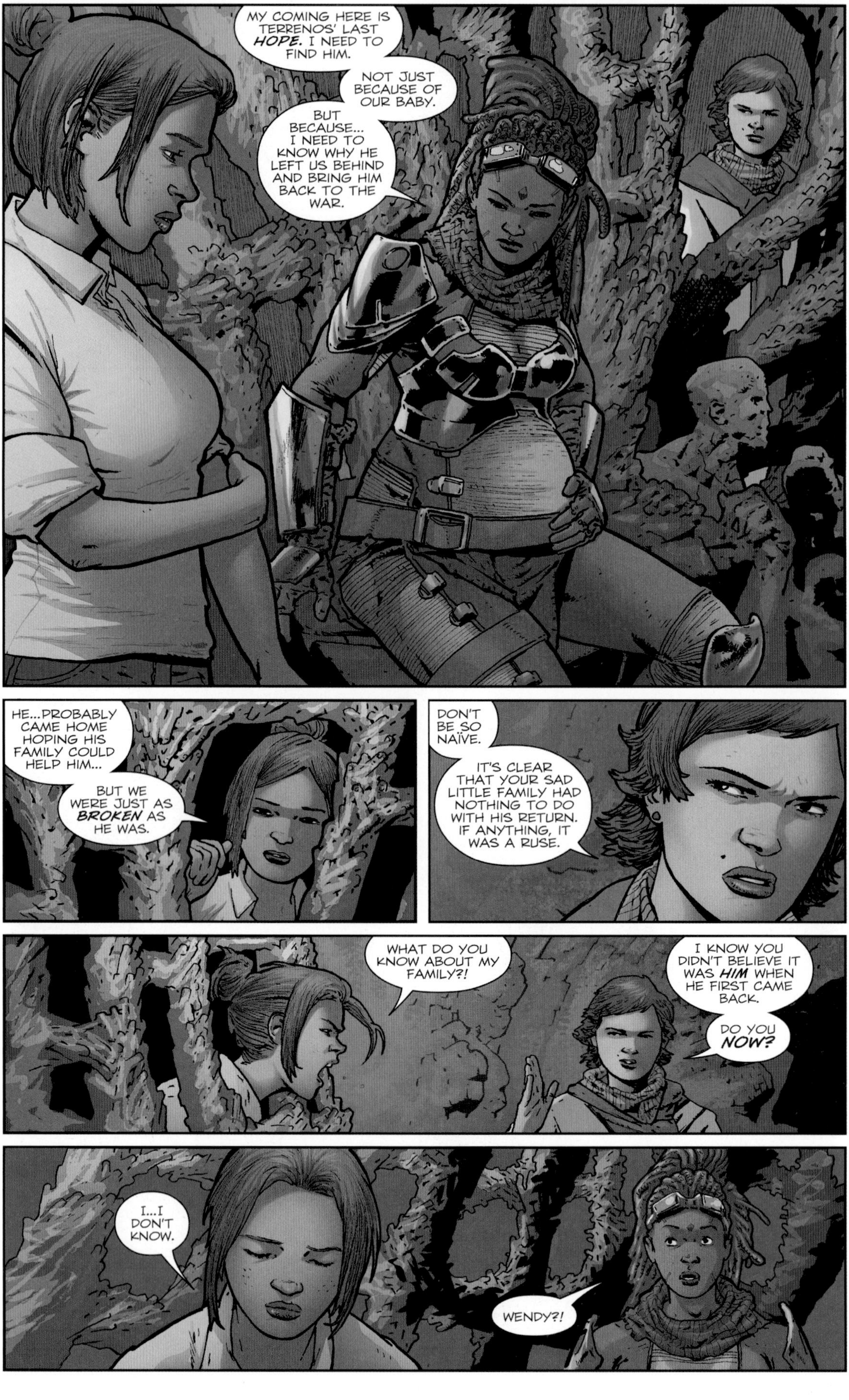
MY COMING HERE IS TERRENOS' LAST HOPE. I NEED TO FIND HIM.
NOT JUST BECAUSE OF OUR BABY.
BUT BECAUSE... I NEED TO KNOW WHY HE LEFT US BEHIND AND BRING HIM BACK TO THE WAR.
HE...PROBABLY CAME HOME HOPING HIS FAMILY COULD HELP HIM...
BUT WE WERE JUST AS BROKEN AS HE WAS.
DON'T BE SO NAÏVE.
IT'S CLEAR THAT YOUR SAD LITTLE FAMILY HAD NOTHING TO DO WITH HIS RETURN. IF ANYTHING, IT WAS A RUSE.
WHAT DO YOU KNOW ABOUT MY FAMILY?!
I KNOW YOU DIDN'T BELIEVE IT WAS HIM WHEN HE FIRST CAME BACK.
DO YOU NOW?
I...I DON'T KNOW.
WENDY?!

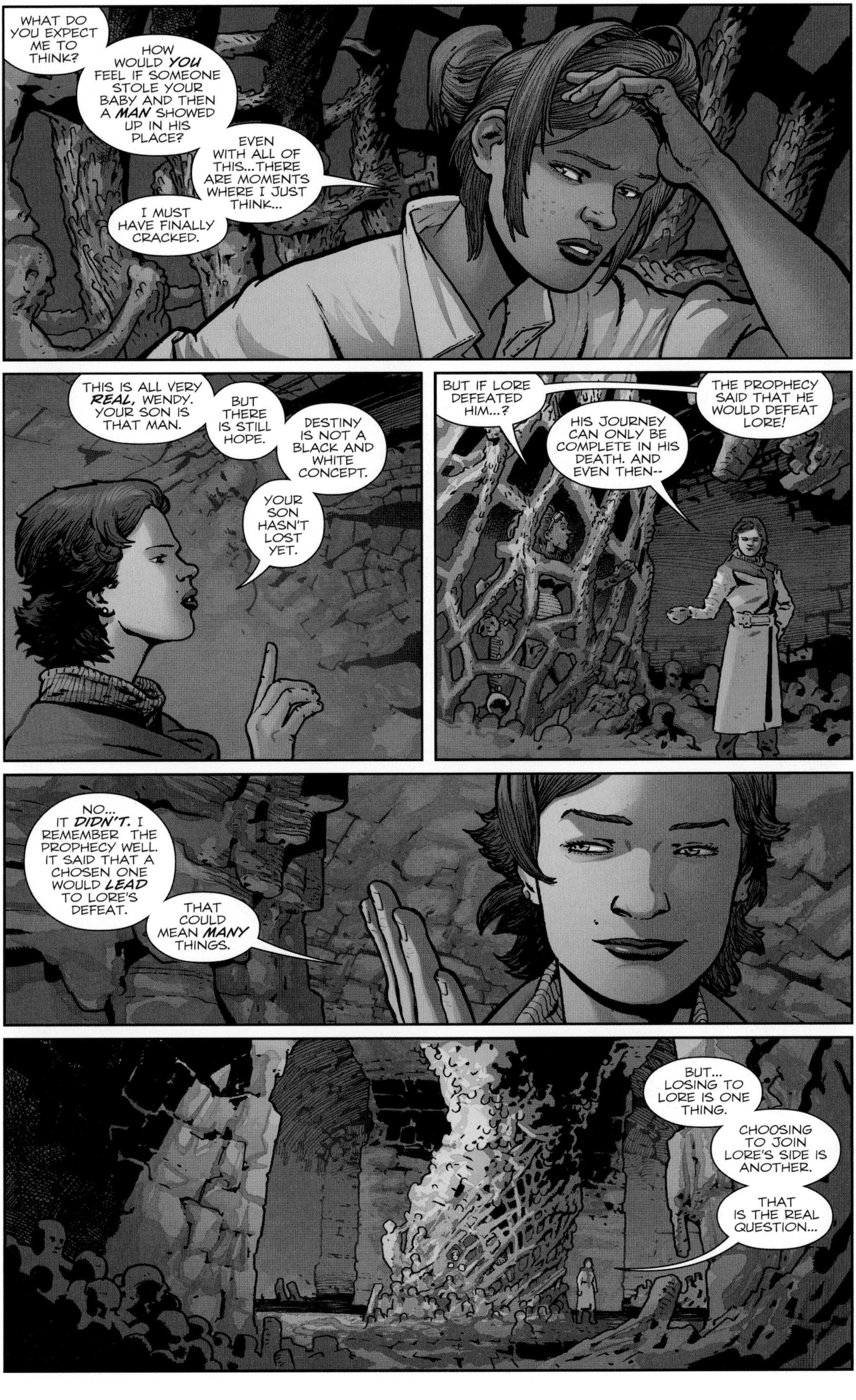
WHAT DO YOU EXPECT ME TO THINK?
HOW WOULD *YOU* FEEL IF SOMEONE STOLE YOUR BABY AND THEN A *MAN* SHOWED UP IN HIS PLACE?
EVEN WITH ALL OF THIS...THERE ARE MOMENTS WHERE I JUST THINK...
I MUST HAVE FINALLY CRACKED.
THIS IS ALL VERY *REAL,* WENDY. YOUR SON IS THAT MAN.
BUT THERE IS STILL HOPE.
DESTINY IS NOT A BLACK AND WHITE CONCEPT.
YOUR SON HASN'T LOST YET.
BUT IF LORE DEFEATED HIM...?
THE PROPHECY SAID THAT HE WOULD DEFEAT LORE!
HIS JOURNEY CAN ONLY BE COMPLETE IN HIS DEATH. AND EVEN THEN--
NO... IT *DIDN'T.* I REMEMBER THE PROPHECY WELL. IT SAID THAT A CHOSEN ONE WOULD *LEAD* TO LORE'S DEFEAT.
THAT COULD MEAN *MANY* THINGS.
BUT... LOSING TO LORE IS ONE THING.
CHOOSING TO JOIN LORE'S SIDE IS ANOTHER.
THAT IS THE REAL QUESTION...

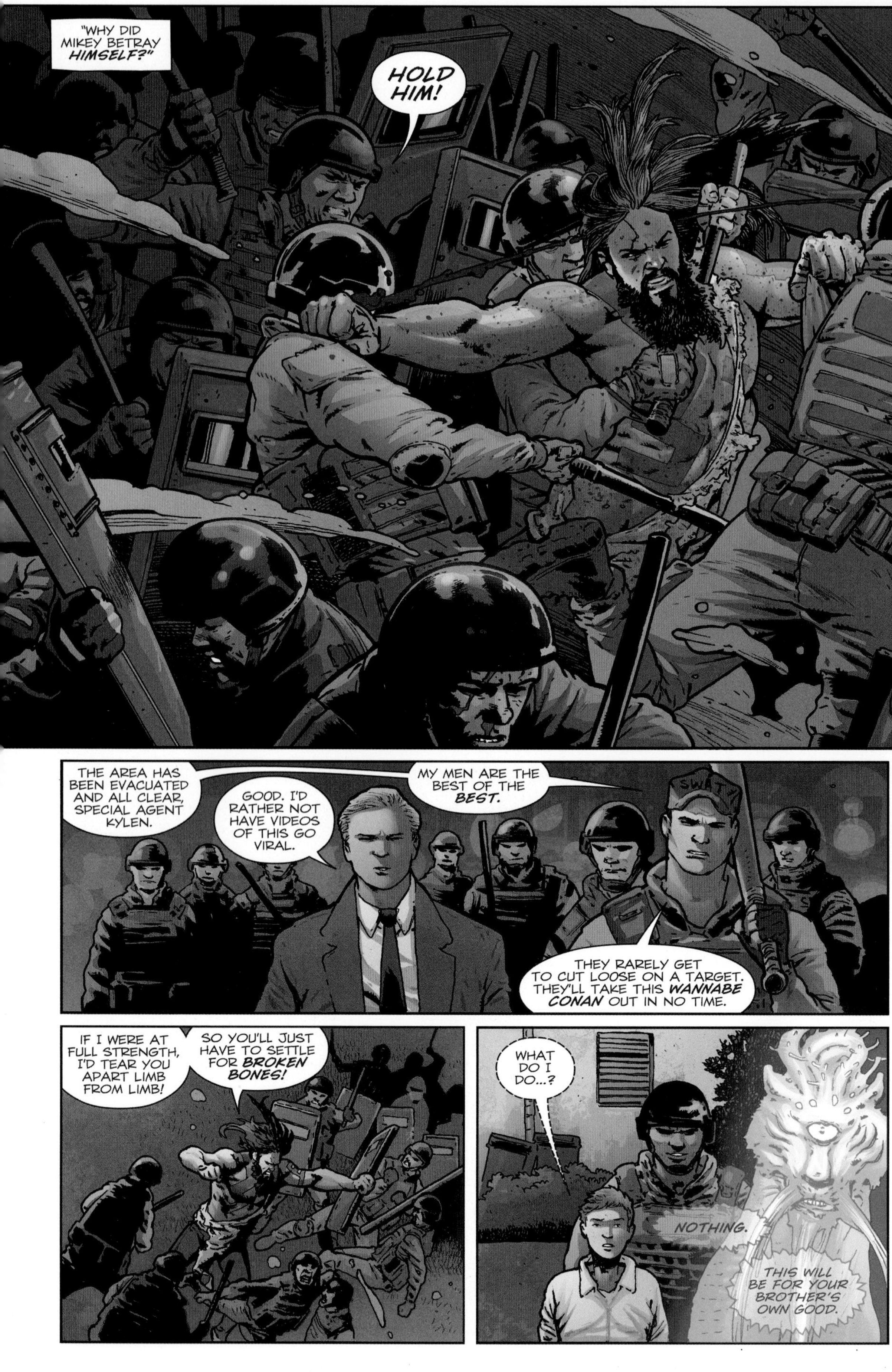
"WHY DID MIKEY BETRAY HIMSELF?"
HOLD HIM!
THE AREA HAS BEEN EVACUATED AND ALL CLEAR, SPECIAL AGENT KYLEN.
GOOD. I'D RATHER NOT HAVE VIDEOS OF THIS GO VIRAL.
MY MEN ARE THE BEST OF THE BEST.
THEY RARELY GET TO CUT LOOSE ON A TARGET. THEY'LL TAKE THIS WANNABE CONAN OUT IN NO TIME.
IF I WERE AT FULL STRENGTH, I'D TEAR YOU APART LIMB FROM LIMB!
SO YOU'LL JUST HAVE TO SETTLE FOR BROKEN BONES!
WHAT DO I DO...?
NOTHING.
THIS WILL BE FOR YOUR BROTHER'S OWN GOOD.

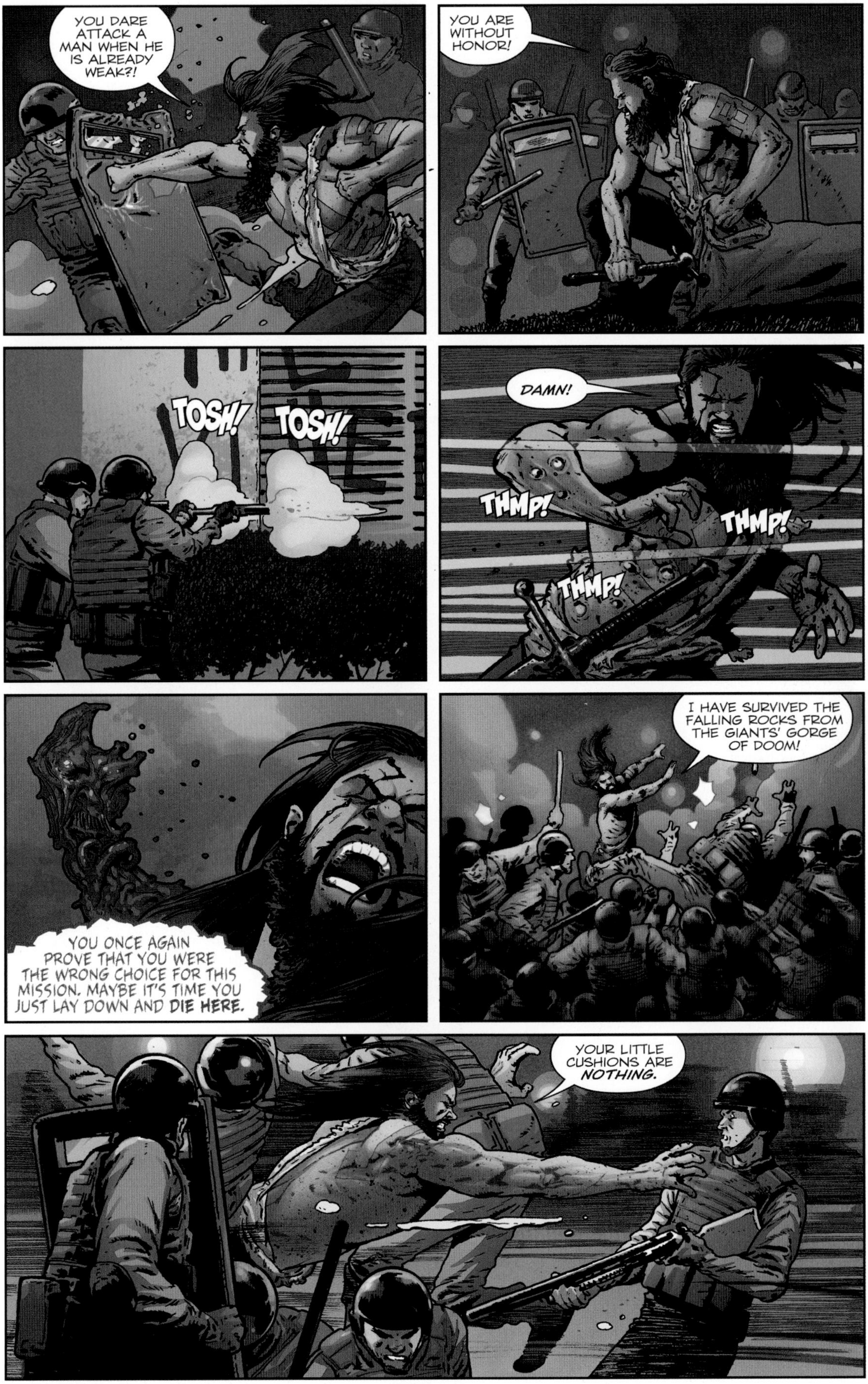
YOU DARE ATTACK A MAN WHEN HE IS ALREADY WEAK?!
YOU ARE WITHOUT HONOR!
TOSH!
TOSH!
DAMN!
THMP!
THMP!
THMP!
YOU ONCE AGAIN PROVE THAT YOU WERE THE WRONG CHOICE FOR THIS MISSION. MAYBE IT'S TIME YOU JUST LAY DOWN AND DIE HERE.
I HAVE SURVIVED THE FALLING ROCKS FROM THE GIANTS' GORGE OF DOOM!
YOUR LITTLE CUSHIONS ARE NOTHING.

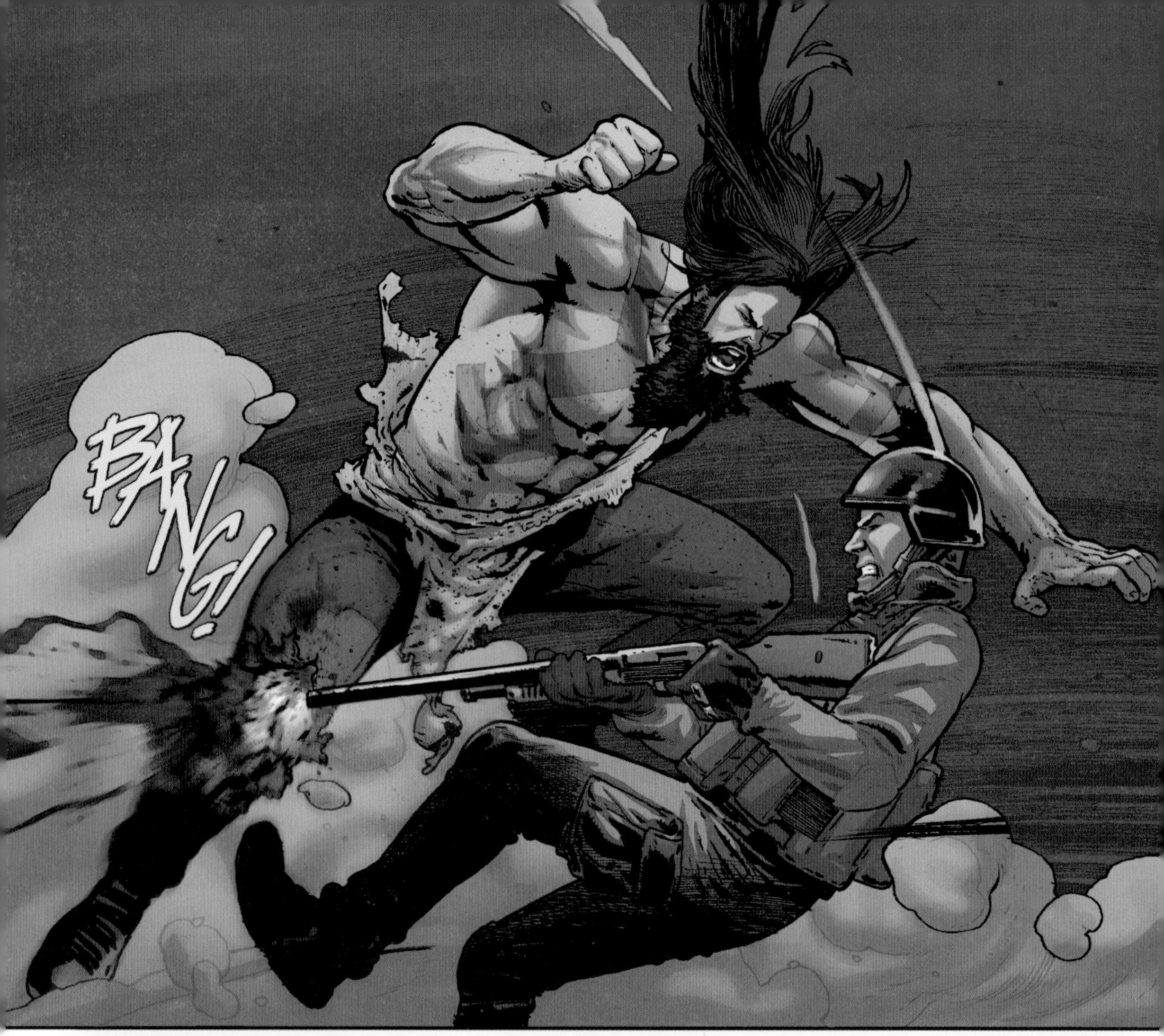
BANG!

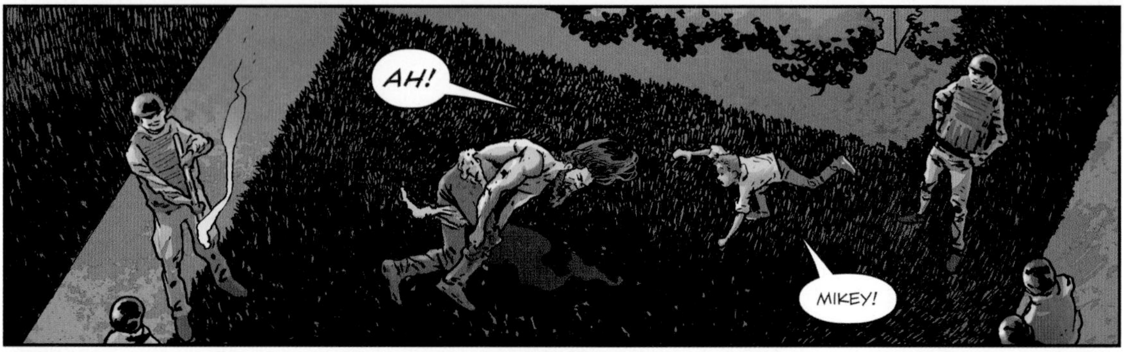
AH!
MIKEY!

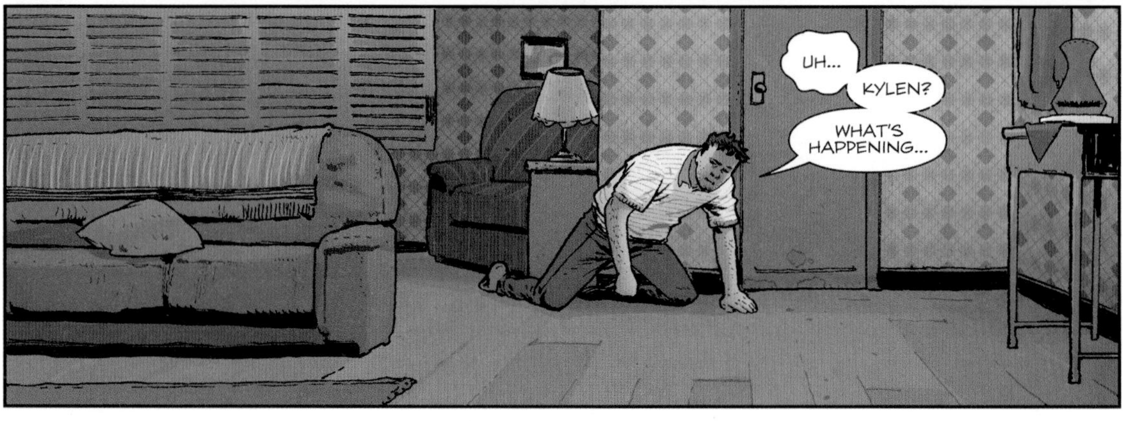
UH...
KYLEN?
WHAT'S HAPPENING...

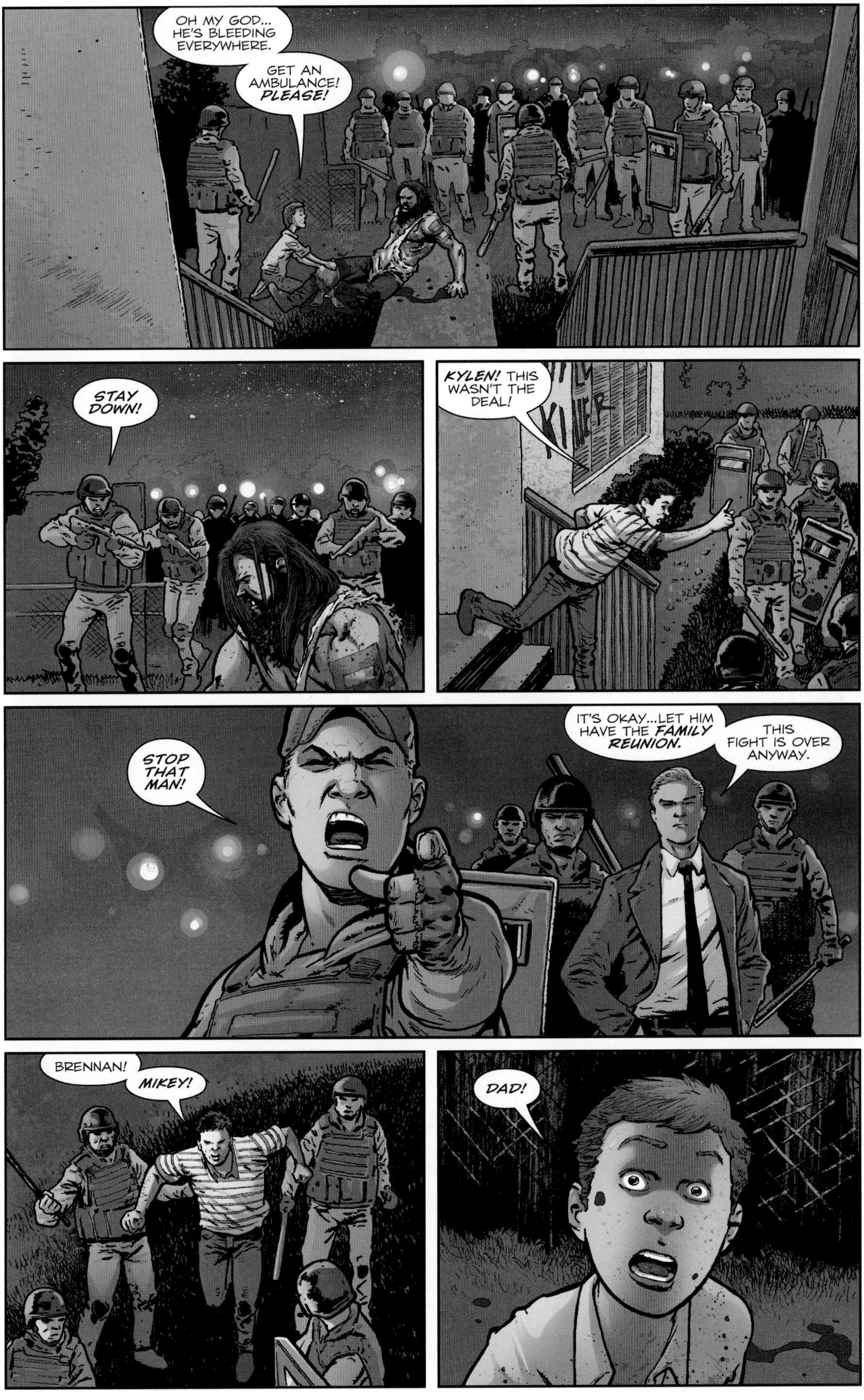
OH MY GOD... HE'S BLEEDING EVERYWHERE.
GET AN AMBULANCE! *PLEASE!*
STAY DOWN!
KYLEN! THIS WASN'T THE DEAL!
STOP THAT MAN!
IT'S OKAY...LET HIM HAVE THE *FAMILY REUNION.*
THIS FIGHT IS OVER ANYWAY.
BRENNAN!
MIKEY!
DAD!

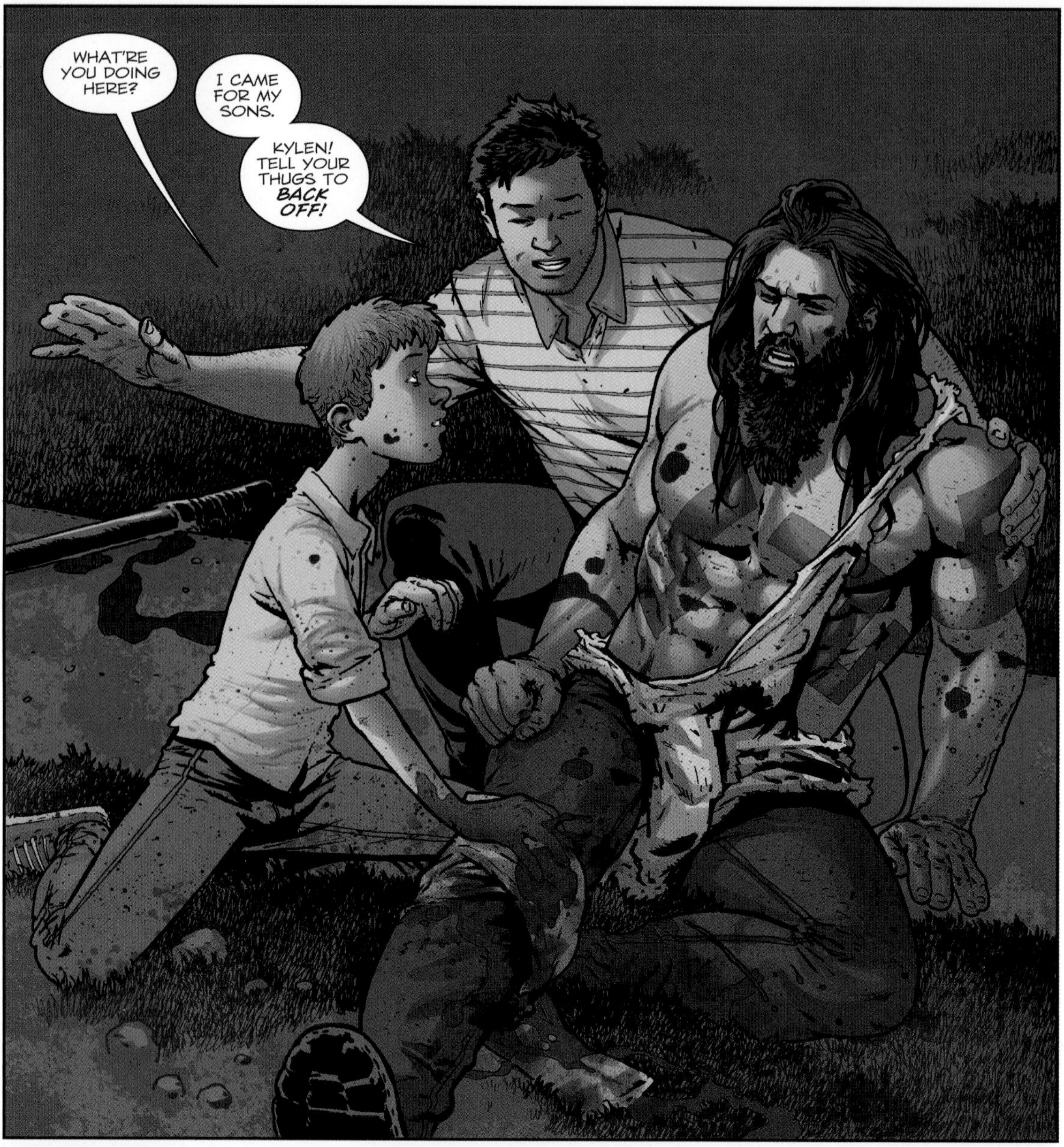
WHAT'RE YOU DOING HERE?
I CAME FOR MY SONS.
KYLEN! TELL YOUR THUGS TO BACK OFF!

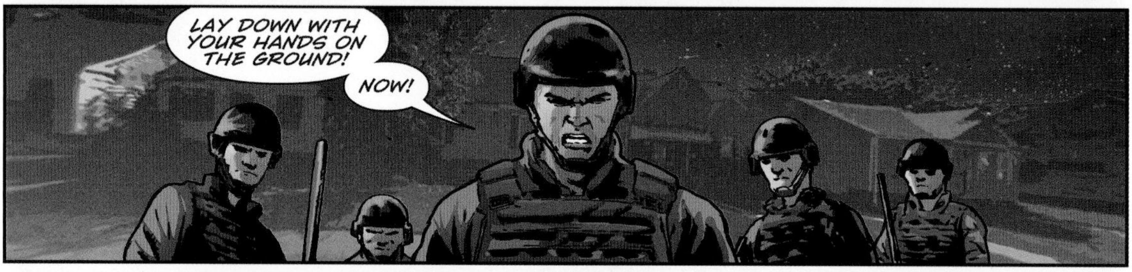
LAY DOWN WITH YOUR HANDS ON THE GROUND!
NOW!

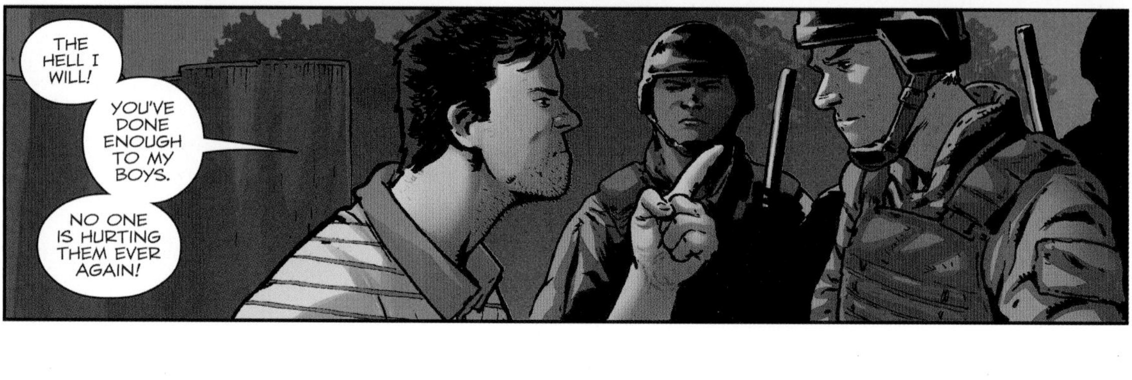
THE HELL I WILL!
YOU'VE DONE ENOUGH TO MY BOYS.
NO ONE IS HURTING THEM EVER AGAIN!

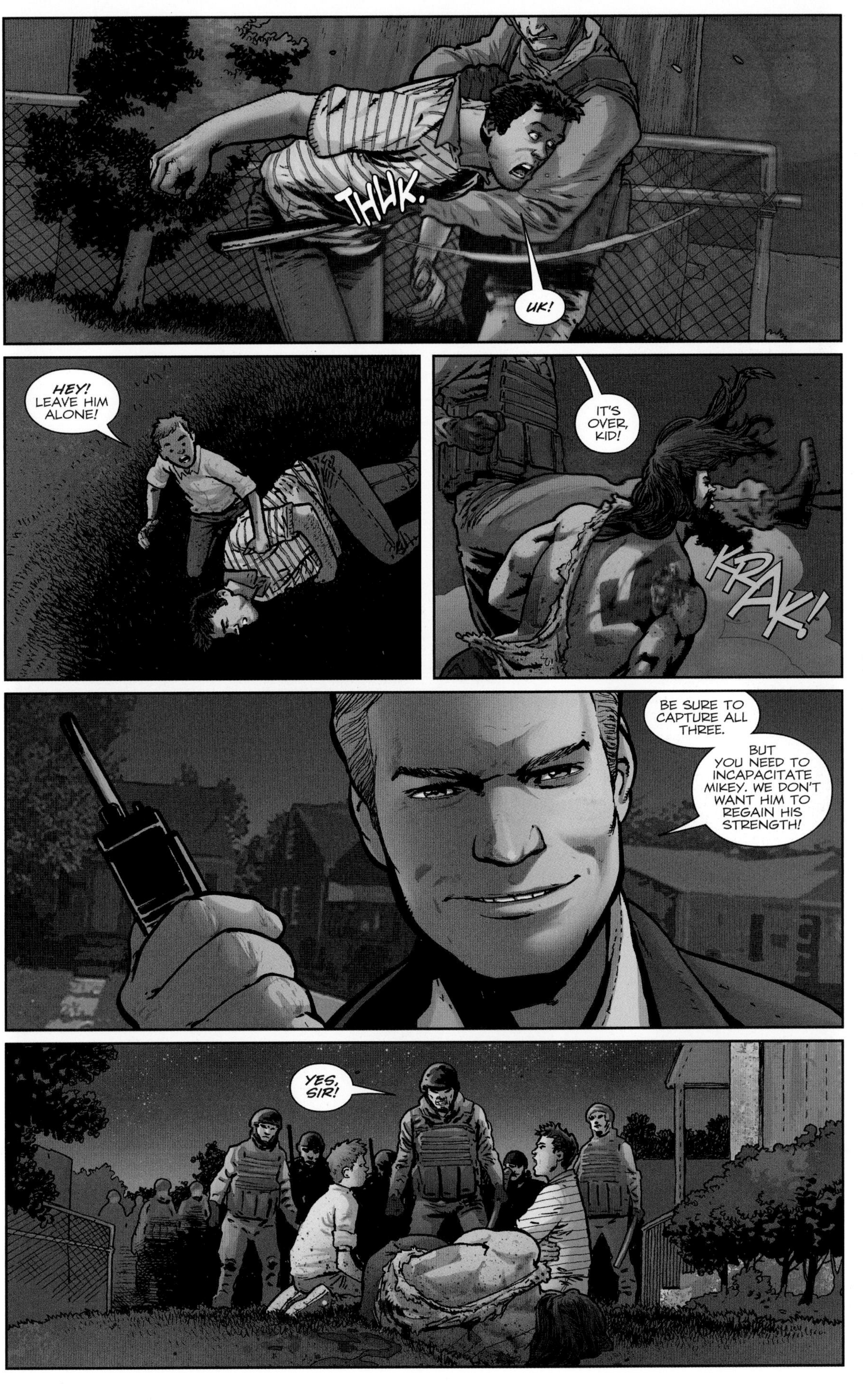
THUK.
UK!
HEY! LEAVE HIM ALONE!
IT'S OVER, KID!
KRAK!
BE SURE TO CAPTURE ALL THREE.
BUT YOU NEED TO INCAPACITATE MIKEY. WE DON'T WANT HIM TO REGAIN HIS STRENGTH!
YES, SIR!

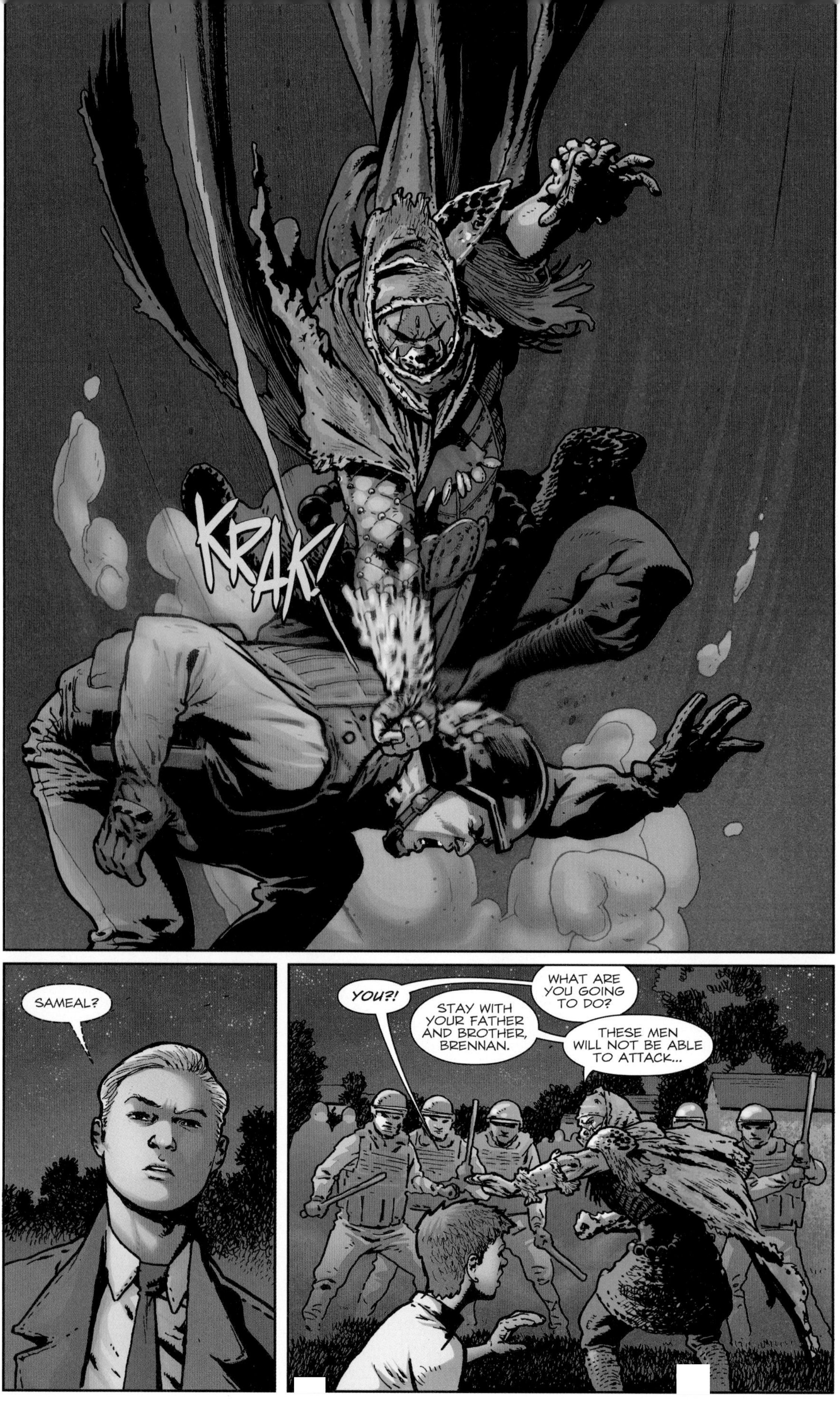
KRAK!
SAMEAL?
YOU?!
WHAT ARE YOU GOING TO DO?
STAY WITH YOUR FATHER AND BROTHER, BRENNAN.
THESE MEN WILL NOT BE ABLE TO ATTACK...

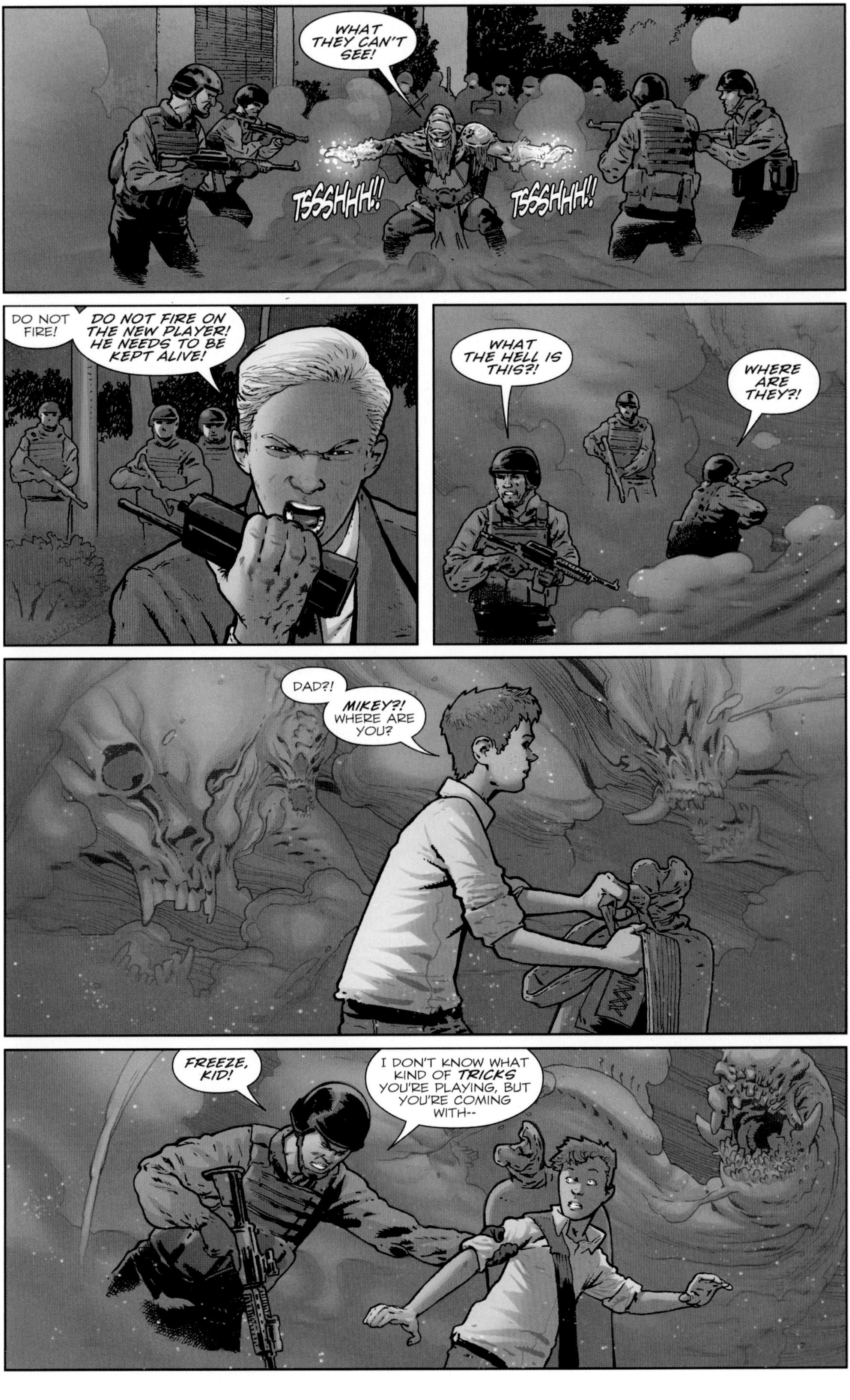
WHAT THEY CAN'T SEE!
TSSSHHH!!
TSSSHHH!!
DO NOT FIRE!
DO NOT FIRE ON THE NEW PLAYER! HE NEEDS TO BE KEPT ALIVE!
WHAT THE HELL IS THIS?!
WHERE ARE THEY?!
DAD?! MIKEY?! WHERE ARE YOU?
FREEZE, KID!
I DON'T KNOW WHAT KIND OF TRICKS YOU'RE PLAYING, BUT YOU'RE COMING WITH--

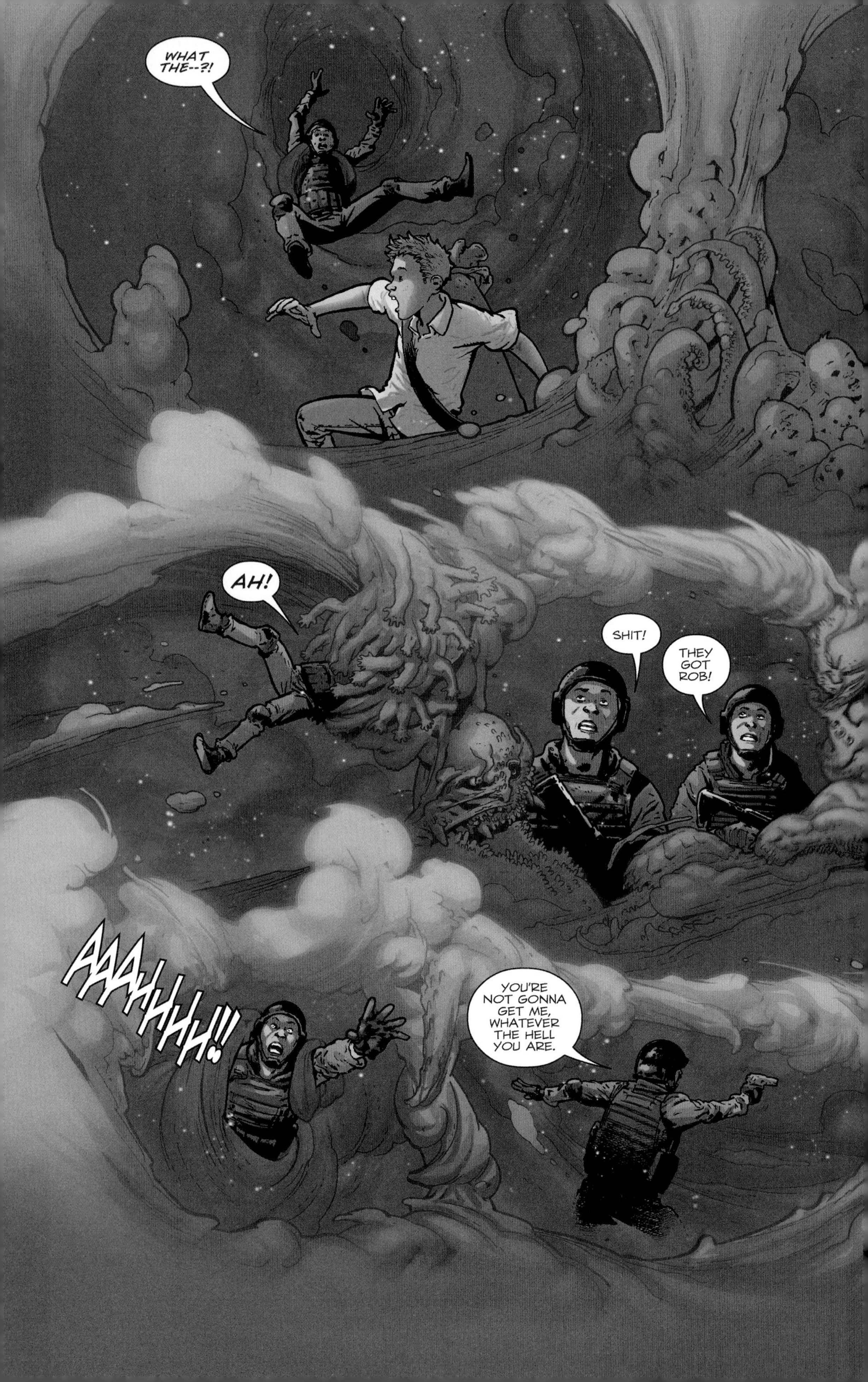
WHAT THE--?!
AH!
SHIT!
THEY GOT ROB!
AAAHHHHH!!
YOU'RE NOT GONNA GET ME, WHATEVER THE HELL YOU ARE.

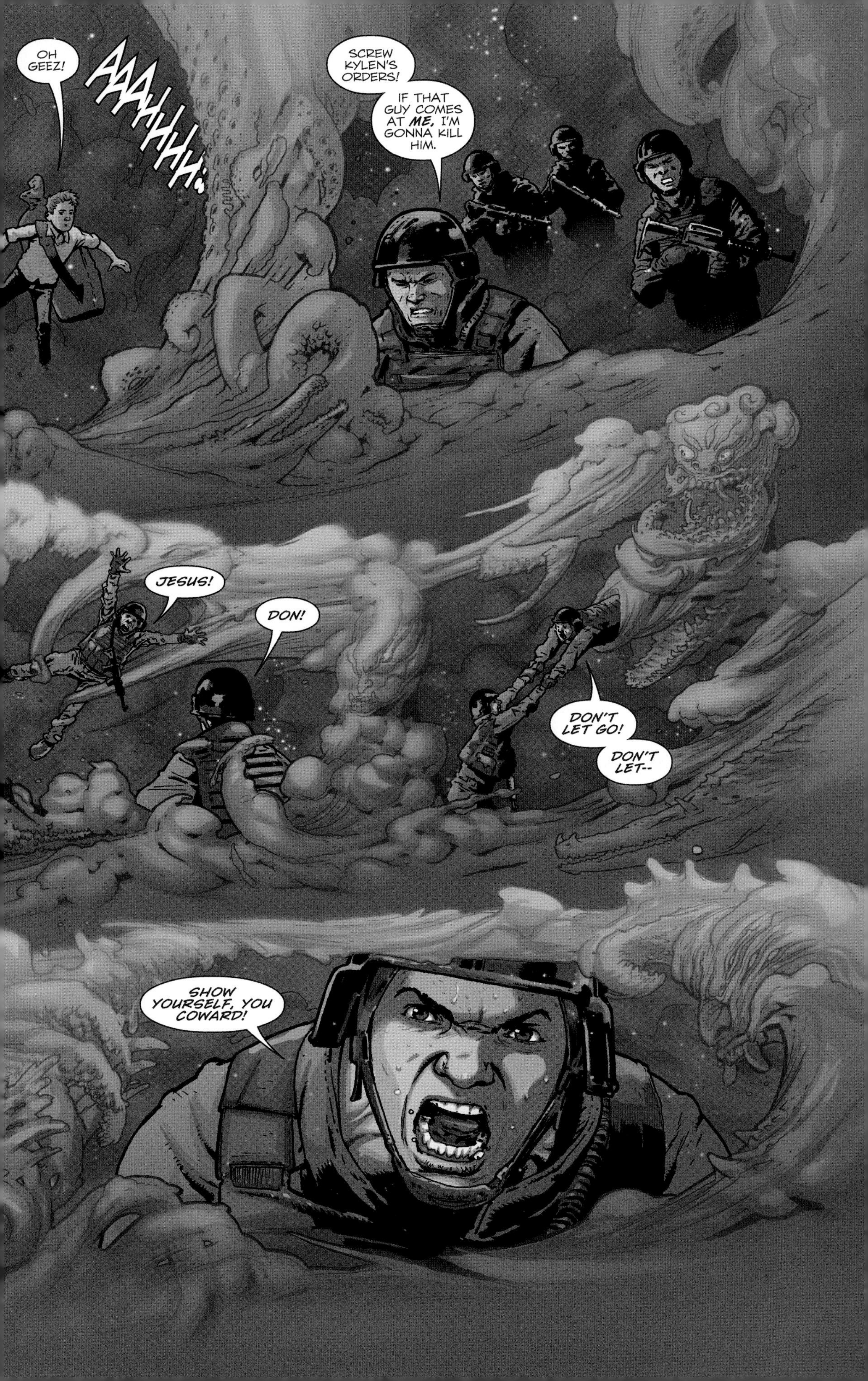
OH GEEZ!
AAAAHHHHH!
SCREW KYLEN'S ORDERS!
IF THAT GUY COMES AT ME, I'M GONNA KILL HIM.
JESUS!
DON!
DON'T LET GO!
DON'T LET--
SHOW YOURSELF, YOU COWARD!

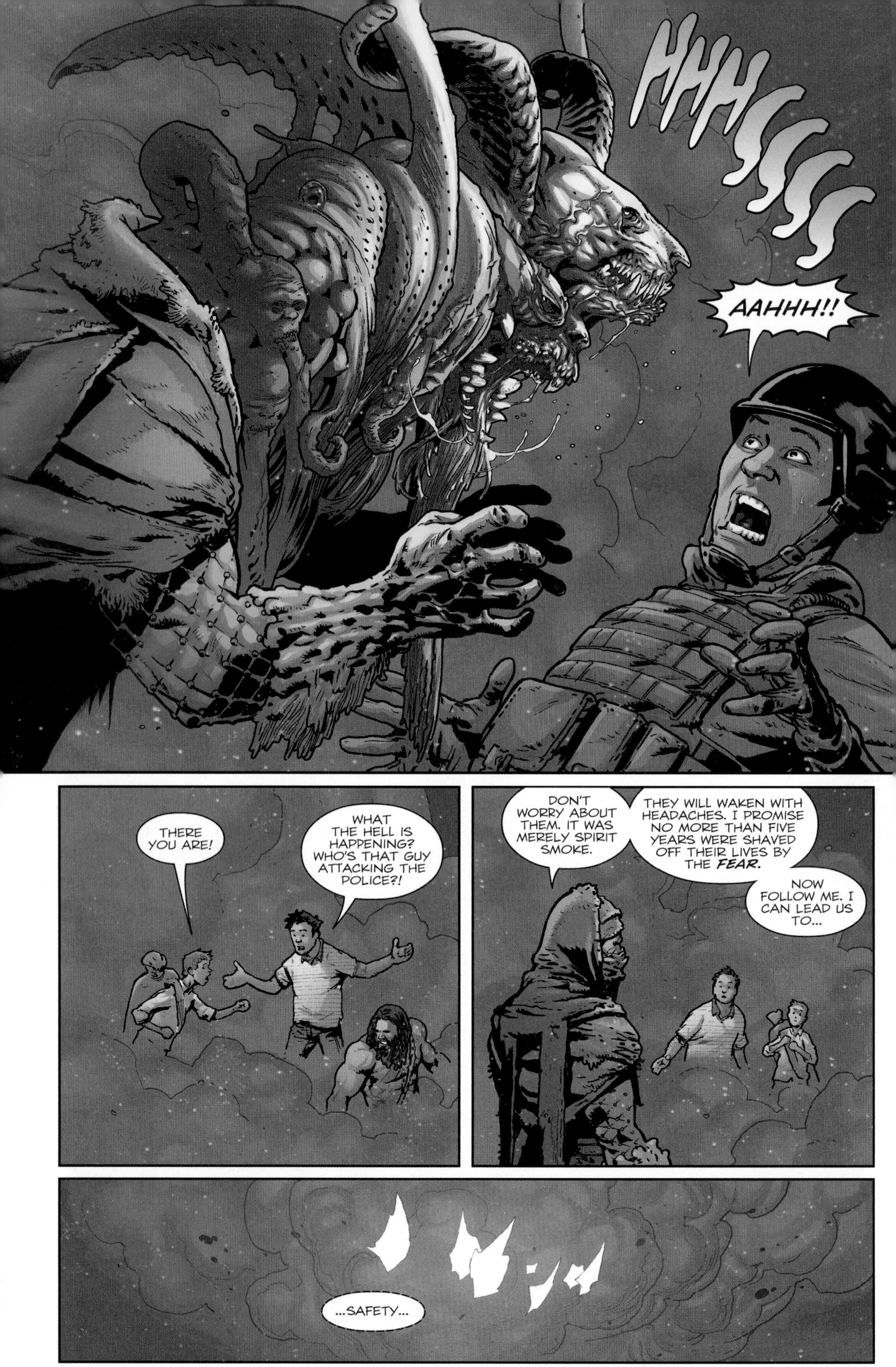
HHHSSSSS
AAHHH!!
THERE YOU ARE!
WHAT THE HELL IS HAPPENING? WHO'S THAT GUY ATTACKING THE POLICE?!
DON'T WORRY ABOUT THEM. IT WAS MERELY SPIRIT SMOKE.
THEY WILL WAKEN WITH HEADACHES. I PROMISE NO MORE THAN FIVE YEARS WERE SHAVED OFF THEIR LIVES BY THE FEAR.
NOW FOLLOW ME. I CAN LEAD US TO...
...SAFETY...

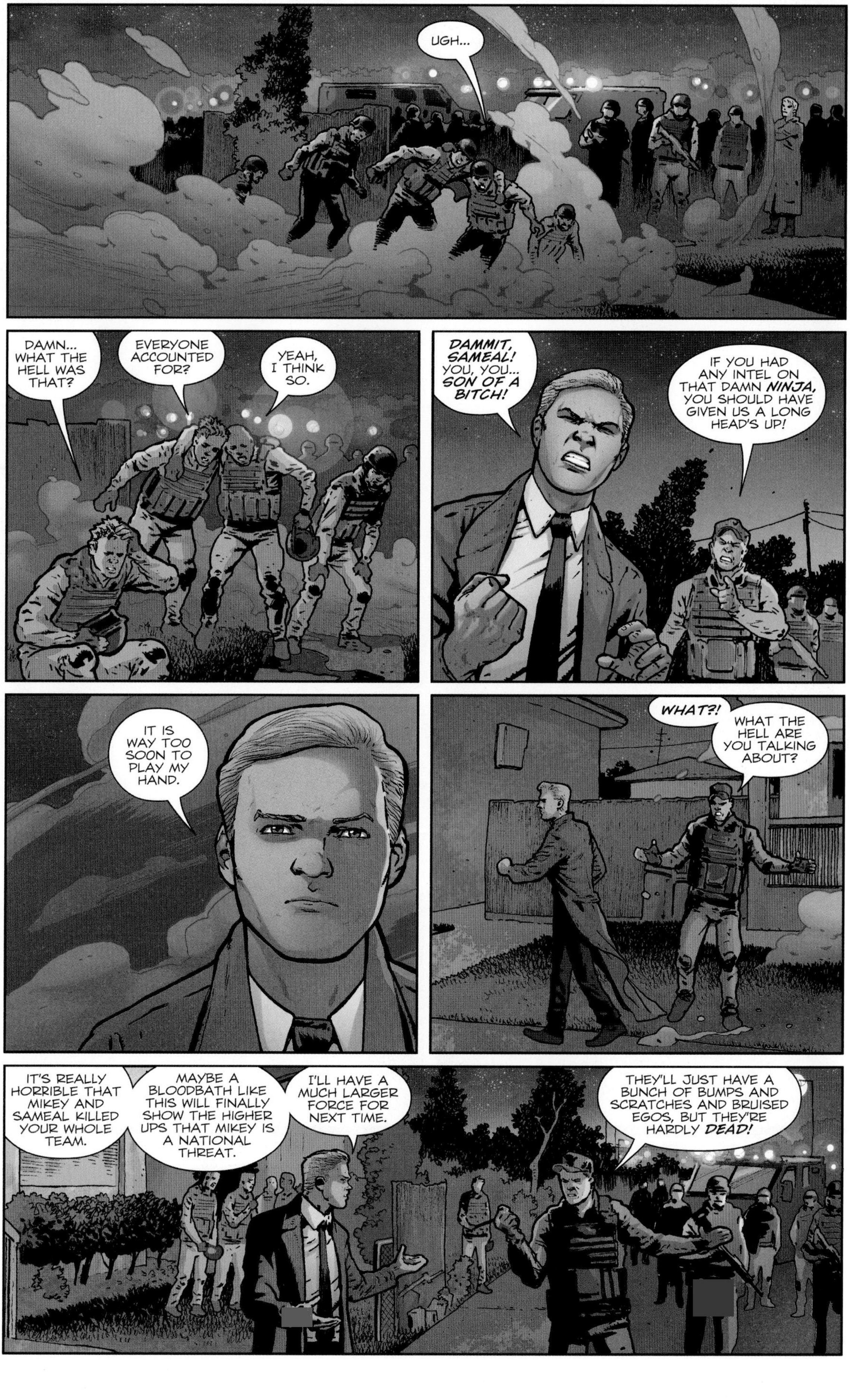
UGH...
DAMN... WHAT THE HELL WAS THAT?
EVERYONE ACCOUNTED FOR?
YEAH, I THINK SO.
DAMMIT, SAMEAL! YOU, YOU... SON OF A BITCH!
IF YOU HAD ANY INTEL ON THAT DAMN NINJA, YOU SHOULD HAVE GIVEN US A LONG HEAD'S UP!
IT IS WAY TOO SOON TO PLAY MY HAND.
WHAT?!
WHAT THE HELL ARE YOU TALKING ABOUT?
IT'S REALLY HORRIBLE THAT MIKEY AND SAMEAL KILLED YOUR WHOLE TEAM.
MAYBE A BLOODBATH LIKE THIS WILL FINALLY SHOW THE HIGHER UPS THAT MIKEY IS A NATIONAL THREAT.
I'LL HAVE A MUCH LARGER FORCE FOR NEXT TIME.
THEY'LL JUST HAVE A BUNCH OF BUMPS AND SCRATCHES AND BRUISED EGOS, BUT THEY'RE HARDLY DEAD!

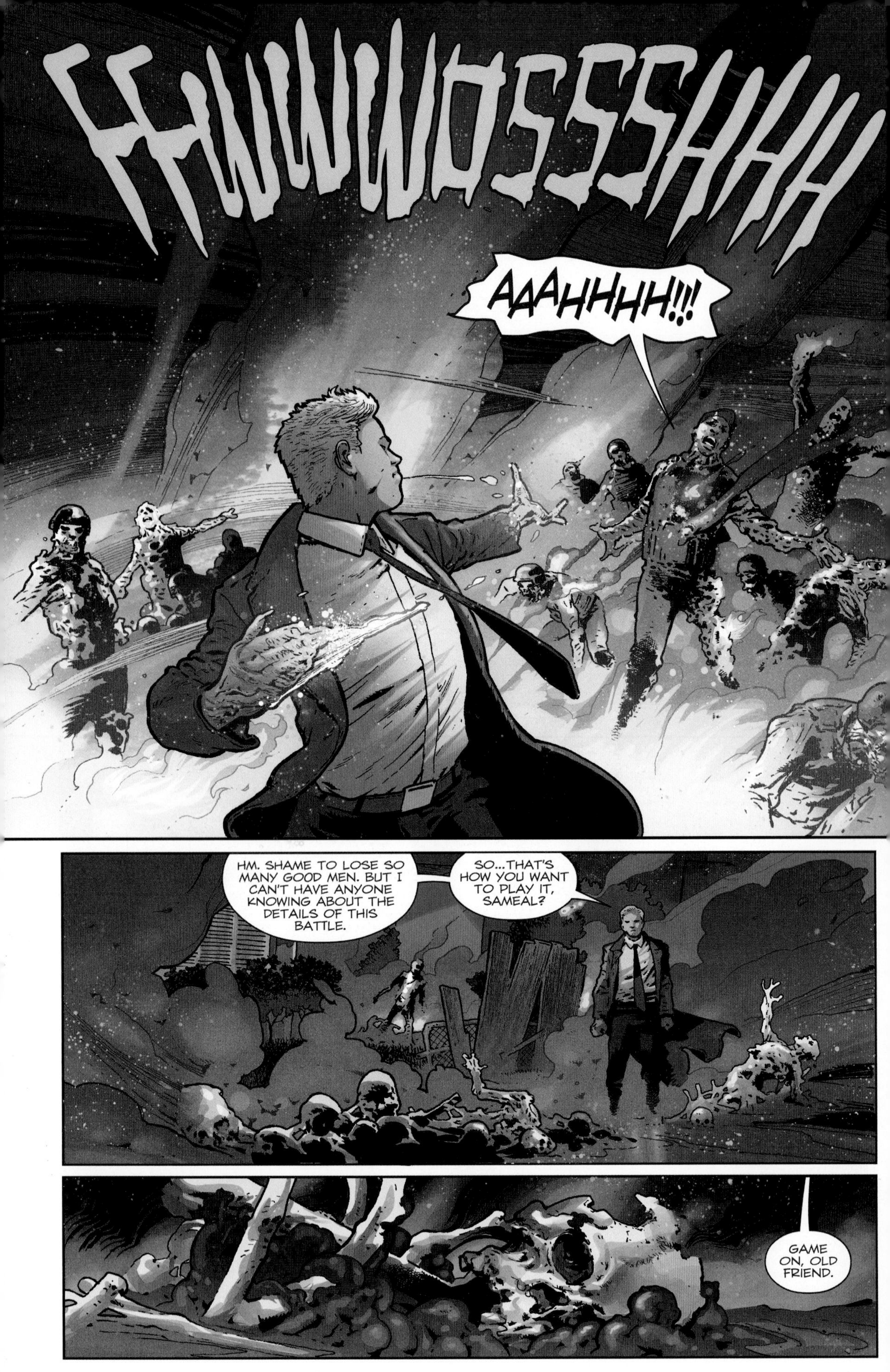
FFHWWWOSSSHHH
AAAHHHH!!!
HM. SHAME TO LOSE SO MANY GOOD MEN. BUT I CAN'T HAVE ANYONE KNOWING ABOUT THE DETAILS OF THIS BATTLE.
SO...THAT'S HOW YOU WANT TO PLAY IT, SAMEAL?
GAME ON, OLD FRIEND.

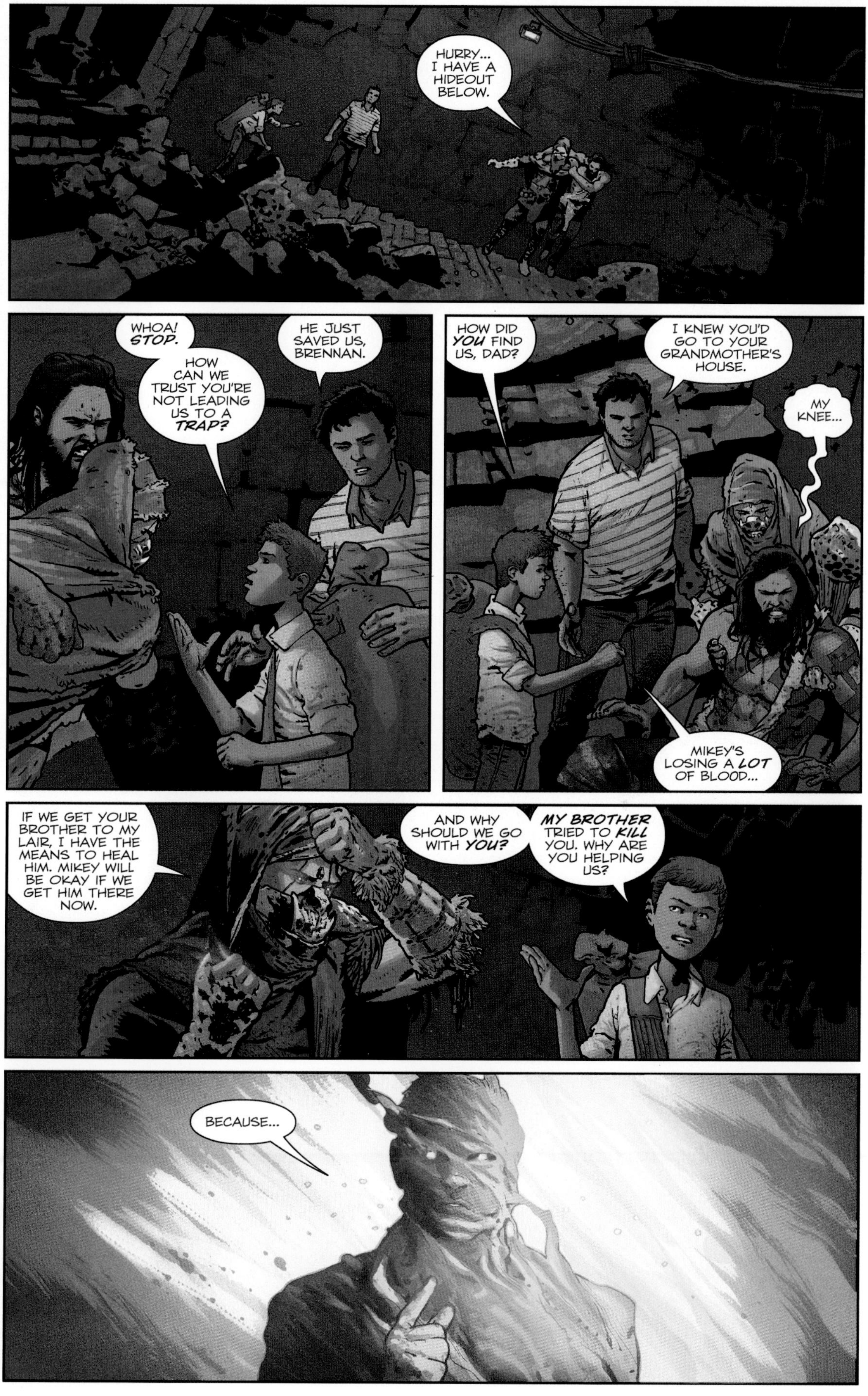
HURRY... I HAVE A HIDEOUT BELOW.
WHOA! STOP.
HOW CAN WE TRUST YOU'RE NOT LEADING US TO A TRAP?
HE JUST SAVED US, BRENNAN.
HOW DID YOU FIND US, DAD?
I KNEW YOU'D GO TO YOUR GRANDMOTHER'S HOUSE.
MY KNEE...
MIKEY'S LOSING A LOT OF BLOOD...
IF WE GET YOUR BROTHER TO MY LAIR, I HAVE THE MEANS TO HEAL HIM. MIKEY WILL BE OKAY IF WE GET HIM THERE NOW.
AND WHY SHOULD WE GO WITH YOU?
MY BROTHER TRIED TO KILL YOU. WHY ARE YOU HELPING US?
BECAUSE...

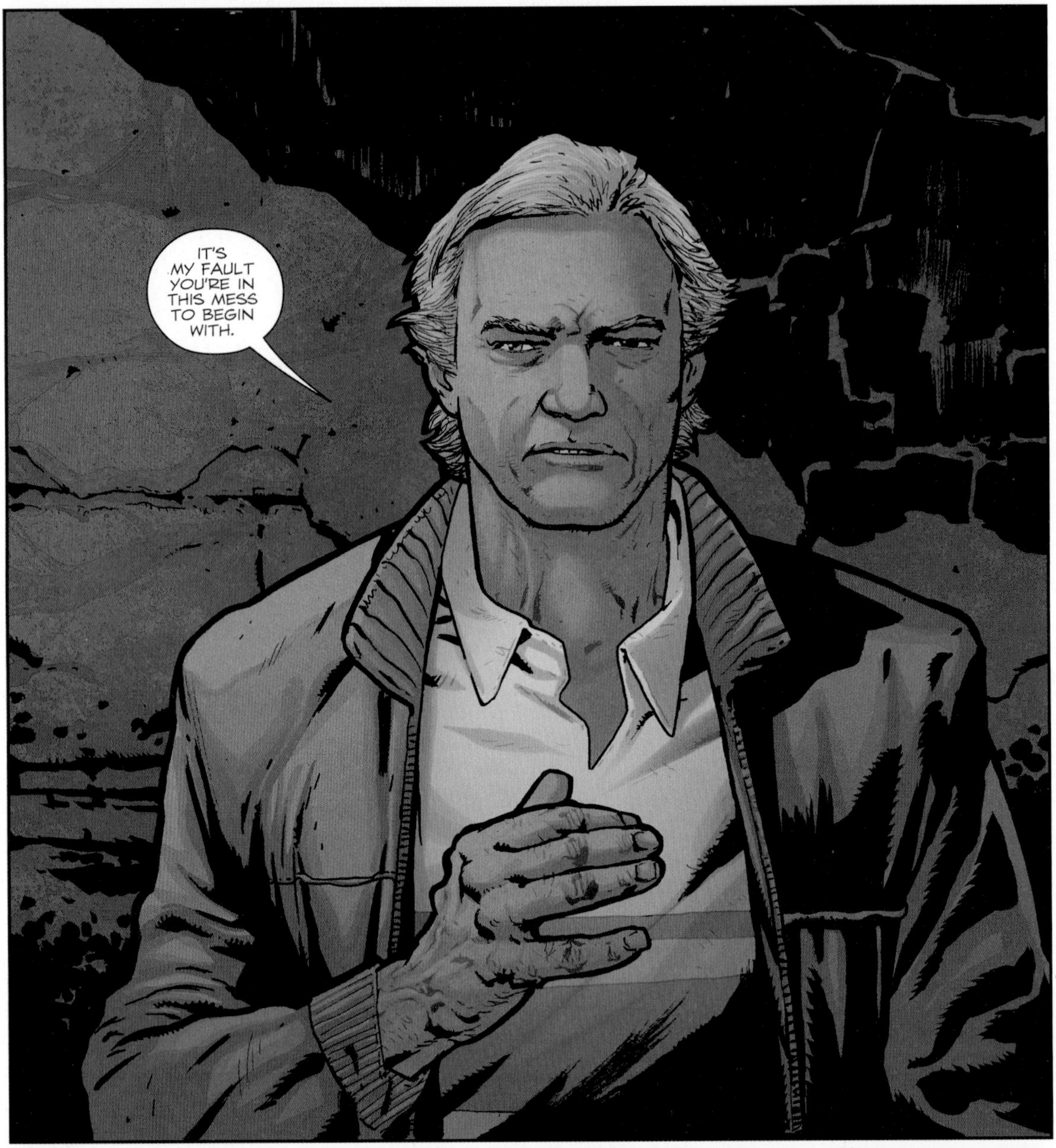
IT'S MY FAULT YOU'RE IN THIS MESS TO BEGIN WITH.

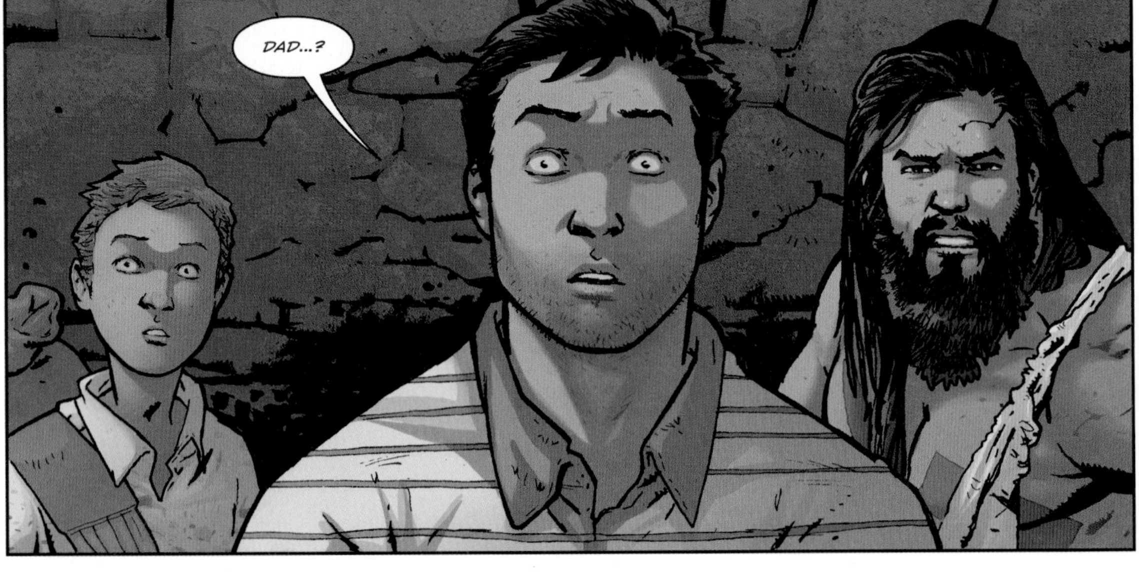
DAD...?

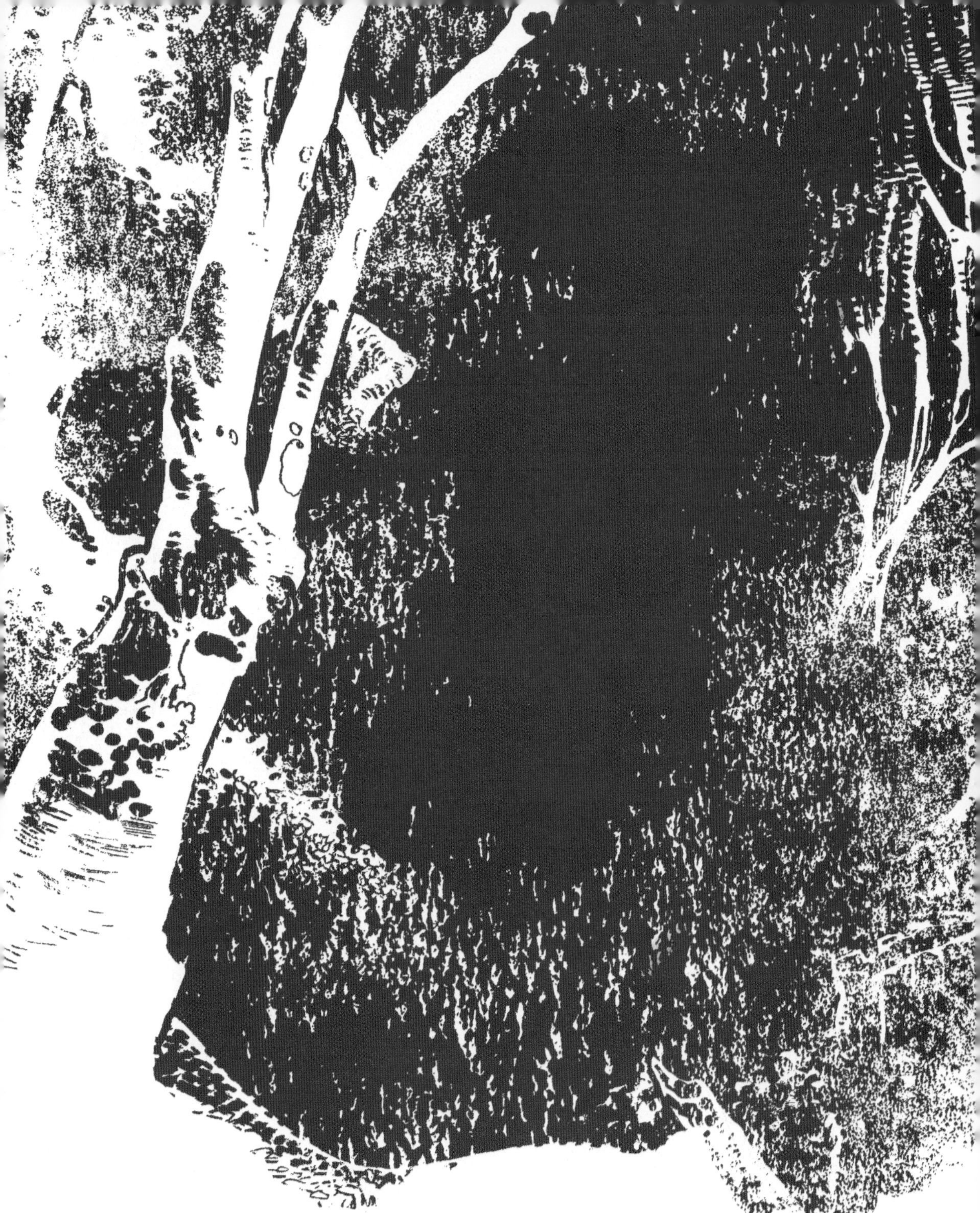

To be continued...

"There are many trials ahead of you."

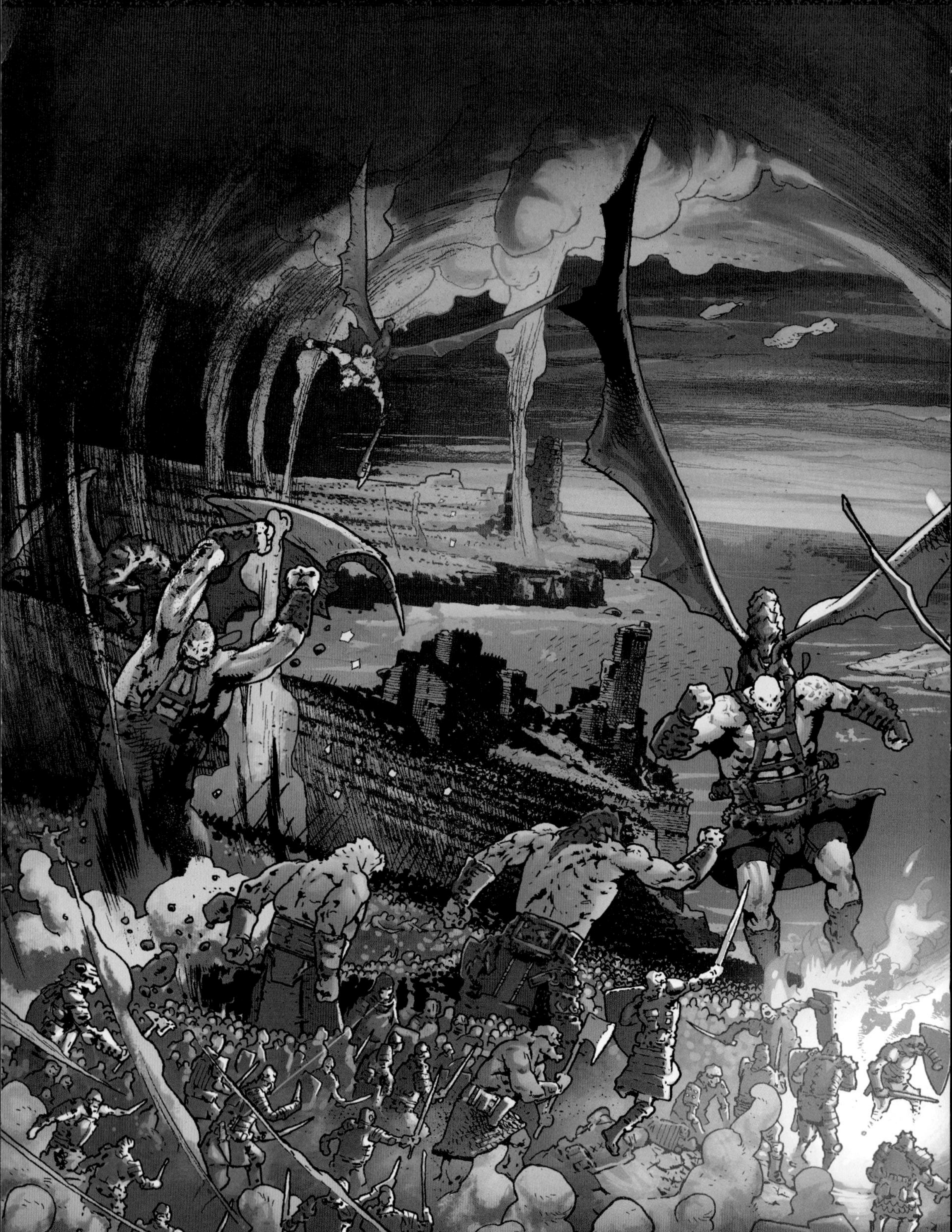

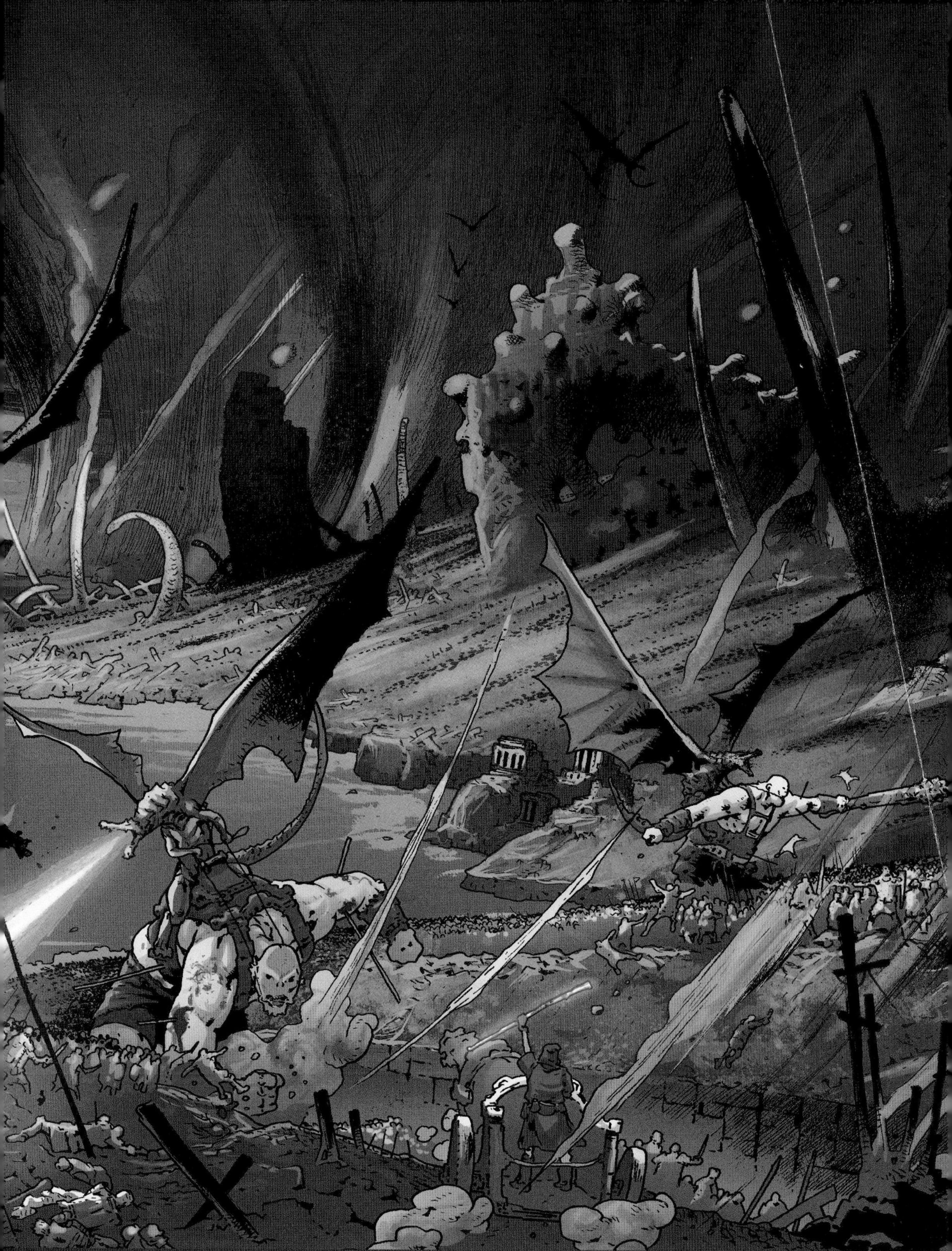

For more tales from ROBERT KIRKMAN and SKYBOUND

VOLUME 3: THIS LITTLE LIGHT
BY KIRKMAN & AZACETA
OUTCAST

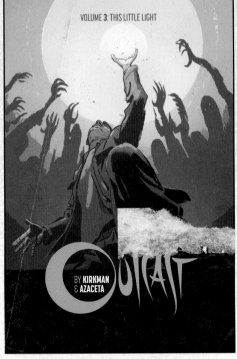

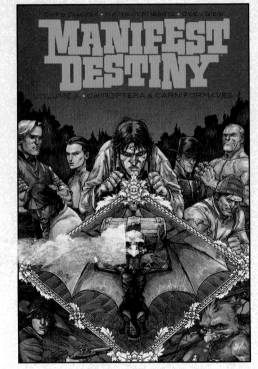

VOL. 1: A DARKNESS SURROUNDS HIM TP
ISBN: 978-1-63215-053-0
$9.99

VOL. 2: A VAST AND UNENDING RUIN TP
ISBN: 978-1-63215-448-4
$14.99

VOL. 3: THIS LITTLE LIGHT TP
ISBN: 978-1-63215-693-8
$14.99

CHRIS DINGESS • MATTHEW ROBERTS • OWEN GIENI
MANIFEST DESTINY
VOLUME 3 • CHIROPTERA & CARNIFORMAVES

VOL. 1: FLORA & FAUNA TP
ISBN: 978-1-60706-982-9
$9.99

VOL. 2: AMPHIBIA & INSECTA TP
ISBN: 978-1-63215-052-3
$14.99

VOL. 3: CHIROPTERA & CARNIFORMAVES TP
ISBN: 978-1-63215-397-5
$14.99

DAVID SCHULNER • JUAN JOSE RYP • FELIX SERRANO
CLONE
VOLUME 1
FIRST GENERATION

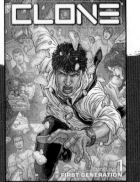

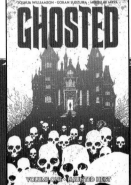

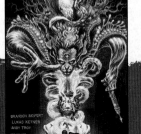

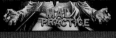

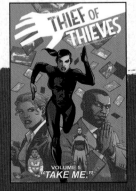

VOL. 1: FIRST GENERATION TP
ISBN: 978-1-60706-683-5
$12.99

VOL. 2: SECOND GENERATION TP
ISBN: 978-1-60706-830-3
$12.99

VOL. 3: THIRD GENERATION TP
ISBN: 978-1-60706-939-3
$12.99

VOL. 4: FOURTH GENERATION TP
ISBN: 978-1-63215-036-3
$12.99

JOSHUA WILLIAMSON • GORAN SUDZUKA • MIROSLAV MRVA
GHOSTED
VOLUME ONE • HAUNTED HEIST

VOL. 1: HAUNTED HEIST TP
ISBN: 978-1-60706-836-5
$9.99

VOL. 2: BOOKS OF THE DEAD TP
ISBN: 978-1-63215-046-2
$12.99

VOL. 3: DEATH WISH TP
ISBN: 978-1-63215-051-6
$12.99

VOL. 4: GHOST TOWN TP
ISBN: 978-1-63215-317-3
$12.99

BRANDON SEIFERT
LUKAS KETNER
ANDY TROY
WITCH DOCTOR
MAL PRACTICE

VOL. 1: UNDER THE KNIFE TP
ISBN: 978-1-60706-441-1
$12.99

VOL. 2: MAL PRACTICE TP
ISBN: 978-1-60706-693-4
$14.99

THIEF OF THIEVES
VOLUME 5
"TAKE ME."

VOL. 1: "I QUIT."
ISBN: 978-1-60706-592-0
$14.99

VOL. 2: "HELP ME."
ISBN: 978-1-60706-676-7
$14.99

VOL. 3: "VENICE."
ISBN: 978-1-60706-844-0
$14.99

VOL. 4: "THE HIT LIST."
ISBN: 978-1-63215-037-0
$14.99

VOL. 5: "TAKE ME."
ISBN: 978-1-63215-401-9
$14.99